The Changeling

The Changeling

PHILIPPA CARR

G.K.HALL&CO.
Boston, Massachusetts
1990

Published in Large Print by arrangement with
G. P. Putnam's Sons.

G.K. Hall Large Print Book Series.

Set in 16 pt Plantin.

Library of Congress Cataloging in Publication Data
Carr, Philippa, 1906–
    The changeling / Philippa Carr.
       p. cm.—(G.K. Hall large print book series)
  ISBN 0-8161-4894-5 (lg. print)
    1. Large type books. I. Title.
  [PR6015.I3C4 1990]
  823'.914—dc20   89-77209

Contents

The Last Summer

I was ten years old when my contented life was disrupted by my mother's marriage to Benedict Lansdon. Had I been older, more experienced of life, I should have seen the inevitability of it. But there I was, happy and snug in my little world, my mother the center of my life—as I believed I was of hers—and it did not occur to me that there could be an intruder to disturb us.

It was not as though he were a stranger to me. He had been there almost as long as I could remember—a rather flamboyant figure in the background, and that was where I wanted, and expected, him to remain.

He had been present on the Australian goldfields when and where I was born. In fact my arrival had actually taken place in his house.

"Mr. Lansdon," my mother explained, "was different from the rest of the miners. He owned a moderately successful mine and he employed men who had given up trying on their own. We all lived in shacks. You never saw the like unless, it was the hut in the woods where that old tramp stayed last winter. Quite unsuitable for babies! And it was decided you should be born in his house. Pedrek was born there too."

Pedrek Cartwright was my greatest friend. His parents lived in London but his grandfather owned Pencarron Mine which was near Cador, my grandparents' home in Cornwall—so we were often together both in London and Cornwall. If his parents were not going to Cornwall and we were going to see my grandparents, he travelled with us; and my mother was very friendly with his parents in London; so we were really like one family.

Pedrek and I used to play at gold mining when we were smaller. There was a great bond between us because we had both been born in a mining township on the other side of the world—and in the house of Mr. Benedict Lansdon.

I should have guessed what was happening because when my mother spoke of Benedict Lansdon her voice would change, her eyes would sparkle and her mouth smile. But I did not attach any significance to that at the time.

Not that it would have made any difference. I should have hated it just the same, but if I had been prepared, it would not have been such a shock.

It was not until after the marriage that I realized how good life had been. I had taken so much for granted.

There had been my happy life in London not far from the park where I would go each morning with my governess, Miss Brown, to walk through the paths under the great trees—chestnut, oak and beech. We would sit with the other nannies to whom Miss Brown wanted to chat while I played with their children. We would feed the ducks on the pond and run about on the expanse of grass which was there for that purpose.

I loved the shops; there was a market some little distance from us and I was sometimes taken there on winter afternoons with Miss Brown. How exciting it was to wander among the crowds and watch the people at their stalls, particularly when it began to get dark and the naphtha flares were lighted. Once we ate jellied eels at a stall about which Miss Brown was a little uneasy because she thought it unsuitable; but I cajoled her. I loved to see the ladies in their wonderful clothes and the gentlemen in their top hats and morning coats. I loved winter evenings when we sat by the fire and listened for the muffin man's bell when Emmy our maid would run out with a dish and buy some which my mother and I would toast by the fire.

They were happy days which I thought would go on for ever, because I was then unaware of Benedict Lansdon lurking in the background, just waiting for the appropriate time to change it all.

When the trees in the Park began to bud, and even the one in our little square garden showed signs of a few inedible pears that it might in due course produce, my mother would say: "It is time we went to Cornwall. I'll speak to Aunt Morwenna. I wonder what their plans are this year?"

Aunt Morwenna was Pedrek's mother, and my mother and I would go to their house which was not very far from ours and Pedrek would take me up to his room to show me his new puppy or some toy he had just acquired; we would talk of Cornwall and what we would do when we arrived there—he to his grandparents, me to mine.

There would follow the excitement of the train. Pedrek and I would endeavor to have a window to ourselves; we would shriek to each other to look at this and that as the train rushed by meadows, streams and woodlands before pulling into the stations.

And at the end of this journey there would be our grandparents waiting for us and making us feel that it was the most wonderful thing that could happen because we were coming to be with them. Then Pedrek would go on his way to Pencarron and I to Cador.

Cador, that most magnificent and exciting house, had been the home of Cadorsons for hundreds of years. There were no Cadorsons there now. The name had died out when my great-grandfather Jake Cadorson and his son Jacco were drowned in Australia and the house had passed to my grandmother who had married Rolf Hanson. I always thought it was a pity the name had died out, for Cadorsons would have been so appropriate at Cador.

Thankfully, however, the house was still in the family; and although my grandfather had come to it through marriage, he loved it, I believe, more than any other member of the family did.

I could understand his feelings for it. There it stood—grey stone, with its towers and turrets, like a medieval fortress. When I was alone in the big lofty rooms, I could imagine myself back hundreds of years. It was exciting and when I was young rather frightening; but there was always the reassuring presence of my mother and my grandparents. My grandfather would tell exciting stories of the past involving roundheads and cavaliers, of storms and shipwrecks and of adventurers who had gone off to the hitherto undiscovered places of the world.

I loved Cador. There the days seemed longer and the sun seemed to shine for days on end. And when the rain came it was just as exciting. I loved the sea. Sometimes we would be allowed to take a little trip on it, but my grandmother never liked that. She could not forget that her parents and brother had been drowned.

I used to go down to the two towns of Poldorey with my mother and grandmother. We would stroll past the cottages on the quay and watch the fishermen mending their nets or talking about the catch. Sometimes I would go down with Mr. Yeo, the butler, to buy fish. I was fascinated by the fishes squirming on the weighing machine which was spattered with silver scales. I would listen to the fishermen's talk. " 'Twas a good catch today, 'Arry. The Lord calmed down them old waves, 'e did and all." At other times it was a gloomy story. "No fish today. Jesus Christ Himself wouldn't venture out on a sea like this." I knew most of them by name—Tom, Ted, Harry. Some of them had grand-sounding names: Reuben,

Solomon, Japheth, Obediah . . . names taken from the Bible. Most of the families had been ardent Wesleyans since John and Charles Wesley had roamed through Cornwall bringing its people to righteousness.

Cador was about a quarter of a mile from the two towns East and West Poldorey which were separated by the River Poldor and were connected by an ancient bridge. I loved the steep streets of the town which wound up to the cliff-top where one could look out across the sea. There was a wooden seat so that people might sit and rest after the climb and there I would sit with my grandfather and persuade him to tell me stories of smugglers and wreckers who lured ships to disaster along this coast. I would search on the beach for the semi-precious stones which were reputed to be found there, but the only ones I ever saw were in the window of Mr. Bander's shop, marked with the inscription "Found on Poldorey Beach."

I was proud to belong to Cador Folk as the family were respectfully referred to in the Poldoreys.

All this was mine—and there was the London home, too. The tall narrow house which my mother and I shared with the servants . . . not many of them. There were of course my governess, Miss Brown, who would have been horrified to be called a servant, then Mr. and Mrs. Emery; she was cook and housekeeper and he a man of all work who tended our tiny garden; and there was a housemaid Ann and a parlormaid Jane.

It was an intimate household. My mother was not one to stand on ceremony, and I think all the servants were devoted to her. They felt themselves to be part of the family. There was not that inpenetrable barrier between up and below stairs as there was in larger establishments such as that of Mr. Benedict Lansdon and my Uncle Peter and Aunt Amaryllis. Not that they were really my uncle and aunt; they were not even my mother's. They were very old and the family connection went back some generations. Benedict Lansdon was Uncle Peter's grandson, so there was even a link with him.

Uncle Peter, though very old, was an important man; he was rich and had lots of interests—some of them rather mysterious; but he was quite an awe-inspiring figure. His wife, Aunt Amaryllis, was one of those very feminine women who seem endearingly helpless and somehow hold the family together. Everyone loved her—including myself.

They entertained lavishly, although Uncle Peter's daughter Helena and his son-in-law Martin Hume, the well-known politician, were often hostess and host at the functions held at their home. It was an exciting family to belong to.

I remember the incidents from what I thought of afterwards as the Last Summer, for it was after Christmas of that year that I had my first inkling of what was to come.

My mother and I had arrived in Cornwall.

Pedrek had travelled down with us and the days seemed to have been spent between Cador and Pencarron Manor. Both Pedrek and I had to do lessons for a certain number of hours each day and these were allowed to coincide by an accommodating Miss Brown and Mr. Clenham who was Pedrek's tutor. Pedrek was to go to school the following year so that in itself would bring change. We rode a great deal but were not allowed to go out on our own. There always had to be an adult with us which was rather restricting. So we spent a good deal of time in the paddock practicing jumping and showing off our equestrian skill to each other.

On this occasion we were with my mother and, as it seemed on many occasions, we found ourselves at St Branok's Pool.

I was fascinated by it. So was Pedrek. It was an uncanny spot with the willows hanging over it. The still waters of the Pool were said to be bottomless, and it had a reputation for being a place to avoid after dark. I suppose that was why it attracted me. My mother always appeared to be fascinated by it.

As usual we tied up our horses and stretched ourselves out on the grass leaning against the boulders which protruded from the ground in certain places.

"They could be the stones of an old monastery," my mother had told us.

We had heard the story many times of the bells which were reputed to ring if a disaster threatened. They were at the bottom of the pool according to the legend.

Pedrek, who was very logical, said that if they were at the bottom, the pool could not be bottomless, to which my mother replied that flaws could often be found in most legends if one tried hard enough.

"I don't want flaws to be found," I told them. "I like to think it is bottomless and that the bells are there all the same."

"A monastery was destroyed by floods because the monks turned from the path of righteousness," explained my mother.

"There are lots of righteous people about here," I commented. "There is old Mrs. Fenny on the quay who watches everything that goes on and thinks everyone but herself is heading for hell fire. And there's Mrs. Polhenny who goes to church twice on Sundays and tries to make her daughter Leah as holy as she is, so that the poor girl never gets any fun."

"People are very strange," said my mother, "but you have to be tolerant with them. 'Cast the beam out of your own eye . . .' "

"*You* sound like Mrs. Polhenny now, Mama," I said. "She's always quoting the Bible, but she would be sure she hasn't the slightest speck in her eyes."

Dreamily I would stare at the pool and lure her to tell me the story, which she had told so many times of how, when I was a little girl, I had been taken away by Jenny Stubbs who still lived

9

in the cottage near the pool; they had thought I had wandered into the water because one of my toys was found in the brink.

"They dragged the pool," said my mother, her eyes wide as though she were looking into the past. "I shall never forget it. I thought I had lost you."

She was too emotional to proceed, and as I loved the story I could not hear it often enough: how Jenny Stubbs had rung toy bells hoping to drive them away because she had me hidden in her cottage, how she had cherished me and believed I was the little girl whom she had lost.

Pedrek liked the story too. He had heard it often enough before but he was never impatient when it was repeated. He knew that I liked to hear it over and over again, and he was always careful not to hurt other people's feelings, even when he was a boy.

What I remember of that occasion is that while we were talking Jenny Stubbs herself, the main character in the story, came out of her cottage and walked to the edge of the pool.

She did not see us at first and she was singing to herself. She had a rather high, reedy voice which sounded uncanny on the stillness of the air.

My mother called: "Good afternoon, Jenny."

She turned sharply, as though startled. "Good afternoon to 'ee, M'am," she said.

She stood facing us, her back to the pool. The light breeze ruffled her fine fair hair and she looked fey—someone who is not quite as others are.

"Are you well, Jenny?" asked my mother.

"Yes, thank'ee, M'am. I be well."

She walked slowly towards us. Her eyes scanned Pedrek and myself and I expected to see some interest in her for the child she had once stolen and cherished. But there was no sign that she was any more interested in me than she was in Pedrek. My mother said later that she would have forgotten that it had ever happened. We had to remember that Jenny was strange . . . not as other people; she lived in a world of her own creating; she must do to have taken someone else's child and thought it was her own.

She came and stood near us. She was gazing at my mother and it was easy to see that she drew some comfort from her presence.

"I be expecting this Lammas," she said.

"Oh Jenny . . ." replied my mother, and added quickly: "You must be very happy."

" 'Tis a little girl, I be sure of that," said Jenny.

My mother nodded and Jenny turned away; walking towards her cottage, she started to sing in her strange unworldly voice.

"It is very sad," said my mother, when she was out of earshot. "She can never forget that she lost her baby all those years ago."

"That baby would be the same age as I am now," I said, "because she thought I was her baby once."

My mother nodded. "And now she thinks she is

going to have another. It is not the first time she has thought this."

"What happens when she doesn't?" I asked.

"It is hard to know what goes on in her poor clouded mind. But she does know how to look after a baby. She was wonderful with you during the few days she had you. We couldn't have looked after you better."

"But I wanted to come home, didn't I? When you found me in her cottage I ran to the door, calling for you to take me home."

My mother nodded again. "Oh, poor, poor Jenny," she said. "I feel so very sorry for her. We must be as kind to her as we can."

We were silent, looking at the pool. I was thinking of the days I had spent in Jenny's cottage, and wishing I could remember more of that time; I was thinking of her ringing toy bells to drive people away so that she could have me to herself.

I felt that poor Jenny was a part of my childhood and I must always be kind and understanding towards her. I knew that was how my mother felt.

I was constantly reminding myself of little incidents from that Last Summer. I remember seeing Jenny often walking along the lanes past the pool to her cottage, singing to herself in that slightly out of tune way which gave her an otherworldliness that was, for me, intriguing.

She seemed happy and her happiness was in

constant delusion. She thought she was going to have a child to replace the one which she had lost; it was what she longed for, and in her simple mind she believed that child would be born to her.

It was pathetic, and yet in a way she was happy because she believed in her fantasy.

Another incident I remembered from that summer occurred when I was in the company of my grandmother. We were the greatest of friends; she seemed too young to be a grandmother; she was more like a lively young aunt or an elder sister.

She told me a great deal about my mother. "You must look after her," she said. "She has had a sad time, you know. She was married to a wonderful man—your father—and he died before you were born and she was all alone."

She had explained several times that my father had wanted to go to Australia to make a fortune so that we could all come back to England and live in comfort. He had gone to find gold and Pedrek's parents had been with him and my mother. They had lived in the township which was a very brave thing to do because they were all unused to hardship. Pedrek's father and mine had been partners. She explained to me how the mines could be quite unsafe; they had to be propped up with wood so that they would not cave in, which was what theirs did. Pedrek's father had been down in the mine when it happened, and my father went down and brought him up. He had passed him to the watchers on the brink and before they could help

13

my father out, there was a great fall of earth, and he had been taken down with it.

"He gave his life for his friend," she finished.

"I know," I replied. "Pedrek's mother told me. She said Pedrek and I must always remember this and be friends for ever."

She nodded. "You will," she said. "I know you will be. And you must love your mother dearly, for when he died . . . she gave all that love she had had for him to you."

I understood. It was how I wanted it to be.

On this particular day we walked down to West Poldorey to the ancient church which stood close to the sea. It was small, dating back to Norman times. West Poldorey was very proud of it and East Poldorey a little envious because it wasn't on their side, for people from far off came to look at it and it was said it should never be allowed to crumble away. There were many bazaars and garden fêtes to bolster up its roof which needed constant repair and I heard ominous talk of woodworm and death watch beetle.

I liked to creep in when no one was there and think of all those people who had sat in that church, just as I was doing. My grandfather had said that people had gone in there to pray when the Armada was off our coast and again when Napoleon was threatening to invade us. In the old church—as in Cador—one could easily slip back into the past.

The church door was open and we heard voices inside.

"I know," said my grandmother. "They are decorating the church with flowers for John Polgarth's wedding." John Polgarth was the man who owned the grocer's shop in East Poldorey, quite a worthy member of the community, and he was to marry Molly Agar, daughter of the butcher.

The wedding was to be the next day.

As we stepped through the door I heard the commanding voice of Mrs. Polhenny. She was a very important person in the neighborhood because she followed the profession of midwife and most of the younger generation had been brought into the world by her. I always thought she believed that gave her the right to pass judgment on their actions and superintend their spiritual welfare, for this she did in no uncertain way.

She was naturally not popular with her protégés. That was of no importance to her. She would have said she was not there to make people like her but to put them on the road to salvation.

Mrs. Polhenny was a good woman if by good it was meant that she went to church twice every Sunday and often in the week, that she was involved in most good works for the salvation of the church, and that she could apply the Scriptures to almost every occasion; and as she could not help being deeply aware of her own goodness she was quick to detect the sin in others.

Naturally her life was one long disapproval of almost everyone around her. Even the vicar came in for criticism. He took the Bible teaching too literally, she said, and was inclined to seek the

15

company of publicans and sinners rather than those whose sins had been washed away by the blood of the Lamb because of their devotion to duty and their love of virtue.

I did not like Mrs. Polhenny. I found her a most uncomfortable person. Not that I had a great deal to do with her, but I was sorry for Leah, her daughter, who was about sixteen years old at this time. Mrs. Polhenny was a widow but I had never heard of a Mr. Polhenny; there must have been one, otherwise there could not have been a Leah.

"She must have killed him off pretty quick," was the comment of Mrs. Garnett, the cook at Cador. "Poor fellow, I reckon he had a rare old time of it."

Leah was very pretty but she always seemed cowed as though she were looking over her shoulder, expecting the devil to be lurking somewhere ready to spring out and tempt her.

Leah was a seamstress. She did beautiful embroidery which she and her mother took into Plymouth once a month and sold to a shop there. Her work was exquisite and the poor girl was kept at it.

On this day she was in church with her mother, helping with the flowers, and Mrs. Polhenny was giving orders to her.

"Good morning, Mrs. Polhenny," said my grandmother. "What beautiful roses!"

Mrs. Polhenny looked pleased. "It'll be a good show for the wedding, Mrs. Hanson."

16

"Oh yes indeed . . . John Polgarth and Molly Agar."

"Everyone in the towns will be there to see them wed," went on Mrs. Polhenny, and added significantly: "And it's about time, too."

"I'm sure they will be very suited. Nice girl, Molly."

"H'm," said Mrs. Polhenny. "A bit on the flighty side."

"Oh, she's just high spirited."

"Agar did well to get her married. She's not the sort to be left unwed." Mrs. Polhenny pursed her lips, hinting at secret knowledge.

"Well, it's all for the best then," replied my grandmother.

There was a movement behind us. Mrs. Polhenny was studying the flowers in the container. I glanced around. The newcomer was a young girl. I did not know her. She slipped into one of the pews and knelt down.

Mrs. Polhenny said: "Bring me that spray, Leah. That would go very well here . . ." She stopped short. She was staring at the girl kneeling in the pew.

"Can I believe my eyes?" she said loudly and with indignation.

We were all silent, wondering what she meant. She had left the flowers and walked briskly down the aisle to the girl.

"Get out!" she cried. "You slut! How dare you come into this holy place? It's not for the likes of you."

The girl had risen. I thought she was going to burst into tears.

"I only wanted . . ." she began.

"Out!" cried Mrs. Polhenny. "Out, I say!"

My grandmother cut in. "Wait a moment. What does this mean? Tell me what's going on."

The girl shot past us and ran out of the church.

"You may well ask," said Mrs. Polhenny. "It's one of the sluts from Bays Cottages." Her eyes narrowed and her lips tightened. "And I don't mind telling you she's six months gone.

"Her husband . . ."

Mrs. Polhenny laughed mirthlessly. "Husband? Her sort don't wait for husbands. She's not the first in that lot, I can tell you. They're bad, through and through. It's a marvel to me that the Lord don't smite them on the spot."

"Perhaps He feels more kindly towards sinners than some mortals do."

"They'll come to judgment, never fear." Mrs. Polhenny's eyes glittered as though she were already seeing the girl writhing in the flames of hell.

"Well, she was here in church," said my grandmother. "She must have been repenting, and you know there is great joy over sinners who repent."

"If I were the Lord," said Mrs. Polhenny, "I'd do something about them Bay Cottages, that I would."

"Perhaps some have to be thankful that you are not the Lord," retorted my grandmother somewhat tartly. "Tell me about the girl. Who is she?"

"Daisy Martin. A bad lot, that family. The

18

girl's grandmother called me in. She's repented her ways . . . getting old and frightened of what's to come, I shouldn't wonder. Wanted me to take a look at the girl. I said, 'She's six months gone and what about the man?' She said it was one of them farm laborers who came on to help with the thatching. The girl's only sixteen. Disgraceful, I call it."

"But you'll deliver the child, of course."

"I have to do that, don't I? 'Tis my work, and if a baby's been planted, however sinfully, it's my duty to bring it into the world. God sent me here to do this work and nothing would stop me."

"I'm glad of that," replied my grandmother. "We must not visit the sins of the parents upon the children, you know."

"Well, they're God's children, however they've been come by. As for that creature . . . I hope they cast her out . . . once the child's born. It does the neighborhood no good to have her sort about."

"She's only sixteen, you say."

"Old enough to know better."

"She's not the first, by any means."

"So much for the sinful ways into which we have fallen."

"There is nothing very new about these things, you know," said my grandmother.

"The Lord will take His vengeance," Mrs. Polhenny assured us, looking up to the rafters as though to Heaven—giving the Lord a little prod, I thought, to remind him that He was being lax in performing His duty.

19

I knew my grandmother was torn between the pity she felt for the wayward young Daisy and the secret pleasure she derived from baiting Mrs. Polhenny who went on: "The goings on at Poldorey . . . East and West . . . well, it would give you a bit of a shock, I reckon, if you knew all."

"Then I suppose I should be thankful to remain in ignorance."

"The Lord will take His vengeance one day . . . mark my words."

"I can hardly see East and West Poldorey as Sodom and Gomorrah."

"It's coming, you'll see.'

"I hope not. But what I do see is that we are holding up your work. We'll say goodbye, Mrs. Polhenny."

We stood outside the church and my grandmother breathed deeply, as though she needed fresh air after the atmosphere in the church.

Then she turned to me and laughed. "What a self-righteous woman. I'd rather have a sinner any day. Oh well . . . she's an excellent midwife. There isn't a better in the whole width and breadth of Cornwall. My dear, we must look after that poor girl. I'll go along to the cottages tomorrow and see what I can find out."

She seemed suddenly to remember my age, and possibly it occurred to her that I was being introduced to the facts of life before I was ready to absorb them.

She went on: "We'll go over to Pencarron this

afternoon. Isn't it wonderful that you have Pedrek here with you?"

I thought a lot about Mrs. Polhenny and always scrutinized her cottage closely when I passed by. It was just outside East Poldorey and often I would see clothes drying on the bushes. There were lace curtains at the windows, spotlessly clean, and the stone steps leading to the front door were regularly scrubbed. She obviously believed that cleanliness was next to godliness; and saw herself as an upholder of both virtues.

Once or twice I glimpsed Leah at a window. She would be there with her embroidery frame, stitching away. Sometimes she looked up from her work and saw me. I would smile, wave my hand, and she would acknowledge my greeting.

I should have liked to talk to her. I wanted to know what it was like living with a mother such as Mrs. Polhenny. But she always gave me the impression, if ever I hesitated, that she must get on quickly with her work.

Poor Leah! I thought. It must be hard to be the daughter of a saintly woman who, as she felt it her duty to uphold the morals of the countryside, must be much more strict in her own home.

I thanked God for my mother, my grandparents and the Pencarrons. They might not be so concerned with the laws of God but they were much more comfortable to live with.

So that summer passed as others had. My grandmother visited Bays Cottages and took clothes and food for the young girl; Mrs. Polhenny delivered a healthy boy in due course and my grandmother affirmed that, however irritating she was in other ways, she knew her job and mothers were safe in her hands.

I seemed to see Jenny Stubbs more frequently that year. Perhaps it was because I noticed her more. I would see her in the lanes. She worked for one of the farmers' wives and I heard she was a good worker. They all humored her, it was said, and Mrs. Bullet, the farmer's wife, made sure none of the other workers teased her or disillusioned her as to her state. "It does no harm to none," said Mrs. Bullet, "so let the poor soul have her fancies."

So Jenny, singing in her reedy off-key tone and Mrs. Polhenny preaching righteousness wherever she went . . . that was what I remembered most from that Last Summer.

And now, looking back, that seems somehow significant.

It is all so clear to me; waving goodbye to the grandparents, which was rather sad in a way. I tried to hide from them the excitement I felt at the thought of seeing London again.

"I wish," I said to Pedrek, "that we could all live close together."

He had the same problem. His grandmother was almost in tears at his departure. Like myself, he wanted to show how sad he was and yet he could not hide his eagerness to be reunited with his parents. The similarity of our positions had always drawn Pedrek and me closer together.

Then we were speeding back to London.

Pedrek's parents were at the station to meet us. It was the usual ritual. If I had been travelling with his parents, my mother would have been there. There is something very comforting about normality which I did not appreciate until it ceased to be there.

We drove back to our house first where we would have tea before the Cartwrights went off to their place only a few streets away, taking Pedrek with them.

Innumerable questions were asked and Pedrek and I talked happily about what we had done in Cornwall.

We were all sitting at the table—Miss Brown and Pedrek's tutor with us—when a visitor arrived.

"Mr. Benedict Lansdon!" announced Jane with more dignity than was customary with her. And there he was—very tall and with what I can only describe as a commanding presence.

"Benedict," said my mother, rising.

She went to him and he took both her hands and they stood there smiling at each other.

Then she turned to us. "Isn't this a nice surprise?"

"I discovered what train you were catching," explained Benedict Lansdon.

"Come and sit down and have a cup of tea," said my mother warmly.

He smiled at us all and pleasantries were exchanged.

I felt deflated. We had departed from the normal. We should have gone on chattering about Cornwall, encouraged by our parents, and then Pedrek should have departed with his mother and father after we had made arrangements when next to meet. That was how it usually went.

"How are things in the mining world?" asked Benedict, smiling at Pedrek's father.

"Oh . . . ups and downs," said Justin Cartwright. "I am sure you know as much about the mining world as I do . . . only I suppose tin isn't gold."

"There must be a difference," said Benedict Lansdon. "But my close connection with all that ended long ago."

"Ah, yes, of course," replied Justin Cartwright.

"I'm going into politics again," said Benedict Lansdon, looking at my mother.

Her eyes widened with pleasure. "Oh really, Benedict, that's wonderful. I always said . . ."

He looked at her, nodding and understanding passed between them. I felt shut out. It was as though I had just discovered that she had a life which did not include me.

"I know you did," he went on. "Well, that is what is happening."

"Do tell us the news, Benedict," begged Morwenna, Pedrek's mother.

"It's no secret," he replied. "I am up for selection as candidate for Manorleigh."

"Your old constituency," cried Justin.

Benedict nodded. He was looking straight at my mother. I who knew her so well, felt a twinge of alarm.

"All very fortuitous," said Benedict. "Tom Dollis died suddenly. Poor chap, he was quite young. A heart attack. He had only been in the House a short while. It will mean a by-election soon."

"Isn't it a Conservative stronghold?" asked Justin.

Benedict nodded. "Has been for years . . . but it was almost broken . . . once."

Again that glance at my mother. "If I'm selected," he went on, "we shall have to make sure the seat doesn't change hands again."

We? It was as though he included her.

She lifted her teacup. "Having nothing stronger at hand," she said, "I'll drink to your success in tea."

"What does the beverage matter?" he said. "It's the wish that counts."

"Well, it's most exciting, I must say."

Again that smile between them. "I think so," he said. "I knew you would."

Morwenna said: "I do know you are an ardent supporter of Mr. Gladstone."

"My dear Morwenna, he's the greatest politician of the century."

"What of Peel . . . Palmerston . . . ?" began Justin Cartwright.

Benedict dismissed them with a flick of the hand.

"And they do say that Mr. Disraeli is quite brilliant," added Morwenna.

"That upstart! He owes his rise to his oily flattery of the Queen."

"Oh come," said Justin. "Surely there is more to it than that? The man's a genius."

"With a flair for self-advertisement."

"He did become Prime Minister."

"Oh, for a month or so . . ."

My mother burst out laughing. "I can see that we are going to be deeply involved in the politics of the day. When is the by-election, Benedict?"

"In December."

"They'll have to make a decision quickly."

"It's not much time to prepare. I should manage though."

Neither Pedrek nor I had spoken during this discourse and I was wondering whether he was thinking the same as I was which was, that they had completely forgotten that we were there. Usually after long separations, they wanted to hear all that had been going on, how our riding had improved, how high we could jump, how the grandparents were, what the weather had been like and such things.

Then they were talking about Mr. Gladstone's plans for reform in Ireland. Benedict Lansdon, of course, knew all about that. He took control and the others were his audience. We heard how Mr. Gladstone was concerned about the distressed state of the Irish and the growing discontent in that country and he was convinced that the remedy lay with the government.

And that was our homecoming—spoilt, I commented to Pedrek, by Benedict Lansdon.

Our lives from then on were dominated by the man. He was a constant caller. When I walked in the Park with my mother he often joined us. They would talk together and seem to forget that I was there, though sometimes he addressed a remark to me. He asked me how I was getting on with my riding and said we must all go riding together.

He had been selected—as my mother had known he would be—and was thinking of buying a house in Manorleigh; he wanted my mother to go down there and give her opinion.

I was longing for him to go. He had rented a furnished house there while he looked round. But he was frequently in London.

November was almost with us. They were sweeping up the leaves in the parks and there was a lovely smell of burning in the air. It was misty and a blue haze hung over the trees which made them look mysterious. Pedrek and I had always loved this time of year; we would shuffle through the leaves and conjure up all sorts of fantastic adventures in which we triumphed and astonished everyone with our bravery, ingenuity and skill.

But the dreams would not come that year. A faint uneasiness was creeping into my mind.

And then . . . I learned the worst.

I had gone to bed and was sitting up reading as I often did and which was allowed by Miss Brown before she came to put out the light.

My mother entered the room. Her eyes were brilliant. I had heard talk about people being radiant and that was how she was. She glowed with an inner light. I had never seen such unadulterated happiness.

She lay down on the bed and put her arms round me.

"Rebecca," she said, "I wanted you to be the first to know."

I turned to her and buried my face against her shoulder.

She stroked my hair. "There has always been just us . . . hasn't there? You and I together. Oh, there was the family, of course, and we loved them all dearly . . . but for us . . . you and me . . . there was always something very close and dear . . . and it is always going to be like that for as long as we both shall live."

I nodded. I was beginning to be rather frightened for some instinct told me what she was going to say.

Then it came: "I'm going to be married again, Rebecca."

"No . . . no," I murmured.

She held me tightly. "You will grow to love him, as I do. He is a wonderful man. I knew him when I was young . . . not much older than you are now. There has always been a very special friendship between us."

"You married my father," I reminded her.

"Yes . . . yes . . . but I have been a widow for a long time . . . a very long time."

"It's ten years," I said. "He died just before I was born."

She nodded. "You don't ask . . ." she began.

I did not have to. I knew. In any case, before I could speak, she said: "It's Mr. Benedict Lansdon."

Even though I had known it must be he, a shock ran through me.

She said: "You will be very fond of him, Rebecca. He is a most unusual man."

I did not speak. The answer to the first sentence was: Never. And to the second: Yes, I know he is unusual. But I did not like unusual people. I liked them to be ordinary, understanding nice people.

"Everything will be just as it was," she went on.

"It can't be," I said.

"Well, there will be a little change . . . for the better, though. Oh, Rebecca, I'm so happy. I have loved him for a long time. He's different from anyone I have ever known. When we were children we shared adventures and then he went away . . . and I met your father."

29

"My father was a great man . . . a hero . . ."

"Yes, I know. We were happy together, but he is dead . . . and he would not want me to go on mourning him for ever. Rebecca, you are going to be happy. Everyone should have a father."

"I have a father."

"I mean one who is here with you . . . to help you . . . to advise you and love you."

"But I am not his daughter."

"You will be his stepdaughter. Rebecca, don't spoil this. I am so happy tonight. I never thought to be so happy in my life. You'll get used to the idea. What are you reading?"

"Robinson Crusoe."

"That's exciting, isn't it? I noticed Pedrek was reading it the other day."

I nodded.

She kissed me. "I just wanted you to be the first to know. Goodnight, my darling."

She was faintly uneasy because I had cast a cloud over her happiness—but only a little one. I knew that she was thinking I was only a child and I was perhaps a little jealous and afraid of Benedict Lansdon coming between us.

It was natural, she was telling herself.

Perhaps I should have pretended to be pleased, but I could not be as deceitful as that.

The family were delighted. There was a dinner party at Uncle Peter's to celebrate the engagement. The wedding was to be soon.

My grandparents would come up to London for the ceremony. They had written sending congratulations and expressing their pleasure in the forthcoming marriage. Uncle Peter was clearly delighted. He was fond of my mother and very proud of Benedict who had become so rich without any help from him. I think he cared more for him than his son Peterkin who had devoted his life to good works at the Mission, and Helena who had been such a perfect wife to Martin Hume.

It was rather different in our house where I was conscious of an atmosphere of brooding apprehension.

The servants did not speak to me about their fears but I used to listen shamelessly to their conversations because it was imperative that I should know what was in their minds. It was possible in a smallish house like ours to listen to talk and I made the most of it.

I heard Mr. and Mrs. Emery once. She was putting things in the linen cupboard and he was handing them to her. It was just outside my room and if the door were a little open—which I had contrived that it should be—it was possible for me to hear quite a bit.

She was saying: "It don't do to worry. We'll know in good time."

"There is this new house they're getting. But if I know Mrs. Mandeville, she's not the sort to forget them as has been good servants to her."

"Oh, it'll be all right if it's left to her . . . but . . ."

"Why shouldn't it be? She'll be the mistress, won't she?"

"Well, yes . . . I reckon he'll leave all that sort of thing to her."

"I doubt he'll buy that house unless he gets in."

"Oh, I don't know. He's been close before, hasn't he? That means if he loses first time round he could win next. There'll be a general election before long . . . bound to be. Yes, I reckon he'll want that house now he's been selected."

"Do you think he'll get into Parliament?"

"He seems the sort to get what he wants."

"Don't forget last time . . . a regular scandal that was."

I crept near to the door. I must not miss this. What scandal? I asked myself. Did my mother know of it?

"Well, it was all cleared up, wasn't it?"

"Sort of. He didn't kill her. That's what they thought at first."

"But it turned out she took the stuff herself instead."

"All nice and convenient, wasn't it?"

"Convenient! Why, it lost him the seat, they said. He was all set to take it."

"Who knows? It was a Tory stronghold and he's a Liberal."

"But, but the Tories was getting really rattled. It looked like he was going to take it . . . make a record. The first time the Tories had been ousted for a hundred years or something."

"But it didn't happen."

"No, his poor unwanted wife died in mysterious circumstances."

"But I told you it was all right. He didn't kill her."

"I reckon it all worked out for the best. It kept the seat for the Tories."

"Oh, you and your Tories. I'm a bit of a Liberal myself."

"What do you know about it?"

"About as much as you do. There! That'll be the lot. Come on. I've got the dinner to see to."

I crept away from the door.

I felt excited, and the same time full of misgiving.

He had been married before. His wife had died . . . mysteriously. His *first* wife! And my mother was proposing to become his second.

I wondered what I could do. Warn her? But she must know about that long-ago scandal. She ignored it. She was bemused. She was bewitched by him.

I wished people would talk to me. I knew it was no use asking the Emerys or either of the maids. They would not tell me.

There was only one thing I could do and that was call on Pedrek's help. Together we might discover what it was all about.

He was eager to help and asked their butler with whom he was on very friendly terms; he was told that some time ago Benedict Lansdon had stood for election in Manorleigh and just before it took place his wife had died; she had been a quiet, rather nervous woman and he had been very friendly with Mrs. Grace Hume. It had been hinted that Benedict murdered his wife to get her out of the way. It was all rumor and nothing was proved at the time of the election, and if this had not all come out, Benedict Lansdon would almost certainly have won the seat. But he was defeated at the polls because of the scandal and lost his chance of becoming a Member of Parliament. A note was discovered later . . . which had been written by the wife before she died. In it she said she was taking her life because she was suffering from some uncurable disease and was beginning to be in great pain.

So he was exonerated, but it was too late for him to win the election and in any case he had gone out of politics.

So there was some secret in his past. And this was the man who was to marry my mother and take her away from me!

From then on it grew worse. I saw less of my mother. They were making plans for the wedding. Uncle Peter wanted a grand one.

"There is nothing people like better than romance," he said. "And if you are going to stand for Parliament, it is a good idea to get into the public eye . . . in the right way, of course."

"That is just like Uncle Peter," my mother said, laughing. She was always laughing at that time.

"Personally I don't care what sort of wedding it is."

Aunt Amaryllis sided with Uncle Peter. She always did.

Benedict Lansdon was in the process of buying the house at Manorleigh. My mother had taken me down to see it. "It will be our home for much of the time, I imagine," she said. "We shall have to nurse the constituency."

"What of our house?" I asked.

"Well, I think I shall sell it. We shall have your . . . stepfather's house in London."

I felt my face grow red. My stepfather! I thought. What am I going to call him? I can't call him Mr. Lansdon. Uncle Benedict? He is not my uncle. But there were a lot of people in our family called uncle although they had no right to the title. Uncle was just a nebulous form of address. It made a mockery of the title, I told Pedrek, who agreed with me. It seemed to be a major problem and I marvelled that so small a thing should matter so much. But what was I going to call him? Father? Never! It would have to be Uncle, I supposed. It was both confusing and embarrassing.

My mother went on trying to pretend she had not noticed my embarrassment and understanding it perfectly.

"We shall have *that* house in London and goodness knows, that is spacious enough—and the place at Manorleigh. Oh, it will be fun, Becca." She reverted to my old childhood name when she wished to be especially tender. "You will love it. The Manorleigh house is just outside the little town and it will be in the country. You'll love that. There will be plenty of scope for riding. You'll have a lovely schoolroom. Miss Brown . . . and all of us . . . will be expecting great things from you."

"What about Mr. and Mrs. Emery . . . ?"

"Oh, I have spoken . . . *we* have spoken . . . about that. I am going to ask them if they would like to come with us to Manorleigh."

That made me feel a good deal better. There would be those familiar faces near me. Moreover I knew they had been worried about their jobs.

I cried: "Oh, they will be so pleased. I heard them talking . . ."

"Oh? What did they say?"

"They didn't know what would happen to them, but they reckoned you would see they were all right."

"Of course. I'll tell them at once. Then they can decide whether they want to come. What else did they say?"

I was silent. I could hear the clock ticking and the seconds passing. I was on the point of telling her what they had said about *his* wife. I could warn her perhaps. The moment passed. She did not seem to notice the hiatus.

"Oh, nothing . . . I can't remember . . ." I said.

It was the first lie I remembered telling her.

He had indeed come between us.

36

My grandparents arrived in London.

I was disappointed that they seemed to be overcome by their admiration for Benedict Lansdon and delighted by the prospect of the marriage.

There was a great deal of excited talk about the constituency and the possibility of a general election.

"Not much chance yet," said my grandfather. "Gladstone is well in . . . unless he comes a cropper over Ireland again."

"It will come in time," said my mother. "And we don't want it too soon. Benedict has to make his presence felt before that."

"He will do that," added my grandmother with conviction.

She soon noticed that all was not well with me.

We went for a walk in the Park together and I quickly realized that she had arranged it so that we could talk in peace.

It was one of those late autumnal days—the mist only faintly disturbed by the softest of winds which blew from the southwest—dampish, leaving the skin glowing. There was a smell of autumn in the air and a few bronze leaves remaining on the trees.

As we walked by the Serpentine, she said to me: "I believe you are feeling a little . . . left out. Are you, my dear?"

I was silent for a moment. She put her arm through mine.

"You mustn't think that. Everything is the same between you and your mother."

"How can it be?" I demanded. "He will be there."

"You will enjoy his company. He will be like your father."

"I can only have one father."

"My dearest child, your father died before you were born. You never knew him."

"I know that he died saving Pedrek's father's life—and I don't want any other father."

She pressed my arm. "It has been a surprise to you. People often feel like that. You think there will be a change. Yes, there will be. But had you thought it might be a change for the better?"

"I liked it as it was."

"Your mother is very happy," she said.

"Yes," I agreed bitterly. "Because of him."

"You and she have been together so much. The fact that your father died made that inevitable. I know there is a very special relationship between you—and there always will be. But she and Benedict . . . they have been such good friends . . . always."

"Then why did she marry my father? *He* must have been a closer friend to her."

"Benedict went to Australia. He was out of her life. They both married different people . . . at first."

"Yes, and my father died saving another man's life. *His* wife . . . she died too."

"Why do you say it like that, Rebecca?

"Like what?"

"As though there was something odd about it."

"There was something odd about it."

"Who said so?"

I closed my lips firmly. I was not going to betray the servants.

"Tell me what you heard," she urged.

I remained silent.

"Please, Rebecca, tell me," she begged.

"She died and they thought he had killed her because he didn't want to be married to her any more . . . and he did not win the election because of it. And afterwards they found that she had killed herself."

"It's true," said my grandmother. "People will always blacken the case against others, particularly if they are in a prominent position. It's a form of envy."

"But she did die."

"Yes."

"I wish my mother was not going to marry him."

"Rebecca, you must not judge him before you know him."

"I do know him."

"No, you don't. We don't even fully know those who are closest to us. He loves your mother. I am sure of that, and she loves him. She has been so long alone. Don't spoil it."

"I? Spoil it?"

"Yes. You can. If she thinks you're not happy, she won't be."

"I don't think she is aware of anyone or any-thing . . . except him."

"Just at the moment she can think of little but her new life . . . her state of happiness. Don't show hostility to him. Let her enjoy this. You *will* . . . in time. But you are building up prejudices against him . . . and that won't do. You'll find everything is more or less as it was. You'll live in a different house, true. But what are houses? Just places to live in. And you will come down to Cornwall and be with your grandfather and me. Pedrek will be there . . ."

"Pedrek's going away to school."

"Well, there'll be holidays. You don't think he won't be coming to see his grandparents just because he's going to school, do you?"

"He's very rich, this er . . ."

"Benedict. Yes, he is now. You are not going to hold that against him, are you? This is not an uncommon situation, you know. Lots of young people get uneasy when their parents remarry. You mustn't make up your mind that he is some sort of villain. Stepparents often acquire an un-healthy reputation since Cinderella. But you are too sensible to be influenced by such things."

I began to feel a slight relief. I always felt cosy with my grandparents. I kept saying to myself: "And they'll be there. All I have to do is go to them."

She pressed my arm. "Come on," she said. "Tell me what's worrying you."

"I . . . I don't know what to call him."

40

She stopped short and looked at me; and then she started to laugh. To my surprise I found myself joining in.

She composed her features and looked very serious.

"Oh, what a weighty matter!" she said. "What are you going to call him? Step-papa? That won't do. Stepfather? Step-pa . . . or simply Father."

"I can't call him that," I said firmly. "I have a father and he is dead."

She must have noticed the stubborn line of my mouth.

"Well, Uncle Benedict."

"He's not my uncle."

"There is a family connection somewhere . . . a long way back . . . so you could do that with a fair conscience. Uncle Benedict. Uncle Lansdon. So that was what was worrying you!"

She knew it was more than that; but we had become lighthearted.

I had known that a talk with my grandmother would do me a lot of good.

I continued to feel better. I assured myself that, whatever happened, I had my grandparents. Moreover the atmosphere in the house had lightened considerably, for the servants were no longer anxious about their future. They were going to Manorleigh—all of them; and as the new house would be much bigger than our present one, there would probably be more servants. This would mean a rise in the status of the Emerys. Mrs. Emery would become a sort of housekeeper and he a full-time butler. Their anxieties had turned to pleasure and I could not spoil the happiness of those about me.

Then I heard more conversation. I must have been adept at keeping my ears open, partly because I was frustrated. On account of my youth, facts were often kept from me. There was nothing new about that, but in the past it had seemed less important.

This time it was Jane and Mrs. Emery and they were talking about the forthcoming wedding which was not surprising because it was everybody's favorite topic.

I was coming up the thickly carpeted stairs so my footsteps would not be heard, and the door to Mrs. Emery's sitting room was half open. She and Jane were turning out a cupboard, preparing for a move to Manorleigh, which we were all doing in some form or other at this time.

It was wrong to eavesdrop normally, I knew; but there must be occasions when it would be foolish not to do so.

I must find out all I could about this man my mother was going to marry. It was of the utmost importance to me . . . as well as to her. Thus I made excuses for myself and shamelessly, I paused and listened, awaiting revelations.

"I'm not surprised," Jane was saying. "I mean, the way she is . . . Goodness me, you can see she's in love with him. She's like a young girl.

Well, you've got to admit, Mrs. Emery, there's something about him."

"He's got something about him all right," agreed Mrs. Emery.

"What I mean is," went on Jane, "he's a real man."

"You and your real men."

"I reckon he'll be Prime Minister one day."

"Here. Hold on. He's not in Parliament yet. We've got to wait and see. People remember things . . . and even if they don't there's them to remind them."

"You mean that first wife of his. Oh, that's all settled now. She did it herself."

"Yes, but he married her for her money. She wasn't what you'd call 'all there' . . . if you know what I mean. A bit simple like. What would a man like him be doing marrying a girl like that? Well, you see, there was this here goldmine."

"Goldmine?" whispered Jane.

"Well, that's where his money come from, didn't it? See, there was gold on her father's land and Mr. Clever found out. So what did he do? There wasn't a son and the daughter got it all. So . . . he married her, then got his hands on the gold . . . and it was this goldmine that made him the rich man he is today."

"Perhaps he fell in love with her."

"Fell in love with the gold, more like."

"Well, it's not Mrs. M's money he's after, 'cos he's got a lot more himself."

"Oh, I reckon that's different, but it goes to show you . . ."

"Show you what?"

"The sort he is. He'll get what he wants. He'll be in that House of Commons before you can say Jack Robinson . . . and when he gets there, there'll be no holding him."

"You're pleased about all this, Mrs. Emery, I do believe."

"I've always wanted to be in one of them houses where things go on . . . above stairs. Mr. Emery feels the same. I'll tell you something. Things is going to be a bit lively in this new place, mark my words. Here! What are we doing gossiping? That's enough, Miss. We'll never get these things sorted out at this rate."

Silence. I made my way quietly up the stairs.

I did not like it. He had married a woman because of the gold found on her father's land; and then . . . she died mysteriously.

He might possess all the assets to make him Jane's Real Man. But I did not like it.

There was great activity. The by-election was soon to take place. My mother went to Manorleigh and Grace Hume left the Mission to give a hand. She was very efficient and had helped Benedict before.

I heard a certain amount of speculation about that, for Grace had been a close friend of Benedict's first wife. Nothing was said about this in

44

the press however. I only heard it from scraps of whispering from the servants.

My mother, as the prospective member's fiancée, was a great success.

Uncle Peter said: "There is nothing like the romantic touch for getting people's votes."

I felt alone—apart; it seemed as though my mother had already gone. They were all so busy. No one could talk of anything but elections; and Miss Brown had started a series of lessons on the Prime Ministers of England. I was heartily tired of Sir Robert Peel and his Peelers and Lord Palmerston and his gun-boat policies.

"If you are going to be a member of a political family, you must know something of the country's leaders," said Miss Brown archly.

Everyone was certain that Benedict Lansdon was going to win the seat although it had been in the hands of the Tories for over a hundred years. He was working indefatigably in Manorleigh, they said, speaking every night. My mother was often with him.

"She's a natural," commented Uncle Peter, who had travelled to Manorleigh to attend some of the meetings. "She's the politician's ideal wife . . . another Helena. Wives are a very important part of a member's ménage."

Nothing else seemed to exist for them. I was surprised by my attitude. I was wishing he would not win and reproaching myself for it. It would be such a great disappointment to all the people I loved best—most of all my mother. A little failure would be good for him, I told myself virtuously; but I knew in my heart that I hated him because he had spoilt my contented and peaceful existence when he came to play such a prominent part in my mother's life.

To the great delight of all the family, he won. I had always known that he would. He had taken the first step. He was now the Member of Parliament for Manorleigh. There was a great deal of publicity about it, because he had snatched the seat from the Tories who had held it for over a hundred years.

I was able to read about him in the papers. Writers tried to assess the reasons for his victory. He was knowledgeable; he had a ready wit; he was good-tempered with hecklers. They admitted he had fought a good campaign and he appeared to have the qualities necessary to make a good Member of Parliament. He was connected with Martin Hume who held cabinet rank in the Tory administration—albeit on the other side of the fence. It was a triumph for the Liberals. Mr. Gladstone expressed his satisfaction.

Benedict had been fortunate in having a newcomer to the neighborhood in his opponent, whereas he had fought the seat some time earlier; he had been set for victory then but the scandal attaching to his wife's death happening at such a critical moment had let in his opponent.

Well, here he was and Manorleigh could be congratulated on electing its new member, one who promised to show energy and enthusiasm if his campaign was anything to go by.

Uncle Peter was delighted. He was tremendously proud of his grandson. There was great rejoicing throughout the family and my mother was particularly excited.

"Now," she said, "we have to settle into that house in Manorleigh. Oh, Becca, won't that be fun?"

Would it? I wondered.

Christmas had passed and spring was approaching. The wedding day grew near.

I had tried hard to shake off my foreboding. I had on one or two occasions tried to talk to my mother about Benedict. She was eager enough to talk but did not tell me what I wanted to hear.

Often in the past she had told me about those days she had spent with my father and Pedrek's parents in the mining township. I had heard so much that I could see it clearly; the mine shaft, the shop where everything was sold, the shacks in which they lived, the celebrations when someone found gold. I could see the eager faces in the light of the fires on which they cooked their steaks; I could almost feel the hungry greed for gold.

I always saw my father as different from the others—the debonair adventurer who had come half way round the world to make his fortune. He was always merry, lighthearted, my mother told me; he always believed that luck would come to him. I could picture him so clearly I glowed with pride; I was desperately sad because I had never had the privilege of knowing him; and there followed his heroic end which fitted into the picture of my ideal. Why hadn't he lived? Then there would have been no possibility of my mother's marrying Benedict Lansdon.

Desperately I hoped that something would happen to prevent this marriage, but the days passed and the wedding day was fast approaching.

Benedict Lansdon had been fortunate in finding an old manor house on the market. It needed a good deal of restoration but my mother had said she would love to help in doing that. It had been built sometime in the early 1400s and restored in the days of Henry VIII—at least the two lower stories had; the upper one was pure medieval.

I should have been greatly interested in it if it had not been *his* house, for it was quite impressive if one did not compare it with Cador. It was shut in by red brick walls and there was an overgrown garden. I did like the garden. It was a place to lose oneself in. My mother was very excited. She was in a mood to find everything connected with her life wonderful. I wanted to remain aloof, but I could not. I was completely fascinated by Manor Grange, which was the name of the house, and I was drawn into discussions on medieval tiles and linen fold panelling, for the roof was faulty and we had to find the right tiles for repair, which was not easy, as they had to be both ancient and in good condition.

There was a long gallery for which my mother was collecting pictures. Aunt Amaryllis gave her some and my grandparents said she could choose what she wanted from Cador. I could have shared her enthusiasm if Benedict had not been part of it.

Above the gallery were the attics—big rooms with sloping ceilings which would be the servants' quarters. Mr. and Mrs. Emery had been down to see the rooms they would have and had expressed their delight.

"You must move in before the wedding," my mother had told her, "just to get everything ready for when we return . . . Perhaps you could go about a week before."

Mrs. Emery thought that would be excellent.

"It will be necessary to engage more staff," said my mother. "We'll have to go into that carefully."

Mrs. Emery agreed, bristling with pride which the responsibility of being in charge of a larger household brought her.

It was arranged that the furniture my mother wanted to keep should go down a week or so before the wedding. Our house would be put up for sale and the week before the wedding my mother and I would stay with Aunt Amaryllis and Uncle Peter. My grandparents, who would be coming to London for the wedding, would stay there also.

It was with great pleasure that the Emerys installed themselves in the new house, taking Jane and Ann with them. The Emerys immediately set about engaging more staff. They had changed overnight; they bristled with importance. Mrs. Emery affected black bombazine which rustled as she walked; she had also acquired jet beads and earrings which seemed to be the insignia of housekeeping dignity. She had assumed a new aura; she was imperious and formidable. Mr. Emery was only slightly less so. He was most carefully dressed in a morning coat with striped trousers. There was a world of difference in being butler to Mr. Benedict Lansdon, M.P., from handyman at the small residence of Mrs. Mandeville.

My mother laughed immoderately about the attitude of the servants and I laughed with her. So there were times when we seemed as close as we had ever been.

Then there was the house which was to be our London residence. It was tall, elegant and Georgian, situated in a London square opposite enclosed gardens. It was similar to that of Uncle Peter and Aunt Amaryllis, only Benedict Lansdon's—naturally—was even more grand. There was a spacious hall and a wide staircase, ideal for receiving guests before they were conducted to the lofty drawing room on the first floor where of course a Member of Parliament with high ambitions would do a great deal of entertaining. It was furnished with expensive simplicity—red and white with a touch of gold here and there. I wondered if I should ever feel it was home to me. I believed I would always think longingly of my room in our old house which was about half the size of the one allocated to me here. Miss Brown's was almost as large. Then we had a schoolroom on the same floor—very different from the little box of a room where Miss Brown and I used to work.

Miss Brown was as delighted by the change as the Emerys but she did not show it so blatantly. I wondered if I should have shared their pleasure in our more opulent way of life if I had not had to accept Benedict Lansdon with it.

It was coming closer. The servants had left for Manorleigh; my mother and I had moved in with Uncle Peter and Aunt Amaryllis and the preparations seemed more intensive than ever. Nobody spoke of anything but the wedding.

My grandparents arrived. I was allowed to join the dinner party. Uncle Peter had said that as soon as children came of a reasonable age they should do so because it was good for them to listen to the conversation of adults which gave them confidence. I have to admit to being a little fascinated by him. He was always so charming to everyone and made me feel that, young as I was, I was of some importance. There was none of that "not for the children" attitude from him. He would often address me and sometimes when he was talking at the table his eyes would meet mine and it was almost as though there was a secret understanding between us. What made him so attractive was that aura of wickedness about him. I knew there was something, but I was not sure what. It set him apart, some scandal from the past which he had overridden and from which he had emerged triumphantly by snapping his fingers at conventions. Mystery was very attractive. I was constantly trying to find out what he had done but no one would tell me.

It was strange because he reminded me so much of Benedict. I had the feeling that when he was Benedict's age he must have been rather like his grandson. Scandal had touched them both . . . and neither of them had allowed it to destroy him. There was something indestructible about him. I hated Benedict. I had admitted it at last. And it was because I was afraid of him. But on the other hand, because I had nothing to fear from Uncle Peter, I was fond of him.

There was no doubt that Uncle Peter was delighted by the coming marriage; he beamed his approval. He was certain that Benedict was going to succeed and politics had always fascinated him. He himself had planned such a career and whatever that scandalous thing was in his past, it had put an end to it. But he lived politics through his son-in-law Martin Hume. I had heard it said: "Martin is Peter's puppet." I wondered if this was so. I could well believe it. And now Benedict was to follow that tradition. But of one thing I was certain: Benedict would never be anyone's puppet.

Uncle Peter was very rich. So was Benedict. I had an inkling that they had both come to be wealthy in a rather shady way.

I wished I knew more. What frustration it is to be young . . . when people hide things from you and you can only glean little pieces of information. It is like fitting together a jigsaw puzzle with the most important bits missing.

Conversation at the dinner table was all about the wedding and the honeymoon which was to be in Italy. They would not go to France because that was where my mother had had her first honeymoon with my father. She used to tell me about the little hotel in the mountains overlooking the sea, where they had stayed.

"I wouldn't stay away too long," said Uncle Peter. "You don't want the people of Manorleigh to think their new M.P. is deserting them."

"We shall be away a month," my mother told him, and, seeing Uncle Peter looked a little shocked, she added: "I insisted."

"So you see," said Benedict, "I had to agree."

"I am sure the electorate of Manorleigh would realize that a honeymoon is a rather special occasion," put in my grandfather.

My mother smiled at Uncle Peter. "You are always saying that the people love romance. I think they might have been disappointed in us if we had cut it short."

"Good reasoning perhaps," conceded Uncle Peter.

When we went to our rooms that night, my grandmother followed me up.

"I wanted to have a little talk," she said. "Where shall you be while you are waiting for them to come back?"

I said: "I can stay here."

"Is that what you want?"

I hesitated. The tenderness in her voice touched me deeply, and I was horrified to discover that I was near to tears.

"I . . . I don't know," I said.

"I thought you didn't." She smiled brightly. "Why don't you come back with us? Your grandfather and I were talking about it coming up in the train and said how nice it would be if you decided to come and stay with us for a while. Miss Brown could come and . . . well, you might as well be at Cador as here."

"Oh . . . I'd like that."

"Then it's settled. Aunt Amaryllis won't mind. She'd understand that you might feel a little lonely here, whereas a complete change of scene . . . we all know you love Cador . . . to say nothing of how we should love to have you."

"Oh, Granny," I cried, and flung myself into her arms.

I did weep a little but she pretended not to notice.

"It's the best time of the year for Cornwall," she said.

So they were married. My mother looked beautiful in a dress of pale lavender and a hat of the same color with an ostrich feather to shade her face. Benedict looked very distinguished; everyone said what a handsome pair they made.

There were many important people there and they all came back to the house where Uncle Peter

54

and Aunt Amaryllis played their accustomed role of host and hostess.

Uncle Peter was obviously pleased by the way in which everything had gone. As for myself, my depression had deepened. All my hopes for the miracle which was going to stop the marriage had come to nothing. Heaven had turned from me and my prayers had fallen on deaf ears. My mother, Mrs. Angelet Mandeville, was now Mrs. Benedict Lansdon.

And *he* was my stepfather.

Everyone was assembled in the drawing room; the cake had been cut, the champagne drunk, the speeches made. It was time for the departure on the honeymoon.

My mother had gone to her room to change. As she passed me she said: "Rebecca, come with me. I want to talk."

Willingly I followed her.

When we were in her bedroom she turned to me, concern showing on her face.

"Oh Becca," she said, "I wish I hadn't got to leave you."

I felt a rush of happiness and, fearing to show my true feelings, I said: "I could hardly expect to go with you on your honeymoon."

"I'll miss you."

I nodded.

"I hope you'll be all right. I am so glad you are going to Cornwall. It's where you'd rather be, I know. You do love them so much, don't you . . . and Cador . . . ?"

I nodded again.

She held me tightly in her arms.

"When I come back . . . it's going to be wonderful. You'll share things with us . . ."

I just smiled and pretended that I was content. I had to. I could not spoil the happiness which I knew was hers.

I stood with the others waving goodbye.

My grandmother was beside me. She took my hand and pressed it.

The next day I was with them on our way to Cornwall.

The Waiting Months

My grandmother was right. Spring is undoubtedly the best time in Cornwall. I felt better when I smelt the sea. I stood at the carriage window as we chuffed through red-soiled Devon where the train ran close to the sea for a few miles . . . then leaving lush Devon behind and crossing the Tamar into Cornwall which had its own special fey quality to be found nowhere else.

And in time we had arrived. The station master greeted us and one of the grooms was waiting with the carriage to take us to Cador. I felt more emotional than usual when I saw the grey stone walls and those towers facing the sea; and I knew I had been right to come.

My familiar room was ready for me and soon I was at the window watching the gulls swooping and screeching and the white frothy waves slightly ruffled by the breeze blowing in from the southwest.

My grandmother looked in and said: "I'm glad you came. Your grandfather was afraid you might not."

I turned and smiled at her. "Of course I came," I said, and we laughed together.

Miss Brown was pleased to be in Cornwall although I think she was looking forward to being in her new grand quarters at Manorleigh and in London.

"The change will be good," she said. "A bridge between the old and new way of life."

I slept more deeply that night than I had for some time and was undisturbed by the vague dreams which had haunted my sleep lately. Benedict Lansdon was usually somewhere in those dreams . . . a rather sinister figure. I told no one of them. I knew people would say I was building up feelings against him for no other reason than that I resented a stepfather. And perhaps they would be right.

The next day at breakfast, my grandmother said: "What shall you do today?"

"Well, Miss Brown thinks we should waste no more time. Lessons have been a little interrupted lately and she thinks we should get down to normal work without delay."

My grandmother grimaced. "What does that mean . . . lessons in the morning?"

"Yes. I'm afraid so."

"Is that the law?" asked my grandfather.

"As unalterable as that of the Medes and the Persians," replied my grandmother.

"I was hoping we'd have a ride together today," he went on. "Perhaps this afternoon, as this morning seems to be devoted to work."

"You ought to go and see Jack and Marian," said my grandmother. "They'll be put out if you don't take Rebecca along."

Jack was my mother's brother. One day he would inherit Cador and he had been brought up to manage the estate. This he did with the same single-mindedness which his father had always shown. He did not live at Cador now although I supposed in due course he would come back to the ancestral home. He, with his wife and five-year-old twins, lived at Dorey Manor—a lovely Elizabethan manor-house. They were often at Cador. On his marriage he had expressed a desire for a separate household, which I think was due to his wife who, although she was very fond of my grandmother, was the sort of woman who would want to be absolute mistress in her own household. It seemed an excellent arrangement.

Dorey Manor had been the home of my grandfather before his marriage, so it was all part of the Cador estate.

"We'll look in on them this afternoon," said my grandfather. "Agreed, Rebecca?"

"Of course. I am longing to see them."

"Then that's settled.'

"I'll tell them to get Dandy ready for you."

"Oh yes, please."

It felt like coming home. This was my own family. My likes and dislikes were remembered. My dear Dandy, whom I always rode in Cornwall, was waiting for me. He was so called because there was an elegance about him. He was beautiful and seemed fully aware of the fact. He was graceful in all his movements and seemed fond of me in a certain rather disdainful way. "He's a regular dandy," one of the grooms had said of him, and that was the name he became to be known by.

Galloping along the beach, cantering across the meadows, I would forget for a while that Benedict Lansdon had taken my mother from me.

My grandmother said suddenly: "Do you remember High Tor?"

"That lovely old house?" I asked. "Weren't there new people there?"

"The Westcotts, yes. But they were only renting. When Sir John Persing died there was no family left. The trustees of the estate wanted to sell . . . and they let it in the meantime. That was how the Westcotts came. Well, there are some new people there now . . . French."

"A kind of refugee," said my grandfather.

"How interesting. Do you know them?"

"We are on nodding terms. They've come over from France after the trouble there . . . or before perhaps . . . seeing it coming."

"The trouble?"

"Now don't tell your grandfather you don't know what's been happening in France. He'll be horrified at your ignorance."

"Wasn't there a war, or something?"

"A war indeed—and a mighty defeat of the French by the Prussians. And it is because of this defeat that the Bourdons are here."

"You mean they have left their own country?"

60

"Yes."

"And are they going to live here?"

My grandmother shrugged her shoulders. "I don't know. But at the moment they are at High Tor. I think they have taken the place on approval as it were with a view to buying. I expect a great deal will depend on what happens in France."

"What are they like?"

"There are the parents and a son and daughter."

"How interesting. Do people here like them?"

"Well, there is always prejudice against foreigners," said my grandfather.

"The girl is rather sweet," said my grandmother. "She's Celeste. I'd say she was about sixteen, wouldn't you, Rolf?"

"I imagine so," replied my grandfather.

"And the young man . . . he's very dashing . . . what would you say . . . twenty . . . twenty-one . . . ?"

"Very likely. We might ask them over some time. Would you like that, Rebecca?"

"Oh yes . . . of course. I suppose most things are just the same here as they always were."

"Oh, we have our changes. As we've told you, we've had the French invasion. Apart from that, much remains the same. The October gales were a little more fierce last year and there was even more rain than usual, which did not please the farmers. Mrs. Polhenny is still sorting out the sheep from the goats, preaching the gospel of eternal damnation awaiting the sinners, which include most of us, herself being the only exception. And Jenny Stubbs is as bemused as ever."

"Does she still go about singing to herself?"

My grandmother nodded. "Poor soul," she said softly.

"And thinks she is going to have a baby?"

"Just the same, I'm afraid. But she is happy enough . . . so I suppose it is not as tragic to her as it seems to us."

"It's going to be a fine day," said my grandfather. "I'll look forward to our ride this afternoon."

I left them at the breakfast table and went up to my room.

In the schoolroom Miss Brown would be waiting for me.

Dandy was saddled and ready for me in the stables.

"Nice to have 'ee back, Miss Rebecca," Jim Isaacs, the groom, told me.

I told him it was nice to be back and as we were talking my grandfather arrived.

"Hello," he said. "Are we all ready? Well then, we might as well go, Rebecca."

It was good to be riding through those lanes. Everywhere was a profusion of wild flowers and the air was damp with the balmy smells of spring. In the fields the dandelions and daisies, the lady smocks and cuckoo flowers were blooming; and the birds were singing rapturously because spring was here. I told myself I had been right to come.

"Where would you like to go after Dorey Manor? Down to the sea, back over the moors or just a ride in the country lanes?"

"I don't mind. I'm just glad to be here."

"That's the spirit," he said.

We made our way to Dorey Manor. Aunt Marian came out to greet us, holding a twin by each hand.

She embraced me warmly.

"Jack," she called. "Come and see who's here."

Uncle Jack came running down the stairs.

"Rebecca." He hugged me. "Lovely to see you. How are you, eh?"

"Very well, Uncle, and you?"

"Better than ever now I've seen you. How did the wedding go?"

I told them that all had gone according to plan.

The twins were tugging at my skirts. I looked down at them. They were adorable—Jacco and Anne-Mary. Jacco after that young man who had drowned in Australia with his parents, and Anne-Mary taking part of my grandmother's name Annora and part from her mother Marian.

They leaped round me, expressing their pleasure. Anne-Mary asked with great gravity if I knew that she was four and three-quarters and would be five in June. She added, as though it were a matter for great surprise: "Jacco will be too."

I expressed great interest in the fact and then

listened to Jacco telling me how well he could ride.

We went into the house in which my grandfather took great pride. It had been almost beyond repair when he and his parents had restored it. They had been lawyers and my grandfather was trained in his profession but he had abandoned all that most willingly to devote himself to Cador.

Jack proudly showed us the recent restoration of the linen fold panelling while Marian brought out a decanter of her homemade wine. There was talk about the estate and of course the wedding. Marian wanted to hear all about that.

"What a different life it will be for Angelet," said Jack.

"Most exciting, I am sure," added Marian.

And I felt one of those twinges of sadness and resentment which I knew would be with me for a long time.

We left them in due course and continued our ride. We went inland for a mile or so. I looked ahead to the grey stone house built on a slight hillock.

"High Tor," commented my grandfather. "Hardly a tor. Just a little high ground."

"All the same, it must be draughty when the winds blow," I said.

"But compensated by the superb views of the countryside. The walls are thick and they have stood up to the storms for at least a couple of hundred years. I daresay the Bourdons manage to keep snug enough inside."

"It must be rather sad to be driven out of one's country."

"There is an alternative. Stay and take the consequences."

"It must be a difficult decision. I could not see *you* ever leaving Cador."

"I hope such an eventuality would never occur."

"Cador would be quite different without you, Grandfather."

"I loved it the moment I saw it. But I can understand those people in a way. Remember, the great revolution is not so far back; and the defeat by the Prussians must have unnerved them."

We were walking our horses along a winding path when we heard the sound of hoofs a little way off. Then we were confronted by two riders—a girl of about sixteen and a young man a few years older.

"Good morning," said my grandfather.

"Good morning," they both replied, their French accent discernible in those two short words, so I guessed who they were.

"Rebecca," said my grandfather, "this is Monsieur Jean Pascal Bourdon and Mademoiselle Celeste Bourdon. My granddaughter Rebecca Mandeville."

Two pairs of bright, alert, dark eyes studied me intently.

The girl was attractive with her dark hair and eyes and olive skin. Her riding habit fitted her womanly figure perfectly and she sat her horse with a grace which was immediately apparent. The

65

same description could also be applied to the young man. He was lithe and handsome with smooth almost black hair and a ready smile.

"Are you settling happily?" asked my grandfather.

"Oh yes . . . yes . . . we settle very well, do we not, Celeste?"

"We settle very well," she repeated carefully.

"That's splendid. My wife wanted you all to come over and have luncheon one day," went on my grandfather. "Do you think that will be possible?"

"It would be a *grand plaisir*."

"Your parents . . . and both of you . . . how's that?"

The girl said: "We like very much . . ."

Her brother added: "Yes, very much."

"It must be soon," added my grandfather. "Rebecca's home is in London and we don't know how long she will be staying with us."

"Very nice," they said.

The men doffed their hats and we went on our way.

"They seem very pleasant," said my grandfather; and I agreed.

"I think it is time we started back," he said. "We spent longer than I intended at Dorey. Still, you had to see Marian and Jack and the twins."

On our way home we went past Mrs. Polhenny's cottage with the prim curtains drawn across all the windows. I thought of Leah working away at her embroidery behind one of them and started once more to wonder about her.

My grandmother was interested to hear of our encounter with the Bourdons. "I'll think about making a date right away," she said.

There were no schoolroom meals at Cador. I took them with my grandparents. They said that they did not see me often enough and did not want to lose a moment of my company. Miss Brown had her meals with us too.

That evening we talked of the Bourdons. My grandmother had already sent a note over to High Tor inviting them.

"I am so sorry for people who find it necessary to leave their countries," my grandmother was saying.

"We had a great number of them over here at the end of last century," added my grandfather.

Miss Brown remarked that the French Revolution was a dreadful piece of history. "We shall be covering it when you have finished with the English Prime Ministers, Rebecca." She added, turning to my grandparents: "I thought she should know something of them, as she will soon be living in political circles."

"An excellent idea," said my grandfather. "How interesting it must be."

"These leaders are so important," said my grandmother.

"The trouble is," said Miss Brown, "that some

of them are not truly fitted for the post. Perhaps all great men have some flaws."

"As the rest of us do," said my grandfather.

"Napoleon the Third certainly had his."

"You know who he is, Rebecca?" My grandfather had turned to me. He never left me out of the conversation.

"Well, he was the French Emperor before the war, wasn't he?"

"Exactly. It is a great mistake for people to have responsibility simply because they are related to the great. There was only one Napoleon. We did not need a second or a third."

"I suppose it is their name," I said. "And they have a right to it."

"His father was Louis Bonaparte, King of Holland, brother of the first Napoleon, and his mother Hortense de Beauharnais, Napoleon the First's stepdaughter," said Miss Brown, who could never resist turning any conversation into a lesson. "From an early age he wanted to follow in his uncle's footsteps."

"So he succeeded in becoming Emperor," said my grandmother.

"And his early career was one disaster after another," continued my grandfather who was as interested in history as Miss Brown. "His vainglorious attempts to call attention to himself resulted in a term of imprisonment. First he was shipped to the United States and then he came here to England where he was for a while, but he saw his chance with the outbreak of the revolution in '48, returned to France, acquired a seat in the National Assembly, and started to work for the imperial title."

"Well, he succeeded in getting it, apparently," said my grandmother.

"Yes, for a time."

"Quite a long time, I believe," she replied.

"He wanted a name to compare with that of his uncle. But he hadn't the same genius."

"And where did Napoleon's genius lead him?" demanded my grandmother.

"Elba and St Helena," I cut in, eager to show them that I knew something of what they were talking about.

Miss Brown threw me a glance of approval.

"All might have been well," continued my grandfather, "if he had not become jealous of the growing power of Prussia, and underestimated it. He provoked war with Prussia. He thought he could defeat them easily and win glory for himself. He reckoned without the discipline of the Prussians. He must have known his fate was sealed at Sedan."

"And then the Bourdons decided to get away," I said, trying to turn the conversation to a subject of more immediate concern to us.

"Very far-seeing indeed," said my grandfather. "Revolution in Paris . . . disaster for Napoleon III. And as a consequence we have the Empress and her son at Camden House in Chislehurst . . . and the Emperor has now joined her . . . no longer a prisoner . . . but an exile from his country."

"Like the Bourdons," I said.

My grandmother smiled at me. "You should never let your grandfather get on to history," she said. "There is no stopping him once he gets started."

"A fascinating subject," said Miss Brown with a smile.

Just as we were leaving the dining room, one of the grooms came in with a note for my grandmother.

The Bourdons were all delighted to accept her kind invitation to luncheon.

They came as arranged and it was a very interesting meeting.

Monsieur and Madame Bourdon were, as my grandmother commented afterwards, typically French. He had a trim pointed beard, crisp dark hair and a very gallant manner. He kissed hands . . . even mine . . . and the look he gave my grandmother was clearly one of admiration. Madame was a good-looking woman and her vivacity and charm made her seem ten or fifteen years younger than she must have been. She was inclined to be plump; her hair was faultlessly dressed and her large brown eyes gave the impression that she missed little. Their English was barely adequate, but I found that quaint and charming.

The son and daughter were like their parents

and I detected similar qualities. The young man's gallantry and awareness of feminine society for instance; the girl's svelte appearance.

They admired Cador's impressiveness and antiquity; and my grandmother said she would show them the house after luncheon if they wished to see it. Monsieur Bourdon said it would be a great pleasure, Madame declared it would give her immense delight, and the son and daughter echoed their parents' words.

Over lunch they talked of the terrible events in their country which had led to their exile.

I gathered that Madame Bourdon was acquainted with the Empress Eugenie and that Monsieur Bourdon had, on several occasions, been admitted to the society of Napoleon III.

"Now that our Emperor and Empress are in England . . . we feel that we must be with them," said Monsieur Bourdon haltingly.

My grandmother asked them how much they liked High Tor.

"Very well . . . very well," was their reply.

"Do you think you will return to France?" asked my grandfather.

Monsieur Bourdon put the palms of his hands together and shook his head from side to side, shrugging his shoulders at the same time.

"It could be . . . yes. It could be . . . no. La République." He grimaced. "If the Emperor returns . . ."

"I should hardly think he would do that for a very long time," said my grandfather.

71

"And in the meantime he lives in exile," added my grandmother. "I wonder how they feel about that. It must be strange to go from all the pomp and ceremony of the French Court to quiet Chislehurst."

"Perhaps he is happy to escape to that quiet spot."

I noticed that Jean Pascal was watching Jenny, the parlormaid who was serving at table. Their eyes met as she held a dish of vegetables for him. She was flushed. Jenny was interested in young men, I knew. I promised myself that I would try to find out what she thought of this one.

When the meal was over we showed them over Cador.

I was with them. I liked to hear my grandfather explain the history of the place. He loved the topic so much and spoke so enthusiastically that my grandmother gently put an end to his discourse which she feared might be boring to the guests.

We were in the gallery in which were displayed some old tapestries, some in the region of five hundred years old, when Madame Bourdon became very excited.

"*Cette tapisserie* . . . it is . . . how you say? . . . er . . . made right?"

"Repaired? Oh yes. We had to have it done. I think it was mended rather well."

"But . . . it is very good."

"You noticed."

"My wife . . . she is very interested," explained

Monsieur Bourdon. "We have some *tapisserie* . . . very good . . . very old . . . Gobelins . . . You understand?"

"Indeed yes," said my grandmother. "That must be wonderful."

Jean Pascal, who was more fluent in our language than his parents were, said that they had brought some of their most valuable tapestry with them. They had been going to have it repaired in France, but if there was someone who could repair it as well as ours had been done, perhaps it would be possible for theirs to be done here.

"It was a young girl living quite near here who restored these two years ago," said my grandmother. "She is very clever with her needle, as you see. She is a professional seamstress and does embroidery on garments and such things which are sold in the shops in Plymouth . . . at quite high prices I imagine."

Madame Bourdon became very excited.

"If you could tell my mother where to find this embroiderer, she would be very grateful to you," said Jean Pascal.

My grandmother was thoughtful. She glanced at my grandfather. "It's Leah," she said, "and that makes it a little awkward. You know how Mrs. Polhenny was about letting Leah come up here."

She turned to our guests. "I will speak to the girl's mother and ask her if she will allow the girl to go to High Tor. You see, her mother likes her to work at home."

"We will pay well . . ." began Jean Pascal.

"Leave it to me. I will do what I can."

We left it at that and there was a great deal of talk about tapestry. Apparently the Bourdons had some priceless pieces in their collection—one from the Château of Blois and another which had been in Chambord.

"It was risk bringing them over," said Jean Pascal, "but my mother could not bear to leave them behind, and some of them did get a little damaged in transport."

When they left, my grandmother assured them that the next day she would go to the Polhenny cottage and would let them know the result immediately.

The next afternoon my grandmother said she was going to beard Mrs. Polhenny in her den and would I care to accompany her? I said I would.

We walked into the town, talking about the Bourdons and the possibility of Mrs. Polhenny's allowing Leah to go up to High Tor to do the work.

"It would mean she would have to stay up there for several weeks, I expect."

"Why should she not go each day?"

"Well, I think she needs the very best light to do the work. She might get there and find the light no longer any good. I think she would have to be on the spot."

"Why shouldn't Mrs. Polhenny want her to stay there?"

"Mrs. Polhenny sees evil all around her . . . even where it doesn't exist . . . and she expects the worst. She wants Leah to live in the shelter of her own home where a watchful eye can be kept on her."

We reached the cottage. The windows gleamed, the pebbles on the path looked as though they had been freshly polished, the porch steps had been recently scrubbed. We knocked at the door.

There was a long pause. We listened and thought we could hear a movement within. My grandmother called out: "It's Mrs. Hanson and Rebecca. Is that you, Leah?"

The door opened and there was Leah. She looked flushed, uncertain and very pretty.

"My mother is not in," she said. "She was called up to Egham Farm. Mrs. Masters has started."

"Oh," said my grandmother, and then: "May we come in for a moment?"

"Oh, yes . . . of course. Please do," replied Leah.

We were taken into the parlor. I noticed that the brass ornaments had been polished to a dazzling brilliance. There was a sofa with two cushions placed at symmetrical angles; the antimacassars on the backs of the chairs were spotless and there were arm covers on the chairs to prevent contamination from those who sat in them.

We scarcely dared sit.

"Shall I ask Mother to come and see you when she returns? I don't know when it will be. You can never be sure with babies."

"Well, this actually concerns you, Leah," said my grandmother. Leah must be about eighteen years old after all. It was an age to make one's own decisions. But she was clearly a meek girl and Mrs. Polhenny was a formidable parent. "You know the French people?"

"Those at High Tor," said Leah.

My grandmother nodded. "They took luncheon with us yesterday and while they were there they saw the work you had done on the tapestries."

"Oh, I loved doing that, Mrs. Hanson."

"I know you did. It was a change, wasn't it? Well, apparently they have some fine tapestries up there. They mentioned Gobelins. You know of them, Leah? Of course you do. They are some of the finest in the world. They are very ancient and in need of repair. Having seen what you did to ours . . ."

Leah looked excited.

"In fact, they would like to talk to you about repairing theirs."

"Oh, I should love to do that. I get a little tired of working rosebuds and butterflies on ladies' petticoats."

"This would be different, wouldn't it? And fancy . . . they have been worked by people hundreds of years ago."

"Yes, I know."

"You would be expected to stay up there while

76

you did the work. You would need the best of light and the journey to and fro would be a little too long . . . there and back."

She nodded. Then she said: "My mother did not like my being away from home . . . even with you."

"Well, that is what I came to discuss. I promised Monsieur and Madame Bourdon that I would ask you. They would pay you very well. I imagine you could name your price."

I studied her. She was very pretty; and now that she was excited, this was more obvious.

"Would you like a cup of tea?" she asked.

"That would be very acceptable," replied my grandmother.

She left us. We looked round the little room and I knew what my grandmother was thinking. It had an unlived-in look. I could not imagine that this was a very happy home. There would be too much striving after what was right and proper in the eyes of that martinet Mrs. Polhenny—and little thought of pleasure.

While we were drinking tea and nibbling home-made biscuits that lady herself came in.

She came straight into the parlor. She was surprised. Her eyes rested momentarily on me and I wondered if I was doing something I should not and perhaps spoiling the perfection of her brown velvet-covered armchair.

"Mrs. Hanson . . ." she began.

"You must forgive the intrusion, Mrs. Pol-

77

henny," said my grandmother. "Leah has given us tea and your oatmeal biscuits are delicious."

"Oh," said Mrs. Polhenny, smiling, "I'm glad she made tea for you."

"How was it at the farm?"

"Another boy." Her face softened. "A lovely healthy boy. They're pleased. Rather a long labor but everything going well. I shall be keeping my eyes on them. I'll be getting back later today."

"I'm glad all went well. We came to talk of a rather interesting proposition. We have mentioned it to Leah."

"Oh, what was that?"

"You know we have those French refugees up at High Tor?"

"Yes, I do."

"And Leah made such a good job of our tapestries. When they came to luncheon with us they saw what she had done. The fact is they would like her to do the same for them. Apparently they have some valuable pieces up there and they want someone to repair them. They would like Leah to do it."

Mrs. Polhenny was frowning. "Leah has plenty of work here."

"This would be different and more highly paid, I imagine."

That did bring a glimmer of interest into Mrs. Polhenny's eyes.

"It would mean her staying up there for a week or two . . . perhaps even more."

Mrs. Polhenny's face hardened. "Why couldn't she go every day?"

"Well, it is a little far . . . that journey twice a day . . . and then there is the matter of catching the best of the light. It's intricate work."

"Leah wouldn't want to be away from home."

"Don't you think she would enjoy a change? She'd be very comfortable up at High Tor and they would be very grateful to get the work done. Madame Bourdon was quite lyrical about her tapestry. You can see she loves it."

"Leah has plenty of work here."

"Do think about it, Mrs. Polhenny."

"I think a young girl's place is home with her mother."

"But she wouldn't be far away."

"Couldn't they send the tapestries here?"

"Impossible. They are big, I expect . . . and very valuable."

"They could get somebody else."

"They like Leah's work. She is especially talented. This would be good for her. People might visit them and see her work . . . as they visited us. You don't know what would come of it. You know we have the Emperor Napoleon and Empress Eugenie in England now. They are friends of Monsieur and Madame Bourdon. Who knows, Leah might be working for royalty."

Mrs. Polhenny looked skeptical. "They're a sinful lot, from what I hear."

"Oh, Mrs. Polhenny, you can't believe all you

hear. I think this would be an excellent chance for her."

"I don't like my daughter to be away from home at night. I like to know she's here . . . and I'm in the next room to her."

"Don't refuse right away. Think about it. Leah loved doing our tapestry. How much more interesting such work is than plain embroidery."

"With foreigners!"

"They are the same as we are," I said.

Mrs. Polhenny gave me a stern look. In her opinion, I was sure, young girls should be seen and not heard.

"Let's leave it like this," said my grandmother. "But think what it would be worth . . . financially."

"I'd want her home every night."

"I don't think that would be feasible. She has to catch the best of the light and you know how predictable the weather is. A light morning can turn to a dull one and her journey would be wasted. And it is a little far. Just think about it. In the meantime, I'll have a word with Madame Bourdon."

So we left it at that.

As we walked away my grandmother said: "Sometimes I think Mrs. Polhenny is a little unbalanced. It's a pity. She's such an excellent midwife."

"And a good housewife too, it seems. There's nothing out of place in that cottage. It's uncomfortably clean."

My grandmother laughed. "It's what is called a fetish and I don't think that is a very healthy thing to have. Then, of course, there's Leah. She can't have a very happy life. Poor girl, it must be difficult to live up to that perfection. And the way she guards the girl . . . it's really unnatural."

"She seems afraid that Leah might do something . . . terrible."

My grandmother nodded and said: "I do hope she will see sense. I tried to persuade her. I thought I detected a glimmer of interest when I talked of money."

"Yes, so did I."

"Well, we'll have to wait and see. I'll write a note to Madame Bourdon and tell her of the reluctance. Perhaps if the money were tempting enough . . ."

So we should have to wait and see.

A letter came from my mother. She was wonderfully happy, she wrote, and she hoped I was enjoying Cornwall. What she was looking forward to about coming home was seeing me. She hoped I would be in London when she arrived. We would stay a few days there and then go down to Manorleigh. It was going to be so exciting.

"You will be able to help us in the political work. It will be great fun and I know that you will enjoy it. Oh, Becca, we're going to be so happy together . . . the three of us."

81

So she wanted me there when she returned.

I showed the letter to my grandmother.

"She's very happy," she said smiling. "It comes out, doesn't it? You can sense it. We must be happy for her, Rebecca. She deserves to be happy."

"I must be there when she comes back," I said.

"Yes, your grandfather and I will go up with you. I should like a few days in town."

So it was arranged.

The last day arrived. I rode in the morning, Miss Brown was busy packing. In the afternoon I took a walk to the pool. I saw Jenny on the way. She was singing softly to herself happy in the certainty that she would soon have her baby.

She was certainly, as my grandmother would say, unbalanced. I suppose the same description could be applied to Mrs. Polhenny because of her preoccupation with sin.

We heard that she had succumbed to the lure of money, that Leah had completed her commitments to the Plymouth customers, and was going to take a rest from such work and go up to High Tor to repair the Bourdons' tapestries.

The next day we left for London. We went to Uncle Peter and Aunt Amaryllis as we usually did. My mother and her husband were due to arrive in London the day after we did.

I was apprehensive, realizing how peaceful it had been in Cornwall and how preoccupied I had been with the matter of the Bourdons' tapestries and Mrs. Polhenny's addiction to virtue, as well as with Jenny Stubbs singing happily in the lanes.

That was far away and now I had to face the grim reality.

I thought Uncle Peter was strangely quiet. Usually he dominated the scene. When I asked him how he was he said he was well and busy as usual and very much looking forward to the return of the married couple.

"Now we shall see something," he said. "Benedict is not the man to stand still."

The pride and admiration in his voice annoyed me. Why must everyone have this immense respect for the man!

The day came. The cab arrived at the door. We were all waiting to greet them. And there was my mother, looking beautiful and I noticed with a pang—half regret, half pleasure—looked as radiant as she had before she left, or perhaps even more so.

I flung myself into her arms.

"Oh Becca, Becca," she said. "How I've missed you! Everything would have been perfect if you had been there."

Benedict was smiling at me. He took my hands in his. My mother was watching us . . . willing me to show my pleasure. So I smiled as brightly as I could.

She had brought a china plaque for me to hang on my wall. On it had been painted a picture of a woman who bore a strong resemblance to Raphael's

Madonna della Sedia of which I had once seen a copy and had loved it. She had remembered this.

"It's lovely," I said.

"We chose it together."

And again I smiled at him.

After dinner, I was to go back with them to his London house and I was not looking forward to it. I felt it would indeed be the beginning of a new life.

There was a great deal of talk at dinner. Aunt Amaryllis wanted to hear about Italy and the honeymoon; Uncle Peter was more interested in what plans Benedict had.

"We shall go down to Manorleigh as soon as possible," said Benedict. "I don't want my constituents to think that I am an absentee Member."

"There'll be lots for you to do, Angelet," said Aunt Amaryllis. "I know how it is with Helena."

"Garden fêtes to open . . . bazaars . . . charities for this and that," said my mother. "I'm prepared."

"It will be nice to be at Manorleigh," went on Aunt Amaryllis, "and you'll have the town house as well. What could be more convenient?"

"It's a blessing that Manorleigh happens to be so near London," said Benedict. "It'll make the journey to and fro so much easier."

"What on earth would have happened if your constituency had been in Cornwall?"

"I can only thank Heaven that it was not."

I wished it had been. Then I could have been with my grandparents for much of the time. But

I would still visit them . . . frequently. I must remember that. If ever life became too difficult with *him* . . . I had my escape.

When the meal was over I left with my mother and her husband for his house. My grandparents were staying with Uncle Peter and Aunt Amaryllis and going back to Cornwall in a few days.

As we walked to the house, my mother linked her arm through mine. He was on the other side of her; they were arm in arm. Anyone seeing us would have thought what a happy family we were and none would have guessed at the turmoil within me.

I felt lost in the big house and a desolate sense of not belonging. It was such a grand house. As soon as I entered it I felt as though every part of it was looking down its nose, demanding to know what I was doing there. Everything looked as though it had cost a great deal of money. There were heavy red curtains, their rich folds held in place by thick bands which in any other house one would have dismissed as brass. The walls were white and looked as though they had been freshly painted. The furniture was elegant—of an earlier period—Georgian, I think, to fit the house. Above the wide staircase hung an enormous chandelier. It was at the top of that staircase that my mother and her new husband would receive their guests. Beyond, on the first floor, were the enormous dining and drawing rooms. I could never feel at home in such a house.

My room was large and lofty with a tall window which looked down on the street. It was heavily curtained in deep blue velvet and there were lace curtains to shut out the street. My bed had a blue headpiece to match the curtains and there were hints of blue in the carpet. It was a beautiful room but not one to feel at home in.

I was glad when we left for Manorleigh.

There was a house which I could really love if it had not been his. I felt I could escape a little more in the country. There were the stables, so it was possible to ride often. Manorleigh itself was a small town but as Manor Grange was a short carriage drive outside it, it seemed to be in the country.

This was the constituency so there was a good deal to do here. Benedict was determined to show all the people who had elected him what an excellent M.P. he was and they were encouraged to call and discuss their problems.

Eager to be the perfect wife, my mother threw herself wholeheartedly into his life. It was a busy one. They would travel round the constituency which extended several miles into the surrounding countryside and it included many villages and several small towns.

"Your stepfather does not wish anyone to feel neglected," said my mother.

It was an embarrassment to mention him. She would have liked me to call him Father but even for her I could not do that. As for him, I was not sure what he wanted. He was too clever not to know how I felt about him, even though my mother tried to pretend that my hostility did not exist. He would not let it be of any great concern to him. It was my mother who was unhappy about it although she showed nothing. I was glad of that because if she had told me how unhappy my attitude made her I should have had to do something about it and I did not want to. I realize now that I had a certain satisfaction in harboring my resentment.

Still, I did like Manorleigh. So did Miss Brown.

We were still working on the Prime Ministers and were now concerned with Mr. Disraeli and Mr. Gladstone.

"Of course," said Miss Brown, "it is not easy to discover little facts about our contemporaries. It is only when people are dead that their little secrets come out."

We used to ride together and sometimes I went out with my mother and her husband. He liked that. It gave a good impression. I imagine he liked people to think that we were a happy family and in spite of his insouciance he must have realized he had something to live down on that score.

I grew to like my room. It had leaded windows, a great beam across the ceiling and the floor sloped a little. But what I liked best was that it looked down on the garden to an ancient oak tree under which was a sundial and a wooden seat. It was very picturesque and I felt a sense of peace when I looked out on it, past the pond on which floated water lilies and over which the figure of Hermes—winged sandals, staff wreathed with serpents, broad hat, sporting wings and all—was poised.

I found a great pleasure in making my way through the overgrown rosetrees and sitting for a while on that seat. It seemed so peaceful there.

As soon as we were settled in, the round of visits began. There were dinner parties and what were called *soirées* when perhaps some well-known musician would come and play the piano or violin. There were always important people to entertain. Fortunately I did not have to be present on these occasions. My mother seemed to enjoy them.

She said to me one day: "Do you know, Rebecca, I think I am turning into a good politician's wife."

"You mean, Mama," I replied, "the good wife of a politician. The way you say it makes it sound as if it is the politician who is good."

"Well, he is, isn't he?"

"I don't think that was what you meant to say."

"I am glad to see Miss Brown is keeping you well versed in your grammar." She looked faintly disturbed as she always did when Benedict—though not mentioned by name—crept into the conversation.

But it was true that she was enjoying her new way of life.

"I love meeting all those people," she said.

"Some of them are a trifle pompous. We have a good laugh over them afterwards."

Yes. She shared things with him from which I was shut out.

I knew in my heart that I was being foolish and unfair. It was I who was deliberately shutting myself out. Sometimes I tried to accept the situation, and I would for a while. Then all the old resentments would flare up.

Mrs. Emery said she was unable to do justice to her new position as she was expected to do so much cooking.

"But, of course," replied my mother. "How thoughtless of me. We must get someone to cook."

Mrs. Emery was secretly delighted.

"I suppose," I said to my mother, "a housekeeper is of higher rank than a cook . . . hence her delight."

"Mrs. Emery will, of course, be in charge of the household."

"As we have become grander, so has she," I commented.

"Well, naturally so," retorted my mother.

The news quickly circulated that the new member needed a cook at Manorleigh and Mrs. Grant appeared.

My mother liked her from the first and when she heard that her mother had been cook at Manorleigh and before that her grandmother, she knew that Mrs. Grant was the one for us.

She was a fat jolly woman with rosy cheeks and sparkling blue eyes. She had masses of rather untidy fair hair and her ample figure suggested that she liked eating food as well as cooking it.

"All to the good," said my mother. "You have to feel enthusiastic about something to do it well."

Mrs. Grant took charge of the kitchen and it soon became clear that we had a treasure in her. She and I took a fancy to each other from the start and she soon discovered my fondness for the garden.

She was a great talker and liked me to go into the kitchen when she was, as she said, pampering herself with a nice cup of tea and giving her feet a treat at the same time.

"It's my time of life," she said. "I don't like to stand more than I can help and a little sit-me-down in the afternoon . . . that's a bit of heaven to me."

One day she said to me: "You like the garden, don't you?" She filled up her cup and poured one out for me. "Did you feel there was something special about it?"

"Yes," I replied. "There is something about it. I think it is because of those overgrown trees. I hope no one touches them."

"So do I. They wouldn't like that."

"Who?"

She grimaced and pointed upwards. I looked astonished and she drew her chair closer to mine.

"You've heard of houses being haunted, have you?"

I nodded.

"This is a bit different. This is a garden that's haunted."

"Is it really? I've never heard of a haunted garden."

"Any place can be haunted. Doesn't have to be within walls. I just had the feeling you'd found out something out there. You're always sitting under that old oak. Why?"

"Well, it's shut away. It's peaceful there. When I'm sitting there I feel . . . apart."

She nodded. "Well, that's it. That's the spirit. That's where the ghost used to come."

"Used to?"

"Well, there'd be no call for it now . . . not after Miss Martha went."

"Tell me the story."

"It was in my grandma's day. She was the cook here. Lady Flamstead came . . . a lovely lady, my grandma said. She came here as a bride. He was a lot older than she was, Sir . . . what was his name? . . . Ronald, I think."

"What happened?"

"It was a happy marriage. Like two love-birds, they were, my gran said. They all loved her. She was so young . . . so excited by it all. She hadn't been used to a grand way of living . . . till he married her. She just enjoyed everything. Then came the day when she was going to have a baby. My gran said you should have seen the fuss. Sir Ronald . . . well, he wasn't all that old, I suppose, but he was beside himself with joy . . . and as for Lady Flamstead, she was in heaven."

"And . . . ?" I prompted.

"Well, everyone was so pleased. They were making such plans. My gran said you'd have thought nobody had ever had a baby before. Nursery done up . . . little toys everywhere . . . and then . . . Lady Flamstead . . . she didn't come through it. There was the baby they'd longed for . . . a little girl . . . but she was the end of her mother."

"How terribly sad!"

"Yes, wasn't it? The change in that house! They were all going to be so happy . . . You see, she was the one who had made it all like that. Without her . . . it was all changed. My gran said Sir Ronald . . . well, he was a good enough master, but he didn't have much to do with any of them. She'd changed all that. They'd all loved her . . . and now she was gone."

"They had the baby," I said.

"Oh, poor Miss Martha. You see, he didn't want her. I reckon he thought that but for her his little ladyship would still be there. And all he'd got was Miss Martha . . . a squalling red-faced little bit of nothing, in place of his lovely wife. He didn't want to look at the child. It turns out like that sometimes. Oh, there was all the best for her . . . nurses, and later on governesses. She was a nice little thing, my gran said. She'd come to the kitchen like you are now. But there was no laughter in that house and a house without laughter is not much of a place . . . not if there's a whole houseful of servants and all you get is the food to

92

eat and fires in every room to keep you warm . . . if you know what I mean."

"I do know what you mean, Mrs. Grant. Where does the haunting come in?"

"Well . . . Miss Martha was about ten years old . . . your age, I reckon, when they started to notice. She'd go out there and sit under that tree on that seat you like so much. She'd be talking . . . we thought to herself. She changed at that time. She was a bit difficult to manage before. Into mischief rather. My gran said she was trying to remind people she was there because she thought her father had forgotten all about her."

"It was very wrong of Sir Ronald to blame the child for her mother's death."

"Oh, he didn't do that, exactly. He just couldn't bear to be with her. I suppose he was reminded of what he had lost."

"So she changed, you were saying."

"She was more satisfied . . . peaceful like, so my gran said. And every day she'd be out there, talking away. They thought she was getting a little bit . . . peculiar."

"What happened then to change her?"

"One of the maids thought she saw a figure in white there. It was dusk. It might have been the shadows. But she came running into the house, scared out of her wits. Miss Martha was there. She said, 'It's nothing to be afraid of. It's my mother. She comes here to talk to me.' That explained a lot . . . the change in her . . . why she was always at that spot in the garden. Why she seemed to be talking to herself. She wasn't talking to herself. She was talking to her mother."

"So her mother came back . . ."

"Like as not she couldn't rest . . . because she knew her daughter was unhappy. Miss Martha . . . she was apart from the rest of us like. A strange young lady. She never married. In time she inherited the house. They used to say she was a bit of a recluse. She wouldn't have the garden changed. The gardeners used to get wild saying that this ought to come down and this and that be cut back. But she wouldn't have it. She was quite old when she died. My mother was in the kitchen then."

"Do you believe Lady Flamstead really came back?"

"My gran said she did and anyone who'd been there would have said it."

"It does seem the sort of garden where anything could happen."

Mrs. Grant nodded and went on sipping her tea.

After that I visited the seat often. I would sit there and think about Miss Martha. I felt a sympathy with her, though our situation was by no means similar. I had my mother, even though she had partially been withdrawn from our close relationship. But I did understand Martha's feelings. She was unwanted because her coming had resulted in the departure of one who had been greatly loved;

she was a poor consolation for what her father had lost.

One day my mother came out and found me sitting there.

"You're often here," she said. "You like it, don't you? I think you are beginning to love this house."

"It's a very interesting house . . . particularly the garden . . . It's haunted."

She laughed. "Who told you that?"

"Mrs. Grant."

"Of course . . . a descendant of the old retainers. My dear Rebecca, every self-respecting house over the age of a hundred years must have its ghost."

"I know. But this is a rather unusual ghost. It's in the garden."

"Good Heavens! Where?" My mother looked round with an air of mock expectancy.

"In this very place. Please don't mock. I have a feeling that ghosts don't like to be laughed at. They are very seriously dedicated to their purpose in returning."

"How knowledgeable you've become! You haven't learned that from Miss Brown, I'm sure. Is it Mrs. Grant whom you have to thank?"

"Let me tell you about the ghost. Lady Flamstead was the young wife of Sir Ronald. He doted on her and she died when her baby was born. Sir Ronald couldn't like the child because through her his wife had died. Poor little thing, she was very unhappy. Then one day she came out to the garden . . . she was about my age . . . and she sat in this seat and Lady Flamstead came back."

"I thought you said she had died."

"I mean she came back to Earth."

"Oh . . . so she is the ghost."

"She's not a mischievous one or anything like that. She was kind and gentle and much loved in her life and she came back because her child was unhappy. Mrs. Grant said her grandmother believed it and so did those who had been there at the time. You don't believe it, do you?"

"Well, these stories grow, you know. Someone imagines they see something . . . and someone else adds a bit . . . and there you have your ghost."

"This was different. Miss Martha changed when her mother came back. She wouldn't have the garden altered."

"Is that why you're here so often . . . hoping to see this ghost?"

"I don't think she would come to me. She doesn't know me. But I do feel there is something special about this spot, and when I heard the story it made it even more interesting. Mama, do you think it possible?"

She was silent for a few seconds. Then she said: "There are those who say all things are possible. There is a special tie between a mother and her child. It is thought the child is part of oneself . . ."

"Is that how you feel about me?"

She turned to me and nodded.

I felt very happy.

"I always shall, my darling," she said. "Nothing will alter that."

She was telling me that it was just the same as it ever was, and I felt happier than I had for a long time. I began to believe that eventually I might even accept Benedict Lansdon's intrusion into our lives. I was not like poor Martha. My mother was with me. It was really the same as it had ever been. Nothing could alter that.

The next few months flew past. We had now fully settled into Manor Grange and the days had taken on a routine. My mother was deeply immersed in my stepfather's life; she clearly enjoyed it. Now and then they went to London. I was always asked if I would like to accompany them but sometimes I preferred to stay in the country. Miss Brown said it was better to. She did not like lessons to be interrupted and travelling to and forth must necessarily do that.

I often thought of Cornwall . . . so different from Manorleigh country, where the fields were like carefully fitted patches into a quilt; and even the trees looked as though they had been pruned. I rarely saw the strange, twisted and often grotesque shapes I encountered frequently in Cornwall . . . those trees which had been victim to the southwest gales. Here in the Manorleigh constituency the little country towns clustered round the greens, with the church spires rising among the trees. It all seemed comfortable, orderly, completely lacking that fey quality which one took for granted in Cornwall.

I often thought of Cador—and not without nostalgia. There were letters from the grandparents. They were constantly asking when we were going down.

That seemed a remote possibility now. Constituencies had to be nursed and Benedict Lansdon, his eyes on far-off goals, was assiduous in his treatment. And my mother was committed to help him. So it was a question of leaving my mother for my grandparents, or vice versa. At this time I wanted to be with my mother, for since our conversation in the garden I was reaching out for an understanding, and trying hard to cast off my prejudices against my stepfather—which in my heart I was not sure that I wanted to do.

November had come. I thought often of Cornwall. The pool looked eerie at this time of the year when it was often shrouded in mist. I had loved to go there with Miss Brown . . . never alone because I felt something fearful might happen to me there. So it had to be Pedrek, my mother or Miss Brown. Then I was disappointed because I did not hear the bells which were supposed to be at the bottom of the water. I was a fanciful child—perhaps because my grandfather had told me so many of the legends which abound in Cornwall. In Manorleigh, we were more precise. But at least it had the ghost of Lady Flamstead.

I was in bed one night when my mother came into my room.

"Not asleep yet?" she said. "Oh good. I have something to tell you."

I sat up, and she lay on the bed beside me, putting her arm round me as she had done many times before.

"I wanted you to know before it became common knowledge."

I waited eagerly.

"Rebecca," she said, "you would like a little brother or sister, wouldn't you?"

I was silent. I might have guessed that this was a possibility, but I had not done so. It was a complete surprise to me and I was unsure how I felt about it.

"You'd love it, wouldn't you, Becca?" she repeated appealingly.

"Oh . . . you mean . . . there is going to be a baby?"

She nodded and turned to me. The radiance was on her. Whatever I felt, it was clear that she wanted this.

"I always felt that you would have liked a little sister, but you wouldn't mind a brother, would you?"

"Yes . . ." I stammered. "Of course . . . I'd like that."

Then I clung to her.

"I knew you'd be delighted," she said.

I thought about it. Our household would be

different. But a brother . . . or a sister. Yes, I did like the thought of it.

"It will be very young," I said.

"Just at first . . . as we all were. I am sure it will be a wonderful child but not quite clever enough to jump right into maturity."

"When will it be . . . ?"

"Oh, not for a long time yet. The summer . . . June perhaps."

"And what does he . . . ?"

"Your stepfather? Oh, he is delighted. He wants a boy, of course. All men do. But I am certain that if it is a little girl she will be just what he wanted. But tell me, Becca, are *you* pleased?"

"Yes," I said slowly. "Oh, yes."

"That makes me very happy."

"She won't be my full sister, will she?"

"You've made up your mind the baby will be a girl. I suppose that is what you prefer."

"I . . . I don't know."

"Well, the child will be your half-brother or half-sister."

"I see."

"It's wonderful news, isn't it? Everyone in the family is going to be so pleased."

"Have you told the grandparents?"

"Not yet. I shall write tomorrow. I didn't want to before I was sure. Oh, it is going to be marvelous. Of course, I shall not be able to get about so much later on. I shall be here . . . at home . . ."

She held me tightly against her.

She was right. It would be wonderful.

The news was out. My grandparents were delighted. They were going to spend Christmas with us. Uncle Peter thought the news was excellent. The voters liked their members to have satisfactory married lives. They liked to see the children coming along.

Mrs. Emery thought it was good news and Jane and Ann, together with the new maids who had been engaged, were all excited at the prospect of having a baby in the house.

It was wonderful to see the grandparents for Christmas. It was our first at Manor Grange. The house was decorated with holly, ivy and mistletoe; the yule log was ceremoniously drawn in; Christmas Day was a family affair but on Boxing Day there was a dinner party for Benedict's important friends in the Party. Mrs. Grant said she was run off her feet, but that was how it should be and she doubted Manor Grange had ever seen such entertaining before, which came of my stepfather's being the M.P.

"As long as I can get my cup of tea and my little 'feet-up' I can cope with it," she said. And she did, magnificently. Mr. Emery was able to play the dignified butler and Mrs. Emery to show us all that her post of housekeeper was no sinecure.

On Christmas morning we all went to church and walked back across the fields to the house. My grandmother slipped her arm through mine and told me how pleased she was that I seemed to be happier, and added that it was wonderful that I was to have a little brother or sister.

Christmas was the time of peace and good-will and everything seemed hopeful on that day. I even liked Benedict Lansdon . . . well, not exactly liked, but admired. He was so gracious to every-one . . . all those dignitaries from the Party. His manners were easy—not quite so suave as some of the gentlemen but that gave them a touch of sin-cerity which people liked.

He kept a watchful eye on my mother and admonished her now and then for not resting enough. My grandparents looked on with approval at this. They were very happy indeed, and now that my grandmother had convinced herself—and I expect my grandfather—that I was becoming reconciled to the situation, there was nothing to disturb her.

My mother complained laughingly that we were all treating her like a semi-invalid. They should remember that she was not the first woman on Earth to have a baby. She was perfectly all right . . . and would they stop fussing? "And that includes you, Benedict," she added.

Everyone laughed and so it was a happy Christ-mas, even for me . . . the last I was to know for a long time.

It seemed that my mother had returned to me to a certain extent. There were days when she felt the need to rest. I was with her. I used to read to her; she loved that. We were reading *Jane Eyre* which Miss Brown thought might be a little old for me, but my mother believed it was quite suitable.

Neither my mother nor my grandparents had tried to shield me from the facts of life as most guardians of children did. They believed that as I had to live a life I might as well know as much about it as I was able to absorb.

I realize it had made me a little old for my years. Pedrek was the same.

So this was a happier time than I had known since I had first heard that my mother was going to marry.

Then came the blow.

My stepfather was in London for the House was sitting. My mother had been going with him but just before they were about to leave she had been tired and Benedict had insisted that she remain at Manorleigh to rest.

I was delighted.

It was a bright March day, I remember. There was a chill in the air but I fancied I could feel the first signs of spring; there were masses of yellow blossoms among the shrubs. We made our way to what was known as my seat and sat there, looking across the pond where Hermes stood poised for flight.

We were talking of the baby . . . our main topic of conversation these days. When next we were in London, my mother was saying, she wanted to find some special baby linen she had heard about.

"You must help me choose," she said.

Then one of the maids appeared. She told us that one of the servants from the London house had just arrived and wanted to see my mother. It turned out to be Alfred the footman.

My mother rose in alarm. "Alfred!" she cried.

"Pray do not be alarmed, Madam," said Alfred.

My mother interrupted: "Something is wrong. Mr. Lansdon . . ."

Alfred found it difficult to discard his dignity even in a crisis. "Mr. Lansdon is well, Madam. It is on his orders that I am here. He thought it better for me to come than to communicate in the normal way. It is Mr. Peter Lansdon. He has been taken ill. The family is gathering at the house, Madam. Mr. Lansdon thought, that if you were well enough to travel, you might wish to be there."

"Uncle Peter . . ." said my mother. She looked at Alfred. "What is wrong? Do you know?"

"Yes, Madam. Mr. Peter Lansdon suffered a stroke during the night. His condition is said to be . . . not good. It is for this reason . . ."

She said: "We will leave as soon as possible. Alfred, have you had something to eat? Go to Mrs. Emery. She will see to you while we prepare ourselves to leave."

I took her arm and we went indoors. I could see that she was shaken.

"Uncle Peter," she murmured. "I do hope

he won't . . . I do hope he'll be all right. I always thought of him as . . . indestructible."

We caught the three-thirty train to London and went straight to Uncle Peter's house. Benedict was there. He embraced my mother tenderly and hardly seemed to notice me.

"I was afraid after I'd sent Alfred that it might have been a shock, darling," he said. "I guessed you'd want to be here . . . but . . . actually he was asking for you."

"How is he?"

Benedict shook his head.

Aunt Amaryllis came out, looking lost and bewildered. I had never seen her like that before. She seemed unaware that we were there.

"Aunt Amaryllis," said my mother. "Oh . . . my dear . . ."

"He was all right just before," said Aunt Amaryllis. "I didn't have a notion . . . and then suddenly . . . he just collapsed."

We stood round his bed. He looked different . . . handsome, distinguished but different. He was very pale and seemed old . . . much older than when I had last seen him.

I looked at those round the bed . . . his family . . . the people who had been closest to him. I was struck by the incredulity in those faces. He was dying and they all knew it, and death was something one had never thought of in connection with Uncle Peter. But it had overtaken him at last and there he lay . . . the buccaneer who had adventured on the high seas of life . . . winning most of the time and often not too scrupulously, I had heard it whispered in the family. Only once had he come near to disaster. That was in connection with the rather notorious and disreputable clubs which he ran at great profit and on which his fortune had been founded. Then he had become a philanthropist, and a great deal of that money which had come through questionable sources had gone back into good works like the Mission run by his son Peterkin and his wife Frances.

I think we had all loved him. He was a rogue, yes, but a very wise one. I knew my mother had loved him as my grandmother had. He had always been kind and helpful. Amaryllis had adored him; she had refused to see any fault in him. The others realized his rogueries . . . and loved him none the less because of them.

And now he was dying.

There were pieces in the papers about him—the millionaire philanthropist, they called him. They were all saying flattering things about him and there was no hint of the manner in which his fortune had been acquired. To be dead is to be sanctified. I supposed it was because people ceased to be envious. Everybody wants to be a millionaire but nobody wants to be dead. So envy evaporates. Moreover, people often feel uneasy about defaming the dead . . . especially the newly dead. Perhaps there is a fear of haunting. "Never speak ill of the dead," they say.

So Uncle Peter was remembered for his good deeds rather than his evil ones. There were many people at the funeral. Aunt Amaryllis was dazed with grief; and even Frances, whose brilliant work at the Mission had been so outstanding and who had never pretended to have a good opinion of her father-in-law, was sad. As for the rest of us, we were quite desolate.

I was only just beginning to be aware of change and now I found it everywhere.

In due course the will was read. I was not present at that ceremony, but I heard about it later.

The servants were pleased. They had all received their legacies. Everything had been taken care of, I was told, which one would expect of Uncle Peter. Aunt Amaryllis was well provided for; Helena, and Martin, Peterkin and Frances all had their portions. He had a great fortune to leave but the larger part of it was in his business which meant the notorious clubs; and these he had left to his grandson, Benedict Lansdon.

They were whispering about it and I wondered what differences this would mean.

I was soon to discover. The relationship between my mother and her husband had undergone a slight change. She was no longer idyllically happy. In fact there was a certain uneasiness about her.

I had seen them in the garden together. Instead of laughing and now and then touching hands, they walked with a slight distance between each other, yet in earnest conversation . . . frowning . . . emphatic . . . in fact one might say arguing.

It dawned on me that it had something to do with this new inheritance from Uncle Peter.

I wished my mother would talk to me about it. But of course she did not. It was one thing to be considered mature enough to read *Jane Eyre*, but to be involved in discussion of this delicate affair was quite different.

My mother was very worried.

I did overhear her discussing it with Frances. Frances was one of those rather uncomfortable people who are kind and considerate when dealing with the masses and less so with individuals. She was of sterling character; she had devoted her life to good works; she had said she accepted money from Uncle Peter with gratitude for she did not care how that money had been come by as long as it came her way and she could use it to the good of her Mission. But she had always been more critical of Uncle Peter than any other member of the family. She had accepted him for what he was and was like Elizabeth of England, gratefully receiving plunder which her pirate-heroes brought her and pouring it into the treasury for the good of her country.

This was logical reasoning of course and one would never expect anything else from Frances.

She said: "Benedict should sell off the clubs.

They'd bring him a fortune. Surely he doesn't mean to continue with them?"

"He feels it is what Uncle Peter wanted him to do," said my mother. "It was for that reason he left them to him."

"Nonsense. Peter would expect him to do what was best for himself . . . as *he* always did."

"Nevertheless . . ."

"He fancies himself in the role, I daresay. Well, my father-in-law sailed very near the wind sometimes . . . and that's no way for a politician to go."

"It's what I tell Benedict."

"And he thinks he can go on reaping rewards from the underworld and increasing his riches. There is no doubt that money is a great asset in a political career."

"It frightens me, Frances."

"Well, like grandfather like grandson. There is no doubting Benedict is a chip off the old block."

"Benedict is wonderful."

A brief silence while Frances was no doubt implying her disagreement with that statement.

"Well," she said at length, "those clubs nearly finished my father-in-law, remember."

"I know. That's why . . ."

"Some men are like that. Offer them a challenge and they've got to take it. It's something to do with their masculine arrogance. They think nothing on Earth can beat them and they have to prove it."

"But it could ruin him . . ."

"Well, his grandfather came sailing through, honored and sung to his grave. Men like that don't think they are living if there is not a bit of danger around them for them to overcome. Don't worry, Angel. It's bad for you in your condition. Take care of yourself and let Benedict fend for himself. His kind always come through . . . and I daresay he knows what he's doing."

So that was it. He was going to continue in Uncle Peter's business. It was dangerous, but then, as Frances had said, that was how men like Benedict and Uncle Peter lived.

Aunt Amaryllis had aged considerably. She was listless and had lost those youthful looks which had been characteristic of her. She caught a chill and could not shake it off. It seemed that now Uncle Peter was dead she could find no purpose in living.

My grandparents came to London. They were concerned about my mother.

I heard them talking together. "She doesn't look at all well," said my grandmother. "Quite different from when we saw her last."

"Well, it's getting near the time, I suppose," replied my grandfather.

"No . . . it's more than that."

I was worried.

"Granny," I said, "is my mother all right?"

She hesitated just a fraction of a second too long. "Oh yes," she said at length. "She'll be all right." But she did speak without conviction. "I was wondering . . ." she went on, and paused.

"Wondering what?" I asked.

"Oh, nothing," she answered, leaving it at that.

Later I realized what she had in mind. She and my grandfather wanted my mother to go back with them to Cornwall and have the child there. I did not think she would agree to that for it would mean leaving Benedict. But then . . . it was not quite the same between them as it had been. This inheritance had come between them. She did not like it and he apparently did. I knew she was trying to persuade him to get out of the business and he was strongly resisting.

My grandfather had long conversations with him and my grandmother talked a little to me.

"I think it would be a good idea if you and your mother came back to Cornwall with us. We ought to go soon while your mother can travel. It could be a little difficult in a few weeks' time."

"She won't want to go. *He* couldn't go with her."

"You mean your stepfather. No, of course he couldn't. But he could come down for the occasional week-end. It is not so very far and he is used to travelling about."

"Oh, Granny, I hope she agrees."

My grandmother squeezed my hand. "We must try to persuade her. You see, it was different before Uncle Peter died. Everything has changed here. We always thought Aunt Amaryllis would look after her in London but she, poor soul, is hardly in a condition to do so. I know your step-father would make sure that she had the best attention, but somehow I think people want those nearest and dearest to them at such a time. If she were with us you could be there too."

"Yes," I said. "Oh yes."

I spoke to my mother about it.

"Grandmother wants you to go to Cornwall."

"She is fussing over me."

"Well, you are her daughter."

She smiled at me. "Cornwall," she said. "Sometimes I think of it, Becca. I feel very tired now and then. I do feel as though I want my mother. Isn't that childish of me?"

I reached for her hand. "I think people do want their mothers at certain times."

"I believe you are right. I should always be there if you wanted me. You'd tell me, wouldn't you, if anything was worrying you."

I hesitated and she did not pursue the matter. I was aware then that she knew how deeply I resented my stepfather. Perhaps it seemed to her nothing out of the ordinary; it must have happened thousands of times when a mother remarried.

I wished she would tell me how deep was this rift between herself and her husband. Sometimes I thought it did not exist at all and that she was so much in love with him that he might do anything he pleased without changing that love. And what did he feel? How could I know? I was too young and inexperienced to understand these situations.

There were long discussions about the advisability of my mother's going to Cornwall; and I sensed that she was wavering.

She talked to me more openly. "You would like to go, wouldn't you, Becca?"

I admitted that I would.

"Poor Becca. You haven't been very happy lately, have you? You have felt it hasn't been quite the same with us. First I go away on a honeymoon . . . and we are apart as we never have been before . . . and then I am caught up in all this political work."

"It had to be," I said.

She nodded. "But you haven't liked it. I know how you love Granny and your grandfather. I know how you feel about your father. You put him on a pedestal. It doesn't do to put people on pedestals, Becca."

What did she mean? Had she discovered that her idol Benedict had feet of clay? She must have done so. He had inherited Uncle Peter's shady business connections and would not give them up although she begged him to.

What a difference Uncle Peter's death had made to us all. Aunt Amaryllis no longer provided that rest house in London; no longer did we have the benefit of his advice; and his death had caused a rift between my mother and her new husband.

She went on: "I am not much use . . . politically . . . now and I shall not be for some time. I had to cancel an engagement the other day because I suddenly felt quite unable to carry it out. I think it would be better for everyone if I retired from the scene for a while . . . and if I went to Cornwall I should be less of a burden than if I were here."

"And my grandparents would be delighted."

"Yes, bless them. I shan't mind being a bother to them."

"A bother! You would be the reason for rejoicing."

I skipped round the room and she laughed at me.

"When do we leave?" I asked.

Even then I was scared that he might raise some objection. It was clear that he did not like the idea. He was very tender and loving towards her and I thought I saw her wavering again.

My grandparents had a long talk with him. My grandmother was a most forceful lady. She was the one to look after her daughter in such circumstances, she said, and she knew exactly what was best for her. It would be simple. We should travel to Cornwall with her; the nursery there would be made ready. Dr. Wilmingham was a friend of the family. He had brought Angelet herself into the world. The very best of midwives lived nearby. She should be engaged at once. He must realize that Aunt Amaryllis was no longer able to help and Uncle Peter was not there in case of emergency. He, Benedict, could come down whenever he had the time. There would be no need to make arrangements. All he had to do was arrive. It was true that Cornwall was not exactly close to London but the train was convenient. At week-ends he would be more free than during the week . . . and he could come at any time.

At length he saw the wisdom of this and I and my mother made preparations to leave for Cornwall.

I was happier than I had been for a long time. It was as it had been before the marriage. I think I must have showed it.

He stood on the platform, waving us farewell. He looked so desolate that not until we began to glide out of the station was I able to cast off my fears that she might change her mind.

She was sad at the parting and I was aware once more of the great attraction between them.

I took her hand and clung to it. She kissed mine and said: "The time will soon pass."

"I daresay that Benedict will be down before long," comforted my grandmother.

I grew happier as we sped along and crossed the Tamar. One of the grooms was waiting for us and soon we were rattling along through those winding lanes and there was Cador—a sight which always filled me with emotion but never more than at this time when a kindly fate had given me back my mother . . . if only temporarily.

I vowed that I would make the most of the weeks during which I should have her to myself.

I thought of the baby as Our Baby. We should look after it together.

One has to have been unhappy to appreciate real happiness; and on that journey I believed I had never in the whole of my life been happier than I was then.

What a joy it was to settle. It was like coming home. My mother's spirits revived. Naturally she loved Cador, for it had been her home when she was a child and she and my grandparents were devoted to each other. If anything could make her stop grieving for the loss of Benedict's company it was this.

It was the beginning of April when we arrived and the countryside was especially beautiful. Spring came a little earlier in Cornwall than it did in London. One could feel it in the air. I could smell the sea and listened contentedly to the gentle rising and falling of the waves. How pleasant it was! My grandparents shared my contentment. They had their beloved daughter back home with them.

The first thing my grandmother did was summon Mrs. Polhenny. She came at once. I thought she looked a little older than when I had last seen her, but if anything even more self-righteous.

She was delighted at the prospect of a new baby.

" 'Twill be a marvelous thing to have a little one up at Cador, Mrs. Hanson," she said. "Why, it seems only yesterday that Miss Angelet arrived."

"Yes, my daughter's child will have *her* old nursery. It is wonderful for us to have her here.

I told them in London, Mrs. Polhenny, that they couldn't find a better midwife than you."

" 'Twas kind of 'ee, Mrs. Hanson. It's doing God's work . . . bringing little children into the world. That's how I see it."

My grandmother and I exchanged amused glances.

"Well, I'd like to have a look at Miss Angelet . . . when it's convenient like."

"Certainly," said my grandmother. "I'll take you up to her room."

My grandmother disappeared with her and shortly after joined me.

"Still singing the Lord's song in a strange land," commented my grandmother.

"It must be gratifying to be so sure you are so good," I said. "I wonder how many share her opinion?"

"Oh, Mrs. Polhenny doesn't care about the opinions of others. I don't think I ever knew a more self-satisfied person."

"I wonder what her name is . . . her Christian name?"

"I have heard it. Something quite unsuitable. Violet, I think. Anything less like a violet, I cannot imagine."

"There hasn't been a Saint Violet, has there?"

"I don't think so, but there will be now . . . at least in Mrs. Polhenny's reckoning. Still, she is a very good midwife and we'll have to put up with her little foibles on that account."

Mrs. Polhenny was a little serious when she joined us.

My grandmother said sharply: "All is well, isn't it?"

"Oh yes." She looked at me. My grandmother nodded. I knew what that meant. Mrs. Polhenny had something to say which was not for my ears.

I left the room but I did not go away. This was my mother and I intended to know what was happening for Mrs. Polhenny's look had alarmed me.

So, though I went outside, I left the door a little ajar and stood there listening.

"She seems exhausted, Mrs. Hanson."

"She's just had a long train journey from London."

"H'm," said Mrs. Polhenny. "Ought to have come earlier. I'd like her to take a good rest."

"She'll have that here. There's nothing wrong, is there, Mrs. Polhenny?"

"No . . . no . . ." She spoke rather hesitantly. Then she went on: "I think we are a week or more farther on than we thought."

"Oh, do you?"

"I think so. Anyway, she's here now. I'm glad she didn't leave it any longer to travel. We'll take good care of her, never fear. She's in the right hands now. With the good Lord's help we'll see she's all right."

"Oh yes, Mrs. Polhenny, of course."

As soon as Mrs. Polhenny had gone I sought out my grandmother.

"She's all right, isn't she?" I asked.

"Oh yes. Mrs. Polhenny wants her to rest more. Naturally she's rather tired after the journey. She's going to be all right now she's here."

"I thought Mrs. Polhenny sounded rather worried."

"No . . . not really. She wants to think we can't do without her. That's just her way."

We laughed together; then we went up to my mother.

"The holy Mrs. Polhenny thinks you should rest more," said my grandmother.

My mother lay back on the pillows and laughed. "I'm willing," she said. "I feel so tired."

My grandmother went over and kissed her.

"I'm so happy you came home," she said.

We were all seated at the dining table. My mother, considerably refreshed in a long rose-colored teagown, looked beautiful. Miss Brown was having something in her room. Meals were always a little difficult. My grandparents did not like her to eat alone and she certainly could not join the servants in the kitchen. It was different at Manorleigh or in the house in London. There Miss Brown and I often ate together, but here there was a more intimate family life. Miss Brown would often plead work to prepare and would eat in her room. I think she preferred it sometimes. In any case she did on that night.

So it was just my grandparents, my mother and myself.

"I daresay Jack and Marian will be over to see you tomorrow," my grandmother was saying. "They are so pleased you are here. Marian will be a great help . . . such a practical girl. And then, of course, there's Mrs. Polhenny . . . she'll be over." She looked at me. "A pity Pedrek's not here. Poor boy! School has put an end to his frequent visits. He's growing up fast."

"Tell us what has been happening here," said my mother.

"Oh, nothing much. Life goes on in the same old way in remote places, you know."

"Well, you did have the French refugees here. Are they still at High Tor?"

"No. They bought the place though. They probably wish they hadn't now. They've got another place near Chislehurst. They pride themselves on their aristocratic connections."

"Oh yes," said my mother. "The Emperor and Empress went there, didn't they?"

"Yes. Exiles. I believe they have a fine house there. When the Emperor died, the Bourdons thought they ought to go and comfort the Empress. I've not doubt she keeps a little court there."

"I heard of his death," said my mother. "In January . . . I think."

My grandmother nodded.

"And what about Mrs. Polhenny's daughter?" I asked.

"Oh, Leah is staying with an aunt now. St Ives way, I think."

"An aunt! Who's that? Mrs. Polhenny's sister?"

"I should think so."

"I didn't know she had any relations," I said. "I thought she just descended from Heaven to lead the unrighteous back to the fold."

We all laughed and my grandfather said: "I must say it seems strange to think of her as a child with a sister . . . and growing up like an ordinary little girl."

"It may be that she was quite normal then," said my mother, "and suddenly she was made aware of her mission . . . like St Paul on the road to Damascus."

"I am sure Mrs. Polhenny would appreciate the comparison," put in my grandmother.

"Did Leah do the tapestries at High Tor?" I asked.

"Yes. She was there for some weeks . . . well, all of a month, I believe. It changed her. I saw her once or twice. She looked so well . . . and happy. Poor girl, it must have been wonderful to get away from her mother."

"Why do good people so often make others uncomfortable?" I asked.

"I doubt whether they are as good as they think they are," replied my grandmother, "and the rest of us are not as bad as they think *we* are."

"The thing is not to let such people bother you," added my grandfather.

"It's not easy if you happen to be the daughter

121

of one," retorted my mother and added: "Poor Leah!"

"Well, I'm glad she enjoyed her spell at High Tor," I said. "And now she's gone to this aunt. It looks as though she has developed a taste for adventure."

"I'm surprised that Mrs. Polhenny allowed it," said my mother.

"Well, she was at length persuaded to let her go, though she stood out against it at first."

"Leah is growing up now," said my mother. "Perhaps she is developing a will of her own as well as a taste for adventure."

We went on chattering about life in the Poldoreys, my mother asking after all the people whom she had known as a child.

It was wonderful to be together like this. It was my happiest day since I had heard she was going to marry Benedict Lansdon.

The days sped by. My mother protested when she had to take her enforced rests. Dr. Wilmingham called. He was pleased with her condition. He stayed to luncheon for he had been a friend for many years. He shared my grandmother's opinion of Mrs. Polhenny. "She can be irritating at times," he said, "but she is one of the best at her job. A really dedicated midwife. We could do with more like her."

I used to go for little walks with my mother.

"Fresh air and exercise is good," Dr. Wilmingham said, "as long as it is not overdone."

We walked in the gardens but my mother liked to go farther afield. She was very fond of the walk to Branok Pool. The place had a strange fascination for her. She told me the story of how it had been dragged when she thought I had strayed into it so many times that I knew every word by heart.

Such places change little. It must have been exactly like that all those years ago with the willows trailing in the water and the marshy ground round the brink. My mother liked to sit on one of the protruding boulders and she would watch the water as though her thoughts were far away.

Now and then we would catch a glimpse of Jenny Stubbs, sometimes singing in that strange voice of hers which had an uncanny otherworldliness about it, and sounded very eerie by the pool.

She would call: "Good day to 'ee, Miss Angel . . . Miss Rebecca."

My mother answered her in a specially gentle voice. Jenny seemed to have a fondness for her. She hardly noticed me which was strange as I was the one she had kidnapped and she had believed was her own.

"Good day, Jenny. A lovely day, isn't it?"

Sometimes Jenny would pause and nod her head. She would look at my mother wonderingly. It was obvious that she was pregnant now.

Once Jenny said: "I see you be expecting, Miss Angel."

"Yes, Jenny."

Jenny lifted her shoulders and giggled. She pointed to herself. "Me too, Miss Angel. Little girl I be having . . ."

"Yes, Jenny," said my mother.

Jenny smiled and walked back to her cottage, singing as she went.

Benedict came down several times. We never knew when he was coming. He would suddenly appear, to cast a cloud over my days. Then it seemed that I lost her. He was the sort of man who seemed to fill a room with his presence. At the dinner table he was the center of conversation. It was all about what was happening in the Party, when the next election could be expected. It was almost as though Mr. Gladstone and Mr. Disraeli joined us at the dinner table.

He and my mother were constantly together during his stay. There was no place for me.

I heard him say to her once: "It seems so long. I wish I had never let you go so far away from me."

She laughed softly and happily and replied: "It won't be long now, darling. Then I'll be home . . . with the baby. It will be wonderful."

I felt then that I must enjoy every moment. This happiness could not last.

May had come. In another month the baby would arrive. Mrs. Polhenny was now sure that it would be earlier than we had at first thought.

"I shan't be able to walk so far soon," said my mother.

"Perhaps you should not walk so far now," I replied.

"I want to see the pool once more."

"I don't think those boulders are very comfortable for you to sit on."

"Nothing is comfortable just now, Becca."

"And they might be a little damp."

"In this weather? There's been no rain for weeks. Come on."

"Well, if you get tired we shall turn back."

"I can get there. I want to."

"Why does the place fascinate you so much? It's gloomy and it always seems to me that there is something evil about it."

"Perhaps that's why."

"They ought to put railings round it to prevent accidents," I said.

"That would change the place completely."

"Well, perhaps that would be a good thing."

She shook her head.

We sat there on the boulders. There was a stillness in the air.

At length she said: "Becca, I want to talk to you."

"Yes, I'm listening."

"You are very dear to me. I shall never forget the day you were born."

"In those goldfields . . ."

"You made a difference to my life . . . you always have. You mustn't ever think that I don't

125

love you as much as I did. You won't mind about the new baby, will you?"

"Mind? I already love the baby."

"I want you to love it . . . dearly. It's very important to me. It's suddenly come to me . . . as though I'm seeing ahead. There is something about this place . . ."

"Yes," I agreed. "There is something about it. You think that because I'm jealous of . . . him . . . I might be of the baby."

"I don't love you any less because I love others."

"I know."

"So never think it."

I shook my head. I was too moved for words.

She took my hand and laid it against her body. "You are young," she said. "People would say you should not know of such things . . . but I have never thought of you as young. You are my own . . . part of me. That is why we have been so close together always . . . until . . . well, so you thought. Stop thinking that, Becca. He wants you to care for him as much as I do. He is hurt because he thinks you resent him. Can you feel the movement? That is the child, Becca . . . our child . . . yours, mine and his. Promise me that you will always love it . . . care for it . . . look after it . . ."

"Of course I will. It will be my sister . . . or my brother. Of course I'll love it. I promise."

She put my hand to her lips and kissed it.

"Thank you, my darling child. You have made me very happy."

For a while we sat looking at the pool. Then she rose suddenly and took my hand.

"Let us go," she said. "Dearest child, always remember . . ."

I was with her all the time. It seemed as though a great burden had been lifted from my shoulders. When the child was born and we went back, he would be there. I was going to try to stop hating him. I could see now that I had been to blame.

He wanted me to be part of the family. He did not want to shut me out. I had shut myself out.

I was going to be different when the child was born.

My mother had stopped going out. Mrs. Polhenny came every day. She was ready, she said. "At the first sign, I'll be here."

Dr. Wilmingham often came to luncheon. My mother would join us, but she was quickly exhausted.

Pedrek came down for a brief stay at Pencarron Manor. He and I would ride together. It was more like the old days, but I never stayed away from Cador for long for I liked to be as much as possible with my mother.

One afternoon Pedrek and I had been riding together and as we approached Cador he said goodbye before going back to Polcarron and I turned my horse to go home. The day had been overcast. There would be rain before long. On the way I passed Mrs. Polhenny's cottage. We had always laughed at its prim appearance—the scrubbed doorstep, the gleaming cobbles, the windows shrouded with heavy curtains at the sides and dazzling white net across them to protect the inmates from seeing sin outside the house, we always said.

Mrs. Polhenny was, I guessed, at the Peggotys' in West Poldorey. I had heard that she had been called there that morning to attend Mrs. Peggoty.

As I glanced up at the windows I saw a shape, so Mrs. Polhenny was at home. That would mean the Peggoty child was born. The shadow was there for a moment and then it had gone.

I hesitated. My grandmother had been a little anxious about Mrs. Peggoty for it was her first child and she was forty years old, which was old to have children. It would be good to know that the child was safely born. So I slipped off my horse and tethered it to a bush. Then I went and knocked at the door.

I stood there smiling to myself, wondering what Mrs. Polhenny would think if I asked if the baby had arrived. I had heard through one of the maids that she thought I was a "forward piece" and that it wasn't right for children to know what I knew and she could not imagine what them up at Cador was thinking about to allow it.

I must say I felt rather a mischievous delight in shocking her.

I waited. There was no answer, The house seemed silent. Yet I was certain I had seen her at the window . . . at least it must be her for Leah was away with the aunt in St Ives.

I waited for ten minutes. Then I mounted my horse and rode away. I was puzzled. I had been sure someone was in the house.

I forgot about the incident until the next morning when my grandmother announced that Mrs. Peggoty had a fine boy.

"He was born at three o'clock this morning, Mrs. Polhenny tells me. She says she was there for all those hours and is really worn out."

So she had not been there, in the house. How odd! I must have imagined the shape at the window. But I knew I had not. It was rather mysterious.

June came. Mrs. Polhenny was, as she said, "at the ready." She had become a little preoccupied which worried me a little. I asked myself if she were a little less sure of herself.

One morning she said to my grandmother: "You could have knocked me down with a feather. I'd never have believed it. I just thought there was something about her . . . the trained eye, you know. Then I said to her, 'Jenny,' I said, 'I'd like to take a look at you.' She was pleased enough to let me and when I examined her . . . well, I tell you, I couldn't believe it . . ."

I listened to this. I was constantly on the alert. I had a feeling that all was not going as it should with my mother and although they told me a little I guessed there was a great deal which was held back. I was determined to find out. I had to know. So I listened quite shamelessly to everything I could in the hope of finding out the true state of affairs concerning my mother.

That was how I learned that Jenny Stubbs was in fact expecting a child. It was a nine days' wonder in the Poldoreys. How could it have come about? Everyone was thinking back to harvest time. September or October . . . to June. It was remembered that Peggotys had had labor in to help with the harvest. Last time with Jenny people guessed the father had been one of the itinerant workers. And Jenny, of course, half dazed as she was, wanted so much to have a child that it had been one of her fantasies to believe she was to have one. According to wiseacres like Mrs. Polhenny, this sort of dreaming made conception more likely.

The news was about and it reached my alert ears. Jenny Stubbs, who had dreamed for years of having a baby, was about to have one, according to Mrs. Polhenny, whose word could not be doubted in such matters.

She had taken on the task of looking after the girl. She wanted no help, no payment. She had presumably had a private conversation with God who had led her to discover that Jenny was really about to give birth and she knew it was her duty to look after the girl.

My mother was pleased when she heard the news.

"I know how wonderful it is to bring a child into the world," she said. "It's the most exciting adventure."

My grandmother commented that when Jenny had previously had her own child she had been so happy that she had improved in every way. This could be the making of a new life for her. She might be quite normal again.

"Well," said Mrs. Polhenny, "I shall have my hands full. Two babies about to appear . . . and at the same time. God will give me strength."

"How gratifying it must be for Mrs. Polhenny to feel that God is working with her . . . a sort of auxiliary midwife, on this occasion it seems," said my grandmother.

My mother laughed. "You are quite irreverent, Mama," she said.

I treasured those moments with her. I should never forget them.

The day came. There was expectation in the house. Soon the ordeal would be over. My mother would be exultant and there would be a new member of the family.

Mrs. Polhenny had arrived. She said: "I delivered Jenny Stubbs' baby last night . . . a lovely little girl. Jenny's beside herself with glee."

"Who is looking after her?" asked my grandmother.

"I've taken her over to my place . . . I did just before the birth was about to take place. I thought

131

it best as I had Mrs. Lansdon's coming. Leah's home. She's helping."

"That's good of you, Mrs. Polhenny."

Mrs. Polhenny preened herself and looked more virtuous than ever.

"Well . . . she's through. Now it's Mrs. Lansdon's turn."

Later my grandmother said to me: "Her heart's in the right place in spite of all that self-congratulation. It was good of her to take Jenny in."

All seemed normal at the time. Jenny's delivery had been an easy matter. We thought my mother's would be the same.

Mrs. Polhenny arrived at eleven in the morning and by midafternoon we knew that all was not well. Dr. Wilmingham was sent for.

Benedict arrived. No one had met him at the station, but we were not surprised to see him for we guessed he would come to Cador for the birth. He wanted to go to my mother at once, but that was not allowed.

"But she will know that you are here," said my grandmother, "and that should comfort her."

Then began one of the most terrible periods of my life. I cannot remember it clearly. I have tried to shut it out of my mind because it brings so much anguish to recall it. I have succeeded to some extent, for now it is just like a blurred memory.

I do recall vividly though how terrible the waiting was, so I sat with my grandparents . . .

and him. He could not sit still and kept pacing about the room, firing questions at us. How had she seemed? Why had he not been sent for earlier? Something ought to have been done.

My grandfather said: "For God's sake, be calm, Benedict. She'll be all right. She has the best attention."

He said angrily: "She should have stayed in London."

"Who knows?" said my grandmother. "We thought it was for the best."

"Some petty country doctor! An old woman . . ."

I felt angry with him. He was blaming my grandparents. But I knew, as they did, that it was his excessive anxiety which made him as he was, and that it was an outlet for his fears and misery to blame someone.

The hours dragged on. I felt the clocks had all stopped. Waiting . . . waiting . . . and with every passing moment growing more afraid.

I cannot dwell on it. Cold fear had taken possession of me. And I knew it was an emotion I shared with them all. I was aware of my grandmother beside me. We looked at each other and neither of us attempted to hide what we felt. She took my hand and gripped it hard.

Then the doctor came. Mrs. Polhenny was with him. They did not have to speak. We knew. And the greatest desolation I had ever felt swept over me.

A Christmas Tragedy

I remember in flashes—flashes of sheer despera-
tion and the most absolute wretchedness I have
ever known. I can see us standing round her
bed. How different she had been in life! She
looked beautiful; there was a serenity in her face;
she looked so white, so young—and so apart from
us. I could not grasp the fact that I had lost her
forever.

We hardly looked at the baby. I don't think we
could bear to do so. But for it, this would not
have happened.

My grandparents were heartbroken. They had
loved her so dearly. They were as stunned as I
was. As for Benedict, I had rarely seen such
misery as I saw in his face. In it there was a
baffled anger against the world. I knew in that
moment how deeply he had loved her. I think we
all felt the need to get away, to be alone with our
grief.

The doctor and Mrs. Polhenny concerned themselves with the child, I sensed, however, that they
did not expect her to live. Feeding was a problem, but Mrs. Polhenny understood all about that.
We were too stunned by our grief to be able to

tear ourselves away from it and I do not know what we should have done without Mrs. Polhenny.

My grandmother said afterwards that we should always be grateful to her. She made little fuss but just continued caring for the child while we nursed our sorrow.

Later, arrangements would have to be made. I supposed the child would stay at Cador. I knew that when my grandmother recovered a little from this terrible blow it was what she would want . . . as I should. But just at first I could not bear to think of her and, miraculously it seemed to us afterwards, Mrs. Polhenny seemed to understand. She ceased to be the Lord's avenging angel and became a practical nurse, giving herself to the care of the living while the rest of us mourned the dead.

We struggled through the remainder of that day and night, and in the morning, after I rose from my bed in which I had slept little, I realized that I had to go on with my life. My mother was dead and I had to accept that fact. This time I had really lost her.

We all seemed to be walking round in a state of shock—Benedict more than any of us. My grandfather tried to be calm and reasonable; he was trying to look ahead—anything to shut out the misery of the moment. The day for the funeral was decided on. She lay there in her coffin . . . she, who had been so alive, so merry, the most important person in my life.

I had my grandparents, of course, and I thanked

God for them. And there was the child. She was weak, said Mrs. Polhenny, and she did not want us fussing over her. "Leave her be . . . just at first. Leave her to me."

So we left her to Mrs. Polhenny and I think we were rather glad to do so.

The day of the funeral arrived. I shall never forget it . . . the coaches, the hearses, the undertakers in their morning dress, the scent of lilies. I was never able to smell them after without recalling that scene.

We stood round the grave; Benedict, my grandparents and I, holding my grandmother's hand. I watched him as the clods fell on the coffin and I had never seen more abject despair in any face.

And then back to Cador which had become a house of mourning.

It had to change. Nothing lasted forever, I consoled myself.

The next day Benedict left. It was as though he could no longer bear to see any of us.

The carriage was at the door to take him to the station and we went down to say goodbye to him. My grandmother tried to console him. She was deeply conscious of his grief.

She said to him: "Leave everything for now, Benedict. We'll work out something later on . . . when we are more settled. Rebecca and the child will stay here with us for the time being."

I saw the look on his face when she mentioned the child. It was a bitter resentment, bordering on hatred. I knew that he had to blame someone to assuage his unbearable grief. He had to replace it with a stronger emotion. I could see he already resented the child and would always say to himself; But for her Angelet would be here.

I understood his feelings, for I too had experienced that bitter resentment and knew how it could take possession of one and warp one's feelings—for just as he resented the child I had resented him. He was telling himself: But for this child she would be here today, and I was saying: But for you, Benedict Lansdon, I should have my mother as I always had before you came.

It was a relief when he had gone.

Pedrek's grandparents, the Pencarrons, now showed more than ever what true and loyal friends they were. Their daughter Morwenna and my mother had had a London season together; Morwenna and her husband had gone to Australia with my parents; Pedrek and I had been born out there. There was a lasting bond between us and we were as one family.

After Benedict left, Mrs. Pencarron said to my grandmother: "I am going to take you, your husband and Rebecca back with me to Pencarron. I want you to stay, if only for a couple of nights."

"There is the child . . ." said my grandmother.

Mrs. Pencarron looked sad for a moment. Then she said: "Mrs. Polhenny will look after the child. You need to get away . . . just for a little spell."

My grandmother was finally persuaded and we left.

The Pencarrons did all they could to help us.

It was no good though. My grandmother was very restive. She and I went for long walks together. She talked to me about my mother.

"I feel she is still with us, Rebecca. Don't let's try to shut her out. Let's talk as though she is still with us."

I told her how she had talked to me only a few weeks before.

"She asked me to care for the baby. 'Always look after the child,' she said. It would be my little brother or sister. It was strange the way she talked to me down by the pool."

"That place meant something special to her."

"Yes, I know. And now I look back I remember so well what she said. It was as though she knew she might not be here."

My grandmother slipped her arm through mine. "We have the child, Rebecca."

"At first none of us seemed to want her."

"It was because . . ."

"Because her coming caused my mother's death."

"Poor little thing. What did she know about that? We must love the child, Rebecca. We shall, of course. She is your sister . . . my grandchild. It is what your mother would want . . . it is what she would expect."

"And we have left her . . . already."

"Yes. But we shall go back and it will be different. We shall find our consolation in the child. We'll tell them at Pencarron that we'll go back tomorrow. They're darlings, they'll understand."

They did and the very next day we returned to Cador.

We were greeted by a satisfied Mrs. Polhenny.

"The child is getting on well now," she said. "She's turned the corner. I've been with her night and day. I could see it was special care she wanted . . . though I didn't think at one time I was going to pull her through. You'll see the change in her. Screaming her head off now she is . . . that's if something don't please her ladyship."

We were proudly taken to the nursery.

She was right. The baby had changed. She looked plumper . . . much more healthy . . . like a different child.

"She'll get on like a house afire now," said Mrs. Polhenny. "I can tell you it was touch and go with that one."

I think from that moment we felt better. We had the baby to think of, to plan for.

We had been wise to take those few days at Pencarron.

They put a divide between us and the terrible shock of my mother's death.

On our return it was as though we were brought face to face with the fact that we had our lives to lead. We realized that at the back of our minds had been the thought that the child was not going to survive, that there would be no living reminder of the beloved one's death. Both Dr. Wilmingham and Mrs. Polhenny clearly thought the child would

139

follow her mother, but by a miracle she was not only alive but a healthy baby. And she was here for us to love and cherish as my mother would have wished and expected us to do.

Now the child was all important to us and we began to move, in a small measure it was true, away from our grief.

There must be a christening. She was to be called Belinda Mary. My grandmother chose the name. "It just came to me," she said; and from then on Belinda became a very definite person. We immediately noticed that there was something special about her; she was brighter than other children; we fancied—absurdly—that she knew us.

Mrs. Polhenny, fortunately, was free from other duties and she took on the role of nurse for a time. I was sure the child owed a great deal to her skill.

We needed a nurse, said my grandmother, and Mrs. Polhenny agreed.

It was about a week after we had returned from Pencarron that she came up with the suggestion.

"There's my Leah," she said. "I don't know, but ever since she went up to High Tor to do that there needlework, she's been unsettled like. I thought that a spell down at St Ives with my sister would have made her want to stay at home for a bit . . ."

My grandmother and I exchanged meaningful glances. We could not imagine Leah's wanting to return to that cottage where cleanliness ranked almost as high as godliness.

"Leah gets on well with little ones," went on Mrs. Polhenny. "I've taught her a few things . . . and I'd be on hand. What I think might be an answer is for Leah to take on this job of nurse to the little 'un."

"Leah!" cried my grandmother. "But Leah is a skilled needlewoman."

"That means she'll be able to make for the baby. She'd like that."

"Have you talked to her about it?"

"Oh yes, I have that. And, believe me, she wants to do it. She's tired of sitting over a piece of needlework. It's bad for the eyes, too. She's already feeling the need to rest them a bit. She's been getting headaches. She wants to come here as the baby's nurse. What she wouldn't know, I'd tell her . . . and she'd have a real fondness for the little one."

"Well," said my grandmother, "if Leah would really like that, I think it would be an excellent idea."

"I'll send her along. She can have a talk with you."

"It would solve the problem . . . and we'd have someone we know. I should like that."

So Leah came and very soon was installed in the nursery. The baby seemed to take to her at once and it appeared to be an excellent arrangement.

We liked Leah. We always had, although, of course, we had not previously seen very much of her. She had always been shut away in the cottage and hardly ever emerged unless in the company of her mother.

Now she seemed like a different person . . . happier, I thought, and that did not surprise me. She was gentle and quiet. My grandmother said we were very lucky to have her.

Leah was blossoming into a beauty—a rather mysterious one with long dark hair and rather soulful brown eyes. Her care for the child was obvious. My grandmother said that when they were together she looked like a Renaissance portrait of the Madonna; and as soon as the baby began to show awareness it was to Leah she looked.

Our interest in the nursery helped us through those melancholy months. My grandparents and I talked constantly of Belinda. The first smile, the first tooth became a matter of great importance and interest to us.

At least we were recovering from the shock and bracing ourselves to accept the fact that my mother was no longer with us.

We were at the breakfast table—myself and my grandparents—when the mail was brought in. Among it was a letter from Benedict. My grandmother looked at it with alarm and I could see that she was afraid to open it.

She said unnecessarily to my grandfather: "It's from Benedict."

He nodded gravely.

"Of course . . . he'll want the child. Perhaps."

My grandfather said gently: "Open it, Annora. I am sure he realizes it is best for Belinda and Rebecca to be here."

Her fingers shook a little and her expression changed to one of relief as she read. I watched her avidly.

"He says the child and Rebecca are his responsibility."

"I'm not," I said.

"Well, I suppose he would be considered your guardian now that he is your stepfather," said my grandfather.

"No. *You* are my guardians."

He smiled at me. Then: "What else does he say?"

"That he will consider making arrangements which he will talk over with us later on. In the meantime, if it is no inconvenience to us, it might be better for the children to stay here."

My grandmother laughed. "Inconvenience indeed!"

I laughed with her. "He doesn't want us . . . any more than we want him."

"So all is well," said my grandmother.

"He just doesn't want us to think he doesn't realize all we are doing," said my grandfather.

"He will reimburse us for the expense," she went on.

"What on Earth is he talking about?"

"I suppose he means the nurse and all that."

"What nonsense!"

"Well, all's well. We carry on as before."

It was a great relief to us all. But it did set me wondering. I did not like to be reminded that he was my guardian and Belinda's father; and that he would be the one to decide our future.

I ran to my grandmother and clung to her. "We're going to stay with you," I said. "I won't leave you."

"It'll be all right," my grandfather assured me. "It's his way of saying he cares about you. He's glad you're here and we're looking after you —which we can do better than he could . . . in a place like this."

When I mentioned the matter later to my grandmother she said: "Don't worry. It wouldn't be easy for him to set up a household in London or Manorleigh without a wife. He will be immersed in his career. He just wants us to know that he is aware of his responsibilities, but he must realize that the best place for Belinda is here. But you have to remember that he *is* her father."

"I wish he were not," I said.

My grandmother shook her head sadly.

She was wishing as I was that we had all gone on as it had been when we were all happy together.

A year passed and the anniversary of my mother's death had come. During the last year Benedict had paid two visits to Cornwall. He inspected the baby. I was in the nursery at the time. Belinda regarded him with indifference. Leah picked her up and placed her in his arms. He held her gingerly and Belinda set up a wail of protest until Leah took her back when she chuckled with gratification.

Leah said: "She's a very bright baby, sir. You will be proud of her."

He looked at Leah intently. She lowered her eyes and flushed a little, looking more than ever like a painting of the Madonna.

My grandmother talked to him afterwards about Leah.

"She's exceptionally good with Belinda," she told him. "And she's knowledgeable. She's the daughter of the midwife and I think she has learned a lot about babies from her mother."

He said: "She seems efficient."

He talked to me in that restrained way which suggested that he knew of my dislike for him, and possibly felt the same towards me.

"Rebecca, you will have to go to school at some time," he said. "It simply isn't good enough to be merely governess-taught."

"I'm quite happy with Miss Brown."

"There is more to education than happiness. It was what was planned for you."

He meant he and my mother had planned it for me. So she had discussed me with him.

"Perhaps next year," he said.

So I was safe for the time being.

I was glad when he left for London. My grandmother was relieved too. I think she always had it in mind that he was going to take Belinda and me away from her.

I might be sent to school, but I was sure he would not want Belinda. Something in the way he looked at the child convinced me that he blamed her for my mother's death.

Pedrek came to Cornwall for the summer holidays, bringing a school friend with him. Of course, the friend did not want a girl to join them. So it was different. Pedrek was a very kind person and always careful of other people's feelings—he took after his mother in that—so he was aware that I was feeling shut out. He was half apologetic but what could he do? He must entertain his guest. We were all growing up and that was another aspect of change.

I used to go down to the pool often and I would think of my mother and when we had sat there and talked. I remembered how she had asked me to care for the child then unborn. It was as though she had had a premonition of what was going to happen, as though she knew she were going to die.

The pool had meant something special to her and while I was there I would have an uncanny feeling that she was there beside me . . . that she was trying to talk to me.

It was at the pool that I first became aware of Lucie.

I was interested in her because no one had

believed her mother was going to have her until almost the time of her birth—and no one knew who her father was.

Mrs. Polhenny mentioned her now and then.

She said; "You couldn't find a better mother than Jenny Stubbs, which is a strange thing, her being a penny short in the head so to speak. But she's nothing short when it comes to babies. Little scrap of a thing that Lucie was . . . now she's bonny; and I reckon it's due to Jenny. Her sort's meant to be mothers. A pity the good Lord saw fit to cut her a bit short."

It was the nearest criticism I had ever heard her utter against the Lord, so she must have felt rather strongly.

My grandmother marvelled too. Mrs. Granger at the farm where Jenny worked said the change in her was remarkable since Lucie had been born. "Quite sensible she is now," went on Mrs. Granger, "and that Lucie . . . Miss Belinda couldn't be better looked after. Always clean, she is . . . always well cared for. I let her bring her here. It makes no difference to the work and I wouldn't want to lose Jenny. She's a good worker . . . and now she's got her wits about her, all the better."

My grandmother said: "The poor girl had a fixation about a child. You see she lost the child she cared for some years ago. She was always simple and now she's got another of her own she's satisfied. When she took you away she looked after you just as she's looking after little Lucie now. I know that Mrs. Polhenny and her kind deplore the fact that the child is illegitimate but if it changes a life like that there can't be a lot of harm in it."

In any case I was very interested in Lucie and she obviously took a liking to me. I used to go to the pool on most afternoons and Jenny would bring her out of the cottage and they would talk to me.

She was two years old at the time—a lovely child with blue eyes and dark hair. She would stand close to me regarding me gravely; then she would smile.

"She's took a big fancy to you, Miss Rebecca," said Jenny happily.

Sometimes Leah and Belinda would be with me. The two children were of an age and they would play together. I was amused for, young as they were, Belinda was the dominating one.

I should have liked the children to play more often than they did but Leah sometimes made excuses. When the two little ones were together I had noticed her watching them uneasily. I wondered if she harbored some snobbish notion about Belinda's belonging to the big house and therefore she should not be playing with a cottage child.

I mentioned this to my grandmother who agreed that the humbler classes were far more aware of these distinctions than we were. We only had to consider the rigid protocol of the staff to realize that.

She was glad that I took an interest in Jenny

and Lucie. She herself visited the cottage often and made sure there was always plenty of food and comfort there.

The more I saw of Lucie the fonder I became of her and I looked forward to our meetings.

"What will happen to her?" I said to my grandmother. "It's all right now she is a baby but what when she grows up?"

"I daresay she will do some sort of work in one of the houses . . . or farms maybe . . . like her mother."

"I always feel there is something unusual about her."

"We shall keep our eyes on her and do what we can."

"She is very bright, you know. As bright as Belinda, I think, only Belinda is more forceful."

"Can you tell at such an age?"

"I think it shows. I do hope Lucie will be all right."

"Don't worry. We'll keep our eyes on her."

I knew it had to change. Just after Belinda's second birthday I went away to school. Miss Brown, said Benedict, was no longer adequate to teach me.

"What does he know about it?" I demanded. "He is not the least interested in what I learn."

"He and your mother must have discussed it together," soothed my grandmother. "It is probably right for you. You are shut away down here and it will be good for you to meet people."

So I went away to school and for the first weeks hated it, and then grew accustomed to it and quite liked it. I made friends quite easily; I was fairly good at games, slightly better at lessons —Miss Brown had given me good grounding— and I got along very well.

Time passed quickly. I came home to Cador for holidays and looked forward to that but I found I was quite eager to rejoin my fellow pupils. School events such as who was picked for the school concert or with whom I shared my room and the destination of outings seemed of great importance.

My grandparents were pleased that I had fitted in so well. They eagerly read my reports and sent them on to Benedict. I felt sure he never looked at them.

I came home for that Christmas holiday. Pedrek and his parents were at Pencarron for the festivities and we saw a good deal of them. Pedrek brought no school friend with him on this occasion and it was like it used to be without intrusion.

Belinda would soon be four years old. I was amazed how she grew while I was away. She was quite imperious now and could talk quite fluently. Leah said with pride that she was very bright for her age, and she was greatly looking forward to Christmas.

On the day there was to be a party for her; the

twins and several children from the neighborhood had been invited; a conjuror was coming from Plymouth to entertain them.

My grandmother looked happier than she had for a long time. Planning for Belinda had been good for her.

My thoughts went to Lucie. How different her Christmas would be!

I asked my grandmother about her. "Oh, we've seen that they don't want for anything. I've had some coal and wood delivered to the cottage and I thought you'd like to take over a basket for them."

"I'd like that. When?"

"My dear, you've only just come home. In good time for Christmas."

"I shall go down tomorrow. Perhaps I could take something then."

"You're very interested in that child, aren't you?"

"Well, yes. Her birth was so unexpected, wasn't it? We none of us believed that Jenny was really going to have her. And I think she is a very intelligent child. I can't imagine how Jenny could have one like that."

"Oh, parents often have the most unlikely children. But I agree she is a nice child."

"I compare her with Belinda . . . who has so much."

"Well, that's how the world goes. There are always these divisions."

"Yes, I suppose so. But I would like to take something really good."

"You shall."

So the next day I was at the cottage. The pool looked dreary. It was a damp dark day and the willows trailing over the pool and the brownish green water looked sinister in the gloom.

The cottage was welcoming though. It was very neat and clean. Lucie came running out when I knocked. She caught me round the legs and hugged me.

It was a spontaneous and warm welcome.

"I've been away to school," I said.

"I tell her," said Jenny. "She does not know about school."

"I'll explain to her."

I sat down on one of the chairs and took the child on my knees. I told her about my school, the dormitories we slept in, the big hall where we assembled, the teachers we had, how we worked at our desks, how we went for long walks in the country with two mistresses, one at the head of the crocodile and one at the rear, how we played games, how we learned to dance and sing.

She listened intently. I don't think she understood half of it, but she watched my mouth the whole time I was talking and her expression was one of enchantment.

Jenny wanted to know how the little one up at Cador was. I told her Belinda was well and looking forward to Christmas. I started to tell her about the party which was being arranged and the conjuror who was coming from Plymouth . . .

then I stopped short. It was insensitive of me. Poor Lucie would not have such a party.

"What is a conjuror?" asked Lucie.

So I had to explain. "He makes things disappear and finds them again as if by magic."

"And he be coming all the way from Plymouth," said Jenny.

Lucie's eyes were wide with excitement. She kept asking questions about the conjuror. I had to go on explaining.

Could she come to the party? I wondered. My grandparents were by no means sticklers for convention. But if Lucie—the child of crazy Jenny —were invited, all the children from the outlying farms and cottages would be expected to attend.

As soon as I reached home I told my grandmother what had happened.

"It was stupid of me," I said. "I shouldn't have mentioned the party, but I did and it slipped out about the conjuror . . . and that was how it came about."

My grandmother raised the point which had occurred to me. If Lucie came all the local children would feel slighted if they were not asked. Then my grandmother had an idea. She would get Jenny to come and help in the kitchen. She could bring Lucie . . . and Lucie should join the party.

And so it was arranged.

When I put the proposition to Jenny her eyes shone with delight. I said: "And Lucie shall come to see the conjuror with the other children."

She clasped her hands together. "She's been

talking of nothing but that there conjuror ever since yesterday."

Lucie jumped up and down with glee when I told her she was to come to the party. I knelt down and put my arms around her. I felt a tremendous tenderness towards the child and a need to protect her.

It occurred to me a little later that all the children would be in their party dresses, and what had Lucie but her little smock? True, it would be clean and neat but there would be a marked difference between her and the others.

Belinda had numerous dresses which she did not need. Why should not Lucie have one of these? I broached the matter to my grandmother and she thought it an excellent idea.

I consulted Leah who found a very pretty dress which she had made for Belinda and which she had not worn for some time. It was pale blue with a frill at the neck and a flounced skirt; and there was a bow of blue ribbon at the waist.

"That is just the thing," I said.

"I don't think it was ever one of Belinda's favorites," said Leah. "I made a mistake with all those flounces."

"I think it is charming and I am sure Lucie will be delighted. She will never have had such a dress before."

When I took it along to the cottage I was immensely gratified. I had never seen such joy in a child's face before. Jenny watched with her hands clasped together.

"Oh, Miss Rebecca," she said, "you be very good to we."

I was touched as I had rarely been. Jenny's love for that child was beautiful to see. The child's happiness meant everything to her. I thought Lucie deprived when compared with Belinda, but how could she be with love like that?

It was a joyous occasion. Now I could talk about the exploits of conjurors with the utmost freedom.

We laughed and chatted. I could not believe that Jenny was the same person whom I had seen singing in the lanes.

Belinda with Leah helped to dress the Christmas tree. She was a little imperious giving orders. "This is where *I* want this . . ." and so on.

There were to be presents for all the children and these would be distributed before the conjuror arrived. I had chosen a doll for Lucie. It had long flaxen hair and eyes which shut when the doll was held backwards.

There were candles on the tree which would be lighted at dusk.

Belinda shrieked with delight when she saw the candles. She said it ought to be Christmas every day.

And at last it came.

All the family from Pencarron were with us. They were going to stay the night because it was a fair way to Pencarron Manor and we did not know what the weather would be like.

Then there were Jack and Marian with the twins, Jacco and Anne-Mary: and the Wilminghams with their son and daughter and three grandchildren were to come for Christmas Day. There would also be another little girl and boy from about a mile away.

My grandparents had said that Christmas Day was for the children and that it should be devoted to their pleasure.

Jenny arrived with Lucie who looked very pretty in her blue flounces. Her eyes lit up with pleasure when she saw me and she ran to me and hugged me round the knees as she usually did. I found this very endearing. I sensed that she was a little overawed and rather eager to keep at my side.

My grandmother kissed her and, taking her by the hand, led her into the hall. I was thrilled to see the wonder in her eyes as she contemplated the tree.

The other children were all gathered there. Belinda came over and I was amused to see with what dignity she greeted Lucie. I had already spoken to her and told her that Lucie was coming and that as she was the hostess she must make sure that all her guests were comfortable.

She had liked the idea of that.

"This is my house," she told Lucie immediately. "I am the hostess."

Lucie nodded but she could not take her eyes from the Christmas tree.

My grandmother and I gave out the presents and when I saw Lucie's joy in her flaxen haired doll I felt a wave of happiness. Then I felt rather guilty to be so contented without my mother. I uttered a little prayer to her. "I have not forgotten you. I never shall. But I am so happy to be able to do this for the child."

In that moment I almost felt that she was beside me, sharing in my happiness and that gave me immense comfort.

The conjuror had arrived. As we arranged the chairs for the children I heard Belinda say: "Lucie, you've got my dress."

Lucie looked down with dismay at the flounces of which she was so proud.

"I didn't say you could have it. It's mine."

I took Belinda's arm and whispered: "Don't be silly. I told you you have to be polite to your guests."

"But she's got my dress. It's mine."

"It's her dress."

"It's just like mine."

"Be quiet or you won't see the conjuror."

Belinda put out the tip of her tongue. It was a gesture of defiance and disrespect. She had done it before and been admonished; she had then sworn that she did not know her tongue was there. Sometimes I had uneasy qualms about her. Even Leah, who doted on her, admitted that she was "a bit of a handful."

There was silence in the hall as the conjuror took his place and began to perform his tricks. He folded paper; he tore it; and when it unfurled it had become a ship. He threw little balls in the air . . . many of them and caught them all. He brought eggs out of his ears and a rabbit out of a hat.

The children were entranced. It had been a brilliant idea to get a conjuror.

Sometimes he wanted help from one of the children—someone to hold his hat and assure the company that there was nothing in it, someone to make sure that the handkerchief was a blue one before it disappeared into his pocket and came out red.

"Now, one of your children . . ."

It was always Belinda. She was the one. If any of the others attempted to get up he or she would be pushed aside. It was as though she could not help reminding them that this was her house and if anyone was going to take part in the show, she was that one.

She was quick and intelligent, of course, but I wished she would sometimes allow one of the others to share the glory.

The last trick had been played; the conjuror was getting his props together and Belinda was dancing round him asking questions.

Jacco boasted that he could do a trick, tried and failed and there was general derision.

It was time that the candles were lighted. The

158

children watched with wonder while this was done. The tree looked very pretty.

Pedrek was at my side.

"He was good, wasn't he?"

"Yes, and I should like to know how he does some of those tricks."

"That's the last thing he'd want you to know."

Belinda was looking round for something to do. She saw Lucie standing there.

She said: "You *have* got my dress."

"It's mine," replied Lucie fiercely. "Miss Rebecca gave it to me.

"It's not hers to give."

I was about to protest when Pedrek said: "Let's go for a ride tomorrow morning."

"Oh, I'd like that," I replied.

Jenny came in with a tray of lemonade for the children. She set it down by the tree. Lucie noticed her and ran to her, possibly to escape from Belinda's taunts. Belinda snatched one of the candles from the tree and brandishing it ran after Lucie.

"It's my dress. It's my dress. I'm a witch. I'm waving my wand. I'm going to turn you into a toad. It's magic."

It all happened so quickly. She touched the flounce of the dress with the candle. I felt stunned as I saw the flames creep round the skirt and up . . . Lucie was a ball of flame.

I heard the screams and shouts, but before any of us could reach the child Jenny was there. She flung herself on top of Lucie, beating out the flames with her hands. She pushed the child away from her . . . Lucie lay on the floor, her dress no longer alight, but Jenny's clothing was a mass of flames.

It had all happened in a few seconds. Pedrek was the first to move. He picked up a rug and wrapped it round Jenny. He battled for a few moments before the fire was extinguished.

Jenny lay there, her hair burned from her head . . . her skin horribly discolored . . . moaning faintly.

My grandmother shouted for Dr. Wilmingham but he was already there, kneeling beside Jenny.

There was pandemonium.

Lucie was in a state of shock and it was to her that Dr. Wilmingham gave his care. There was no saving Jenny.

She had given her life for the child's.

What a terrible ending to that never-to-be-forgotten Christmas.

I was relieved to discover that Lucie was not as badly hurt as I had feared. Jenny had been so quick to beat out the fire with her own body that all the child had suffered from were a few superficial burns which Dr. Wilmingham was able to deal with.

Pedrek too had burns on his hands but fortunately nothing serious.

Leah had taken Belinda away. I was wondering what effect this would have on her. Did she realize that she was responsible for one death and might have been for another?

We should have to talk very seriously to Belinda; but at the moment Lucie was our concern. I asked that she should be put in my bed that I might be with her throughout the night. I wondered what we were going to tell her. There was the even more pressing problem of what would become of her.

At the moment she was deeply shocked and in some pain from the burns. I knew my presence comforted her to a great extent and I was glad that I had had the foresight to insist that she was put into my bed.

What a strangely long day that was. Lucie was given a sedative and I was glad she slept.

Gathered downstairs were my grandparents with Pedrek and his family with the Wilminghams. Jack and Marian had thought it best to take the children home and all the other young people had left also.

"What a terrible thing to happen," said my grandmother. "It is that child I'm thinking of most."

"Miraculously she is not badly hurt . . . physically," said Dr. Wilmingham. "That heroic woman saw to that. But naturally this sort of thing is a great shock to the system. We shall have to watch that. The poor child has lost her mother. I don't know what will come out of this."

"The question will be what will become of her?" said my grandmother.

"We shall see that she is all right, won't we, Granny?" I said.

She nodded reassuringly. "Poor, poor little thing. She was so happy watching the conjuror."

"And Belinda . . ." I began.

There was silence.

My grandmother said at length: "Leah was so anxious about her."

"Anxious about her!" I cried. "She was the one who caused it all. What is she going to think? Jenny Stubbs . . . dead . . . because of her."

"I know," said my grandmother. "It's a terrible thing to happen to a child."

"She deliberately took the candle and set fire to Lucie's dress."

"Children don't understand the dangers of fire. She's very young . . . and seeing all those tricks . . . she probably thought she was going to transform Lucie into a dragon or something."

"We mustn't be too hard on her," said my grandfather. "Something like this could scar a child's mind for ever."

"I know," agreed my grandmother. "It's a terrible situation. It was my fault for giving Lucie Belinda's dress."

My grandfather said: "Oh come. Don't let's start blaming ourselves. We would all have done anything to avert such a tragedy."

"I am glad Lucie is with you, Rebecca," said my grandmother.

"If she awakened in the night, she wouldn't know where she was . . . so I thought it best . . ."

"Yes, you are right."

Silence fell upon us. We were all thoughtful —every one of us preoccupied with Lucie and the terrible tragedy which had come upon us.

I lay beside the child, thankful that she was still sleeping. She looked very young and vulnerable. I wanted to weep for the cruelty of life which had taken my mother from me . . . as Lucie's had been taken from her. That made me feel doubly close to the child.

I would be there when she awoke. I would hold her tightly and comfort her.

On that Christmas night I had a strange experience. I was not sure whether I was awake or sleeping. I thought I was awake but afterwards I supposed I could not have been, for it seemed to me that my mother was in the room. Remembering back I did not see her but I almost felt that I did. It was just that I knew she was there. I did not hear her voice but the words were in my mind. She was calling to me . . . telling me what I must do.

I lay there, my heart pounding. I was exultant suddenly because she was with me . . . because she had come back. I tried to call out to her but I did not hear my voice.

I just know that she was with me . . . urging me to act.

I was wide awake. The room was silent. The

child was still sleeping beside me. I could see the shapes of the furniture in the pale moonlight.

I got out of bed and put on my dressing gown and slippers.

"Where are you, Mama . . . dearest Mama, where are you?" I whispered.

There was no answer.

I went to the window and looked out. There was moonlight on the sea; I listened to the silence all around me, broken only by the gentle swishing of the waves.

I could not stay in my room. Some impulse made me go to the door. I looked out. All was quiet. I went down the great staircase to the hall.

There was the Christmas tree . . . an object of tragedy now. The burned-down candles . . . the symbol of tragedy. I sat down beside it and covered my face with my hands.

"Come back," I murmured. "Come back, Mama. You did come back . . . for a while."

And as I sat there, I heard a soft footfall on the stairs. I looked up eagerly. It was my grandmother coming into the hall.

"Rebecca," she said. "I thought I heard someone moving about. What are you doing down here?"

"I . . . I couldn't sleep."

She came and sat beside me. She took my hand. "My dear child," she said. "I know what you feel."

"It's the child," I said. "There is something I must do."

"Tell me."

"I want to take her. I want her to come here . . . not as the child of a servant. I want her to be here with us . . . I just feel that is what must be."

My grandmother nodded.

"You love her, don't you?"

"Yes. And she is all alone now. What will become of her . . . some workhouse . . . an orphanage? Oh no, I couldn't bear it. Something happened, Granny. Upstairs just now . . . it was as though my mother came to me."

"Oh, my dear . . ."

"Was I dreaming? I don't know. I thought she was in the room. I thought she was telling me what to do."

"It was your heart telling you, Rebecca."

"I don't know. But I have to do it. I don't care if no one will help me. I am going to look after Lucie."

"What do you mean . . . if no one will help you? You know we'll help you."

I turned to her and she took me into her arms.

"Rebecca, you are a dear child and I'm proud of you. We will take her in. She shall share the nursery with Belinda. Belinda owes her that, doesn't she?"

"What of Belinda, Granny?"

"She is a normal highspirited child. She meant no harm. Leah says she has been crying bitterly. It was just a game to her. She did not understand what fire could do."

"Then she has learned a lesson tonight . . . a

165

bitter one. And at what cost to poor Jenny and Lucie!"

My grandmother said: "Rebecca, it is the least we can do . . . if only for the sake of Jenny who, without a moment's hesitation, gave her own life to save the child's."

"You always understood me."

She stood up suddenly as though afraid of her emotion.

"It's chilly," she said. "We should get back to bed. Besides . . . what if Lucie should wake."

"I should be there to comfort her. I always will be, Granny. I always will."

I went to my room. Lucie was sleeping peacefully. I had a feeling that there was a presence there . . . my mother . . . and that she was pleased.

The Engagement

I had just passed my seventeenth birthday. It was six years since my mother had died. I had never forgotten that Christmas night when she had seemed to come to me. I often felt that she was close and that gave me great comfort.

My grandmother had often said we must get on with our lives. We must stop looking back and we were succeeding to a certain extent. I had done something for Lucie and she certainly had for me. I had cared for her—and she needed great care during the weeks which followed Jenny's death—and she had given me a new interest in life. She had been bewildered; she had cried for Jenny. I had to be a substitute for her. It was fortunate that I had already found my way into her affections. I cannot think what would have happened to the child but for that. I was the one she now relied on; she looked to me for everything, and I was deeply touched and gratified that she had this trust in me. During those first weeks she followed me around. Her little face would pucker with fear if I went away. My grandmother tried to help and to stand in for me on those occasions when I had to part from her; but she said Lucie was always uneasy until I reappeared.

167

Everyone was so sorry for the child that they were eager to help in whatever way was possible. Leah was good with children and she took her into the nursery and made it her home. All the servants did their best and there was no resentment—as we had feared there might be—because a child from the cottages was being treated as a member of the family.

Belinda—rather to my surprise—was helpful and shared her toys, showing no rancor at the intrusion into her undisputed domain. I think she must have realized what a terrible thing had happened and that she had helped to bring it about. She was quieter than she had been for some time. Leah stressed that she should not be told that she was responsible for the death of Jenny Stubbs while at the same time she should be made to realize the danger of playing with fire. Leah seemed to have great understanding of children and was proving to be a wonderful nanny which surprised me when I considered the life she had led as the captive of a self-righteous mother, stitching the hours away at her embroidery.

When I had to go back to school I explained to Lucie that I should be home soon and in the meantime there was my grandmother as well as Leah and Belinda to look after her.

She accepted this with a look of sad resignation and the memory of her pensive little face was with me as I made my journey back to school.

When they had reached the age of five a governess had been engaged for them. Miss Stringer was energetic and efficient, brisk but kindly and she had a gift for enforcing discipline in a rather genial way which was very necessary in the case of Belinda.

Leah, of course, remained in charge of the nursery. My grandmother said she made herself more indispensable every day.

Benedict paid periodic visits which I always thought to him were a matter of duty. I wished he would stay away, for I could never see him without remembering how happy I had been before the fatal marriage which had resulted in my mother's death. I believed I never would forget that or forgive him for spoiling my life.

On those occasions Belinda would be presented to him and I could see by his expression that he was remembering that her arrival had caused the departure of my mother. He bore the same resentment towards her which I did towards him; so I understood his feelings well.

Belinda was aware of it, I felt sure. She was a very sharp child. I had seen her regarding him with a hint of hostility in her eyes. Once as he turned away after a rather perfunctory talk about her riding and how she was getting on with her lessons, I saw the tip of a pink tongue protruding very slightly from her lips, and I could not help smiling. So she had retained the habit then. She was really a rather naughty little girl.

Well, there I was, my schooldays coming to an end. I might have guessed there would be speculation among the adult members of the family as to what was to happen to me.

Benedict wrote to my grandparents now and then and I knew something serious was about to happen when they said they wanted to talk to me.

I went to the small sitting room just off the hall where they were waiting for me. They both looked apprehensive.

"Rebecca," began my grandfather, "you are growing up fast."

I raised my eyebrows. Surely they had not asked me to come here to tell me such an obvious fact.

"Schooldays are over," went on my grandmother, "and, of course, there is your future."

I smiled at them. "Well, I shall be at home, I suppose. There is plenty for me to do here."

"We have to think of what is best for you, of course," said my grandfather and my grandmother went on: "Perhaps it is not the place for a young girl. At least your stepfather thinks something should be done."

"My stepfather! What is it to do with him?"

"Well, he is your natural guardian, you know."

"He's not. You are. I've always been with you." I was beginning to be alarmed.

My grandmother saw this and tried to soothe me. "We have to look at this clearly, Rebecca," she said. "Your stepfather is going to be married."

"Married!"

"It is six years since your mother died. A man in his position needs a wife."

"And that is why he is getting married?"

170

My grandmother shrugged her shoulders. "I daresay he is very fond of the lady. It is very natural, Rebecca. I think it is what your mother would have wanted for him. She loved him very dearly, you know, as he did her."

"So he is going to marry again!"

"He is probably lonely. He needs a wife . . . a family. He is a rising politician. A wife is an asset to a man in his position. I know he has been unhappy for a long time. I hope it is a success and he finds some happiness again."

"But what of me?"

"He wants you to go and live in his house . . . you and Belinda."

"And what of Lucie?"

"She would stay here perhaps. Don't worry about her. We'd always care for her."

"But I have promised . . ." I hesitated and went on: "I have sworn to look after her . . . always."

"We know how you feel. But I think we should wait and see what happens. He is coming down soon."

"I shall never leave Lucie."

"It will be best to wait and see."

"Who is he going to marry?"

"He did not say. It must be someone he met in London or Manorleigh. He would meet all sorts of suitable people in the course of his career, I daresay."

"We can be sure she will be suitable."

"Don't be too hard on him, Rebecca. I hope he will find some happiness."

There was a certain amount of apprehension because Benedict was coming.

My grandfather said: "I imagine he is a little disappointed that Disraeli stayed in power so long. It must be five years. But Gladstone's popularity is rising. There'll probably be a new government in a year or two . . . and it won't be Disraeli's."

"That's the worst of politics," replied my grandmother. "There's so much luck in it. So much depends on who's in and who's out. There are all those years of waiting while a man gets older. It can mean that the most promising career never gets a chance to blossom. But I daresay if the Liberals get in Benedict will get a post if it is only an under secretaryship to start with. There is a forcefulness about him and it should be obvious that he is an outstanding man. Surely the sort who would add to his party's stature."

"H'm," said my grandfather.

"I know what you are thinking . . . that matter of his first wife's death."

They talked freely before me now. It was an indication that I was adult. There was no secret in the family that, before Benedict had married my mother, he had married Lizzie Morley and through her had acquired the goldmine which had provided the foundation for his wealth, and that Lizzie had died suddenly and at first mysteriously, until it was discovered that she was suffering from a painful illness which must mean eventual death

172

and she had taken her own life. However before that had been known foul play had been suspected. It had all been satisfactorily cleared up but such events have a way of creating something vaguely unpleasant which clings. People forget the true facts and remember that there was an unpleasant aura about something that happened in the past.

"Well," said my grandfather, "it could be a reason."

"To have a respectable family would do him a great deal of good," added my grandmother.

"I am afraid he will never forget Angelet. Right from the time he came down here as a young man . . . I knew there was some special rapport between them." His voice faltered and my grandmother changed the subject.

"We must wait and see," she said briskly. "I am sure it will all turn out for the best."

Would it? I wondered. He was going to marry again, because a wife was good for his political career. Belinda and I were to be his family for the same reason. There would always be a motive with him. Lizzie had brought him a goldmine; my mother had brought him love; and this new woman and Belinda and I were to provide the happy family which the voters liked their member to have.

One thing I was certain of was that no one was going to part me from Lucie.

On those occasions when I knew that he was coming I always built up a picture of him in my mind. Arrogant, overbearing, knowing I did not like him and therefore despising me because he was so wonderful that anyone who did not recognize this obvious fact must be a fool.

When he came he was always different from my mental picture which was a little disconcerting.

He arrived in midafternoon and one of the first things he did was have a talk with my grandparents.

After that my grandmother came to my room. "He wants to talk to you," she said. "I think he really wants to do everything for the best."

"The best for him," I retorted.

"The best for all concerned," she corrected. "It is better that he explains to you himself."

I went down to him in the little sitting room. He rose and took my hands.

"Why, Rebecca, how you have grown!"

What did he expect, I wondered. That I was going to remain a child all my life?

"Come and sit down. I want to talk to you."

"Yes, so I was told. I believe I have to congratulate you on your coming marriage."

He frowned and looked at me intently. "Yes," he said. "I am to be married next month." He turned to me suddenly and I felt sorry for him as I had never done before. His mouth twisted a little and he said in a voice unlike his normal one: "It is six years, Rebecca. I think of her all the time. But . . . one cannot go on living in the past. You know what she meant to me . . . and I believe she would want me to do what I propose to now. We have to get on with our lives . . . you, too. I know your feelings. I know how it was with you two. She often told me. I was there when you were born. I could be fond of you as my own child . . . if you would allow me. But you never have, have you? You have resented me. I don't reproach you. I understand . . . absolutely. In fact, I believe I should have felt the same had I been you. You see, we both loved her . . . infinitely."

I could not believe that this was the great Benedict speaking. I was deeply moved but, even as I listened, so great was my resentment against him that I was telling myself that he was not completely sincere. He had loved her . . . but in his selfish way. There was only one person he loved wholeheartedly and that was Benedict Lansdon.

He seemed to regret his lapse into sentimentality.

"We have to be practical, Rebecca," he went on. "It is not good for me to go on in this way . . . and not good for you either. You are now a young lady. You cannot be shut away in the country."

"I don't feel shut away. I am very happy with my grandparents."

"I know. They are wonderful people, but you have to come out into the world. It is what your mother would have wanted for you. You have to make a life for yourself. You have to meet people of your own age. You have to mix into a society where you belong . . . where you can meet suitable people."

"Suitable? Everything has to be suitable."

He looked at me in amazement. "What is wrong with that? Of course everything should be suitable. You don't want things to be unsuitable, do you? What I propose is that after the wedding, when we get settled in, you and Belinda come up to London. You will live mainly at Manorleigh. That is most . . . suitable." He looked at me and smiled. "It is a most . . . er . . . satisfactory residence. We shall take the governess and the nurse with us. The nursery will just be transported from Cador."

"You make it all sound very simple."

"It *is* simple. As for you . . . you must have a London season."

"I wouldn't want that."

"You must have it. It would be . . ."

"Suitable?"

"Necessary . . . in your position. You are my stepdaughter, you must remember. It would be expected. Moreover, you would find it very enjoyable . . . exciting even."

"I am not sure about that."

"I am. You have lived too long out of touch down here."

"I have been as happy . . . as I could be in the circumstances."

"I know. Your grandparents have been wonderful."

"I suppose you can take Belinda, but I won't come. I can't. There is a reason."

"What reason?"

"The child Lucie."

"Oh," he said. "That little girl in the nursery. I thought she was the nurse's child."

"She is not the nurse's child. I have adopted her. I would not go anywhere without her. I don't expect you to understand. I am sure you would consider it most . . . unsuitable."

"Why not try and explain?"

"I have told you. I have adopted her."

"You . . . a young girl . . . adopt a child! It sounds absurd."

"My grandparents understand."

"I hope you will give me a chance to."

I told him what had happened at the party. He listened with horror.

"Belinda . . . my daughter . . . did that!"

"She didn't realize what she was doing. However, the mother died from burns and shock. She died saving her child whom I felt to be our responsibility. Belinda is my half-sister. I had to do something. I know it is what my mother would have expected me to do."

He nodded. "What of Belinda? What was her reaction?"

"She was contrite. She did her best to make Lucie welcome in the nursery. She was somewhat antagonistic towards her before. It was that, I think, which caused her to set the dress alight. But we knew she did not understand the danger of fire. But she knew she had done a terrible thing. Leah, the nurse, is wonderful with her. She understands her and manages her as well as anyone can. But I have vowed always to look after Lucie because she lost her mother due to the action of a member of my family. I shall look after her and shall never do anything which prevents my being able to do so."

He was looking at me intently; I fancied—but I may have been wrong—that I saw something like admiration in his eyes.

Then he said: "There was nothing else you could have done, but it would have been better if your grandparents had taken full responsibility for the child."

"I did it. I wanted to. And she is *my* responsibility."

"Well, you have left her while you went away to school."

"With my grandparents . . . yes."

"She can stay with your grandparents."

"But you are going to take Belinda and the nursery with you.

"There is only one answer then. The child must come with us."

"You mean you will take her into your household?"

"What else? You are coming to London. So is Belinda. So the child must come, too."

He was smiling at me triumphantly because he had removed the obstacle I had tried to set up.

He went on: "As soon as we are settled in, you, with the young children, will come to London. I will make all the arrangements with your grandparents. They see the point of your coming.

They liked you to be here, of course, but then you will be coming back and forth for holidays and so on . . . just as you used to before . . . before . . ."

I nodded.

"And, believe me, Rebecca, it is the best thing for you. It is what your mother would have wished. I think you can finish school. I had thought of your going for a year or so to some establishment on the Continent where they are supposed to do wonders for girls."

"I would not leave Lucie for a year . . . or even six or seven months."

"I gathered that, so we will dispense with the finishing school. As soon as you are settled in we will set about your presentation. I think it takes place at Easter so there is plenty of time for next year. You'll be eighteen then. That's about the age, I believe."

"When do you propose to marry?"

"In about six weeks, time. Would you come up for the ceremony?"

I shook my head. He understood. He touched my arm lightly.

"I think you will find it all for the best, Rebecca," he said gently.

I knew, of course, that protests were useless. My grandmother had said that as I was his step-daughter he was my natural guardian. He would take Belinda. She was his natural daughter and Leah and Miss Springer would go with her. It would be best for Lucie and I must accept that.

"I am sure," he said, "that you will get along well with my future wife."

"I hope the children will."

"I do not think she will want to interfere in the nursery. She is considerably younger than I. As a matter of fact, I believe you have met her. Some time ago she was living here in Cornwall . . . at a house called High Tor."

"High Tor!" I cried, "But that was taken over by some French people."

"That's right. I believe the family still own the place and the present tenants rent it from them. They have a place in Chislehurst and also in London.

"Then it must be the Bourdons."

He smiled. "Mademoiselle Celeste Bourdon will be my wife."

I was astounded. I tried to remember Monsieur and Madame Bourdon and found I could not recall their faces, but I did have faint memories of the younger ones. Celeste and Jean Pascal. Celeste must have been six or seven years older than I. That would make her twenty-three or -four years old now, so she was truly considerably younger than Benedict. And Jean Pascal, the rather dashing young man, must be about two years older than his sister.

"I met them in London," went on Benedict, "and of course we were immediately interested in the Cornish connection."

"I see," I said.

But I could not help feeling a twinge of uneasiness. Why was it that I should feel so about people of whom I had a slight acquaintance rather than complete strangers?

There were several weeks' respite. There would be the wedding and then I suppose a honeymoon and after that the new wife might need a little time to put her house in order before we were required to descend upon her.

But as I said to my grandmother, we should prepare the children; she agreed with me and suggested that I should be the best one to do this.

I went to the nursery. It was not lesson time so Miss Stringer was absent. I did not feel she was so important. She could teach anywhere, but to the others Cornwall had been home all their lives and I wondered how they would feel about being uprooted.

Leah was there with the two girls. Belinda was stretched out on the floor doing a jigsaw puzzle. Lucie knelt beside her handing pieces to her. Leah was sitting in the armchair sewing.

Lucie leaped up and ran to me as I entered. Belinda went on with the puzzle.

"Do come and sit down," said Leah.

Lucie took my hand and led me to a chair. She stood leaning against me.

"I have something to tell you," I said.

Belinda glanced up from the jigsaw. "What?" she demanded.

"I'll tell you when you come and sit down."

Belinda looked at the puzzle as though she were going to refuse.

"All right. If you don't want to hear, I'll just tell Leah and Lucie."

"If it's important . . ." she began.

"Belinda doesn't want to know," I said, "so come over here and I'll tell you two."

Belinda jumped up. *"Of course* I want to hear and *of course* I'm going to listen."

She had a habit at the moment of using "of course" rather superciliously in almost every sentence where it could be worked in and it was a little irritating.

"All right. Come and sit down and you shall hear. We are going away."

"All of us?" asked Lucie looking fearfully at me.

"You, Belinda, Leah, Miss Stringer and I."

"Where?" demanded Belinda.

"To London part of the time and partly to Manorleigh. We are going to your father, Belinda."

For once she was taken aback.

"You are going too, Lucie," I went on reassuringly. "It will be just the same only it won't be this house. It won't be Cornwall." I pressed Lucie's hand. "I shall be there, too. It will be our home. Of course, we shall come down here often. It is just that for most of the time we shall be somewhere else."

"Is that all?" said Belinda.

"Isn't it enough?"

"Of course, if I don't like it I won't stay."

"We shall see."

"I don't like my father," went on Belinda. "He's not a very nice man. He doesn't like me."

"You have to make him like you . . . if you can."

"Of course I can."

"Well then, we shall look forward to seeing you do it."

"Of course I shan't if I don't want to."

I turned to Leah. "There'll be a certain amount of packing to do," I said.

"Yes," said Leah. "When do we go?"

"I'm not quite sure yet. We have to wait until he is ready for us."

Belinda went back to her puzzle.

"Do you want me to help?" Lucie asked her.

Belinda shrugged her shoulders and Lucie settled down beside her.

Leah and I left them and went into the adjoining room.

"Mr. Lansdon is going to marry," I told her.

"Oh? Is that why . . . ?"

"Yes. When he has a wife he wants to get the family together, I believe." I could not help adding maliciously: "It is good for his image as an M.P."

"I see."

"You'll be surprised to hear whom he is marrying. You remember the Bourdons? Of course you do. You went up to High Tor to do repairs to their priceless tapestries, didn't you?"

She looked faintly bewildered.

183

"Yes," I went on. "It's quite a coincidence. Mr. Lansdon met the family in London. They are living mainly at Chislehurst now, I gather. Do you remember Mademoiselle Celeste?"

She had turned away slightly. She seemed a little disconcerted. I supposed the thought of our departure from Cornwall, which was after all her home, had upset her a little. She said quietly: "Yes, I remember."

"She is going to be his wife."

"I see."

"You will know the family better than I do. You were there for some little time working on those tapestries, weren't you?"

"Oh yes . . . several weeks."

"Well, she won't be exactly a stranger to you."

"Er . . . no."

"Do you think we shall get on all right with her? Mr. Lansdon seems to think she won't want to interfere in the nursery."

"No. I am sure she would not."

"Well, we shall see. I am afraid it's certain, Leah. Mr. Lansdon insists. After all Belinda is his daughter."

"Yes," she murmured. Her thoughts seemed far away. I wished I knew what she was thinking but she had always struck me as being rather withdrawn . . . mysterious in fact.

The time arrived when we were to leave Cornwall.

My grandmother said: "It's the best thing for

you really. But we shall miss you terribly. It makes it harder for us because all of you are going. But we both agree it is for the best and it is only right that Benedict should have his daughter with him."

"He only wants us so that he can have a family to show his constituents."

"I don't think that is entirely true. Try to be fair to him, Rebecca. He's had a hard time and one thing I do know: he really loved your mother. He has lost her, don't forget, just as you have."

"But he is putting someone else in her place now."

"I do not believe he will ever do that."

I was not sure.

Leah was growing more and more uneasy as time passed. It must have been a great upheaval for her. I believed she had never been out of Cornwall before. Belinda was excited though. She kept talking of the grand house she was going to live in in the big city. She was going to live with her rich and important father whom she did not like much but she would forget about him and enjoy the house.

Lucie watched me and would take her cue from me, I knew. So I tried to pretend that I found it all exciting and not give her an inkling of my feelings of disquiet.

I thought at least I should enjoy Manorleigh where I should find the Emerys, Ann and Jane who had been with us before my mother's marriage. Moreover I had felt a certain attachment to the house . . . particularly the haunted garden.

In a way, although I did not want to share Benedict's house, it was an exciting project—particularly as I was to be presented at Court.

A carriage was waiting for us at the station. Miss Springer, who had come from London, was in good spirits. She had no regrets about the move and it was obvious that she believed we were going to lead lives of much greater interest in the big city than we could in some remote country place.

Benedict and Celeste were waiting to receive us when we arrived at the house. He was quite gracious and seemed very pleased to see us. Celeste hovered in the background until he signed for her to come forward.

She had changed from the girl I had seen all those years ago. She was a young woman now. Attractive, I thought, though not exactly beautiful or even pretty; but she was dressed with elegance in a pale grey gown of what I imagined was a Parisian cut. There were pearls at her neck and in her ears. Her dark hair was beautifully dressed and she moved with becoming grace.

She came forward and took my hands.

"I am so pleased you are here," she said with a very pronounced French accent. "I am touched that you come. You must be happy here. It is what we want . . . the two . . ." She smiled ingratiatingly at Benedict.

"Yes," he said, returning her smile. "It is what we want. And the children . . ." He looked

186

towards them. "Belinda . . ." She gave him a rather defiant look. "And . . . er . . . Lucie."

I took Lucie's hand and brought her forward.

"I hope you will like your new home," said Celeste very carefully as though she had learned the words by heart.

I could see the children were a little fascinated by her.

She smiled at Leah. "But . . . we have met. You came . . . I remember it well."

Leah flushed and the look of uneasiness returned. She did not seem to want to recall her stay at High Tor although, from what we had heard from Mrs. Polhenny, the Bourdons had been delighted by her work.

Miss Stringer was introduced and seemed to make a good impression on Benedict and his wife as they did on her.

We were shown the nursery which was on the top floor of the house. It was simple but elegant with high-ceilinged rooms and long windows looking out on the square with the enclosed garden in the center. Miss Stringer had a room on the top floor as did Leah and the night nursery was there, too.

We left them up there and Celeste took me down to my room which was on the second floor.

"I think you first want to see the little ones . . . how is it?"

"Settled," I suggested.

She nodded smiling. "This is your room."

It was spacious and furnished with the elegance

I found everywhere in the house. The colors were blue and cream; it had the long high windows and the view on the square was just as below the nursery.

She slid her hand through my arm. "I want so much that you be happy here," she said.

"That is so kind of you."

"Your *beau-père* . . ."

"My stepfather."

"Yes, your stepfather . . . he very much wish. He wants you happy here in his house." She lifted her hands and added charmingly: "And because he want . . . I want."

"That is most kind of you. I am sure everything is going to work out very well."

She nodded. "Now I leave." She rubbed her hands together as though washing them. "And when you . . . *prête* . . . you come down, eh? We have tea . . . and talk . . . I think that is what your stepfather want."

"Thank you. By the way . . . what do I call you?"

"Celeste is my name . . . I will not be stepmother . . . oh no. I must be too young to be your *maman* . . . do you not think?"

"Much too young," I assured her. "Then I shall call you Celeste."

"That will be nice." She went to the door and looked back at me. "I see you very soon . . . eh?"

"Very soon."

She was gone and I thought: She certainly seems welcoming. I think I am going to like her.

I dined that evening with Benedict and his wife. There were just the three of us. The children were already in bed, sharing the night nursery. When I went in to say goodnight Lucie put her arms round my neck and clung to me fiercely.

"You are going to like it here," I whispered. "And I am right below you."

She continued to cling.

"It will be almost the same here and later on we'll go back to Cador to stay for a while," I assured her.

I went over to Belinda's bed. She opened one eye and looked at me.

"Goodnight, Belinda. Sleep well." I bent down and kissed her lightly.

"You're going to like it here," I repeated.

She nodded and closed her eyes.

I guessed both children were exhausted after the day's journey and the excitement of arriving.

Leah had glided into the room.

"They will be asleep in no time," she whispered.

The meal was served in a small room leading from the large and imposing dining room, presumably where Benedict entertained his political friends. The small room was intended to be more intimate, but I was deeply conscious of the restraint I always felt in his company.

While the fish was being served, he said: "I thought the children should stay in London for a little while, although of course Manorleigh will be so much better for them."

"Yes," I said. "I think Manorleigh would suit them very well. They will have more freedom in the country."

"Exactly."

"There are parks here, of course. I remember . . ."

I stopped. He knew I would be thinking of my mother and the memory would be as painful to him as it was to me.

To my dismay I realized that Celeste had guessed the gist of the conversation. She was hurt.

I went on quickly: "They can walk in the park and feed the ducks . . . but the country is, of course, better. They can ride there and there is the garden. The garden at Manorleigh is a delight."

"You must be here," said Celeste. "There is this . . . how you say it? . . . "

"Coming out," supplied Benedict. "The London season. Yes, Rebecca will have to be here and . . ." He turned to me. ". . . I . . . we . . . thought the children would be unhappy at first if they were deprived of your company. They have just said goodbye to your grandparents which must have been something of a wrench. Well, the fact is I thought that if you remained in London for a few weeks . . . then perhaps you could all go to Manorleigh for a while for you to settle them in and then you would come back to London."

"I should think that would work out very well.

They would have Leah who is very important to them."

"She is very good," said Celeste.

"Well you know something of her," I said. "She was with you when she repaired the tapestries at High Tor."

"They will soon get used to the change," Benedict said.

I thought: Yes, they will have to. It is necessary that you have your happy family to present to your constituents.

After that, conversation was of a light nature and of so little interest to me that I have forgotten it; but I was aware of a certain tension between them, and it occurred to me that all was not well with this marriage. I wondered why he had married. I had seen him with my mother. His relationship with her had been entirely different, but with Celeste there was a complete absence of that obsessive love. In fact I thought I detected a faintly critical attitude in his manner towards her. As for her, it was easy to see that she was besottedly in love with the man.

I tried to assess him as a man. I had been so hedged in with my own prejudices and resentment that I had not really seen him clearly. My mother had loved him. Something told me that he had been more important to her than even my noble father . . . though of course I had seen nothing of that relationship.

He was distinguished looking though not handsome in the manner of Adonis or Apollo. He was tall and of a commanding appearance; his features were not clearcut but they emanated strength. He was a very rich man and he exuded power and I had come to believe that power is an essential part of masculine attraction. He certainly had that.

I sensed that neither he nor Celeste was happy. There was something between them.

I daresay, I told myself, he married her because she would grace his dinner table. She was to be an asset to his political career and, just as he had acquired a family in Belinda and myself and even Lucie, he had taken a wife.

It would be interesting to watch them and discover what exactly was wrong. I despised myself for taking this attitude, but I could not help gloating a little. After all, he had spoiled my life. Why should his go smoothly?

Morwenna asked me over to the Cartwrights' house which was not very far from Benedict's residence.

She greeted me warmly.

I had always liked Pedrek's mother. There was something very sweet and gentle about her; moreover she and my mother had been close friends and had shared many an adventure together.

"It is lovely to see you, Rebecca," she said. "I am glad you have come to London. Though I must say I am a little scared about this coming out business. I'm to do it."

"I'm glad you are."

She laughed self-deprecatingly. "Helena would have been much better. Wife of a prominent member of the House. She brought us out, you know."

"Yes, I did know." I could talk about my mother more easily with Morwenna than I could with my grandmother. Morwenna and I did not mind showing our emotion when we spoke of her whereas with my grandmother we both tried to hide the intensity of our grief. "My mother often talked about it."

"How awful I was! I was terrified . . . not so much of the presentation . . . that was over in a few seconds . . . just a curtsy and taking care that your train did not trip you up so that you stumbled at Her Majesty's feet. One can imagine what consternation that would cause but there was very little danger of it. It was the parties and the balls . . . and the terrible fear that one was not going to get a partner. I was in agonies. Your mother did not care. But then she didn't have to . . ."

I had heard it all before, but somehow with Morwenna it did not upset me. It was almost as though my mother were there with us in the Cartwright sitting room and that gave me a warm and comfortable feeling of peace.

"Helena is getting a little old now, though she is sprightly enough and Matthew is still high up in politics and a name to be reckoned with. She will help, of course, but she doesn't feel like undertaking the whole thing."

"What shall I have to do?"

"Well, first of all you'll have to have some

dancing lessons, singing too. Her Majesty is very interested in singing and dancing."

"I thought she had gone into seclusion."

"She has been for years . . . ever since the Prince died . . . but the conventions go on."

"Yes. Mama often told me about Madame Dupré who was really Miss Dappry and how she used to dragoon you both."

"And how I was the clumsiest creature she was ever doomed to teach."

"My mother did not say that. She said that all that was wrong was in your mind."

"She was very wise."

We were silent for a little while. Then Morwenna said: "You'll get through easily. The thing is not to worry. I always felt that Mother and Pa wanted a great marriage for me . . . which is, after all, the purpose of the operation . . . and that I was going to fail them. Your mother didn't care because her parents only wanted her to enjoy herself. Mine did too . . . but they just had this idea."

I was suddenly appalled. "Of course, that is what my stepfather will expect of me!"

"But your grandparents . . ."

"I wasn't thinking of them. They would want me to be happy as they did my mother, but he . . . that will be why he wants it. 'The stepdaughter of Benedict Lansdon, the Member for Manorleigh, has become engaged to the Duke of . . . , the Earl of . . . , the Viscount . . .'. I don't think a simple Sir would be good enough for him."

"You mustn't think like that. Just go in and see what happens. If you meet someone and he happens to be a duke or an earl or a viscount . . . well, as long as you're in love with him . . . his title is of no account."

I burst out laughing. "It will be to him."

"This is your future happiness. That's what is important."

"You don't know him, Morwenna."

"I think I do." She was silent for a moment, then she said: "He loved your mother dearly . . . and she him. She was never so close to any other man."

"She loved my father," I insisted. "He was a wonderful man."

She nodded. "Justin and I have every reason to be grateful to him. It is something we shall never forget. But for him . . . well, you know he gave his life to save Justin's."

"He was a good man . . . a heroic man . . . a father to be proud of."

She nodded. "But one does not always love people for their heroic qualities. You see, something happened between your mother and Benedict . . . years before. They met in Cornwall and the spark struck then. I felt theirs was the perfect marriage. And to think it ended in what should have been an additional joy for them."

And there we were, weeping quietly, but giving comfort to each other.

Morwenna stretched for my hand and said:

"We have to go on living, Rebecca. He is your stepfather. He wants to care for you."

"He doesn't. He wants a family because it is good for his image with the voters."

"No . . . no. He wants you here. You are her daughter and that would endear you to him."

"I am another man's daughter. Perhaps he does not like that."

"No . . . no. You must try to understand him . . . try to be fond of him."

"How can you make yourself fond of people?"

"By not building up resentment against them . . . by not looking for their faults but by trying to see the good in them."

I shook my head. "Where?" I asked.

"He wants to love you and Belinda. Help him."

"I wonder what he would say if he thought we were helping him. He would laugh. He doesn't need help. He thinks himself omnipotent."

"He is not a happy man."

I looked at her steadily. "You mean his marriage . . ."

"Celeste is a nice girl. I think she loves him very much."

"He married her because he believed she would be suitable to entertain his guests."

"I think that he mourns for your mother still. I think she is there . . . between those two. It is the last thing your mother would want. She loved him. She would want to see him happy. He has his demons to face, Rebecca, as you do. You should help each other. Oh dear, what am I saying? I am talking about something of which I know nothing which is a silly thing to do. Pedrek will be home from school soon. He'll be glad to know you are in London."

"That's wonderful news. I missed him in Cornwall."

"Well, school makes a difference, you know."

"What is he going to do?"

"We're not sure. He might go to the university. On the other hand he would like to go into business. His grandfather wants him in Cornwall naturally to take over the mine in due course, but his father thinks he needs a spell in the London office with him. We shall have to wait and see."

"It will be wonderful to have him here."

"You'll see him . . . often, I imagine. And now, of course, we shall have to get busy. Court dress . . . deportment lessons . . . dancing. My dear Rebecca, your days from now on will be fully occupied until we get you into that drawing room where you will have to make your curtsy . . . without a wobble, mind . . . and have become acceptable to London society."

Then the preparations began. This was what my mother had done some twenty years before. Morwenna told me that the presentation ceremony was less formal than it had been. In the days of the Prince Consort it had been quite a different matter, with debutantes and sponsors being severely censored to make sure that their families were worthy to come into contact with the Queen.

Time was passing and it would soon be Easter. Pedrek came home for half term which was pleasant. Madame Dupré was past giving deportment and dancing lessons. Her successor was Madame Perrotte, middle-aged, black-haired and sallow skinned, who spoke in mincing tones, over-refined and very precise. I danced with her which was not very inspiring, but I did enjoy the lessons. I sang, too. My voice could naturally not compare with that of Jenny Lind but, according to Madame Perrotte, it was just passable.

The lessons took place in the Cartwright home as Morwenna was sponsoring me.

When Pedrek arrived there was great rejoicing. Both his parents thought him wonderful— and so did I! There was something so dependable about Pedrek. He always seemed to me in command of his own life. He was practical and not given to flights of fancy; he was kind and considerate to everyone.

Dancing lessons became great fun because he was called in to partner me. Madame Perrotte would sit at the pianoforte and rattle out the tunes to which we danced round and round the drawing room, most of the furniture having been pushed to the sides of the room. Madame Perrotte, one eye on the keyboard and the other on us, would cry out: "*Non . . . non*, more *esprit . . . s'il vous plaît*. That is good, good . . . ah, too slow . . , too quick . . . oh . . . oh, *ma foi*." Pedrek and I would be overcome with mirth and the excitement of the dance, feeling almost hysterical with suppressed laughter.

There was my court dress to be tried on; there was deportment and the correct manner to curtsy. It was hard to believe so much had to go into one small gesture. But it had to be right, Madame Perrotte insisted, one false step, one little slip and a girl could be disgraced for ever.

Pedrek and I used to laugh about it and I would go into the nursery and show the children how one had to curtsy before the Queen, and how we danced and sang; they listened intently and used to clap their hands when I showed them how I danced in the Cartwright drawing room with Pedrek. They were both practicing curtsies and playing at presentation. Belinda always wanted to be the Queen and she amused us all by her regal manner.

As for my stepfather, if he were looking for a duke or earl to enhance his political career, I did not feel in duty bound to provide it . . . even if I could. I had not asked to be presented and if I failed, I simply did not care.

There were three weeks to the great day and Benedict thought it was time for the children to go to Manorleigh. He said that I should go down with them to stay for a week or so, then return. I should feel fresh for my ordeal after the respite and I should have a week or so to prepare myself.

Both Morwenna and Helena agreed that it was a good idea. And so it was arranged.

The children were excited. They were going to a big house in the country.

"But it's not as big as Cador," Belinda announced.

"No, perhaps not," I replied. "But it *is* a big house, and you will be able to ride in the paddock and enjoy it very much."

"You are coming," stated Lucie.

"Yes . . . just at first. Then I shall come back to London. But I shall not be far away and I shall be coming to see you. It is going to be great fun."

Arriving at the house was an emotional experience. I was prepared for that. Mr. and Mrs. Emery greeted us in the dignified manner of butler and housekeeper in the establishment of a very important gentleman. Here at least were two who did not resent Benedict.

After the first encounter Mrs. Emery unbent a little. A sentimental heart beat under the black bombazine and jet ornaments.

"It's nice to see you here, Miss Rebecca," she told me, after everyone was settled in and we had a few words alone. "I hope we see you often. Mr. Emery and I often talk of you."

"You are happy here, Mrs. Emery?"

"Oh yes, Miss Rebecca. The master . . . he's very kind. Not one of the interfering sort. Them sort I can't abide. He knows we can manage best on our own . . . and he gives us a free hand. It's a fine old house, as you know."

She was pleased the children had come.

"There's one thing an old house like this wants and that's children," she went on. "All them nurseries going to waste up there. That Leah is a quiet one. She'll be in the nursery most of the time. Miss Stringer . . . well, governesses are always a problem."

"I think she would like her meals in her room."

"That's how it should be."

Mrs. Emery was well versed in the protocol of houses like this and she was one who would like everything to be as it should be.

I heard the children laughing in the nursery and I went in. Leah was with them. She seemed less tense than she had in London.

I said: "You like it here, Leah?"

"Yes, Miss Rebecca," she answered. "I be one for the country. 'Tis better for the children. It's put some color in their cheeks."

"They didn't look exactly wan when they arrived."

"Oh, you know what I mean, Miss."

Yes, I thought. It means you will be happier here. Well, I was pleased for her.

Miss Stringer was slightly less delighted. She was sorry to leave London but at least Manorleigh was not so far from the metropolis as Cornwall and I imagined she would be making little trips to town every now and then.

So everyone seemed satisfied.

Mrs. Emery informed me that she had given me my old room and she looked at me a little questioningly. "I thought that was what you'd want, Miss Rebecca. If not, I can have another made ready on the other side of the house."

I knew what she meant. This was the room I had occupied when my mother was here. Would there be too many memories?

It was natural, of course, that I should remember, but as it was six years since my mother had died, I should have thought that, for people like Mrs. Emery, she had now become a figure of the past. But that was not so, I could see.

I told her I preferred to stay in my old room.

That first night at Manorleigh was an emotional one for me. Perhaps, I thought coward-like, I should have had another room. I sat at the window for a long time, looking down on the pond where Hermes was still poised for flight, now touched by moonlight. And there was the seat under the tree where I had sat with my mother; I remembered how at the pool she had asked me to care for the unborn child . . . almost as though she had known what was going to happen to her.

I spent a restless night. I was haunted by dreams of my mother. I thought I was seated there in the garden and that she came to me.

I should expect this, coming back to the house, but as my grandmother had wisely told me, I had to put the past behind me and live for the present.

So much had happened since her death. I kept saying to myself, it is six years.

But there was a great deal to remind me of

her in this house that at times it almost seemed as though she were there.

There was no doubt that the children loved Manorleigh. They quickly settled in which was a great relief. Leah was happier. The place suited her.

There was great excitement about the children's ponies and each day one of the grooms took them riding in the paddock . . . a treat they had missed in London.

They were both doing well, Thomas, the groom, reported. I was glad. Lucie had changed. She had ceased to cling quite so much to me although I knew I was more important to her than anyone else. But she was more self-reliant now and able to stand up to Belinda. They were quite fond of each other in a way and although they quarrelled occasionally when Belinda exerted her superiority as the daughter of the great man, they were happy in each other's company.

One thing that worried me a little was Belinda's resentment against her father. I understood how he felt towards the child. He was not the sort of man who would understand children in any way, but he could not forget that it was Belinda's coming which had resulted in her mother's departure; and the more I saw of him the more I realized what a deep void her death had made in his life.

I should have been sorry for him. It was a

shared emotion. But I could not forget how happy I had been before he came to change everything.

My mother and he had shared a suite of rooms on the second floor. I had not gone there very much in the past for they were his rooms as well as hers. They were two of the best rooms in the house really—a bedroom with a dressing room adjoining and a sitting room. They had been furnished in blue and white, I remembered.

I felt an urge to see them and on the day after my arrival I went along to them, but when I turned the handle of the door which led to the suite, I found it was locked.

I went straight to Mrs. Emery's sitting room. I knew this was the time when she would be making herself a cup of tea and she would be sitting by the fire reading either *Lorna Doone* or *East Lynne*—that was unless she had changed an old habit. In the past she read only those two books and when she had finished one she would start on the other. It was enough for her, she said. There was nothing that could touch them for interest and she liked to know what was coming next.

I knocked at her door and was immediately greeted by an imperious "Come in." Clearly she thought it was one of the servants about to intrude on the exploits of Jan Rodd or Lady Isabel.

Her expression changed when she saw me.

"Well, come in, Miss Rebecca. I was just waiting for the kettle to boil."

She put *Lorna Doone* aside and looked at me through her spectacles.

"I am interrupting your rest time, Mrs. Emery," I began.

"Oh no . . . think nothing of it. Is it something you wanted, Miss Rebecca?"

"Well, those rooms on the second floor . . . I tried the door and they were locked."

"Oh yes, Miss Rebecca. Did you want to go in?"

"Yes . . . I did rather."

She rose and, going to a drawer, took out a bunch of keys.

"I'll take you along," she said.

"Is there any reason why they're locked?"

"Oh yes, there's a reason. I wouldn't take it on myself, you know."

I thought it was rather mysterious and by that time we had reached the door of the suite. She unlocked it and I stepped into the room.

It was a shock because it looked exactly the same as it had when my mother was alive. Her things were spread around . . . the enameled mirror on the dressing table with her initials embossed on the back . . . the brushes to match. I looked at the big double bed which she had shared with him, the big white wardrobe with the gilt handles. I went to it and opened it, knowing that I should find her clothes there . . . just as she had left them.

I turned to look at Mrs. Emery, who stood beside me, her eyes misty, nodding her head.

"It's his orders," she said. "No one's to come here except me . . . to keep the place dusted like. I do the cleaning myself. He doesn't want anyone else here. When he's at Manorleigh he comes in here and sits for hours. I tell you I don't like it, Miss Rebecca. There's something not right about it."

I sensed that she wanted to get out of the room.

"He wouldn't like anyone in here," she said. "He don't like me in here . . . but someone's got to clean the rooms and he'd rather me than any of the others."

We went out and she locked the door. I returned with her to her sitting room where she carefully put the key into the drawer from which she had taken it. "I'll make a cup of tea and I'd be honored if you'd take one with me, Miss Rebecca."

I said I should be pleased to.

She waited for the kettle to boil, then took it from the hob and infused the tea.

"Let it stand a bit," she said.

She sat down.

"It's been like that ever since . . ." she began. "You see, she meant so much to him."

"She did to me, too," I reminded her.

"I know that. She was a lovely lady, your mother. She had so much love in her . . . and she was so missed . . . that it seems people can't let her go. For a long time it was her he wanted. That was clear enough. It was a tragedy that when they got together it was for such a short time."

"She was happily married to my father."

Mrs. Emery nodded. "I reckon he'd do better to change that room. Send her clothes away. It don't do no good to keep mourning. It's not as though he can bring her back, although . . ."

"Although what, Mrs. Emery?"

"Well, in a house of this sort that's been here for hundreds of years, people get fanciful about bygone days. There's dark shadows in these big rooms and the boards creak something shocking at times. Empty-headed servant girls . . . well, they get thinking things, if you know what I mean."

"Hauntings?"

"Yes, that's what I mean. You see, there was this story about Lady Flamstead and that Miss Martha who lived here all them years ago . . . and this Lady Flamstead was said to do a bit of haunting."

"I did hear the story. She died . . . having a baby."

Mrs. Emery looked at me mournfully. "You see, it's the same story. Your mother died having that Belinda."

"My mother could not have been in the least like Lady Flamstead and Belinda is not like what I have heard of Miss Martha. She was devoted to her mother. So far it seems that Belinda is devoted only to herself."

"It's the way of children . . . but as I'm telling you, I'd like to see them rooms cleared out. Her clothes could be sent away. But he won't have it. Maybe he gets some comfort from going in there. Who's to say? It's as though he can't face his loss and he's trying to pretend she's not gone after all."

"Oh, Mrs. Emery, it's so sad."

"It's life, Miss Rebecca. It's what the good Lord has ordained for us . . . and we needs must accept it."

I nodded.

"But it's not right . . . particularly now he's wed again."

"If he cared so much for her . . . why . . . ?"

"Well, a man needs a woman, I reckon. His sort as much as any. And if you can't have the one you want you'll sometimes take second best. I'm sorry for the new Mrs. Lansdon. She's a strange lady. I never did take to foreigners. All that funny talk and throwing their hands about. It's not natural. But she thinks a lot of him. There's no doubt of that. Well, he married her, didn't he? What does he want to marry her for if he's going to spend all his time in that room moping over what's past and done with?"

"Does she . . . know?"

"Poor young lady, I reckon she does. When he's here, as he is some of every week, she'll come with him. Well, he's in that room. She must know. I think she gets rather cut up about it."

"But he must care for her . . ."

"He's not an easy man to know. There was no question of how he felt about your mother . . . and she about him. But the present Mrs. Lansdon . . . well, she's young—a lot younger than he is—

208

and she's good looking if you like that foreign sort of way which I don't much. And the time she spends on her clothes and her hair and all that . . . and it wouldn't surprise me if some of that nice complexion of hers didn't come out of a box. Then she's got this French maid. Yvette or some such outlandish name . . . well, some of the servants say she must have thrown herself at him . . . helping him with the constituency . . . and of course, as Jim Fedder down in the stables says . . . forgive the expression, Miss Rebecca, but you know what he means . . . he said she was a tasty piece . . . the sort a man would find it hard to say no to if you know what I mean."

"I do, Mrs. Emery."

"Well, I must say you found out about that room pretty quick and I had to take you in there . . . you being mistress of the house so to speak in the absence of him or her. But I think it's what I call unhealthy. I've said it to Mr. Emery and I'd say it to Mr. Lansdon himself if I had half a chance. In a house like this you don't want people to get imagining things . . . servants being what they are. There's some of them already saying she can't rest because of him being so cut up. They'll soon be seeing her under that oak tree . . . and they'll say it's like Lady Flamstead all over again.

"Yes, I do see what you mean, Mrs. Emery," I said. "It is unhealthy."

She sat there nodding her head sagely. Then she said: "Another cup, Miss Rebecca?"

"No thanks. I'd better go. I have things to do. It's been pleasant having a chat."

I left her then. I wanted to be alone to think.

I was sure that by the time I had to leave Manorleigh the children would have settled in. They had the familiar figures of Leah and Miss Stringer; and Mrs. Emery had already become a favorite with them as had Ann and Jane.

But while I was there I spent as much of my time as I could with them.

I was in the nursery one day when Jane brought in the milk and biscuits which they had mid-morning. She was very fond of them and they of her, and she waited while they drank their milk, which was natural as she did not want to make another journey to the top of the house to collect mugs and plates.

Leah was there and we all talked together for a while . . . of the weather, I believe. I said they all seemed very comfortable and I asked if Jane regretted leaving London.

"Well, it was ever so nice working for Mrs. Mandeville," she said. "But it was rather a little house . . . and not convenient like . . . but she was such a lovely lady. It's different here but there is something about working in a big house."

"Owned by a Member of Parliament?" I asked.

"Well, a gentleman like Mr. Lansdon . . . that'd be working for somebody, I reckon."

"It's quiet here, Jane."

"Only when the master's not in residence. When he is . . . well, there's entertaining all the time. It's very exciting . . . all those people coming and going, some of them you've seen in the papers. It's not often we're as quiet as we've been since you've been here, Miss. There hasn't been any guests . . ."

"Do you get many people actually staying at the house?"

"Oh yes . . . friends of the master, they come. And then there's *her* people."

"You mean Monsieur and Madame Bourdon?"

"Mind you, they haven't come. It's different with that Monsieur Jean Pascal."

"Oh . . . Mrs. Lansdon's brother. He's been?"

"That's him. He comes down now and then." She flushed a little and giggled. I remembered when I had met him long ago and, young as I was, how I had noticed that his eyes rested on the young girls.

"Well, 'tis natural like, Miss . . . he being brother to the mistress."

"Quite natural," I said.

Leah had not been well for the last few days and I suggested that she see a doctor.

"Oh no, Miss. I be all right." She was emphatic. " 'Tis just the change of air, maybe."

"There is a difference between here and London, Leah," I reminded her. "But this is more like Cornwall."

"Oh no, Miss, nothing be quite like Cornwall."

211

I thought she looked a little tired. She told me she had had a bad night. "Go to bed for an hour or so now," I told her, "It will do you a lot of good."

At length she agreed and I took the children into the garden.

I was near the Hermes pool, lazily watching the gnats dancing above the water and the girls bouncing a red ball between them, when suddenly I was aware that we were not alone.

I looked up sharply. A man was standing nearby watching us.

He smiled. He had one of the most charming smiles I had ever seen. It was warm and friendly and there was a hint of mischief in it. He took off his hat and bowed low. The children stopped playing and stood still watching him.

"What a charming group," he said. "I must apologize for disturbing it. I believe I am in the presence of Miss Rebecca Mandeville."

"You are right."

"And one of these charming young ladies is Miss Belinda Lansdon."

"It's me," shrieked Belinda.

"If Miss Stringer were here what would she say?" I asked,

"Don't shout," said Lucie. "That's what she'd say. You're always shouting, Belinda."

"People want to hear what *I* say," Belinda pointed out.

"You are forgetting your manners," I said. "And

what Miss Stringer would say is 'Watch your grammar.' It should be 'It is I' not 'me.' "

"Well, it is me all the same however you say it." She went to the newcomer and held out her hand. "I am Belinda," she said.

"I guessed," he told her.

"Are you looking for Mr. Lansdon?" I asked. "He's in London."

"Is that so? Well, I must content myself with meeting his charming family."

"You know who *we* are," I said. "Could you introduce yourself?"

"You must forgive the omission. I have been so overcome with pleasure to meet you in this somewhat unconventional manner. I am Oliver Gerson. I might say an associate of your stepfather."

"I presume you want to talk business with him."

"Not as much as I want to chat in the sunshine with his family."

I thought he was a little too suave—the typical man about town with a talent for paying flattering compliments which were obviously false, although I had to admit that he did so with a certain grace and charm which inclined one to forget the insincerity.

He asked if he might sit with us. Lucie came and stood close to me. Belinda was stretched on the grass; she stared with unconcealed interest at the newcomer.

He surveyed her benignly: "You are putting me under close scrutiny, Miss Belinda," he said.

"What's that?" she asked.

"You are studying me intently, wondering whether I fit into your scheme of things."

She was a little taken aback but pleased to have his attention focused on her.

"Tell us about you," she said.

"I am an associate of your father. We are in business together. I, however, never did aspire to the Houses of Parliament. Now tell me, Miss Rebecca, is it true that you are shortly to be presented to the Queen?"

"I can do the curtsy," cried Belinda, and leaping up proceeded to show him.

"Bravo!" he shouted. "What a pity you are not going to be presented too."

"They don't present little girls."

"But fortunately little girls become bigger in due course."

"But they have to wait until then. I've got *ages* to wait."

"Time will soon pass, will it not, Miss Rebecca?"

I said yes it would and before long it would be Belinda's and Lucie's turns.

"We know how to do it already," Lucie observed.

"You have recently come from Cornwall?" he asked.

"What a lot you know about us!"

"I am very interested in Benedict's family. Are you going to help him hold his seat?"

"I shall help him if I want to," announced Belinda.

"You are a young lady of whims, I see."

Belinda had sidled up to him and placed her hands on his knees. "What's whims?" she asked.

"Passing fancies . . . impulsive acts . . . Is that how you would describe it, Miss Rebecca?"

"I should think that is an accurate description."

He looked at me earnestly. "I shall look forward to seeing you after your initiation."

"Oh, shall you be in town?"

"Indeed I shall. I have wanted to meet you ever since I heard you were leaving the remote land of Cornwall."

"You heard of that?"

"Your stepfather is very proud of his stepdaughter and very eager to see her entry into society."

"Oh, do you know him well?"

"Indeed. We work together."

"Yes, I believe you did tell us this."

"Can you ride?" asked Belinda.

"I came here on horseback. My steed is now in the stables being looked after by your very capable groom."

"We have ponies, don't we, Lucie?" said Belinda.

Lucie nodded.

"Would you like to see us jump?" went on Belinda. "We go very high now."

"Oh really, Belinda," I said with a laugh. "Mr. Gerson won't have time for that."

"I have time." He smiled at Belinda. "And my greatest desire at this moment is to see Miss Belinda take the jump with her pony."

"Will you wait until we get into our riding things?" asked Belinda excitedly.

"Until the end of time," he told her.

"You say such funny things. Come on, Lucie." She turned back to him. "Stay there till we come. Don't go away."

"Wild horses could not drag me away."

They ran off and I looked at him in astonishment. He smiled at me half apologetically. "They were so charmingly eager," he said. "What a bright creature Miss Belinda is."

"Sometimes we feel a little too bright."

"The other one is charming, too. She is the foundling . . . is she not?"

"We don't mention it."

"Forgive me. I am a close friend of Benedict's and I know the circumstances. I have so long wanted to meet his family and this is a great occasion for me."

"I am surprised that you did not know he is in London."

He had a way of lifting one eyebrow when he smiled.

"Will you forgive me? I did know. I wanted an opportunity to meet his stepdaughter in private, so that when we meet at those functions which you as a young lady who has passed the royal test will be attending, I should already have had the pleasure of your acquaintance."

"Why should you bother?"

"I thought it would be more amusing. At those dances and such like functions conversation is not always easy. I wanted to get to know you away from them. You must pardon my forwardness."

"Well, at least you have been frank and there is really nothing to pardon."

"May I say that I have rarely spent such an agreeable afternoon?"

He had such a convincing manner that I almost believed him. His presence in any case had given an interest to the afternoon.

The girls appeared, flushed and excited.

"Do we have to have a groom?" asked Lucie.

"I think you should. Let's go and see who is in the stables."

"We don't need a groom," said Belinda impatiently. "We can do without him. We can ride now. Grooms are for little children."

"I know you are fast leaving childhood behind and are vastly experienced but the rule is that a groom must be present and we must keep to it."

"It's nonsense," said Belinda.

"Don't flout authority, Belinda," I said, "or Mr. Gerson will think you are a rebel."

"Will you?" she asked. "And am I?"

"The answers are Yes and Yes again. Do you believe I am right?"

She skipped round him. "You're a rebel. You're a rebel," she chanted.

"Do I so betray myself to those clear young eyes?"

It was obvious that Belinda was enchanted

by Mr. Gerson. I was afraid she would try to do something rash to impress him.

We stood side by side in the paddock, watching them taking their jumps, under the guidance of Jim Taylor.

"What a charming domestic scene," said Oliver Gerson. "I cannot remember when I enjoyed an afternoon so much."

Afterwards I took the children back to the house.

"Leah will be wondering what has become of you," I told them.

"Oh, she's got one of her silly old headaches," said Belinda.

"You will see that Miss Belinda Lansdon is not of a very sympathetic nature," I said to Oliver Gerson.

"Miss Belinda Lansdon is a young lady of strong opinions," he replied, "nor does she hesitate to express them."

He did not come into the house. He said he had to get back to London; he had business to deal with.

After he had gone Lucie said to me: "I think Belinda liked him a lot . . . and I think he liked you."

I replied: "He is the sort of person who appears to like people . . . that is on the surface. In fact, he might have entirely different feelings about them."

"That's called deceit," said Lucie.

"Often," I answered, "it is called charm."

It was time for me to return to London. The children said a regretful goodbye to me, but I felt that they were happy enough at Manor Grange. In the short time we had been there it had become home to them and it was true that a house in the country was more suitable to their needs than the splendid London residence could be.

Morwenna was waiting for me. There was a great deal to press into a short time, she said. We must go to the dressmaker to make sure everything fitted; moreover Madame Perrotte would be coming until the very last day. She was a little worried about my curtsy.

There followed a week of intensive action and then the great day dawned.

I set out in the carriage with Morwenna and Helena and as was the custom we were inspected by the curious eyes of passers by. It was quite an ordeal. At least we were in the royal drawing room and there was the Queen, a diminutive figure, with an expression of gloom and an air of aloofness which was rather disconcerting.

However, the procedure was short lived. One approached, curtsied, kissed the plump bejeweled little hand, and for a fraction of a second looked into that sad old face, then cautiously walked backwards, balancing the three plumes on one's head and taking the utmost care not to trip over one's three and a half yards of train. I was inwardly amused by all the preparations which had been necessary to make me ready for those few seconds of confrontation with royalty. However, the purpose was served. I had survived the ordeal and was now an accepted member of London society.

I was relieved to take off my feathers—as great a hazard as the train of my dress—and to sit back and say Thank Heaven, that's over.

Morwenna was as relieved as I was.

"I remember it so well," she said.

"I too," added Helena.

"I was in a state of perpetual anxiety throughout the whole business," admitted Morwenna. "I knew I'd be a failure."

"So did I," added Helena.

"Yet," I pointed out, "you are both happily married which is the whole purpose of the affair."

"The whole purpose of the affair," said Helena, "is to parade the girls so that they can aspire to a grand marriage. Our marriages were grand for us but not to the world. Martin wasn't known at all when I married him."

I knew the story of how they had met on the way to Australia with my great-grandparents. Martin had been going out to write a book about convicts. Uncle Peter had helped him when he returned to England and had molded him so that he had become the successful politician he was to-day.

Morwenna said: "And Justin was not considered a good match. He is just a good husband."

"To get a good husband is a more successful way of going about it, I should think," I said.

"You see what a wise woman our little Rebecca has become," said Helena. "I am going to pray that *you* find the most successful way."

We all were pleased that the great ordeal was over but we all knew there could be more to come. There would be the invitations, the gaiety, the splendor and the misgivings of the London season.

My stepfather would be watching me. He after all had borne the cost of the expensive arrangements of getting me launched. There had always been a great deal of entertaining at his London house—and at Manorleigh, of course; but that was political entertaining. Now the parties would be for his stepdaughter. There would doubtless be a strong political flavor about them, I supposed, because that was the circle in which he moved. But on the face of it the balls would be given for *me*. What return did he expect? He wanted to see little notices in the paper. "Miss Rebecca Mandeville, stepdaughter of Mr Benedict Lansdon . . . the debutante of the season . . ." "Miss Rebecca Mandeville announces her engagement to the Duke of . . . the Marquis of . . . It will be remembered that she is the stepdaughter of Mr Benedict Lansdon . . ." Uncle Peter had been like that. His grandson had inherited his talent for advertising himself. My mother used to laugh at Uncle Peter. What had they said of Benedict? "He's a chip off the old block." Well, if he expected me to shine in society and walk off with the big matrimonial prize, I feared he might be in for a big disappointment.

There was to be a ball for me at the London house. It was the first of the season. Great preparations ensued. Celeste was eager to help in any way she could. She was certainly trying hard to be friendly. She came to my room to help me dress for the ball, bringing her maid, Yvette, with her.

My gown was of lavender chiffon. Celeste had chosen it. She had said: "I wish everyone to say . . . Who is that beautiful one? Is her gown not *charmante?* I wanted Benedict to be proud of you."

"He'll hardly notice me."

She lifted her shoulders in a resigned gesture. I thought she was expressing her own disappointment in being unable to please him.

She and Yvette twittered round me while Yvette dressed my hair.

I must admit that the final effect was surprising. I looked different. More attractive . . . yes . . . but older . . . more sophisticated. The person who looked back at me in the mirror hardly seemed myself.

And there I was at the top of the grand staircase under the grand chandelier with Benedict on one side of me and Celeste on the other, greeting the guests. There were many compliments on my appearance and I was aware of Celeste's gratified smile.

I was beginning to like her and somewhere in my feelings was a certain pity. She was not happy and that unhappiness was due to him. All was not well with their marriage. He did not really love her. He had loved my mother and no one else could take her place. I understood that but I felt he had had no right to marry this young woman and then make her miserable by his devotion to someone else . . . even though that someone was dead. It was, as Mrs. Emery had said, an unhealthy situation.

My dance program was full that night. There was none of the agonizing which Morwenna and Helena had told me they had suffered, sitting out just hoping that someone . . . anyone . . . the oldest, clumsiest man in the ballroom, would ask them to dance for even he would be better than no one at all.

I was lucky because there were three men whom I already knew and as it was the very beginning of the season quite a number of young people were unknown to each other.

I danced first with a young politician to whom my stepfather had introduced me. I was glad of Madame Perrotte's tuition which enabled me to concentrate on the conversation as well as on my feet.

The young man told me how delighted he was to meet me and what a wonderful person my stepfather was. This conversation was peppered with comments on the House and comparisons were drawn between Mr. Gladstone and Mr. Disraeli, the former being clearly the favorite which was natural because the young man belonged to the same party as Benedict. I answered as intelligently as I could; and I was rather pleased when the music released me. And no sooner was I returned to my seat between Morwenna and Helena than someone appeared to claim the next dance.

I recognized him at once as the man who had called at Manorleigh. Oliver Gerson.

"I crave the pleasure of the next dance," he said, bowing agreeably to us all. "I have the honor of Miss Mandeville's acquaintance. We met at Manorleigh."

"Oh yes, of course," said Morwenna. "I believe we have met. Mr. Gerson, is it not?"

"How gratifying that you remember. And you are Mrs. Cartwright, and Mrs. Hume, of course, the wife of the great Martin Hume."

"On the other side of the political fence from you, I imagine," said Helena.

He lifted his shoulders. "Although a great friend of Mr. Benedict Lansdon and having an immense interest in all he does, I do not have political inclinations. My vote goes to the side which at the time of the election, seems most desirable to me.

"Which is probably the wisest way," said Helena laughing. "And now you are asking Miss Mandeville to dance."

He smiled at me. "Am I to have that pleasure?"

"But of course."

We went onto the floor together.

"How delightful you look!"

"I owe a great deal to Mrs. Lansdon and her French maid."

"I am sure you owe a great deal more to Nature who made you as you are."

I burst out laughing.

"I have said something amusing?" he asked.

"It amused me. How do you think of these things? They trip off your tongue as though you really mean them."

"That is because they come from the heart and I do mean them."

"Then it would be ungracious of me not to say Thank you."

He laughed with me. "I did enjoy our encounter in the gardens at Manorleigh."

"Yes . . . it was amusing."

"How is the sprightly Belinda, and the somewhat demure Lucie?"

"They are well and still at Manorleigh. Mr. Lansdon thinks it is best for them to be there."

"Miss Belinda made quite an impression on me."

"You made quite an impression on her."

"Did I indeed?"

"Don't congratulate yourself. She is impressed by all who show an interest in her."

"I shall make an excuse to visit Manor Grange again. But I shall be sure that I come when you are there. I suppose you will be from time to time?"

"I shall be in London till the end of the season, I suppose."

"During which time I hope to see more and more of you."

"Have you the time to spend in frivolous pursuits such as balls and functions for debutantes?"

"I do not find enjoying the company of interesting people a frivolous occupation."

"But occasions like this . . ."

"When there are moments such as the present there is nothing more I would ask for."

"You know a great deal about me. Tell me about yourself."

"Benedict Lansdon's grandfather was a benefactor of mine. I suppose I was a sort of protégé of his. My father knew him well and Peter was always interested in me. He said I had vitality . . . I reminded him of himself. It is always a point in one's favor if one reminds people of themselves. It gives them high hopes of you."

"Do I detect a note of cynicism?" I asked.

"You may. The truth can sometimes appear so. But we all have the utmost admiration for ourselves and if people are made in our image we must admire them too."

"I expect you are right. So Uncle Peter regarded you favorably?"

"Most favorably. You were fond of him, I see."

"It was impossible not to be fond of him. There was something about him. He was very worldly wise but at the root of it was great kindness . . . and understanding."

"It is often easier for the not-so-virtuous to be

more lenient towards sinners. Have you not found that in life?"

"Yes, I think so. So you were a friend of his and he took you under his wing."

"He never struck me as a bird or a celestial being who, I believe, are the only creatures who possess wings. You could say that he showed an interest in me, guided me, taught me a good deal of what I know and made a business man of me."

"I don't suppose it was such a difficult task."

"Now who is paying the compliments?"

"I meant it. There is something . . ." I paused and he asked:

"Yes? What were you going to say?"

"There is something astute about you."

"Astute? Perceptive. Shrewd. Having insight. It sounds very commendable. But are astute people sometimes a little sly . . . self-seeking . . . having an eye open for the main chance?"

"Perhaps that covers it, too. But everyone would like to be astute surely. Who would wish to be otherwise?"

"Then I thank you."

The music had stopped.

"Alas," he said. "I must return you to your guardians. But the night is just beginning. There will be other opportunities."

"I daresay there will."

"Your dancing program is almost full, is that so?"

"There are quite a number . . . it is after all given by my stepfather and people feel in duty bound to dance with me . . . as I am to dance with some of his friends."

He grimaced. "I shall watch for my opportunity and, being perceptive, shrewd and having insight, trust me to leap in and seize my chance."

I laughed. It had been a stimulating encounter.

Morwenna said to me: "Did you enjoy that? You looked as though you did."

"He is very amusing."

"And exceptionally good looking," commented Helena. "Oh, there is Sir Toby Dorien coming over. You're to dance with him, I believe. He's an important colleague of Benedict. Martin knows him well."

How different it was dancing with Sir Toby! He was far from being an expert dancer and there was a certain amount of stumbling and one or two painful jabs at my toes. Madame Perrotte had given me a few hints on how to react on such occasions and I did not emerge from the ordeal as battered as I might have been. His conversation was almost completely political with references to all the well-known politicians of the day. I was very glad when that duty was over.

I had only just returned to my seat when a young man came towards us. He was vaguely familiar—very dark and of medium stature, good looking in a certain way.

I was momentarily puzzled until Helena said: "Oh, good evening, Monsieur Bourdon. I expected to see you here tonight."

He bowed to us all.

"It is an occasion which I was determined not to miss."

"Do you know Miss Mandeville? You must . . ."

"Oh yes. We met long ago. In Cornwall. I remember it well."

"I remember, too," I said.

He took my hand and kissed it.

"This gives me great pleasure," he said. "Then you were a little girl. I knew you would grow into a beautiful young woman."

"I daresay you are longing to dance," said Helena. "I advised Rebecca that she must leave certain gaps in the program. That was absolutely essential."

"And this is one of those gaps? What luck for me. Miss Mandeville, will you allow me the pleasure?"

"But, of course," I said.

He was a polished dancer—by far the most practiced I had had that evening. To dance with him meant an absence of tension. He led the way, guiding me so that all I had to do was follow. I could give myself up to the joy of the dance. Madame Perrotte had said: "With some partners you can forget all the do's and don'ts. You merely dance. Your feet are free from violation. Let yourself rejoice and enjoy. It rarely happens."

Well, it was happening now, for here was the perfect dancer.

"I heard you were home—from Celeste," he said.

"Are you often at the house?"

"It depends. If I am in London, I call. We have a house in London . . . a *pied à terre*. But mostly I am in Chislehurst or France."

"So never in the same place long?"

"I have been at Chislehurst with my family. It is a very sad time. You have heard of the son of the Emperor and Empress . . . the Prince Imperial . . ."

I was puzzled.

He went on: "He was killed in the war. You know of the trouble between the British and the Zulus?"

"There has been a good deal of talk about it but it is over now, is it not?"

"Yes. The Zulus were defeated and now they are asking for the protection of the British. They want to be taken over. They need the protection of a great power . . . but so far that has not come about. The rulers are reluctant to take on new responsibility. There is indecision at the moment and still strife in Zululand. During the trouble the Prince Imperial was killed while in the service of the British army. You can imagine the mourning there has been at Chislehurst."

I nodded.

"The Empress . . . turned from her throne . . . losing her husband . . . and then her son. She has had a hard life. Those of us who were in exile with her have done our best to comfort her. It has kept us in Chislehurst. There. That is the long explanation of why I have not seen you before. But now . . . I hope to see you much."

"I suppose you will be visiting your sister often?"

"I shall with double pleasure now . . . because you and she are under the same roof."

"So you do have your residence in London?"

"Yes, as I said . . . a small place . . . a *pied à terre* merely."

"What of High Tor?"

"It belongs to my parents. They bought it when they thought they would stay there. But later they decided to go to Chislehurst and have bought a house there. High Tor has been kept ever since."

"And the priceless tapestries, are they still there?"

"They were taken to Chislehurst. What do you know of them?"

"I heard of them because Leah Polhenny went to High Tor to repair them, and made a very good job of the intricate work, I believe. She is now in our nursery."

He was silent for a few seconds, wrinkling his brows as though trying to remember.

"Oh yes, she did come to repair the tapestries . . . I remember now how pleased my mother was with her work. So you know her well."

"Nobody knows Leah very well. Even now I am not sure that I do. Everyone knew her mother because she was the midwife and had assisted at the birth of quite a number of the inhabitants of the Poldoreys."

"Well . . . so now the young lady is here and the tapestries are safe in my parents' house in Chislehurst and I am sure I cannot fully express what a great pleasure it is for me to meet you. I hope you too are pleased to renew our acquaintance."

"So far," I said, "it has been a pleasure."

"Why do you say . . . so far? Do you expect it will not continue to be a pleasure?"

"I meant nothing of the sort. I am sure it will continue to be as it is now."

"We are relations now, eh . . . in a way. My sister married to your stepfather."

"Well, a connection, shall we say."

"We shall meet often. That I look forward to with great pleasure."

I was sorry when the dance came to an end. It had been so comfortably easy to dance with him. And when he returned me to my seat I was delighted to see Pedrek there.

Jean Pascal stayed and chatted with us and Pedrek remarked that he was late in arriving because his train had been delayed.

"Better late than never," commented Morwenna, "and I believe Rebecca has left the supper dance free. I advised her to because I knew you would want it."

"How is it going?" Pedrek asked me.

"As well as can be expected."

"That sounds like a sick patient."

"Well, I always felt it would be touch and go . . . According to these gruesome accounts I had from your mother and Aunt Helena, these occasions can be fraught with anxieties. Will this man or that man ask me to dance? Will *any*body ask me? I am going to be a failure. The wallflower of the season."

"That could never happen to you."

"Perhaps not in my stepfather's house where it would be a breach of good manners for no one to ask me. So far I have got through with slightly mutilated toes but my pride intact."

One could be easy and frank with Pedrek. But then we had been friends from babyhood; and the most enjoyable dance of all was the supper dance which I shared with him.

Not that he could dance well. He was no Jean Pascal, but he was Pedrek, my dear friend with whom I felt fully at ease.

"It is long since I have seen you," he said. "It's not always going to be like that."

"What are your plans, Pedrek?"

"I'm starting next month at a Mining Engineering College near St Austell. Pencarron Mine will belong to me one day. My grandfather thinks I should take the course. The college is one of the finest in the South West."

"Well, that's good. I am sure your grandparents are delighted. You won't be far away from them."

"And I shall be there for two years. It will be extensive study, but when I emerge I should be ready to take over the mine and, as my grandfather says, with a full knowledge of modern improvements. I'll tell you more about it over supper. And, Rebecca, let's find a table for two. I don't want anyone joining us."

"It sounds intriguing."

"I hope you'll find it so. I'm sorry . . . I think I went the wrong way then."

"You did. Madame Perrotte would despair of you."

"I noticed the graceful movements of the Frenchman."

"He's the perfect dancer."

"Few possess his talents."

"You sound envious. Surely you know there is more to life than being able to dance well?"

"I breathe again."

"Oh, Pedrek, what's come over you? You're unlike yourself tonight."

"A change for the better or worse?"

I hesitated, then I said: "I'll tell you over supper. Look. They are going in now. Do you think we ought to look after your mother and Aunt Helena?"

"They can look after themselves. Besides, I suppose they will be with other chaperones."

"I see they have joined my stepfather and his wife."

"Come on. We'll find a table for two."

We found it—slightly shaded by a pot of ferns.

"This looks inviting," said Pedrek. "You sit down and I will go and get the food."

He returned with the salmon I had seen being delivered that morning. On each of the tables was a bottle of champagne in an ice bucket. We sat down opposite each other.

"I must say your stepfather knows how to manage these affairs in style."

"It is all part of the business of being an ambitious member of Parliament."

"I thought that was done by distinguishing oneself in Parliament."

"And keeping up appearances outside . . . knowing the right people . . . pulling the right strings and keeping in the public eye."

"That can sometimes be disastrous."

"I mean keeping in a favorable light."

"That's different. But enough of politics. I don't ever intend to take part in them. Does that please you?"

"Do you mean does it please me that you don't intend to?"

"I mean exactly that."

"I don't think you'd make a politician, Pedrek. You're too honest . . ."

He raised his eyebrows and I went on: "I mean that you are too straightforward. Politicians always have to think of what is going to please or displease the voters. Uncle Peter was always saying that. He would have made a good politician. We were all fond of him but he was a manipulator . . . not only of things but of people. Look how he made Martin Hume. I don't think a man should have to be made. He should do it by his own efforts."

"You are looking for perfection in a less than perfect world. But enough of politicians. I want to talk about myself . . . and you."

"Well, go ahead."

"We've always been friends," he said slowly. "Isn't it wonderful that we were both born in extraordinary circumstances . . . both of us seeing the light of day in the Australian goldfields? Don't you think that makes us special friends?"

"Yes, but we know that, Pedrek. What was it you wanted to tell me?"

"I shall not be able to marry for two years . . . not until I finish with the college really. How do you feel about that?"

"What should I feel about your marriage?"

"The utmost interest because I want it to be yours as well."

I laughed with pleasure. "For the moment, Pedrek, I thought you were going to tell me that you had fallen victim to some alluring siren."

"I have been in the coils of an irresistible siren ever since I was born."

"Oh Pedrek, you are talking of me. This is so sudden."

"Don't joke about it, Rebecca. I am very serious. For me there is only one siren. I always knew you would be the one. To me it was a foregone conclusion that one day we should be together . . . always."

"You have never consulted me on this important matter before."

"I didn't think it was the time; and I thought it was something between us . . . something you knew as well as I did. That it was . . . inevitable."

"I don't think I thought of it as inevitable."

236

"Well, it is."

"So this is a proposal?"

"Of a sort."

"What do you mean, 'of a sort'? Is it or isn't it?"

"I'm asking you to become engaged to me."

I smiled at him and touched his hand across the table. "I'm so proud of myself," I said. "It is not many girls who get a proposal the instant they are launched into society."

"That's not the point."

"I haven't finished yet. I was going to say get a proposal from Pedrek Cartwright. That's what makes it so wonderful . . . because it's you, Pedrek."

"This is the happiest night of my life," he said.

"Of mine, too. Won't they be pleased?"

"My mother will. I am not so sure of your stepfather." He was frowning.

"What is it, Pedrek?" I asked.

"He has planned all this for you because he wants you to make a grand marriage."

"I am going to make a grand marriage in exactly two years from now."

"Let's be sensible, Rebecca. It's not what he would call a grand marriage. A mining engineer with a mine in remote Cornwall."

"It's a very successful mine. In any case I wouldn't care if it was an old scat bal, as they call a useless old mine down there, if you went with it."

"Oh, Rebecca, it's going to be wonderful . . .

237

the two of us . . . I can't wait. You make me want to abandon the idea of going to college. I could go into my father's office and we'd be married right away."

"You have to be sensible, Pedrek. This is marvelous. Two years . . . they will pass and all the time we'll be thinking of what's to come. They would say we are too young anyway. It doesn't matter so much for women . . . eighteen is all right . . . but for a man it should be older. Let's do it the right way, Pedrek."

"Yes. I'm afraid we'll have to."

"We want to do it all absolutely right. You'll go to your college knowing I'm waiting . . . longing for the day . . . and that will help you to come through with flying colors. Then there will be a riotous feast at Cador. My grandparents will be pleased and I shall be rid of my stepfather forever."

"You've never liked him."

"Well, I suppose I blame him for spoiling our lives. If he had never been there my mother would be alive today. I can't get that out of my mind."

"I don't think you should blame him for that. But I do think he is very ambitious. He married his first wife for a goldmine. Money is important to him . . . money and fame."

"He sees himself as a Disraeli or Gladstone. He wants to be Prime Minister one day."

"He probably will."

"At the same time he happens to be my step-father and my grandparents say he is my guardian because of it. I don't want a guardian. If I have to be guarded my grandparents can do it."

"Let's try to look at this logically. He is your guardian until you are twenty-one or married, I suppose. I have a feeling that he might not give his consent to our marriage. At best he would insist that we wait until you were twenty-one."

"Do you think he could . . . if I wanted to and my grandparents approved? I do feel absolutely sure that they will be pleased."

"He could stop it, I suppose."

"It's three years before I'm twenty-one."

"When I'm through with college we shall be twenty. Then we'll get married and say nothing about it until after the deed is done."

I laughed. "How exciting!"

"In the meantime," he went on. "Let's not announce it . . . just yet. We can leave it until later."

"All right. For the time being it is our secret."

He gripped my hand and held it tightly. Then we lifted our glasses and drank to the glorious years ahead of us.

That was my first grand ball and I had enjoyed almost every minute of it. I was ecstatically happy. Pedrek and I were engaged—secretly for the moment, it was true, but that added to the excitement.

I looked beyond the next two years. They would pass quickly, lightened by the knowledge that when they were over I should be Pedrek's wife. We should have a house on the moor possibly. I loved the moor, and I should not be far from Cador. Pedrek's grandparents would be close by. We should have ten children and they would be loving and as devoted to me as Lucie was. That was another problem which had been solved. Some husbands would not have wanted Lucie in their households and I would never be parted from the child. I regarded her as my own and my husband must do the same. Pedrek had understood at once.

This was the happy ending which all romances should have and mine with Pedrek had lasted for years already. We had been destined for each other from the moment we had been born on that dusty goldfield in Australia.

Life was now a round of gaiety. This was the Season. Eager mothers, and those who were bringing out young ladies, gave balls, dinners and parties to the newly emerged young people. The fact that Benedict was my stepfather meant that I was invited to many of them.

I saw a great deal of Pedrek during the next three or four weeks. He would be at the functions as the good-looking son of one of the sponsors. He might not have been in the highest echelons of society, lacking the necessary blue blood, but his grandfather was well known in mining circles and a man of great wealth, and money and blood were often weighed equally in the social scales.

We used to meet in the park where I often

walked with Morwenna, for it was permissible for her son to join us.

Long happy days they were but at last the time came for him to go off to his college. He would write every week he told me and I must do the same. I swore I would.

I was lonely after he had gone, but there was always a great deal for me to do. There were the constant social engagements and during these I often met Oliver Gerson and Jean Pascal Bourdon. The latter, having connections with exiled royalty at Chislehurst, was acceptable; and Oliver Gerson's links with my stepfather gave him the entry, if not to all, to a great number of occasions.

I was rather glad of their company. I found them both interesting and in a way amusing. Moreover they expressed admiration for me and I was vain enough to enjoy this.

Jean Pascal was an excellent dancing partner. I loved dancing and, thanks to Madame Perrote, when I danced with him I thought I did really well. People actually commented on how well our styles matched.

I learned a little about both men. Jean Pascal had become a wine importer and paid periodic visits to France.

"I must do something, you understand," he said. "I cannot dance all day."

There was something completely sophisticated about him. He was a cynic and a realist at heart, I believed. It was his great hope that one day the monarchy would be restored in France and then he would return to his own country and live in the old château in the style to which he had become accustomed under the rule of his good friends the Emperor Napoleon III and the Empress Eugenie.

"Will that ever be?" I asked him.

He lifted his shoulders. "There have been movements. There is trouble with the government. It sways this way and that. Our great tragedy came with that accursed revolution. If we had kept our monarchy then all would be well today."

"But that happened a hundred years ago."

"And nothing has been right since. We had Napoleon. Then we began to be great again . . . but now . . . these communards . . . I always hope . . . So I go to France. I bring in the wine. I do England a great favor. There is no wine in the world like French wine."

"The Germans wouldn't agree with you."

"The Germans!" He snapped his fingers with contempt.

"They beat you, you know," I reminded him maliciously.

"We were foolish. We did not believe in their strength. They ruined everything when they came."

"And now we have a big power in Germany in Europe."

"A tragedy. But one day perhaps we shall come back."

"You mean the French aristocrats?"

"And then you will see."

"Well, now you have connections in England.

Your sister is married to one of our members of Parliament."

He nodded. "Yes, that is good."

"For your sister?"

"Yes, for my sister."

I wondered if he knew of his sister's sadness. But he would not consider that, I imagined. It would be a good marriage because Benedict Lansdon was a wealthy and rising politician with very likely a brilliant future before him.

It came out that Jean Pascal had plans to marry in France. The lady in question was a member of the deposed royal family. At the moment she was of little importance but if the monarchy returned, well then Jean Pascal could find himself in a very exalted position. He was not marrying her yet though. The situation was too uncertain. He did not actually tell me this, but he did not attempt to disguise it either.

Although I found him amusing, there were some aspects of his character which filled me with distrust and a certain apprehension. It was the manner in which he looked at me and some other women. It was almost with speculation and what I had begun to think of as lust. That he was a man of deep sensuality, I was sure. I had gathered that long ago, for I had seen him glance at the more attractive of the maids; but in his conversation there would be certain innuendoes which I pretended not to understand; but I fancied he was so knowledgeable about the feminine mind that he was aware that I understood very well.

He seemed to have a contempt for my innocence, for my lack of sophistication, for my youthful inexperience and I fancied he was hinting that he could initiate me into a world of pleasure and understanding.

I hoped I had shown him that I was not interested in acquiring experience through him; but he was so sure of his infinite wisdom in such matters that he believed he knew what was good for me far better than I did myself.

It was an intriguing situation and I was missing Pedrek. I had only his weekly letters to compensate for his absence and I found the time passed quickly in the company of Jean Pascal.

There was always Oliver Gerson. He was amusing, witty and charming. He was not at all the functions. I think some of the more aristocratic mammas thought he was not quite worthy. However, I did see him fairly frequently and he did make it clear that he enjoyed my company.

So with my secret engagement to Pedrek, I was able to enjoy the functions without that feeling of apprehension that I was failing to become a success, which had dogged poor Morwenna and Helena during their seasons. I was able to give myself up to the enjoyment of those occasions, as much as I could without Pedrek's company.

So the months passed and the season was drawing to an end.

It was time that Benedict and his wife went to Manorleigh for a spell—and of course I went with them.

The Ghost in the Garden

To come to Manorleigh after having been away from it for some time was an emotional experience. Memories of my mother came flooding back. I could not forget those locked rooms, untouched since her death; and there was a certain intimacy in the house which the London one lacked.

For instance, in London I used to go out with Morwenna and Helena; there had been shopping expeditions and visits to their houses and I did not see Benedict for days when he was busy at the House of Commons. Celeste had had her friends —wives of members like herself who met frequently. But in Manor Grange it was different. We all seemed closer together and I found that disconcerting.

The children were delighted to see me and for the first few days I spent my time mainly in the nursery, catching up on what had been happening during my absence.

They had been progressing with their riding and I went down to the paddock to watch them. They were good enough now to leave the paddock and take to the road with a groom in attendance. They both loved their ponies dearly.

Leah looked a little better than she had in London. I asked if her headaches no longer troubled her.

"Very rarely now, thank you, Miss Rebecca," she said. "I trust you had a successful season in London."

"Oh yes," I told her. "Mr. Cartwright unfortunately had to leave town. He's gone to Cornwall to a mining engineering college. We shall see him when he comes down to visit his grandparents there."

"Are we going to Cornwall soon?"

"My grandparents are suggesting we go."

"The children always enjoy it."

"And I daresay you are looking forward to seeing your old home."

A blank expression crossed her face. She must love Cornwall but it did contain her mother. I gathered that Mrs. Polhenny was still plying her trade. My grandmother had written that she had acquired a bicycle with wooden wheels and iron tires—what was called an old bone-shaker—and that she rattled up and down the hills getting to and from her patients. It was daring for a woman of her age but I supposed she had commanded the Lord to look after her.

I could well understand that Leah, who had lived in her mother's holy shadow for so many years, would be glad to escape and could not have any great desire to get within a few miles of it.

Back in Manorleigh we were plunged into a whirl of activity. Benedict was rarely at home; he went travelling round the constituency which covered a large area, speaking at meetings, attending conferences and on certain days attending what was called "the surgery" which was conducted in a small room leading from the hall where he listened to complaints and suggestions from his constituents.

We all seemed to be caught up in parliamentary duties.

When he was not at home people sometimes called with problems and Celeste was expected to listen to their accounts and answer sympathetically, explaining the unavoidable absence of her husband before whom the matter would be put on his return.

On one occasion, when Benedict was away for a few days, one of the farmers called. He was concerned about a right of way which people were using indiscriminatingly and damaging his corn.

Celeste was not at home and I happened to be there so I took him into the little room called the surgery and let him talk to me.

Having been brought up at Cador, I did understand what he was talking about.

"I remember something very like it in Cornwall," I told him. "The farmer put up a fence leaving just a narrow path. His workmen were able to do it very quickly and his crops were safe."

"I've been thinking of it, but I didn't want to go to the expense."

"It's worth it," I assured him. "You see, there is this law about rights of way."

"You have a point," he said. "I was wondering

if there was anything Mr. Lansdon could do about it."

"The law is the law, and unless it's changed it stands."

"Well, thank you for your attention. You're his stepdaughter, I believe."

"Yes."

"Well, it's better talking to you than to the foreign lady."

"You mean Mrs. Lansdon."

"She doesn't know what you're talking about half the time. It's different with you. You've got good sense."

"It is on account of my being brought up on my grandparents' estate."

"That's what I say. You know what you're talking about. It's a pleasure to talk to you."

A few days later Benedict returned home. He met the farmer who told him that he had called at the house and what a bright and intelligent young lady his stepdaughter was.

I always avoided Benedict when I could and the relationship between us was as uneasy as it had ever been. Belinda was the same with him. It was his fault. He could not bear to look at her. Oddly enough, he was happier in Lucie's company with whose existence he need not concern himself, She did not arouse any sad memories in him. Lucie was attractive and well mannered; she caused him no annoyance, whereas Belinda was the one left to him as a substitute for Angelet— and he could not forgive her for that. It was unfair. Belinda was not an easy child to handle but she was blameless on that score.

"I understand you took surgery the other day," he said to me.

"Oh, there was no one else about."

"They shouldn't come when I am not here. There is a special day for it."

"The farmer must have forgotten that."

"You impressed him."

"Oh . . . it was about a right of way . . . similar to a case we had in Cornwall."

"He said it was good to talk to someone sensible who knew something about things."

"Oh . . . I'm flattered."

"Thank you, Rebecca."

I said: "Well, I happened to be around and he caught me."

My resentment was as great as ever. I did not want him to think I was going out of my way to help him.

I left him quickly. I hoped the farmer had not mentioned that he preferred to talk to me rather than to Celeste.

I was growing sorry for Celeste. The marriage was a great mistake. I could see that and it was his fault mostly.

He did not care. He had a wife which was what was expected of him. She was a good hostess and so elegant that her appearance carried her through. That was what *he* had needed. Did he ever think that she would not be content to be a puppet set up to further his ambitions? Did he not think she might want a loving husband? I knew enough to see that she craved his affection; I believed she was a passionate woman who needed to be loved. It was cruel to have married her if he intended to remain aloof . . . mourning one who was lost to him for ever.

There was something very wrong in this house. There was a brooding feeling of tragedy. Perhaps I was fanciful. It might be because I knew something of the deep passion which had existed between him and my mother—a feeling of such intensity that it could not die because one of them had. What happened in that silent room behind the locked door? Her brushes were on the table . . . her clothes hanging in the wardrobe. Could she come back to him there? I had thought she came to me once. Perhaps when a person is deeply loved that person becomes part of the one left behind; there is a bond which even death cannot break.

But poor Celeste was living flesh and blood. Warm and passionately, earnestly desiring . . . the unwanted one, brought in because the people who had put him into Parliament expected him to have a wife. That was what was wrong in the house and it was more obvious here than it had been in London because behind that locked door my mother seemed to linger.

I was in my room one day, thinking of going for a ride. I was about to change into my riding habit and sat for a moment at the window looking down at the seat under the oak tree, that haunted part of the garden where Lady Flamstead was said to have returned to be with the daughter she had never seen.

There was a gentle tap on the door. I turned sharply. Such was my mood that I almost expected to see my mother standing there.

The door opened slowly and Celeste came in.

"I thought you were here, Rebecca," she said. "Were you just going out?"

"Yes, but it is not important. I was only going for a ride."

"It's Mrs. Carston-Browne. She always terrifies me. She is downstairs now. She speak so that I cannot follow all."

"Oh, she is an indefatigable worker for good causes. What does she want?"

"She talks about a fête . . . a pageant . . . I think she say. I tell her I believe you were in and that you are interested in that kind of thing."

"Celeste!"

"Forgive . . . I am desperate."

"I'll come down," I said.

Mrs. Carston-Browne was in the drawing room. Large, benign and bland, she regarded me with relief. This was the second time within a week when I realized that the Member's stepdaughter was preferable to his wife.

"Oh . . . Miss Mandeville . . . good morning. How nice that you are at home."

"Good morning, Mrs. Carston-Browne. It is good of you to call. I am afraid Mr. Lansdon is out."

251

"I did not want to see him exactly. I daresay he is too busy and that is no man's business. It is for us women . . . the pageant, you know."

"Well, you see, I have only just arrived here."

"I know. It is necessary for us to be represented at Westminster certainly and we cannot expect the Member to be here all the time. But this is something we have been planning for some time. It is done every year and I wanted to enlist your help. We are doing scenes from Her Majesty's youth and we thought that as it is forty years since she came to the throne we might have a coronation. *Tableau vivant*, you know. Some people manage so much better if they don't have to speak. We're collecting clothes . . . anything that could be made over to fit the period."

"I see," I said. "I don't know if we have any clothes. I'll look."

"We thought the little girls might appear. Children are so appealing. The Member's daughter should certainly be there . . . and the little adopted one as well."

"You mean taking part in the *tableau?*"

"Exactly. We are doing as one scene the Queen's being awakened to be told she is Queen . . . and then her coronation and her wedding. A great deal of organizing has to be done and it does help raise funds. It is for the church, of course. I thought the little girls might be in the wedding scene. They could be attending on the Queen."

"I am sure they would enjoy that."

"We usually do very well and the proceeds are

252

for the church. Reverend Whyte is very concerned at the moment about the roof. He said if we can get it done now it will save pounds later."

"Was the bazaar a success?"

"An immense success."

"I am sure Mrs. Lansdon is very sorry she was not here to help you."

Mrs. Carston-Browne gave Celeste a cool nod in acknowledgment of her regret.

"It was *nécessaire* to be in London," said Celeste. "Did you know that Rebecca was having a season?"

"Yes, we do read the papers."

"Oh, was it mentioned there?" I asked.

"The local paper. As the Member's stepdaughter . . ."

"Oh, of course."

"I am sure, Miss Mandeville, that you will be able to dress the children."

"Mrs. Lansdon will, *I* am sure. And perhaps help you with the costumes. She is very clever at that sort of thing."

"Oh?" said Mrs. Carston-Browne, almost disbelievingly.

"Yes, she has a special eye for what is right for all occasions."

"I am sure that will be most useful. Could I expect you at The Firs tomorrow morning at ten thirty for discussions?"

I looked at Celeste who seemed bewildered. "I am sure that will be all right," I said.

Mrs. Carston-Browne rose, her feather in her hat quivering as she leaned forward on her parasol and surveyed us—me with approval but Celeste with a certain suspicion.

I walked with her to the front door where her carriage was waiting.

"It was such a pleasure to find *you* in, Miss Mandeville," she said.

I stood for a few seconds, listening to the clip-clop of her horses' hoofs on the gravel.

I thought: What is happening to me? I am being drawn in to help *him*. I shall go down to Cornwall as soon as I can. I wanted no change in our relationship. I still felt my mother's death bitterly and resentfully. I really did not *want* anything to change. On the other hand I was sorry for Celeste. She was trying to take my mother's place and that was something she could never do.

She was beside me and she slipped her arm through mine.

"Thank you, Rebecca," she said.

And then I felt a little better.

The pageant occupied us for the next two weeks. It was to be held on the first of September. Lucie was delighted to be taking part. So was Belinda but she pretended that it meant little to her.

Celeste looked through her store of materials. Leah was an expert with her needle and with Celeste's designs and Leah's ability to make up the materials, the children were going to make very attractive attendants of the Queen.

Celeste would have made a good Queen; she

was petite but perhaps too slim and elegant to play the plump little Queen. Moreover the spectators would have been shocked to see a foreigner in the part.

Benedict was to open the pageant and the *tableaux vivants* would be shown with intervals of half an hour between each—it was taking all that time to prepare for the next. There were stalls where all sorts of produce could be bought—cakes, homemade jam and all sorts of farm produce as well as flowers. The usual sideshows were in evidence—wishing wells with fishing rods and if these could be hooked on to the toy fishes this entitled the successful to a prize. It was the usual fun of the fair, the highlight being the *tableaux vivants* which had never been attempted before.

Celeste and I were behind the scenes most of the time, helping to fix up the *tableaux*. Belinda was running round in a state of excitement. Lucie was equally thrilled. Their dresses were identical. They wore white satin trimmed with lace and round their heads were mauve anenomes. They looked very attractive.

The first scene, with the Queen in her dressing gown receiving the Archbishop of Canterbury and the Lord Chamberlain to be told she was Queen, was a great success. It was really quite effective with the Lord Chamberlain kissing her hand and the Archbishop standing by preparing to do the same. The coronation was even more grand but the scene which won the most applause was the royal wedding—the Queen, her husband beside her and her attendants . . . among them Belinda and Lucie, who, because of their connection with the Member, were placed in prominent positions.

The applause rang out. The curtain was lowered and the *tableau* came to life with the participants coming forward to take their bows.

Belinda's eyes sparkled. I knew how hard she found it to stand still and I thought she was going to leap in the air at any moment.

She smiled and bowed and waved to the audience which delighted them.

All that evening she could talk of nothing but the part she had played on the stage. She made us all laugh when she said: "I was afraid my enemies were going to fall off my head. Lucie's nearly did, too."

"They are anenomes," Lucie corrected her.

Belinda could never accept that she was wrong. "Mine were enemies," she said.

They were starry-eyed when I said goodnight to them. "Actresses are on the stage," said Belinda. "When I grow up I am going to be one of them."

Belinda's desire to be an actress lasted for some weeks. It was dressing up which appealed to her. One day I found her in my room trying on a hat of mine and a short coat. I couldn't help being amused. She wanted to go down to the kitchen and show them and I allowed her to do this.

"I am Miss Rebecca Mandeville," she announced

in haughty tones which were unlike any I was likely to use. "I have just had my London season."

They were all highly amused.

Mrs. Emery, seated at the head of the table, for they were all having tea, said she was a real caution. Jane, the parlormaid, clapped her hands and soon they were all doing the same. Belinda stood in the middle of the kitchen bowing and kissing her hands to them. Then she flounced off.

"A regular little Madam, that one," said Mrs. Emery. "You have to watch her though. She's up to tricks . . . and she drags that Miss Lucie with her."

Leah, who had watched the little show, tried to suppress the pride she felt in her charge. I had long ago guessed that Belinda was her favorite. I supposed her exuberant personality was certain to make her outstanding; and then there was the fact that Belinda was the daughter of the house whereas Lucie was a foundling whom, in a rather eccentric manner, I had been allowed to adopt by my rather unconventional grandparents.

I supposed Lucie was aware of this too. I must make her understand that she was as important to me at any rate as my half-sister Belinda.

Her successful impersonation of me must have aroused the desire in Belinda to attempt further success and she announced that she and Lucie were going to do a *tableau* for us but there would be talking in this one. We must all go to the kitchen and wait there.

I was very glad afterwards that Celeste was unable to come. She was visiting the agent's wife which was a duty she had rather reluctantly to perform.

However it worked out for the best on this occasion.

The servants were all laughing together as we arranged ourselves in the chairs, Mrs. Emery, hands folded in bombazine lap next to me with Leah and Miss Stringer on the other side.

I felt a twinge of alarm when the children burst in, for Belinda was wearing a top hat and a morning coat which had obviously been taken from Benedict's wardrobe. She really did look incongruous. I was wondering what was coming next and whether we should have to put a stop to this intrusion into people's rooms.

And there was Lucie, her hair pinned up on top of her head, strangely unlike herself in one of Celeste's elegant gowns which trailed along the floor and hung on her like a sack.

There was silence.

"I am your Member of Parliament," announced Belinda. "And you have to do what I say . . . I have a big house in London which would be too good for any of *you*, because I have grand servants there . . . and we have important people coming. The Prime Minister and the Queen sometimes . . . when I ask her." Lucie came forward, "Go away," went on Belinda. "I don't want you. I don't like you very much. I like Belinda's mother. I go to see her in the locked room. That's why I don't want *you*."

Miss Stringer half rose in her seat. Leah had turned pale. Mrs. Emery was staring open-mouthed and I heard Jane mutter something under her breath.

I was terrified of what Belinda would say next.

I stood up and went to her.

"Take those things off at once," I said. "Both of you. Go and put them back where you took them from. You are never . . . never to take clothes from other people's wardrobes. You have some things which you have had given you for dressing up. You may use those . . . and those only."

Belinda looked at me defiantly.

"It was a good play," she cried. "It was a true play . . . like the Queen at her wedding."

"It was not true," I said. "It was very silly. Now take them off at once. Leah . . ."

Leah hurried forward. So did Miss Stringer. Leah took Belinda by the hand. Miss Stringer took Lucie's and they were gone.

There was silence in the kitchen. I turned and followed them upstairs.

I went to see Mrs. Emery in her private sitting room.

"It's that Miss Belinda," she said. "There's no knowing what she'll do next. She's got to be watched. She's got her nose into everything."

"How does she know about that room?"

"Well, how do they know anything? Little

259

pitchers have long ears and that Miss Belinda's are ten times as long as normal. Eyes on everything. What's this? What's that? And she talked to the maids. I can't stop the gossiping. They don't dare do it in front of me but I reckon it's chitter chatter all the time behind my back."

"I'm only thankful that Mrs. Lansdon was not here."

"Yes. That would not have been very nice."

"Mrs. Emery, how could she have *known?*"

Mrs. Emery shook her head. "There's not much that goes on in a house that the maids don't know about. They see little things . . . we know how different it is with the French lady than it was with your mother. He worshipped her. They was like one . . . the two of them. The whole house knew it and when she went it broke him. Then he kept that room."

"I don't like it, Mrs. Emery."

"You're not the only one, Miss Rebecca. There's bound to be talk. They're already saying her ghost is in that room. Orders is that I'm the only one that's to go in. That's all very well, but to tell you frank like, I'd never be able to get any of the others *to* go in . . . not alone by any road. I reckon if we had that door open and things moved out and changed round a bit . . . it would be a lot better. It's like a shrine, Miss Rebecca . . . and people gets ideas when there's that sort of thing in a house."

"You're right, Mrs. Emery, but what can we do about it?"

"Well, it's up to him. If only he'd try to forget her . . . make a normal life for the present Mrs. Lansdon . . . you see what I mean."

"I do see what you mean."

"If someone could tell him . . ."

She looked at me and shrugged her shoulders. "You'd be the only one who could, I suppose. But I know how it is between you. You're not what you might call loving father and daughter."

I thought: Our lives are exposed to our servants. They are aware of everything that is going on. They know in this house that Celeste is passionately in love with a husband who rejects her because he is still so deeply in love with his dead wife that he makes a shrine to her and spends nights in that room from which the present Mrs. Lansdon is shut out.

"We'll have to wait and see," I said. "Perhaps if the right moment comes it might be possible to say something."

She nodded.

"While that room stays locked it's unhealthy. That's what I've always said and I'll go on saying it. I don't like it, Miss Rebecca, I don't like it at all."

I agreed with her. I did not like it either.

Belinda was very sullen after that. She hardly spoke to me and Miss Stringer said she was more difficult than usual.

Lucie was also in disgrace. She was a sensitive

261

child and what upset her most was that she thought I was angry with her.

I explained to her: "I am not angry. I just want you to understand that it is not polite to imitate people. It is all right to play the Queen or the Archbishop of Canterbury and the Lord Chamberlain because they are far away and it is a long time ago when the Queen was called from her bed to be told she was Queen and had her coronation and marriage, but to pretend to be people around you could be hurtful to them . . . and so it is different."

She saw the point and was contrite.

It took several days for Belinda's sullen mood to pass but finally she reverted to her old exuberant self. I remarked to Miss Stringer that she appeared to have given up her theatrical ambitions.

Miss Stringer said: "It was a passing fancy . . . all due to Mrs. Carston-Browne and her *tableaux vivants.*"

I agreed.

The children were in the garden with Leah one day when I joined them. We had not been there long when one of the maids came running out. She was breathless. "It's that new gardener's boy, Miss Rebecca. He's cutting down the oak tree."

"He can't be," I cried. "It's far too big."

I went across the lawn to that spot past the pond below my window onto which I looked down so often. All the boy was doing was trimming the branches.

"Who told you to do that?" I asked.

"Nobody, Miss. I just thought it needed a trim like."

"We don't like the oak tree being touched."

The maid who had told us what was happening said: "The ghosts wouldn't like it."

The boy stared open-mouthed at the tree.

"It's an old legend attached to the house," I said. "I don't think we want it trimmed. Of course, if Mr. Camps thinks it should be done, he should speak to someone about it. But for the time being leave it."

"Well, I never," said the maid. "It was a good thing, Miss Rebecca, that I saw him in time. Cutting up that tree. Goodness knows what would happen."

"Why is it haunted?" asked Lucie.

"Oh, that's just a story."

"What sort of a story?" asked Belinda.

"Something that was once said. I've forgotten."

"Ghosts don't like it if people forget about them," said Belinda. "They come back and haunt them to remind them."

"It was nothing," I said. "Would you two like to go for a ride?"

November had come—misty autumnal with the days drawing in so that it was dark soon after four.

Ever since the gardener's boy had attempted to lop the branches off the oak tree there seemed to have been a revival of the hauntings. One of the maids swore she saw a shadow at the window of the locked room. She ran screaming into the house. Some of them would not go into the garden after dusk and certainly not in the vicinity of the oak tree.

I began to be affected by it and often at night I would go down to my window and look down on it, in spite of myself, expecting to see Lady Flamstead or her daughter there . . . and I would have given a great deal to see my mother.

I thought about what Mrs. Emery had said regarding the locked room. How could one stop young people having fancies in a house like this? It seemed to be enveloped in the unhappy atmosphere created by a husband who did not love the wife he had recently married and continued to mourn the one he had lost. I understood his passionate obsession; I had one of a kind myself for I could not forget her either; but I still blamed Benedict. Perhaps it was due to living in a house of shadows where the past seemed to intrude on the present where neither he nor I could come to terms with life as it was and were both craving to be back in those days when she was with us.

I wondered if I might speak to him about the locked room. But how could I? He would not listen to me. He found his solace there. He communed with her. I had once felt that she came back to me. Surely she would come and try to comfort him if that were possible.

Celeste talked to me about the servants' obsession with ghosts.

"I suppose in a house like this," I said, "in which many people have lived over the centuries, there would be a feeling that those who have gone before have left something behind."

"What is the story of this oak tree?"

"It was about a woman who lived here long ago. She was the young wife of an older man who adored her. She died in childbirth and she came back to commune with the child she had never known on Earth. They were supposed to meet under the oak tree."

"She would be a kind ghost?"

"Oh yes . . . quite benign."

"Where is the daughter now?"

"She is dead. All the people in the story are dead. They had to die before they became ghosts."

"And she died giving birth. It is like . . ."

"Yes," I said, "but I am afraid it is not an infrequent happening."

She nodded. "I see. Why does Lady Flamstead come back now?"

"Because the servants have been reminded of her. When the gardener's boy tried to prune the tree he is supposed to have disturbed the ghosts. They will tell you they have come back to warn people not to touch their sanctum."

"I see. That is it."

"This talk of ghosts adds a spice to their lives. My grandmother used to say that people whose lives are a little dull have to invent things to make them lively. Well, ghosts have provided this little diversion."

"I see . . . how it is. And we need not listen for the clanging of chains."

"There would be no chains attached to Lady Flamstead nor to her daughter. They never acquired them . . . they lived pleasant, uncomplicated lives."

It was a few days later when Celeste fainted in the garden. Fortunately Lucie happened to be nearby and called for help. I was in the hall and was the first to get out there.

"It's Aunt Celeste," she said. "She's lying on the ground."

"Where?"

"Near the pond."

"Go and call Mrs. Emery or anyone you can find," I said and ran out.

Celeste was lying on the ground, looking pale. I knelt beside her. I saw that she had fainted.

I lifted her up to a sitting position and held down her head. I was greatly relieved to see the color coming into her face. She turned her head and looked fearfully over her shoulder.

"It's all right, Celeste," I said. "I think you just fainted. Perhaps it was the cold . . ."

She was shaking.

"I saw her," she whispered. "It's true . . . she was there . . . under the tree."

I shivered. What did she mean? Was Celeste seeing ghosts now?

I said: "We'll get you into the house."

"She was there," she went on. "I saw her clearly."

Mrs. Emery had appeared.

"Oh, Mrs. Emery," I said. "Mrs. Lansdon has fainted. I think she must have left a warm room and the cold was too much for her." I was battling to find reasons. I did not like this talk of ghosts.

"Let's get her in . . . quick," said Mrs. Emery practically.

"We'll take her to her room," I said. "Then I think a little brandy . . ."

She was on her feet but shaky; she turned and looked over her shoulder at the seat under the tree.

"You're shivering!" I said. "Come on. Let's get in."

We took her to her room.

"Get her to lie down," said Mrs. Emery. "I'll go and see about that brandy. I'll send up one of the girls to see to the fire. It's nearly out."

Celeste lay on the bed. She took my hand and held it tightly. "Don't go," she said.

"Of course I won't. I'll stay here. Don't talk now, Celeste. Wait till Mrs. Emery brings the brandy. You'll feel so much better after that."

She lay back; she was still shivering.

Mrs. Emery came in with Ann.

"Make up the fire, Ann," she said. "Mrs. Lansdon is not feeling very well. And here's the brandy, Miss Rebecca."

"Thank you, Mrs. Emery."

"Shall I pour out, Miss?"

"Yes, please."

She did so and handed it to me. Celeste sat up and sipped it. The fire was now blazing brightly.

"I think Mrs. Lansdon would like to be quiet for a while," I said.

Celeste looked appealingly at me and I knew she wanted me to stay. I nodded reassuringly and the door closed quietly on Mrs. Emery and Ann.

"Rebecca," she said. "I saw her. She was there . . . looking for me. She was telling me that this is her place and there is no room for me here."

"This . . . er . . . ghost spoke to you?"

"No, no . . . there were no words . . . but that was what it meant."

"Celeste, there was no one there. You imagined it."

"But I see clearly . . . she was there."

"She?"

"She has come out of the locked room. She has come to where the ghosts are."

"Celeste, this doesn't make sense. You didn't see anyone there. Lucie was near. She saw you fall. She did not say she saw anyone else."

"She has come for me . . . I saw her clearly. Her head was turned away at first . . . but I knew who she was. She was in a pale blue coat with a cape edged with white fur . . . and a blue hat with white fur round it . . . a little old-fashioned in style."

A blue coat with a fur-edged cape. I had seen my mother in such an outfit—and yes, there had been a hat to match. She had worn it in the house,

268

I remembered. I could visualize her walking under the trees, laughing and talking about the brother or sister I was to have.

I gripped my hands together because they were shaking slightly.

"You imagined it, Celeste," I said without conviction.

"I did not. I did not. I was not thinking of her. My thoughts were far away and then . . . I saw the movement under the trees . . . I saw the figure in the blue coat. She was sitting on the seat . . . and I know who it was . . . I have felt her in the house many times. There are those rooms in which she lived . . . that locked room . . . and now she has come to the garden to join the other ghosts."

"This is all fancy, Celeste."

"I do not think so."

"It is all in your mind."

She stared at me. "In my mind . . ." she stammered.

"Yes, you are thinking of her and you fancy you see her."

"I saw her," she said firmly.

"Celeste, it has to stop, you know. Perhaps you ought to leave here for a while."

"I cannot go."

"Why not? You could come to Cornwall with me. Come for Christmas. My grandparents would love it. We'll take the children."

"Benedict . . . he could not go."

"Then we could go without Benedict."

269

"I could not, Rebecca."

"It might be good."

"No. He needs me . . . here. I have to be at the dinner parties. It is the duty of the Member's wife."

"There is too much emphasis on duties and not enough on . . . on . . ." She waited and I added lamely: "On . . . er . . . home life. You should go away. Then perhaps he would miss you and realize how much you do for him."

She was silent. Then suddenly she turned to me and I knew by the heaving of her shoulders that she was weeping.

"What am I to do?" she asked. "He does not love me."

"He must do. He married you."

"He married me because he wanted a wife. All Members of Parliament should have wives. If they want big office they need a wife . . . the right wife. But, alas, Rebecca, I am not the right one for him. Your mother was."

"You must forget that. You are good. You are wonderful at parties. You always look so elegant. They all admire you."

"And when he look at me . . . he think of another."

I was silent.

"Was she very beautiful?" she asked.

"I don't know. She was my mother. I never thought whether she was beautiful or not. To me she was perfect because she was my mother."

"And to him . . . she was perfect and there

could never be another to take her place. Do you believe that when people are so deeply needed they can be lured from the tomb and come back to those who cannot live without them?"

"No," I said.

"Your mother . . . she must have been a wonderful person."

"She was to me."

"And to him."

"Yes, to him. But they both married someone else in the first place."

"I know he married the girl in Australia. She brought him the goldmine."

"My mother married my father first. He was very handsome and charming . . . like Hercules or Apollo . . . only better because he was so good. He gave his life for his friend."

"I know. I have heard."

"And my mother loved him . . . dearly," I said fiercely. "But it is all over, Celeste. That is in the past. It's now that matters."

"He doesn't care for me, Rebecca."

"He must. He married you."

"Did he care for the first one, I wonder?"

"This is different."

"How is it different?"

"I am sure of it."

"I love him so much. When I first saw him I thought he was the most wonderful man I had ever seen. When he asked me to marry him I could not believe it. I think I am dreaming. But we marry . . . and now he does not want me. All

271

he wants is her. He dream of her. I have heard him say her name in his sleep. He has drawn her back from the grave because he cannot live without her. She is here. She is in this house. And now she is tired of being in that locked room. She has come out to join those other ghosts in the garden."

"Oh, Celeste. You must not think like that. He needs time . . . time to recover."

"It is years since she died. It was when Belinda was born."

"She would not wish you to suffer like this. She was the kindest person in the world. If she came back it would be to help you . . . not to harm you."

I wished that I knew how to comfort her. I hated him then. He was responsible for her unhappiness. He was selfish and cruel. He had married her because he needed a wife to enhance his career, just as he had married Lizzie Morley because he needed her money for the same reason. My mother he had truly loved; there was no doubt of that, and God . . . or Fate . . . was repaying him. He had lost the one he loved and would not try to make a happy life for the woman he had taken up to serve his own ends.

He was a monster, I thought, and I whipped up my hatred and contempt of him.

I said: "It will come all right one day, Celeste."

She shook her head. "But I pray that he will turn to me," she said. "I lie here sometimes waiting . . . waiting . . . You cannot understand, Rebecca."

"I think I do," I replied. "And you must rest now. Do you think you could sleep?"

"I am very tired," she said.

"Shall I get Mrs. Emery to send up a little supper on a tray? I could have mine with you if you liked. Then you could rest. You'll feel better in the morning."

"I've never fainted before," she told me. "It's strange to feel the Earth slipping away."

"People often faint for various reasons. There are no after effects. Perhaps you were not feeling well and the change of air . . ."

"But I saw . . ."

"It really could have been the mist in the air."

"It wasn't mist. I saw her clearly."

"How did you know who it was?"

"I knew."

"People see a sort of mirage sometimes. There are shadows and they don't recognize them as such and the brain starts to work out what it is . . . and imagination comes in. It's all this talk about ghosts. Just suppose it was a ghost. It might have been Lady Flamstead or Miss Martha."

"I know who it was. Instinct told me."

"Will you have something to eat?"

"I couldn't manage it . . . not tonight."

"Do you think you could sleep?"

"Perhaps."

I stood up and kissed her.

"I am so glad you are here, Rebecca," she said.

"I wondered a lot . . . how would you like me . . . the one who took your mother's place."

"I never felt like that for a moment. It is so long since she died." I smiled at her. "If you want me . . . later on . . . if you can't sleep and would like to talk . . . ring the bell and tell one of the servants. I'll come along and talk."

"Thank you. You would comfort me much . . . if I could be comforted."

"You will be, and I am going to see that you are."

She smiled faintly. She looked a little better and very young with the traces of tears on her eyelashes and a faint flush in her cheeks.

I was glad to be alone. I wanted to think. She had shaken me. Although I had told her that I did not accept the theory that she had seen a ghost, I was impressed by her description of the clothes. Being so interested in the subject she would see them more clearly than most people and she had been so emphatic in her description of them.

I kept seeing my mother walking across the garden with her hair escaping from under that becoming hat and mingling with the white fur on the edge of it.

Celeste had described it accurately.

It was not possible. If my mother returned, it would not be to show herself to poor little Celeste, but to me . . . or to him . . . and she would not do it in a frightening way.

I recalled that occasion when I had thought she was in my bedroom. I had not seen her. I had not heard her voice. It was just a conviction that she was close. I had been overwrought at the time, worried about Lucie and what would become of her.

At such times one could have hallucinations. But I had never seen her and Celeste would have it that *she* had seen her so closely that she could describe the clothes she was wearing.

She did not send for me that night but before I retired I went to her room to see how she was and found her sleeping peacefully.

I tossed and turned all night and it must have been about five in the morning when I found myself wide awake.

I sat up in bed and said in a whisper: "I don't believe it." The clothes were real though. My mother did possess them at some time. Was it possible that someone could have found those clothes and worn them and come to the spot to play the ghost?

I could not get the idea out of my mind.

I was up early. I had thought a great deal about what I could do. I would enlist the help of Mrs. Emery. I could take her into my confidence and I knew that she would respect it.

The first thing I did was to go along to Celeste.

She looked exhausted and drawn and I was relieved when she suggested staying in bed, for the morning at least.

She was very tired, she said.

275

I told her I would have a light breakfast sent up to her room and after she had partaken of it she should try to sleep. I would look in later to see how she felt.

Mrs. Emery was a woman of routine. She was a great believer in the beneficial effects of a good cup of tea and she took it at eleven in the morning as well as in the afternoon.

It was safe to go along to her room at eleven o'clock.

She was always pleased to see me. Celeste was, of course, the mistress of the house, but now that I was no longer a child, Mrs. Emery regarded me as such. She could not give foreigners the same respect she applied to her own countryfolk, therefore, I was as important—perhaps more so—in her eyes than Celeste.

"I do want to talk to you, Mrs. Emery," I said.

She preened herself. "Well, it is always a pleasure, Miss Rebecca."

"Thank you."

"And you're just in time for a cup of tea. I'll have it ready in a jiffy."

"Oh thank you. That would be nice."

I did not speak until the ritual of teamaking was completed. I watched her. I had heard her tell the servants many times. Warm the pot with very hot water, dry thoroughly before putting in the tea . . . one teaspoonful for each person and one for the pot. Infuse, stir and allow to stand for five minutes . . . not a second more . . . not a second less.

The tea was poured into the cups which she kept specially for honored visitors. I was flattered that I was one.

"Mrs. Emery," I began, "I am concerned about what happened yesterday."

"Oh . . . Mrs. Lansdon, yes . . . she was really shook up."

"Do you know what caused it?"

"I didn't. I just wondered. Well, it seems hardly possible. I wondered if she was expecting."

"Oh no . . . nothing like that, I think. She thought she saw . . . something . . . under the oak tree."

"Mercy on us, Miss Rebecca. Not the ghost!"

"Mrs. Lansdon believed she saw one . . . on the haunted seat."

"My goodness gracious me! What next?"

"She described the clothes. I recognized them as my mother's."

Mrs. Emery stared at me open-mouthed.

"Yes," I said. "She thinks it was the ghost of my mother."

"But . . ."

"You see . . ."

"Yes, I see all right. You can't help knowing how things are. Oh, how different it was when your dear mother was here. Then we were a happy household."

"We should try to make it happy now, Mrs. Emery."

"Well . . . what with him and that locked room . . . and her . . . well, it's not easy, is it?"

"She must have imagined something. She is not very well."

Mrs. Emery nodded. "She's a sad lady. There are times when I feel sorry for her."

"Yes, but I don't think she imagined this. I think she really did see something under the trees and whoever it was was wearing my mother's clothes."

"Lord a' mercy!"

"I may be wrong but the fact that she described the clothes so accurately makes me believe that someone in this house was playing a trick."

Mrs. Emery nodded thoughtfully.

"You go to that room regularly and everyone knows you do that. I think someone got into your room, found the key and took the clothes from my mother's wardrobe."

"The door is always locked and I have the key."

"You always keep it in the same place?"

"Yes, I do."

"Possibly someone discovered where you kept it."

"I can't see how."

"I can. The door of your room . . . this room . . . is never locked, is it?"

She shook her head.

"Someone could come in when you are busy and there was no chance of being disturbed. Whoever it was could have taken the key, gone to the locked room, taken the clothes, locked the

278

door and returned the key back to this room. That's possible."

"No one would dare."

"There are some daring people around, Mrs. Emery."

"But what for? What's the good of it?"

"Mischief. That is very attractive to some."

"You mean someone did it to frighten the wits out of that poor lady?"

"It's possible, and I intend to find out. You have the key here now?"

She rose and went to a drawer. She opened it and triumphantly held up the key.

"I want you to take me up to that room now, Mrs. Emery," I said. "I want to see if those clothes are there. If they are, and I think they should be because my mother was wearing them right to the time she left here, then we shall know that whatever Mrs. Lansdon saw under the oak tree was not a figment of her imagination. But because this happened only yesterday, whoever took the clothes might not have had time yet to return them."

"Well, the key was there, and if anyone took it they'd have had to return it pretty prompt like. They wouldn't know when I was going to pop in . . . and it would be dangerous to bring it back when I might come in and catch them at it."

"So it is fair to say that if the clothes are still there what Mrs. Lansdon saw was something very likely to be supernatural. And if it was someone playing a trick . . . well then, the one who played the trick could still have them."

"I can't believe anyone would go to all that trouble just to frighten her. And run the risk of getting caught into the bargain."

"Some people like mischief. They like to take risks, too. In any case, let us take the first step towards solving the mystery. Let's go and see if the clothes are still there."

Mrs. Emery rose immediately and we went to the room.

Even at such a time I was deeply moved as I stepped over the threshold. It was exactly as it had been in the old days and I could imagine myself a young girl again . . . secure in the love of my mother, though that resentment I felt towards my stepfather was already with me.

The sight of her things unnerved me; but I had come here for a purpose.

I went to the wardrobe. Her clothes were hanging there but there was no sign of the blue coat. I reached up and in between a tweed costume and a riding habit was an empty coat hanger.

I turned to look at Mrs. Emery.

I said: "I think someone has been in here and taken the clothes."

"I can't believe that," cried Mrs. Emery. "I kept that key in my room. Nobody comes in but him and me. We are the only two with keys."

"Could anyone have stolen his key?"

"I'd hardly think so. He keeps it on his watch

chain and it is always with him . . . and he hasn't been here this past week or more."

She locked the door and we went back to her sitting room.

When we were seated she said: "Of course, there is no knowing that this coat and hat was in the wardrobe."

"Not for certain," I agreed. "But I know my mother liked it particularly and she did have it right to the time she went down to Cornwall. You always keep the key in that drawer, I suppose. Could you put it in a different place?"

"Well, perhaps I could . . ."

"Then if someone came in to steal it again they wouldn't be able to find it. I am presuming that whoever took the clothes might want to return them. Or perhaps they are keeping her clothes and intend to be a series of hauntings."

"You're giving me the shivers, Miss Rebecca. I'm not sure I wouldn't it were rather the real thing than all this plotting."

"I am going to see if I can find the clothes, Mrs. Emery. I feel they are somewhere in this house and if I did find them I should discover who played this wicked trick on Mrs. Lansdon."

"It could have been really serious . . . if she's been carrying . . ."

"Mrs. Emery, will you guard the key . . . absolutely? Put it in a different place and make sure that none but yourself knows where. I do not want anyone to be able to get into that room until I have solved this mystery."

"I'll do just as you say, Miss Rebecca, and I would like to know who played such a nasty trick . . . I would that . . . and if it's any of my maids . . . well, they won't be on my staff much longer, I can tell you."

As soon as I left her I went to the schoolroom. Belinda and Lucie were seated at the table with Miss Stringer.

"Good morning, Miss Mandeville," said Miss Stringer. "Did you want me?"

I said: "No . . . no. How are the lessons going?"

"Oh!" She raised her eyes to the ceiling. "As well as can be expected."

"We're doing history," said Lucie.

"I'm glad to hear it."

"About William the Conqueror who came over here and killed King Harold."

"That must be very interesting. Belinda is quiet this morning. Are you all right, Belinda?"

She nodded curtly.

"Thank Miss Rebecca for her enquiry and answer graciously," said Miss Stringer.

"I'm all right, thank you," mumbled Belinda.

"I thought you might have been anxious about your stepmother," I said.

She did not look up.

"How is Mrs. Lansdon today?" asked Miss Stringer.

"She's resting. It was quite a bad turn she had yesterday."

"I heard she had fainted in the garden. I hope she did not hurt herself when she fell."

"She could have done so, of course," I said. "Fortunately she fell on soft earth. But it was a shock to her."

I was looking at the cupboards. They would be full of books and schoolroom accessories. No clothes could be hidden there. Miss Stringer would soon discover them if they were.

"Well, I'll leave you to William the Conqueror," I said and came out.

However, I did not want to confront Belinda without evidence. I did not want to speak to Lucie who might well be in the conspiracy. I hoped she was not but I understood from Miss Stringer and what I had observed that Belinda often required her to join in games in which she took the leading role.

Just above the schoolroom was an attic. The children used it as a playroom. There were trunks up there as it was also a good storeroom. If one wanted to hide something it could be the ideal spot.

It was approached by a short spiral staircase. I went to it.

The roof sloped and at either end it was impossible to stand upright. Old pictures were stacked against the wall and there were certain pieces of furniture there. At one end of the room were three large trunks. I noticed at once that one of them was not properly shut. I opened it.

It was simpler than I had anticipated. There, on

the top of other garments, lay the blue coat and hat. My suspicions had been confirmed.

There was an armchair close by. I sat down on this and thought about what had happened. Belinda, of course, had been in my mind and I wondered what went on in hers. She alarmed me. How would my mother have dealt with such a child? She would have loved her as she loved me; but sometimes I thought there was more than a hint of mischief in Belinda. I thought of the scheme she had made Lucie play with her. It was calculated to hurt. It seemed unnatural that she—my own sister—could behave so.

I tried to make excuses for her. That brought me back to him . . . to Benedict Lansdon. He had been an unnatural father to her. He seemed to forget that she was his child. My mother would have wanted him to care for her. The fact that she herself was not there to do so would have made her doubly anxious that he should. Yet he was so aloof. Perhaps he did not try very hard. He was unable to forget the fact that she was the one responsible for my mother's death—although she knew nothing of this.

I had heard of such cases and I had always thought such an attitude was unforgivable in a parent.

And because of being unwanted by her father . . . relying on Leah for that love and care which all children need, she was forever trying to show how clever she was, how she could score over other people.

I must try not to be angry with her. I must try to understand. After all, she was a child . . . a lost child.

I knew that sooner or later she would come up to the attic, for she would have to make sure that the clothes had not been discovered. She may have guessed my suspicions for she was sharp beyond her years. She was shrewd and cunning by nature.

I sat for an hour in the attic waiting, for I guessed that as soon as lessons were over she would come up.

I was right.

I braced myself when I heard light footsteps on the spiral staircase.

"Come in, Belinda," I said. "I want to talk to you."

She stared at me in amazement. I was glad that I had waited for I had feared that after our encounter in the schoolroom she would have guessed my suspicions and stayed away.

"What are you doing up here?" she demanded.

"That's not very polite, is it?"

I saw the fear in her face. "What do you want?" she asked.

"I want you to go over to that trunk and take out what you find lying on the top."

"Why?"

"Because I want you to show me and to tell me how they came to be there."

"How should I know?"

"We'll see about that."

I stood up and, taking her hand, led her to the trunk. "Now open it," I said.

"Why?"

"Open it."

She did so.

"You put those things there," I said.

"No."

I ignored the lie. "How did you get into the locked room?" I asked.

She looked sly. She thought she had been rather clever and it was hard to resist boasting of that. But she remained silent.

I went on: "You stole the key from Mrs. Emery's sitting room. You knew it was there because she went in to clean twice a week. You knew when she would not be in her room and you went there and found it."

She stared at me in amazement. "Lucie's been telling tales."

"Lucie knew . . . ?"

"A bit," she said.

"And what did Lucie do?"

"Nothing. Lucie never thinks of anything. She's too silly."

"I see. Well, having got the key, you took the clothes. You knew they were there and that they were your mother's. She would be very sad if she knew you did things like this, Belinda. Don't you care about hurting people?"

"People hurt me."

"Who? Who hurts you?"

She was silent.

"Leah is good and kind to you. Miss Stringer is too. Lucie loves you, so does Mrs. Emery. And have I been unkind to you?"

For a moment her defiance wavered and she looked like a frightened little girl.

"*He* hates me," she said. "He hates me because . . . because . . . she died having me."

"Who tells you these tales?"

She looked at me scornfully. "Everybody knows. You know. You only pretend you don't."

"Oh Belinda," I said, "It's not like that. It wasn't your fault. It happens to hundreds of children. Nobody blames them."

"He does," she said.

I wanted to put my arms round her and hold her against me. I wanted to say: We are sisters, Belinda. I know we have different fathers, but your mother was my mother. That makes a special bond between us. Why don't you talk to me . . . tell me how you feel?

She said: "You don't like him either."

"Belinda . . ."

"Only you don't tell the truth. I do. I hate him."

I was in despair. I wondered what to say to her. It was true that he avoided her and was cool towards her, that he could not take to her, he could not forget that her coming had meant the departure of his beloved wife.

I wished afterwards that I had been older, wiser, more experienced, and could have comforted the child in some way.

But at the time I could only think of what she had done to Celeste.

"Why did you want to frighten her like that?" I asked.

Her defiance had returned. The softness I had glimpsed, the craving for affection, was no longer there. She was Belinda, the clever one, who knew how to take revenge on those who hurt her.

She lifted her shoulders and smiled.

"They were so big," she said. "I had to be careful." She laughed almost hysterically. "I nearly tripped over. The hat was all right but it did press down on my ears. I had to keep sitting down."

"She fainted," I reminded her. "Fortunately she fell on soft earth, but she could have been badly hurt."

"Serve her right for marrying him. She'd no right to marry him. I didn't want a stepmother."

"There are many things in life you don't understand. Perhaps you will when you grow up. She is not to blame for anything. She wants to do what is best."

"She can't even speak English properly."

"I should imagine her English compares favorably with your French. Doesn't it worry you that you may have caused her some injury?"

She looked at me steadily, her eyes almost expressionless.

She shook her head.

"I was very good," she said complacently. "She thought I was a real ghost."

"You weren't clever enough."

"Lucie told you."

"Lucie has told me nothing. Tell me what part she played in this."

"None. She couldn't. She's not clever enough. She would have spoilt it. She just knew . . . that was all. And she told you. Because . . . how else would you have known?"

"I know *you*, Belinda. I suspected you almost at once."

"Why?"

"Because of the clothes for one thing. I knew where you found them. Then I checked with Mrs. Emery and discovered they were missing, so I knew someone had taken them. Belinda, I want to talk to you very seriously."

"What are you going to do? Tell him . . . tell my father?"

I shook my head. "No. You must see your stepmother and tell her how sorry you are and you will never do anything like that again. Don't you see how wrong it is to hurt people?"

"I was only being a ghost."

"I told you before . . ."

I saw the tip of her tongue protruding.

"Belinda, listen to me. You want people to like and admire you, don't you?"

"Leah does."

"Leah has been your nurse since you were a baby. She loves you and Lucie as though you were her own."

"She loves me best."

"She loves you both. If you are kind to people they will love you in return. Believe me, you will be happier if you are good and do not play unkind tricks on people . . . especially those who have done you no harm."

On impulse I put my arms round her and to my amazement and joy she suddenly clung to me. I held her to me for a few minutes. Then I looked into her face. Her tears were genuine.

"Always remember, Belinda," I said, "that we are sisters . . . you and I. We lost our mother. I knew her and loved her dearly. She was everything to me. We have to remember that he loved her dearly, too. When she died he was deeply and bitterly hurt. He cannot forget her. We each have to help him, Belinda, and in helping him we shall help ourselves. Promise me you will talk to me more. If anything happens, come to me, tell me about it. Will you?"

She looked at me steadily and nodded.

Then she threw her arms about my neck and I felt happier than I had for a long time. I was breaking through. I was beginning to make headway with this strange child who was my sister.

I said: "Now we understand each other. We are friends, eh, Belinda?"

She nodded again.

"There is one other thing," I went on. "We have to go to your stepmother."

She shrank back.

"It is necessary," I went on. "She has had a bad fright. She thinks she saw a ghost."

The old Belinda was back and I saw a look of triumph cross her face.

"She will be looking for that ghost everywhere she goes. It will haunt her."

Belinda nodded, her eyes sparkling at the prospect of future hauntings and I realized I had been premature in my belief that I had aroused something good in her nature.

"We have to put her mind at rest," I said firmly. "We have to tell her the truth. So we are going to her now. We are going to tell her exactly what happened and ask her forgiveness. It was a silly childish prank but you are sorry you did it. You just did not think what harm you were doing."

"I don't want to."

"We often have to do things we don't want to in life. I shall give these clothes to Mrs. Emery and she can put them back where they were. She will be glad to hear that there was no ghost—only a little girl playing tricks."

She looked stubborn.

"Come along," I said. "Let's get it over."

I put the coat and hat back in the trunk to be dealt with later and took Belinda down to Celeste's room.

Celeste was sitting by the window in her dressing gown.

I said: "Belinda wants to tell you something."

She looked surprised and I led Belinda over to her.

Belinda said in a sing-song voice as though she were repeating a lesson: "I took the clothes out

291

of the wardrobe in the locked room. I took them to the garden and when I heard you coming I put them on. It was only a game and I'm sorry I frightened you."

I could see the relief in Celeste's face.

I said: "Belinda is really sorry. You must forgive her. She thought she was playing a game. You know how she likes dressing up and acting . . . ever since the *tableaux vivants*."

"Oh . . ." said Celeste, faintly. "I . . . I see."

"Belinda is very, very sorry for what happened."

Celeste smiled at her. "I see it," she said. "It is just a little joke, eh? It was silly of me."

Belinda nodded. I put my arm round her and she was not exactly responsive but she did not reject me.

"Are you riding this afternoon?" I asked her.

"Yes."

"You and Lucie? I'll come with you. You can go now."

She was clearly glad to escape.

I said: "She really is contrite."

"She hates me . . . I think."

"No. She is bewildered . . . lost. I wish her father would give her a little attention. That is what she needs. I think she admired him . . ." I paused. "But you see . . ."

"Yes, I see," said Celeste.

Their problems were similar.

I could not help feeling a certain pleasure because, due to this episode, Belinda and I had come a little closer. I must keep it that way. The child

292

—and she was only a child although we forgot it at times—wanted affection. It was the reason why she was always showing off, as it were, seeking admiration. If only Benedict would cast aside his bitter grief. If only he would give a little thought to the living.

It all came back to him.

The Treasure Hunt

Benedict had returned and Christmas was almost
upon us. I had hoped I could take the children
with me to Cornwall but this was not to be. Christmas was an important time in Manorleigh. There
would be a great deal of entertaining at Manor
Grange with special dinner parties as well as the
usual celebrations. People who worked in the constituency would have to be invited. My stepfather
would want his family around him at such a time
for Christmas was an occasion when all the family
should be together.

It was a great disappointment, for not only
would I have loved to be with my grandparents,
but Pedrek was there with his parents and grandparents; and I daresay they would be often at
Cador.

It was very frustrating and I consoled myself
with the fact that time was passing, and next Christmas we should be planning our wedding. So . . . I
must be patient.

Miss Stringer was to join her family in the
Cotswolds for three weeks. There would be no
lessons during that time. "Hurrah!" said Belinda.
Lucie joined in and they danced round the schoolroom singing: "No lessons for three weeks."

"There will be so much to do for Christmas," I reminded them, "that you will find yourselves fully occupied."

It was to be a traditional Christmas. The great hall would be decorated with holly, ivy and bay. Besides the sprays of mistletoe, there were the old Christmas bushes—two hoops fastened at right angles and trimmed with evergreen leaves which were hung on the rafters; they served the same purpose as the mistletoe and were even called Kissing Bushes.

Belinda was very excited. She and Lucie were dashing about helping with the decorations, running into the kitchen to take a stir at the puddings which, decreed Mrs. Grant, the cook, should be stirred by everyone in the household, high and low.

So we all had a stir—apart from Benedict. I could not imagine anyone's suggesting he should take part in such a procedure.

The smell of the boiling puddings permeated the kitchen and we all went down to listen to them bubbling away in the copper in the laundry house. Mrs. Emery said that all the staff should join in the tasting ceremony and the children were allowed to share in it too. This was indeed a ceremonial occasion when Mrs. Grant, like a priestess in some holy temple, served everyone with a mouthful from one of the small basins which contained a specimen of the rich mixture; and which we all declared was perfect.

Then there were the mince pies to be made and

the Christmas cake to be iced with the words "Merry Christmas" and "God Bless This House" written on it in blue; and then this was placed in state on the kitchen table where all might inspect and admire it before it was put away.

It was all very simple and exciting; and I was glad to see Belinda looked happier than she had for some time; and what was most gratifying was that she seemed to want to please me. I said to Celeste that this incident, regrettable as it was at the time, might be a turning point.

"I think I am closer to her than I have ever been," I said. "She has always seemed so overbearing, but, poor child, what she needs is love and tenderness."

Celeste was inclined to agree with me.

I said: "She admires her father, I know. She is deeply hurt by his neglect. If only he would show a little interest in her it would make a world of difference, I am sure."

"He seems to like Lucie more than he does her."

"Lucie is easier to like perhaps."

"That may be. But Belinda is his daughter."

"Perhaps one day . . . one of us will be able to make him see . . ."

"Perhaps," sighed Celeste.

I received letters from Cornwall. Pedrek had kept his promise to write once a week and I had kept mine to reply. So I knew exactly what was happening in Cornwall. He was getting on well at the Mining College. Working hard helped him to endure the separation. I tried to write amusingly about life in London and at Manor Grange, telling him of the political world and what it was like to be on the edge of it.

The day before Christmas Eve I received a batch of letters from Cornwall with gifts from everyone. There was a necklace of amethyst from my grandparents and a gold bracelet from Pedrek.

I kept the letter he sent with it.

Dearest Rebecca,

If only we could be together! I kept hoping that you would come for Christmas. So did we all. I have a confession to make. I have told them. I could not keep it to myself. They were talking about you and saying how they wished you were here . . . and somehow it came out.

We did say we wouldn't . . . and I should have waited until we could tell them together . . . but if you could have seen their joy you would have been glad they knew. My mother and your grandmother hugged each other and I thought my grandparents were going to burst into tears . . . tears of absolute bliss. They all said it was what they had always hoped for and prayed for. And my grandfather said there was going to be such a wedding as had never been seen in Cornwall.

But they all think it is wise that we should wait until I am through with college. They said we are both very young and need a little time to prepare. I don't agree. I'm just telling you what they said. I am just wishing the time away.

Oh, Rebecca, it would be wonderful if you were here. It would be such a happy Christmas. Your grandparents said you are certain to come down in the Spring, but that seems far away. But I suppose it will come in time and I must be patient until then. The only way I can do that is by telling myself that we shall be married and then together all the time.

My love to you . . . today, tomorrow and

forever,
Pedrek

My grandmother had written:

My dear Rebecca,

Pedrek has just told us and I must write and tell you how happy that has made your grandfather and me. Pedrek was a little contrite. He said you had agreed not to tell yet. You wanted to wait until he was out of college . . . or almost. Don't blame him. It slipped out. He was so happy and wanted to share that happiness with us.

If only you could have been here!

Your grandfather says he would not have wished anything else for you and that goes for me. You should have seen the Pencarrons. They are a dear, sentimental old pair and as you know Pedrek and his mother are the sun, moon and stars and the whole universe to them. They are such *family* people.

They are so happy about Pedrek's going eventually into the mine and this of course has made everything quite blissful for them.

We drank your health and talked of you continually. Mrs Pencarron is already working out what she will wear for the wedding as the bridegroom's grandmama and Mr P is wondering who shall be honoured with the order for the catering for the grand feast he has in mind. Then there are Pedrek's parents. Morwenna is completely delighted and so is Justin. Morwenna says our families have always been close and she went on about the way the two of you were born in your stepfather's grand house in that grim mining township and how close she and your dear mother always were. Oh, Rebecca, I am sure your mother would be delighted. Your happiness meant everything to her . . . as it does to us. Pedrek is a really *good* young man and we all love him dearly. It is wonderful.

Now to more mundane matters. Things in the Poldoreys go on much as usual. Mrs Arkwright has given birth to twins—predicted of course by our wise Mrs Polhenny. One of Joe Garth's fishing boats was lost in a gale recently. All on board were saved, thank God, but the loss of the boat was a blow. Somebody thought she heard the bells of St Branok recently. But that happens periodically, as you know. Mrs Yeo and Miss Heathers had their usual fight over who should be in charge of church decorations for Christmas. Mrs Polhenny still pursues her calling, fighting the good fight and travelling round on her old bone-shaker. You would be amused to see her. She really is one of the sights of Poldorey.

It is such a disappointment that you are not with us. You must come in the Spring. That's the best time really. But it would have been lovely to have you for Christmas—particularly now that Pedrek has broken this wonderful news.

All our love, darling,

> Your loving and deprived (of your company, of course) Grandparents

They were lovely, heartwarming letters. I put them in the silver box which my mother had given me and I kept them in a drawer because I knew I should want to read them again and again.

A few days before Christmas Oliver Gerson arrived. I was surprised. I had heard that a business associate of Benedict's would be spending Christmas at Manor Grange but Oliver's name had not been mentioned.

I had been out riding with the girls which I did frequently. Miss Stringer had already left and that meant that I was even more frequently than usual in their company.

As we returned into the drive I saw a carriage at the door and Mr. Emery was standing there giving instructions for the gentleman's luggage to be taken into the house.

Then he turned and I saw who it was.

"Mr. Gerson!" I cried.

Belinda surprised me. She leaped from her pony and ran to him. She stood before him, looking up and smiling. There could not have been a warmer welcome.

He took Belinda's hand and solemnly kissed it. "What a pleasure it is to see you," he said.

Then he walked to me and, taking my hand, kissed it in the same manner. He looked at Lucie. She held out her hand and received the same treatment. I had rarely seen such gracious manners.

He was gazing at me as he said: "I have been looking forward to this pleasure. I must confess I was apprehensive, fearing that you might have decided not to spend Christmas here."

"We shall be here," cried Belinda, jumping into the air.

"What fun that will be!" he replied. "Christmas in the country with the most delightful of companions." He included us all in his smile.

"Are you going to stay for a long time?" asked Belinda.

"That will depend on how long my host wants me to."

"Is your host my father?" asked Belinda a little blankly.

"Indeed he is."

"Let's go into the house, shall we?" I suggested.

The groom took our horses and we went into the hall. As we did so Benedict came down the stairs.

"Oh, there you are, Gerson," he said. "They have your room ready. I'll get one of them to take you up. It's good to see you."

"I am delighted to be here. These ladies have already made me feel welcome."

"So I see . . ." said my stepfather vaguely. "Your bags will be taken up. Good journey?"

"Quite good, thanks."

"I'd like to have a chat about things before dinner."

"But of course."

"Right." He walked with Oliver Gerson across the hall. He seemed hardly to have noticed our presence.

I looked at Belinda. Her eyes were shining. "It's wonderful," she said. "Aren't you pleased, Lucie? He's going to be here for Christmas."

"He's very nice," said Lucie.

"Of course he's nice. He's the nicest man I know."

"You don't really know him yet," I reminded her.

"I *do* know him. I like him. I'm glad he's here."

She skipped up three stairs.

I looked at Lucie and laughed. "It's clear that he has Belinda's approval," I said.

"She talks about him a lot. She says he's like

one of those knights who did all sorts of daring things to win the King's daughter."

"Let's hope she's right," I said.

When I look back it seems that that Christmas was dominated by Oliver Gerson. He devoted quite a lot of time to the children which I thought was kind of him. He seemed to understand Belinda and she was certainly happier in his company than I had known her to be before. She had become a normal fun-loving child. It proved to me that she craved attention and that her waywardness had been a method of calling attention to herself. The change in her was remarkable.

Oliver Gerson was, for the greater part of the day, in my stepfather's company. It was for that purpose, I supposed, that he had been invited to the house.

He told me that he was my stepfather's righthand man.

"I knew that you were in business together," I said. "It's those clubs, isn't it?"

"That and other things. I worked for your step-father's grandfather, you know."

"Oh yes . . . Uncle Peter."

"He was a wonderful man. Astute, knowledge-able and crafty as a fox."

"Did you like working for him?"

"Immensely. It was a great adventure."

"He is very much missed in the family although we all knew there was something rather shocking about what he was engaged in. Is it the same still?"

"Those who are shocked are envious of others' success. The clubs provide a need for certain people. If they want to gamble why shouldn't they? If they lose money it is their affair."

"I believe there are other things besides gambling."

He shrugged his shoulders. "No one is dragooned into attending. They use the clubs of their own free will. It is all legitimate business. There is nothing illegal about it."

"Uncle Peter wanted to be a member of Parliament and there was some scandal about the clubs. It ruined his parliamentary career."

"I know. It happened years ago. People's ideas changed after the Consort's death. It would have been different if it had happened now. It was the Prince who set out these rigid codes."

"But might it not still be dangerous for my stepfather?"

"I think you can say he knows what he is doing."

"My mother was very upset when she knew he had inherited the business. She wanted him to sell out."

"He is too good a businessman to do that. How could he resist the chance of adding to his immense fortune?"

"Easily, I should have thought, as he has enough already."

"You don't understand the mind of a business-man, Rebecca."

"I think family happiness comes before all that."

He put his hand over mine. " 'Oh wise young judge,' " he quoted. " 'How I do honour thee.' "

"I am no Portia but I should have thought that was clear. My mother was very worried. It was just before she died."

I pulled myself up sharply. I was trying to blame him for what had happened. I was telling myself that in his greed for more wealth he had worried her, weakened her so that when her ordeal came she was unable to face it.

It was nonsense. That had had nothing to do with her death.

"You see," Oliver Gerson was saying, "he has a great flair for business. I gathered he did well in Australia before he acquired his goldmine. Didn't he have men working for him?"

"Yes. My mother spoke of it to me many times. He found gold but not enough to make the fortune he had set out for but he was able to employ those men who despaired of ever doing so and wanted a regular wage. Several were working for him so there was more chance of finding gold on his patch."

"You see what I mean about this flair for business? You can't expect such people to take the easy way out just because it offers a more peaceful existence. His sort don't want peace. They want excitement and adventure."

"And you . . . you have this flair?"

"But, of course. But I have not had your step-father's good fortune . . . yet."

"Well, I can only hope that it will come to you in time."

"Needless to say, I fervently share that hope. But don't worry about the business. I can assure you your stepfather will know how to steer our craft past the dangerous rocks."

"You have a great admiration for him."

"If you worked with him, so would you."

When he was not with my stepfather he was with us.

He continued to make much of the children and they admired him. He had a way of treating them as adults, never stressing that he was reducing himself to their level but just as though he accepted them as grown-up intelligent beings simply because they were.

We often went riding together. I had never seen Belinda so happy. I was now convinced that she was a normal child who had for a time been warped by the indifference—and even resentment —of an unnatural father.

I was delighted to see the change in her and I encouraged Oliver Gerson to be with us. Not that he needed any encouragement. I realized that he had a flair for being amusing as well as that of which he had told me, for business. Conversation was always lighthearted and punctuated with laughter from the children . . . not so much the laughter of amusement as of sheer happiness.

He would devise games as we rode along.

He always found something fresh with which to stimulate their interest, so the rides were especially enjoyable.

"A mark for the first one who spots a holly bush with at least ten berries."

They giggled. Lucie cried: "There's one."

"It's not a holly bush, is it, Mr. Gerson?" said Belinda.

"No . . . it's some other thing . . . not holly. We ought to have your governess here to tell us what."

"Oh, we don't want her. She makes a lesson out of everything."

"Well, sorry, Lucie, it's not holly. Try again."

Then it would be the first to see a grey horse.

Thus a spirit of competition was added to the rides and both children enjoyed it.

We all knew what we should do on the morning of Christmas Day. There would be church and then the carol singers would come. Hot punch and fairy cakes would be distributed to them and then there would be midday dinner in the great hall when we would have several guests. The children would be at a table near the screens presided over by Leah, and the meal would be served in the traditional manner, the dishes carried in with a certain ceremony.

Afterwards the grown-ups would be a little somnolent and there would be desultory conversation and some dozing. There would be tea at five o'clock and a buffet supper later. Then the guests who were staying at the house would retire to their rooms and the others leave the house. The children would be allowed to stay up until nine o'clock as a concession to the day.

Oliver Gerson said to me: "What a great deal of preparation for something which has to be over almost as soon as it has begun. I am afraid our two are going to wonder what to do while the grown-ups are resting. We should think up some entertainment for them."

"What an excellent idea. It was different at Cador. There always seemed something to do."

"We must make something to do here. I thought of a treasure hunt."

"How? Where?"

"It would have to be in the garden. We could not have them prowling about the house when people are trying to sleep."

"Suppose it rains or snows?"

"Well then, it would have to be called off or we should have to think of some other indoor pastime."

"What sort of treasure hunt?"

"Oh . . . clues . . . about six, I think. Little couplets, one leading to another. All very simple."

"It sounds wonderful. Who'll do the couplets?"

"We shall. I shall need your help to tell me the right places in the garden."

"It's a wonderful idea."

"Of course. It's mine."

We laughed together.

"How many children will there be?" he asked.

"Oh, six . . . maybe seven. There are the

agent's two and three belonging to those indefatigable workers and our two."

"That's an ideal number. And we'll have a prize for the winner. There must be a prize . . . some goal to work for."

"What prize?"

"You and I will go to the village today and buy a splendid box of chocolates. Big . . . and gaudy . . . so that it looks like a worthwhile prize."

"I am sure they will all love it."

"It will dispense with the boredom of having to be quiet in a houseful of somnolent guests."

"Are you sure you won't be too somnolent to conduct affairs?"

"I? Never! I shall be as wide awake as you will."

"I am glad you thought of it. They will be thrilled. It will make an exciting Christmas Day for them."

"Well, let's get to work. First the clues. We'll hide ourselves away. What about the summerhouse? It will be warm in there with the door shut and they won't think of looking for us there."

"All right. Now do you mean?"

"Well, we shall have to get busy and this afternoon we shall go into the village for the prize."

It was great fun in the summerhouse. Together we worked on six simple clues and distributed them in appropriate parts of the garden. Then we went into the village and bought a large box of chocolates tied up with red ribbon.

When we returned Lucie and Belinda, who were

in the garden, came rushing up to us. Belinda caught Oliver Gerson's arm.

"Where have you been?" she demanded.

"Ah," said Oliver, looking mysterious. "On secret business."

"What secret business? And what's that?"

He put his fingers to his lips and smiled at me secretively.

Lucie hung on my arm. "What is it, Rebecca?" she pleaded.

"This," said Oliver, holding up the parcel, "is the prize."

"What prize? What prize?" shrieked Belinda.

"Shall we tell them?" asked Oliver, looking at me.

"I think so," I replied judiciously. "It's about time they knew."

Belinda was jumping up and down, unable to contain her excitement.

Oliver said: "On Christmas Day . . . after the feast . . . there is going to be a treasure hunt."

"Treasure . . . what treasure?"

"Miss Rebecca and I have planned it for you."

"For us?" cried Lucie, as excited as Belinda.

"For you and all the children who are here. There will be others so there will be fierce competition."

"Tell!" demanded Belinda.

"This, as I told you, is the prize . . . the treasure, you might say. The one who wins it will bring us the clues. We shall give you one to start with and then you will go off and search for the other five. They are all in the garden. When you have them you bring them to us . . . that is to Miss Rebecca and to me. We shall be in the summerhouse waiting for the first one to come in. When she . . . or perhaps he . . . as there will be other children . . . arrives with the six then the treasure will be handed over."

"What a lovely game," said Belinda. "You do think of the loveliest games, Mr. Gerson."

"It is my pleasure in life to please you, Miss Belinda."

"And me?" asked Lucie.

"You too, Miss Lucie . . . and Miss Rebecca, of course . . . and all the others who will join us on Christmas Day."

"When can we have the clues?" asked Belinda.

"Not until you are all assembled. This has to be fair, you know."

They talked about the treasure hunt for the rest of the day. There was no doubt that it had been a good idea.

"Now we have to pray for a fine afternoon," I said. "Disappointment would indeed be bitter if the weather put an end to the treasure hunt."

Christmas Day dawned dry but dull. There was a dampness in the air, but we hoped that the rain would hold off. At least it was not particularly cold.

We all went to the church in the morning and as soon as we were back the carol singers came.

"The First Noel," "The Holly and the Ivy," "The Twelve Days of Christmas" and "O Come All Ye Faithful"—it was always moving to hear the well-loved words and music.

After the performance the singers came into the hall; my stepfather made a little speech of thanks; and all were served with hot punch and mince pies, which were handed round by the children, supervised by Celeste.

After that we dined . . . the children at the small table with Leah, and the rest of us at the great oak one in the center of the hall. There was a great deal of laughter. I watched my stepfather at the head of the table being very charming to his guests and I asked myself: Why cannot he be like that with his family? Celeste, at the other end of the table, was trying to do what was expected of her. I found myself next to Oliver Gerson. I think he had arranged that, but I was not displeased. It meant that I could enjoy a certain amount of lighthearted conversation.

Every now and then he would glance over to the little table. I saw him catch Belinda's eye and lift his hand in acknowledgment. A smile immediately lightened her face. I warmed towards him. He had succeeded admirably in making hers a happy Christmas.

How different from my stepfather who was so completely immersed in his own ambitions that he had no time to spare for others.

I said: "It looks as though all is set fair this afternoon."

"It must be. Otherwise we should have to devise some other entertainment."

"It *must* keep fine. There is so much enthusiasm for the treasure hunt. Belinda and Lucie have been talking of nothing else since they heard of it. Even the excitement of Christmas gifts has taken second place."

The meal seemed to go on for a long time but at last it was over.

All the children had been told of the arranged treasure hunt and were all eager to be there.

"It's always a trial," Mrs. Emery had said, "knowing what to do with them. They're wide awake and everyone else is half asleep. It's a fine way of getting them from under our feet. That Mr. Gerson knows what's what. To see him with those two girls makes you think he should have some of his own."

At last they were assembled and Oliver gave them the first clue.

He told them: "Miss Rebecca and I will be in the summerhouse. The first one who brings us the six clues will be presented with the mystery treasure. Here it is." He held up the parcel which was tied up with red ribbon.

"We shall need six little pieces of paper like this one. Now . . . wait for the signal. Ready. Steady. Go!"

As we made our way to the summerhouse I said to him: "Don't you think Belinda and Lucie have an unfair advantage? They know the garden so much better than the others."

"Life is full of unfair advantages," he replied. "It is impossible to avoid them."

"Well, I suppose one or two others might be a little older. I know William Arlott is."

"There, you see. One has it one way . . . one another."

There were two chairs in the summerhouse and we seated ourselves.

"Do you think we shall wait long?" I asked.

"No. The clues were easy. Someone will triumph before long, never fear."

"Belinda desperately wants to."

"I hope she does," he said. "Poor child."

"You say that with real feeling."

"She's an interesting little girl. Bright too . . . oh, very bright. She is not entirely happy, is she?"

"No. She is often very difficult."

He nodded.

"But," I went on, "she is better lately. You have done a lot for her."

"I think she misses her parents."

"Yes. It is sad when a child is left as she has been. The most important person in the world to a child is its mother and she lost hers before she knew her."

"What of Leah?"

"There couldn't be anyone better in the circumstances. She has done everything for the child. I think she may have indulged her too much. Sometimes I'm worried about Lucie because there is a decided preference . . ."

"Lucie is a friendly child, isn't she? Does it worry her?"

"I don't know. Children are so secretive about some things. They don't always tell you their innermost thoughts. Belinda reminds her now and then that she is the daughter of the house. Lucie's birth was mysterious. Her mother was half crazy and no one knows who her father was."

"And strangest of all . . . you adopted her."

"It was my grandparents actually. I was only about fifteen at the time. But I just had this conviction that I couldn't leave her. I could not have done it, of course, if my grandparents had not been so good. If it had not been possible for me to take Lucie with me they would have looked after her at Cador. But when we came to London my stepfather made no objection to her being with us . . . and she has been here ever since."

"If there had been a reason for a child's lack of feeling of security, one would have thought Lucie might have felt it rather than Belinda."

"Lucie accepts what she is. She knew that she came into the family in an unconventional way but she accepts me as a mother-sister as a family relationship, I am sure; and she and Belinda are as close as two sisters. There are naturally occasional quarrels, but fundamentally they are fond of each other."

He took my hand and held it tightly: "I think it was wonderful of you to take the child in," he said.

"I had a compulsion to do so, as I told you."

"Yes, you must have had."

"And I have never regretted it."

"And if you marry . . . ?"

"I would never marry unless my husband accepted the child."

I smiled, thinking of Pedrek who understood my feelings. My thoughts had slipped away to the future. We should be so happy. They would all understand about Lucie. There would be no problem as there would certainly be if I had contemplated marrying someone else.

The door was flung open. Oliver released my hand which he was still holding. Belinda stood there.

"You have brought me the clues and you have come to claim the treasure," said Oliver.

She shook her head. She was near to tears.

"I have five," she said. "I can't find the last one. I've looked everywhere. Lucie's nearly there . . . I want the treasure. It ought to be mine. This is my house."

"That's nothing to do with it," I told her. "This is a game and you have to win fairly. You must not be a bad loser."

Oliver Gerson held out his hand and she went and leaned against him. He opened her clenched fingers and took out the screwed-up pieces of paper.

"It's the last one," she said in heartbroken tones. "I've looked everywhere."

"What does it say on number five?" he asked. He read aloud:

" 'Over the water you must seek
Beside the winged and noble Greek.' "

He took her by the shoulders and she watched
his lips expectantly.

"You're not thinking hard enough," he said.
"You know where the water is, don't you?"

She shook her head.

"Who is the noble Greek?"

"I . . . I don't know."

"Yes, you do. Who's got wings on his heels?"
She looked blank.

"Where do the water lilies grow?"

"On the pond."

"Well, isn't that water, and what's above it?
The statue, I mean?"

Her eyes widened with joy.

"Well, you know where to find it. So . . . go
and get it."

When she had gone I said: "That's cheating.
You practically told her."

"I know."

"But it isn't fair to the others."

"They won't know."

"But . . . Mr. Gerson . . ."

"Do you think you could call me Oliver? It's
quite a distinguished name really. Oliver Gold-
smith, Oliver Cromwell . . . Oliver Gerson."

"You're straying from the point. You cheated."

"I had to."

Belinda came rushing into the summerhouse,

proudly waving the six clues. "I've found them. I've found them. *I've* won the treasure."

He took the pieces of paper from her hand.

"All present and correct," he said. "You are the first. You have won the treasure. Now we must call in the others and they must witness the presentation."

We came out of the summerhouse. I was still shaken by what he had done.

He called: "Children of the Treasure Hunt, the treasure has been found. All assemble at the summerhouse."

Belinda was jumping up and down with glee. Lucie was already running up.

"I nearly had it," she told me. "I was on the last one."

The others arrived.

Oliver Gerson lifted the beribboned parcel aloft and cried: "The hunt is over. Belinda is the triumphant one. Miss Belinda Lansdon, the treasure is yours."

He put the parcel into her hands. Her face expressed her delight. She put the parcel into Lucie's hands and for a moment I thought she was giving it over to her. But all she wanted to do was put her arms round Oliver and hug him; she kissed him heartily when he stooped to her.

Then she took the parcel from Lucie and held it tightly in her arms.

Never had I seen such joy on her face before. Oliver Gerson had given Belinda the happiest Christmas she had ever known.

For some time Belinda was in a state of bliss. Long after the chocolates were eaten the box, complete with red ribbons, was given a place of honor in the nursery and I often saw Belinda's eyes rest on it, alight with loving memory.

Oliver Gerson was her hero. It did not seem to occur to her that the method by which she had won the trophy was not strictly honorable. She had won it and that was all that mattered. She may have been helped to it by Oliver Gerson but that only endeared him to her the more. He was, to her, the perfect knight.

I talked to him about the treasure hunt the very next day. I was in the garden when he joined me.

He said: "You are looking at me a little reproachfully. Are you still thinking of the treasure hunt?"

"Yes," I admitted.

"Come and sit awhile in the summerhouse. I want to talk and we shan't be interrupted there."

As we sat down he said: "Yes, it was not strictly fair, was it? It wasn't according to ethics. But I am sorry for the child. She interests me. I think she has suffered considerably."

"All she wants is a normal happy life . . . with parents who love her."

"She has lost her mother at birth and her father cannot forgive her for coming into the world at the cost of his wife's life. It is not the first time such a situation has arisen."

"It is so unfair to the child. Sometimes I hate him for what he has done to Belinda."

"He doesn't mean any harm. He just wants to forget . . . and she doesn't help him."

"But it is years since it happened."

"I know. There's nothing we can do about him . . . but we can help the child, and that is what I am trying to do."

"You are succeeding. You have made her very happy, but she should not be led to believe that she can get what she wants by cheating."

"It is often the case in real life."

"That may be and it has to be deplored. At least it is not the way a child should be taught. It is really telling her that this is the way to succeed."

"You are a lady of great virtue, I see."

"That's not the point. We are dealing with a child's impressionable mind. She thinks you are wonderful and what you do will seem to her right. I just feel that—small matter as it may seem to you—it was the wrong way to deal with it."

"Then I offer my humble apologies to you but I think there are times when the rules can be stretched for the sake of a child's happiness."

"Happiness? Every one of those children would have been happy to win. It was a game . . . a test . . . a competition . . . and one of them was helped to the winning post."

"I give you my word that I will not repeat my folly, and if I had known how you would feel, I should never have done it in the first place. But she so desperately wanted to win . . . and, poor child, she has her troubles and I just thought I would let her have this small triumph."

"You are very kind and I expect I am making a fuss about something which is not of great importance."

"I know how you feel and you are right, of course, and I am wrong . . . but I was overcome by my feelings for the child."

"You have done a great deal to help her. I thank you for that. It has given her the happiest Christmas she has ever known. So let us say no more. I expect I am carping a bit."

"You would never carp. You are much too sweet and kind . . . and delightful in every way."

I began to feel a trifle uneasy, for he had brought his chair closer to mine.

"Rebecca," he went on, "I have been trying to tell you something for a long time."

"Trying?" I said.

"Trying to choose the right moment and feeling afraid that I might choose the wrong one and speak too soon."

"What are you trying to tell me?"

"Haven't you guessed? You know how I feel about you."

I drew back and looked at him steadily. He smiled at me very tenderly.

"I love you, Rebecca," he said. "I did from the moment I saw you. I know we haven't known each other long but I knew at once. It was a sort of rapport. Your sweetness and kindness to the children . . . your anxieties about Belinda . . . and taking in that other child, Lucie. It shows me that you are indeed a very special person. I have hoped and dreamed. I can see us together . . . all of us. You need have no qualms in that direction. Rebecca, I love you and want you to marry me."

"Don't say any more," I interrupted. "I am flattered and honored. I do regard you very highly. But I could not marry you."

"I have spoken too soon. That was what I feared I might do. Forgive me, Rebecca. Let us go on as we were. Think about it and we'll talk later."

"No, Oliver, that isn't any good. As a matter of fact I am going to marry someone else."

He stared at me in dismay.

"There is a secret understanding between us. It is not at all sudden. We've known each other all our lives and it is something which is . . . well . . . inevitable. It was arranged only a little while ago . . . at the beginning of the season. So you see . . ."

"Yes," he said soberly, "I see."

"I am sorry, Oliver. I do like you and I appreciate what you have done for Belinda. I shall never forget that."

"Perhaps I hoped for too much."

I shook my head. "If I had been free . . . if it hadn't been the way it is . . ."

"This is definite, is it?"

"Yes."

"And you love this man?"

"Absolutely."

"Without any doubts?"

"Yes, without any doubts."

"And yet it is a secret? Is that because your family do not approve?"

"Oh no . . . they approve entirely."

"Your stepfather . . . ?"

"Oh . . . no . . . not him. He doesn't know. I should not take any notice of him for I don't regard him as family. I mean my grandparents who brought me up . . . and his people. They are great friends and are delighted."

"So they all know and your stepfather does not?"

I nodded. "We can't be married for another year . . . then everybody will know."

He took my hand and kissed it. "There is nothing I can do but wish you all the happiness you deserve."

"Thank you, Oliver. It is good of you to be so understanding."

The door of the summerhouse burst open and Belinda and Lucie were standing there.

"We've been looking all over the place for you," scolded Belinda. "Haven't we, Lucie?"

"We have been right round the garden and then Belinda said, 'What about the summerhouse? Perhaps they're in there, doing new clues for another treasure hunt.' "

"No," said Oliver. "We were not doing that, One treasure hunt is enough for one Christmas. Familiarity breeds contempt. Miss Rebecca and I were just having a little chat."

"It seemed a serious sort of chat," said Belinda. "When are we going to ride?"

"Now if you wish," said Oliver, turning to me. "If that is all right for you?"

"Yes, it is," I said.

"What shall we look for?" demanded Belinda. "We looked for brown horses last time."

"It will be black this time," said Oliver. "They will be hard to find."

"Black horses, black horses," cried Belinda. "I'll find one. Come on. Don't waste time."

She went to Oliver and put her arm through his.

Belinda came to my room that evening. It was just before their bedtime and she would soon be having her glass of milk and biscuits before washing her teeth and going to bed. She was already undressed and in her dressing gown and slippers. I was surprised to see her but felt a thrill of gratification that she had shown a desire to be with me. Our relationship had certainly undergone a change and that gave me great pleasure.

"How nice of you to come and see me, Belinda," I said. "I see you are almost ready for bed."

"Leah will bring in the milk soon."

"Yes. Did you want to tell me something?"

She was silent for a few seconds, then she burst out: "You're going to marry Oliver, aren't you?"

"No," I said.

"I think he is going to ask you. He likes you a lot."

"What gives you that impression?"

"The way he looks at you and smiles when he talks. He's always talking about you."

"You have become very observant, Belinda."

"I know about these things and I know he wants to marry you. I want him to."

"Why?"

"Because I could come and live with you. We could leave here and be in his house. You and I, Lucie and Oliver. We could have games and treasure hunts all the time."

"Life is not all games and treasure hunts, you know."

"It's always fun with him. I think it would be lovely. The four of us . . . and we could take Leah, of course."

"Before you make too many arrangements, Belinda, I must tell you that I am not going to marry him."

"He will ask you to."

"Two people have to want to marry before they do."

"He'll ask. I thought he was asking you in the summerhouse when we came in. We should have waited and then you could have announced it."

"Listen, Belinda. I know you like him very much and would relish him as a brother-in-law but life doesn't work out as smoothly as that. We can't always have what we want, especially if it involves other people. I am not going to marry him."

"Why not?"

"I don't want to marry him."

"Everyone wants to marry when they get old."

"How can you know?"

"Well, they talk about it. It's what you have to do when you get old."

"You don't have to. And I am not going to marry Mr. Gerson."

"But he wants to marry you."

"How do you know?"

"I can tell."

"Then you are very wise."

"You are not planning to marry someone else, are you?"

I hesitated a moment too long and she was very perceptive.

"I believe you want to," she said accusingly.

"Look, Belinda, you don't know anything about these things. I am not going to marry Mr. Gerson."

"But *why* not? It would be wonderful. If you don't, it will spoil everything. We could all be together. It would be such fun."

She looked as though she were going to burst into tears. I put my arms round her.

"Things don't always work out as people want them to. People marry because they believe they have found the one and only person with whom they can live happily. You'll understand one day. Now, go and have your milk. It will be getting cold."

Her face hardened and she flounced out of the room.

I asked myself: Why did I think she had changed? She wants everything her own way . . . even my marriage!

Nightmare

It was late May before we went to Cornwall. I
had been receiving Pedrek's letters regularly, but
they were not enough, so it was with great delight
that I set out. Belinda and Lucie were delighted
at the prospect—Miss Stringer slightly less so. As
for Leah, it was difficult to know what she felt.
I was sure she would be glad to see her native
town, but she would have to pay frequent visits to
her mother and I supposed that was a less attractive proposition.

Life had run smoothly since Christmas. Belinda
seemed more contented than ever before. Mrs.
Emery said: "It's good to see her more settled
like. She's lost that moody broody way she used
to have . . . picking quarrels . . . and wanting to
be better than anyone else." It was true.

Oliver Gerson was a frequent visitor. He came
when Benedict was there and they spent a good
deal of time together but he usually managed
to ride with us. He was as friendly as ever and although I would sometimes find him regarding
me ruefully, he did not refer to his proposal. He
seemed to be biding his time.

He always showed his affection for Belinda and
she blossomed when he was around. Moreover the

pleasure inspired by his visits seemed to linger after he had gone and I was sure she lived in a state of pleasant anticipation wondering when he would come again.

I had thought, when I first told her we were going to Cornwall, she would raise objections for it was hardly likely that Oliver would visit us there and for a time it really seemed as though that was on her mind. But after a while she was as excited as Lucie about going back there.

I was glad of that, for although recently she had changed so much for the better, I remembered how sullen she could be and I did not want the pleasure in the visit to be spoilt in any way.

It was wonderful to arrive at the station and to find my grandparents with Pedrek waiting to greet us.

I was caught up in loving embraces and everyone seemed to be talking at once.

"Wonderful to have you here at last." "How well you look!" "We've been counting the days . . . and Lucie . . . and Belinda . . . how they've grown!" "Everyone in the Poldoreys knows you are coming."

And there we were, getting into the carriage, Pedrek beside me, clinging to my hand as though he feared I was going to run away, Belinda and Lucie talking excitedly . . . memories coming back to them. Was Petal still in the stables? Was Snowdrop?

Yes, they were, and waiting to be ridden.

"Oh, there's the sea," cried Lucie. "It looks just the same."

"Did you expect it to turn black or red or violet?" demanded Belinda.

"No, but it's lovely to see it."

"Oh, look, there's Cador."

And there it was indeed, looking as majestic as ever, having that thrilling effect on me, as it always did after absence, making me feel warm and happy.

My grandparents were smiling contentedly.

"The Pencarrons wanted to come over but thought it might be too many for the first day. They'll come tomorrow."

"That's lovely," I said. "Oh, it is wonderful to be back."

"You've had an exciting time in London and Manorleigh, I daresay," said my grandmother.

"It's still exciting to be here."

"We had a treasure hunt at Christmas," Belinda announced.

"That must have been fun. We could do something like that at Cador."

"Oh, it wouldn't be the same. Mr. Gerson did this one. He wrote poetry and you had to find it. I won, didn't I, Lucie?"

"You just beat me by four seconds," said Lucie.

"It must have been very exciting," said my grandmother.

"It was the best treasure hunt in the world," said Belinda nostalgically.

And then we were at Cador. It was like coming home. I was happy. I should see Pedrek often.

He had told me he returned to his family at week-ends but had contrived to have a few days off because of my arrival.

I think I was happier than I had ever been since the death of my mother.

I went to my room and sat at the window looking out at the sea. Lucie and Belinda had already gone to the stables to assure themselves that Petal and Snowdrop were really there.

My grandmother came to my room.

"Do you want any help with unpacking?" she asked.

"None at all," I assured her.

She came over to the window and I stood up and we were in each other's arms.

"It seems such ages, Rebecca," she said.

"Yes. I was longing to come."

"And now . . . you and Pedrek. It will be wonderful."

"Yes . . . I know."

"The Pencarrons are so pleased. You know how they are."

"Yes, they are a pair of old darlings."

"We've always been such friends . . . more like a family."

"We always thought of ourselves like that."

"Now it will be a reality. Pedrek was saying that if he worked hard and passes the exams, by the end of the course he'll be fully fledged. Old Jos Pencarron said *he* never had any degrees or diplomas and he's managed the mine all these years. But it seems nowadays that bits of paper count. When you marry you'll be near us . . . that's what gives your grandfather and me such pleasure."

There was a knock on the door.

"Come in," said my grandmother.

The door opened and a girl entered the room. She could not have been more than sixteen years old. She had very dark hair—almost black, lovely dark eyes and an olive skin. I should have thought her foreign looking if we had not quite a number of her type in Cornwall. There was a Spanish touch about her. It was said that people of her coloring and type of feature were the result of the visit of Spaniards to the Cornish shores when the Armada had been scattered along the coast and many a shipwrecked sailor had managed to reach land, had settled there, and married the local girls so introducing Spanish blood into Celtic Cornwall. This girl was voluptuous and very attractive.

She stood there expectantly, her lively eyes surveying my baggage.

"This is Madge," said my grandmother. "She's been with us a month now and works in the kitchen."

"I was sent, Ma'am, to see if I could help Miss Rebecca with her unpacking."

"Thank you," I said with a little laugh, "but I can manage myself. I don't really need any help."

Still she hesitated, seeming reluctant to go.

"That's all right then, Madge," said my grandmother. "Just go and tell them Miss Rebecca can manage by herself."

She bobbed a little curtsy and, looking disappointed, went out.

"What a striking looking girl," I said to my grandmother.

"Yes, she's very willing, I believe. I think she is very grateful to be here."

"You say she has only been here a month or so."

"Yes. She comes from Land's End way. Mrs. Fellows heard of her and said she could do with a girl in the kitchen. She's a bit shorthanded since Ada left to get married. So she came here."

"Where had she been before? She seems quite young."

"She's from a family of eight . . . the eldest, I think. The father is one of those fanatical Bible thumpers. All hell fire and the wrath of the Lord type."

"Oh, there are a lot of those in Cornwall."

"They interpret the Bible their way and being by nature sadistic they want vengeance on all sinners which means, of course, people who don't agree with them. If their sort had their way we should have stakes set up on Bodmin Moor and people being burned to death as they were in the days of Bloody Mary."

"What happened to the girl then?"

"He threw her out."

"What had she done?"

"Exchanged pleasantries with one of the cowmen. She must have been heard laughing on a Sunday. Then she was caught, talking with him, we heard, but it might have been something more. In any case she was turned out. Poor child. A sister of Mrs. Fellows took her in and then asked Mrs. Fellows if she could find a place for the girl. Hence she is here."

"What a lot of trouble these people cause. By the way, this reminds me of Mrs. Polhenny. How is she?"

"Still fighting the good fight with all her might. You'll see her on that bicycle of hers. It shakes her up quite a bit but it helps her to get round and, as she tells me every time I see her, she's doing the Lord's work."

"Well, I'm glad this girl Madge found somewhere to go."

"You'll see her around. She's the sort of girl who makes herself seen and heard. Well, we'll talk later on. Just now I think I ought to go down and see what's happening. We're going to eat soon and then you can have an early night."

When she had left me I unpacked, washed and changed my travelling clothes. I went downstairs where the children, freshly washed and combed, were already assembled with the rest of the family for the meal.

Pedrek was at my side. We talked eagerly. He told me how he was progressing at the college and how fortunate it was that it was so near. Being at St Austell enabled him to get to Pencarron for week-ends, and we should be seeing each other frequently while I was at Cador.

It was a very happy evening and I reminded myself it was a prelude. It was wonderful to be at Cador.

I had not been in my room for more than five minutes when there was a knock on the door and my grandmother came in. This was the usual ritual. Whenever we met after a long absence she would come to my room on the first night and we would have what she called a "Catching-up chat."

"Well," I said as she sat in one of the armchairs. "What is the news?"

"I'll tell you the worst first," she said. "There's been an accident at Pencarron Mine. It upset Josiah very much. He's always had such a record for safety, which is due to meticulous and continual checks. So . . . although it wasn't so bad as it might have been, it has upset him."

"That's terrible. Pedrek did not mention it."

"We agreed not to . . . on your first night, and there wasn't an opportunity really. It happened six weeks ago. Something caved in. It was possible to get most of the men out, but one was badly hurt, Jack Kellaway. It was . . . tragic."

"How dreadful! Was he married?"

"Yes, with one child. A girl of eight or nine. Mary . . . Mary Kellaway . . . the poor wife, was distracted. Josiah was in a terrible state. I remember the day the news came through. It was the night shift. It was what happened afterwards which was really so dreadful. Jack Kellaway was so badly hurt that he would never work again. He could just crawl about the cottage. There was no hope for him really. He had always been a good husband and father and it was terrible for him. He could not bear to be a burden. One day when he was in the house alone he set fire to the place and cut his throat. He wanted it to seem as if he had been burned to death. It was something to do with insurance and he thought his wife and child would be better off without him. Some farm laborers happened to be passing and saw the fire and poor Jack's body was found. It was very sad. The cottage was uninhabitable. His plan had gone wrong."

"What a terrible story!"

"Josiah is going to see that Mary Kellaway and the girl are all right. The child is Mary too. He's going to build a cottage for them. In the meantime we had to find somewhere for them to live. There wasn't anything available except Jenny Stubbs' old cottage near the pool."

"So she is there?"

My grandmother nodded.

It was the cottage where Lucie had been born and spent her first years. Once I had been held captive there. I had always felt there was something mysterious about it. It was hardly the place to revive the poor widow's spirits. I said so to my grandmother.

"I think she was glad to be quiet with a roof over her head and it was the only place. She seems to have settled in there. Oh, I know, it's

336

rather eerie. It's that pool really . . . nothing to do with the cottage. It's quite ordinary . . . just like all the others around here. It's all that talk about the monastery being at the bottom of the water."

"A lot of people still believe that."

"Well, the Cornish are notoriously superstitious."

"My mother always had a strong feeling about the pool."

"I know."

We were silent, thinking of her, then I said: "Are they still talking about the bells at the bottom of the pool which are supposed to ring to herald disaster?"

"Of course. They always did. The point is that people remember they heard them after the event."

"What else has been happening?"

"One of the boats was lost in a gale. The gales were worse than usual this year."

"A string of disasters."

"Well, there are always the gales. Mrs. Jones had twins and Flora Grey is expecting a baby."

"Good work for Mrs. Polhenny. How is she?"

"Doing her duty. Now tell me about yourself. The season went well, didn't it? And you emerged engaged to be married."

"That is what all girls are expected to do. But ours is a secret so I don't get the glory."

My grandmother laughed. "It is . . . wonderful. Our dearest hopes realized."

"I did not know you were so dedicated to the idea."

"We didn't feel we could interfere. A marriage should be arranged between the two chief parties concerned."

"But it is nice to find approval all round."

"You haven't told your stepfather?"

"Why should I?"

"He's your guardian, I suppose. He'll have to know."

"You don't think he'll raise objections."

She was silent and I flushed with indignation. Then I was laughing. "He won't care," I said. "He's not interested. All he thinks about is getting on with his political career."

"He did give you that expensive season."

"He probably expected me to marry some great nobleman . . . someone who would bring kudos to him. 'Rebecca Mandeville, stepdaughter of rising politician Benedict Lansdon, is to marry the Duke of . . .' "

"Uncle Peter was like that. He always wanted such things to be noticed. Well, Benedict is his grandson. He might have the same thing in mind."

I faced my grandmother. "If ever he tried to stop us . . ."

She smiled at me. "Don't worry. We would talk him round."

I stamped my foot in sudden rage. "It's not his affair."

"He might think differently."

"I would not have it, Granny."

"Well, don't let's imagine something which has not happened yet."

"I think we were right in not telling people. We should wait until Pedrek and I are married."

She did not answer. I knew it was something she would discuss with my grandfather later.

She changed the subject and said: "The children look well."

"Leah turned out to be good for them."

"She does a lot of sewing and they have beautifully embroidered dresses. She is always stitching. I think she is happy. But one can never be sure with Leah."

"She must enjoy coming back here . . . after all it was her home."

"I think she had a bad time before she escaped."

"There was a change in her after she went up to High Tor. It must have been strange to her to find she was more or less working for the same people. Who would have thought Benedict would have married Celeste Bourdon?"

"It was rather surprising. I think it was their connections with Cornwall which made them interested in each other in the first place."

"I'm glad he married again. We all know how it was between him and Angelet. They were made for each other. I think he suffered terribly. I like to think of him . . . settling down."

"He hasn't settled down."

I told her about the locked room, the sadness of Celeste and the uneasy situation between him and Belinda.

"Belinda is very much aware of it," I said. "It is quite wrong. But she is much better now. Miss

Stringer is very good for her and Leah, of course, dotes on her. She probably lets her have too much of her own way. But what is rather nice is that she seems to be getting fond of me. Lucie is a help."

"Dear Lucie! One would think she might be the one to develop complexes."

"She knows of her birth. I thought it best that she should learn of it through me and not discover some other way. Belinda has a knack of finding out things and I did not want her taunting Lucie with it. Oh, they are good enough friends, but you know what children are. Lucie knows that I brought her into the household because her mother died. She does not know of course that her mother was strange and her father unknown. I said her father was dead . . . as he may well be . . . and that her mother lived near Cador and we had known her for a long time. She seemed content to leave it at that."

"I am sure you will never regret insisting that we take her."

"I had to do it, Granny. It was some compulsion."

"You are a good sweet girl, Rebecca. You know what a comfort you have been to us."

"Granny, we are getting morbid again."

"All right . . . I won't. Tell me about Belinda."

"Christmas was good. There is a friend of my stepfather . . . well, a business associate really. He came down. He's one of those suave men . . . very charming to everyone. Men of the world, I

340

think you call them. He was particularly nice to Belinda and that made her very happy."

"What that child needs is tenderness . . . special tenderness."

"If only her father would notice her. I think that is what she wants. After all he is her father. But I notice that he avoids looking at her . . . and she knows it, too. It makes her truculent, always calling attention to herself . . . always wanting to be better than anyone."

"How does Lucie react?"

"Lucie has a sunny temperament. She takes it without concern. I think she is aware that Belinda is the daughter of the house and that she is the one who is privileged to be brought into it."

"She is a dear child."

I agreed. "And a wonderful companion for Belinda."

"All was for the best then. But what are we going to do about Belinda and her father? How could we show him what he is doing to the child?"

"I don't think he can help it. It's a sad household, Granny. I liked it better at Manorleigh . . . when he was in London. Then Celeste had to be with him and we had the house to ourselves."

"How's Mrs. Emery?"

"Very grand and so is Mr. E. He's developed great dignity. They both have. I get on well with Mrs. Emery who invites me to drink a cup of her best tea . . . Darjeeling . . . which comes from the Strand in London, she tells me. It's only used on special occasions and when I take tea with her that is one of them."

"She's a good woman and I am glad she is with you. Now, my dear, it is getting late and time for bed. I'll see you tomorrow . . . and the next day . . . and the next . . . and the next. Sleep well in your old bed and in the morning we'll talk and talk. Goodnight, my darling."

"Goodnight, Granny dear."

It was a wonderful feeling to have come home.

In a few days I had settled in and it seemed as if I had never been away. I had done all the familiar things. I had walked into the town and been greeted by Gerry Fish wheeling his barrow through the streets and beyond as his father old Tom Fish had before him. He shouted a greeting. "Good day to 'ee, Miss Rebecca. How be to, then? You back with us now for a spell, me 'andsome?" Old Mrs. Grant, who had kept the wool shop when my mother was a girl and still did, although her hands were too crippled with rheumatism to allow her to do her crochet work now, came to the door of the shop to welcome me. There were the young Trenarths who had taken over the Fishermen's Arms from old Penny-leg and were, to the dismay of some, introducing new ways.

They all had a welcome for me.

I paused to chat with the fishermen who were mending their nets and received a detailed description of the gale in which one of the boats had been lost.

It was comforting to realize that life did not change very much here.

The Pencarrons came over the day after our arrival and there was a happy reunion. Both of them had adopted a rather proprietorial attitude towards me. I was now to be their granddaughter-in-law, and they wanted me to know how happy that made them.

My grandmother had warned me not to mention the mine disaster to them.

"It upset Josiah so much," she explained. "No doubt he'll tell you about it later on . . . or I expect Pedrek will. Just don't bring it up. Let him enjoy the reunion."

It was a very happy day. Pedrek was not with us but he would be home for the week-end, and it was arranged that I should go over to Pencarron on Saturday. "So it will be a lovely surprise when he comes in," said his fond grandmother.

I spent a happy week-end at Pencarron and on the Sunday Pedrek came back with me to Cador. There would be many week-ends like that.

Pedrek and I went riding together and we talked of the future as we made our plans. We would not live at Pencarron. We would look for a house and if we could not find what we wanted we would build our own.

We spent happy hours planning it.

"By the sea or on the moor?" asked Pedrek.

"Somewhere between the two perhaps?"

"The best of both worlds."

"Are you going to enjoy it, Pedrek?"

"Superbly. But isn't it frustrating to have to wait?"

I agreed that it was.

"They say that anticipation is the best part of life."

"We will make the realization even better."

"Oh, we will," I said fervently.

I was delighted to see that Belinda was enjoying Cornwall. I had wondered how she would feel when the possibility of seeing Oliver Gerson was removed, for indeed she had seemed to have an adoration—an obsession one might say—for the man. Perhaps I had exaggerated it. She seemed so fond of me now, which was gratifying. I was very content to bask in the affection of the two girls and the love of Pedrek and my grandparents. I was thinking that, in spite of the fact that I had lost my mother and could not forget that, I had a great deal to be thankful for.

Leah took the children into the Poldoreys and on the way she called in to see her mother. The girls were intrigued by Mrs. Polhenny. They rolled about in glee when they described her on her "bone-shaker."

"She looked so funny!" shrieked Belinda.

"We thought she was going to fall off," said Lucie.

"Did she give you an exhibition then?" I asked.

"We went there . . . and there was no one in

and just as we were going away she came up on that . . ."

They were hysterical.

"And what did she say to you?"

"We had to go in and sit in the parlor," said Lucie.

"There were pictures all round the room. Jesus on the cross . . ."

"And another one carrying a little lamb."

"And somebody with a lot of arrows sticking out of his body. She asked Leah if our souls were saved."

"And what did Leah say?"

"She said she looked after us in a right and proper manner," Lucie told me.

"Mrs. Polhenny was looking at me all the time," said Belinda.

She and Lucie could say no more because they were laughing so much.

I told my grandmother about it afterwards. "They found it quite hilarious," I added.

"I am glad they did. I should have thought they would have hated it and wanted to get away."

"You would think they had been to some entertainment."

"Well, I'm glad they see it that way. I daresay Leah would like to go and see her mother now and then and if they would go with her willingly, that's all to the good."

"It would take Mrs. Polhenny's attention off Leah perhaps."

"Yes, that is what I thought."

The new girl, Madge, was often with the children. They obviously liked her very much. I had seen her in the garden where she had doubtless been sent to bring something in from the kitchen garden, and the children would be with her. I liked to hear their laughter.

My grandmother had noticed, too.

"She is young and full of high spirits," she said. "I don't see why she shouldn't relieve Leah a little."

"You mean to give Leah time to go off and see her mother?"

My grandmother grimaced. "No. To give her a little time to herself. And it would be good for Madge. She is little more than a child herself and she is far from home."

I had wanted the girls to enjoy Cornwall and I was delighted that they seemed to be doing so.

I gathered that they often went to St Branok Pool. They talked about it. They also enjoyed the moors and when we went out together they would lead the way either to the pool or the moors.

There had been a great deal of gossip about people's seeing white hares and black dogs, not only at Pencarron Mine, but on the disused one on the moors.

I noticed that Belinda seemed to have a particular interest in disaster. She liked to talk about old superstitions. Lucie did, too. Their eyes would grow wide while they discussed the knackers who were reputed to inhabit the mines and could, by some magic they possessed, bring disaster to any miners whom they disliked. It was the same with the fishermen. There were many superstitions about the evil which could befall them if they broke any of the ancient customs.

Down by the pool they made the acquaintance of young Mary Kellaway. She would often come out of Jenny's old cottage to talk to them.

She was a strange looking child with long straight hair and a sad look in her eyes, which was understandable considering the tragedy in which she had recently become involved.

I discovered that it was she who had told them of the hares and dogs and little old men in the mines.

"It shows what they do," was Belinda's verdict. "Mr. Kellaway must have made them angry and then they made the mine fall down on him."

"That's nonsense," I said.

"How do you know?" demanded Belinda. "You weren't there."

"Because such things don't happen. The accident was due to a fault in the mine."

"Mary says . . ."

"You shouldn't talk about it with Mary. She should try to forget."

"How can she forget it when her house is burned down?"

"She'll soon have a new house."

"But you don't *forget* . . ."

How right she was! One did not forget.

My grandmother said she thought it was good that they had made friends with Mary. "I'd ask her over to Cador to play with them but you know what the servants are . . . and you'd have them saying that if she can come why can't all the other children in the neighborhood do the same?"

"I think they like seeing her at the pool. I wish they had chosen some other meeting place but of course it is so near the cottage."

They both told me the story of the wicked monks who would not repent and were warned by Heaven but they went on doing what they shouldn't and the flood was sent.

"It was like Noah's," Lucie told me.

"No it wasn't, silly," cut in Belinda. "That was a long time ago. This was when they had monks and things they didn't have in Noah's day."

"How do you know?" demanded Lucie.

"I do know. There wasn't an ark for them and they were all drowned. They're still down there at the bottom of the pool . . . because wicked people don't always die. They have to go on living in misery which it must be down at the bottom of the pool with all that dirty water. And the bells ring when something is going to happen. I wish I could hear the bells."

"You wouldn't want something awful to happen, surely?" I said.

"I wouldn't mind."

"As long as it didn't happen to you," I retorted with a laugh.

I often heard them discussing the bells and I

often thought that the reason they went to the pool so frequently was in the hope of hearing them rather than to play with Mary.

I had formed the habit of going in to say good-night to them when they were in bed.

There were two single beds on either side of the room and Leah said they used to talk to each other after she had put out the lights. I thought it was very pleasant for them to have each other and rejoiced once more that I had been able to bring Lucie into the house and give her a good home. It was proving beneficial not only to her but to Belinda as well.

One night I went in and I heard Belinda say: "It must have been exciting when they dragged the pool . . . to look for Rebecca and found the murderer."

I was shocked that they had learned that. I did not mention it. Belinda seemed to know that I might have heard her comment and guessed it was a subject I would not encourage for she immediately said that Petal had to go to the blacksmith the next day. Tom Grimes had said they could go in and see her shod.

I left them, wondering where they got their information. I suppose dramatic events were remembered and it was inevitable that they should hear some of them.

It was one of our Saturdays which had become very precious to us. Pedrek came riding over to

Cador where I was waiting for him. We were to go off riding together.

"Why can't we come, too?" demanded Belinda.

"Because they have a good deal to talk about," my grandmother explained.

"I don't mind listening," said Belinda, which made us all laugh.

She was a little sullen when we left and Lucie showed clearly that she did not like it either. But for Pedrek and me the happy day had begun.

We were in such harmony that we did not always have to speak; we often understood the other's train of thought. This gave me a wonderfully cozy feeling. I was growing closer than ever to Pedrek—as close as I had been to my mother—and that gave me great content.

We would laugh all the time—at nothing often, just out of sheer happiness. Simple things seemed extraordinarily amusing—and there were so many plans to be made.

It was nearly a year since he had gone to college, he reminded me. "Half way there. Just think of that."

"It seems such a long time since you asked me to marry you."

"It seems an age . . . yet half of it has gone. Sometimes I think I can't wait and I am on the point of abducting you."

"That wouldn't be necessary," I told him. "I'd come without protest."

"Then . . . why don't we?"

"What about college?"

He was thoughtful. "There's a good deal to learn."

"You must learn it then. You would hate to think there were things you didn't know. The more you learn the more likely you are to stop accidents like . . ."

"I think so. There is so much known about the soil now. I am finding out all sorts of things which would astonish my grandfather."

"We shall have to be patient for another year."

"I don't see why we couldn't start on the house. It will take some time to get all that settled. Wouldn't it be wonderful to get it all ready . . . so that it is there for us. We could do all that while we are waiting."

"That would be fun. I wonder what your grandfather would say about it."

"He would probably like the idea and I am sure my grandmother would."

"It would make us feel that we were almost there."

"I tell you what we'll do. We'll start looking. Next week-end we'll begin in earnest. How's that?"

"It's a marvelous idea."

"It will have to be in the vicinity of the mine."

"It looks as if we may have to build."

"Yes . . . something in between the families. We want to please both sides."

"They would appreciate it if we were half way. We'll start looking now."

The search added zest to the day.

We stopped at an inn—a charming old place

called The King's Head. There was a picture on the old sign, of Charles II, saturnine in spite of a certain lustful look and a luxuriously curly wig. We went into the parlor with its oak beams, leaded windows and great open fireplace round which sparkling horse brasses were displayed.

We drank cider from pewter pots and ate cheese with hot bread straight from the oven.

We talked of the house we would have. I saw it materialize before my eyes—the hall, the wide staircase, the rooms upstairs, and I realized I was creating a place which was something between Cador and Pencarron Manor.

"You wouldn't like a Victorian house," said Pedrek. "Your heart is in the past."

"I'll tell you something," I said. "I wouldn't mind what period it was as long as we were in it together."

On the way back we looked for likely sites and inspected them critically.

"It would be very open here. Imagine the southwest gales."

"And wouldn't it be lonely?"

"Not with servants. Lucie will be there. Oh, Pedrek, what about Belinda?"

"She can come, too."

"She'll have to be with her father. He will insist. He has to preserve the family atmosphere."

"She can come and stay with us."

"I don't know how she and Lucie will feel about being apart."

"Are they such good friends?"

352

"Not exactly. I think they have become a habit to each other. They quarrel of course as all children do . . . but I don't think they would like to be separated."

"They'll get used to it."

"I wonder what my stepfather will say. He is supposed to be my guardian, you know."

"I shall be your guardian soon."

"I am not sure I like this talk of guardians. I like to think I am my own. But there is a point. I should have to get his consent, I suppose."

"We'll get married first and tell him afterwards."

We agreed that that was a good idea; but it did not answer the question of how the girls would feel to be separated.

They would be a year older then. They seemed so knowledgeable sometimes that I forgot how young they were. But I suppose most children are aware of what is going on. They have sharp enquiring minds; all they lack is the experience which comes through living.

Pedrek came back with me to Cador.

The girls dashed out to welcome me home and they both flung themselves at me. Belinda first . . . Lucie in her turn. It was comforting to receive such a welcome.

"We've been riding this afternoon. Then we went for a walk with Leah . . . to the pool."

"I suppose you did," I said. I turned to Pedrek. "It's one of their favorite places."

"Well, it does have an air of mystery."

"All those legends . . . bells and monks," I said.

"And other things," added Belinda.

"What things?" I asked.

"Other things," she repeated, smiling mysteriously.

My grandmother came into the room. "Oh, you're back. Good. Had a pleasant day?"

We assured her we had had a wonderful day.

Pedrek stayed to dine which was served a little earlier on Saturdays so that he would not be too late getting back to Pencarron.

We talked to my grandparents about our search for a suitable site on which to build our future home.

"Well, did you decide?"

"Not really. We'll look further next week, won't we, Pedrek?"

"Talking of houses," said my grandfather, "I saw the people at High Tor this afternoon. They're leaving."

"Are they? After all this time?"

"Yes. The son is coming home from Germany. He's been living there for some years. He says he fancies getting a place in Dorset and . . . I've forgotten what their name is."

"Stenning," supplied my grandmother.

"That's right. Stenning. Well, he said they will be getting a place there to be near the son. They rented High Tor because they didn't want to commit themselves to buying before their son came home."

"That means High Tor will either be to let or for sale," said my grandmother looking at me.

I glanced at Pedrek.

"High Tor," I murmured. "It's a nice place."

"And ancient," added Pedrek.

"Well," added my grandmother. "It's an idea. I daresay it will be some time before the Stennings are ready to leave, but . . . as I said . . . it's an idea."

High Tor had taken possession of my thoughts and the next Saturday Pedrek and I rode out there. It looked different from what it had before. I suppose that was because there was a possibility that it might one day be our house.

"Do you think," said Pedrek, "that we might call on the Stennings?"

"Why not? They may not know us well but they know who we are."

"Let's go then," said Pedrek.

So we rode in through the cobbled courtyard under the archway to the oak iron-studded door.

A servant came out, and Pedrek asked if Mr. or Mrs. Stenning were at home.

Mrs. Stenning came down. She was a little surprised but extremely hospitable and soon we were seated in the drawing room. We told her that we had heard that she and her husband were contemplating leaving High Tor to settle in Dorset and as we planned to marry in a year's time we were interested in the house.

She opened her eyes wide and said: "What a good idea! I don't know whether the owners want to sell or rent it . . . but I could find out. You probably know them."

"Very well," I said. "My stepfather is married to the lady who was Miss Celeste Bourdon."

"Of course. Well, that *is* interesting. We shall be leaving fairly soon. We are taking a house in Dorchester and there we shall stay until we find a suitable property. This is a very interesting house, this. We shall be sorry to leave it. Most of the furniture is ours though the Bourdons did leave one or two pieces. But in any case you would want your own. Would you like to see over it?"

We spent an interesting hour being taken round. The house had been built in the late sixteenth or early seventeenth century. I liked the gables with their pediments and the casements and leaded lights.

Mr. Stenning joined us and he was quite knowledgeable about architecture. He said he thought the house was in the style of the Inigo Jones period and the architects had learned a great deal from him.

"He went to Italy and studied the buildings there. You can detect the influence of that."

I was not interested so much in the architecture. I was just seeing it as our future home.

The Stennings insisted that we take tea with them and this we did in the drawing room with its gracious proportions and casement windows. It was indeed a beautiful house.

We talked of it incessantly and could hardly wait to get back to Cador and tell my grandparents about it.

They were as thrilled as we were.

"It would be ideal for you," said my grandfather. "I daresay we shall soon hear what the Bourdons intend to do."

We became obsessed by the house. We talked of nothing else.

A few days after we had been shown over it, we had a note from the Stennings saying that if at any time we wished to look at High Tor, or ask them questions about it, they would be delighted to show or tell us if they knew the answer.

We took the first opportunity of calling.

They told us there was a change of plans and they intended to leave a few weeks earlier than they had originally arranged to. In ten days they would be gone.

They could give us the Chislehurst address of the Bourdons or perhaps we would prefer to approach them through Mrs. Lansdon.

The Pencarrons came over to Cador to dine and there was a consultation between the two lots of grandparents. Mine were more romantically minded than Mr. Pencarron. "We didn't want to find we had a ruin on our hands," he said.

Pedrek reminded him that houses which had stood up to the weather for a few hundred years could surely do so for a few hundred more. But

Mr. Pencarron thought that a good solid modern place might be better.

"It's due to being brought up at Cador," said my grandmother. "There is something romantic about living in houses where lots of people have lived before."

"Nevertheless," insisted Mr. Pencarron, "we want to have a good look at the place."

"That can be easily done," said my grandfather.

Pedrek and I knew that we wanted it. We did go round it once more and our rides always took us past it. We would sit in a field where we could look up at the grey gables and dream of the days when it would be ours.

Pedrek had written to the Bourdons and received a reply.

They were not entirely certain what they intended to do but would decide quickly. We sighed with impatience and continued to regard it as our house.

We had just had luncheon. It was one of those week days which I lived through, longing for the week-end to come. The children had gone for a ride, one of the grooms accompanying them. I was with my grandmother who wanted to show me something in the garden. As we came out of the house one of the maids announced a visitor.

I was amazed and excited to see Jean Pascal Bourdon. He took my grandmother's hand and kissed it; then did the same to me.

"What a pleasure!" he said. "I have descended

on you charming ladies to pay my respects. I am to be in Cornwall for a little while. How good it is to see you! And Mademoiselle Rebecca is looking so well . . .”

“Have you had luncheon?” asked my grandmother.

“I have indeed.”

“Then come in. Would you like some wine . . . or a little coffee?”

“Some coffee please. That would be nice.”

When we were in the drawing room I went to the bell pull and very soon Madge appeared. I noticed Jean Pascal’s eyes on her, assessing her; and I remembered that old habit of his. Girls like Madge were always aware of masculine attention. She bridled a little and said demurely: “Yes, Ma’am?”

“Will you bring some coffee please, Madge?”

“Yes, Ma’am.” With a little bob she disappeared.

Jean Pascal said: “I expect you have guessed why I am here? It concerns High Tor, of course.”

“You know we are interested.”

“Yes. May I say that *I* was most . . . interested to hear that you were interested.”

“It’s no secret. Rebecca and Pedrek Cartwright are thinking of buying a house.”

He raised his eyebrows and my grandmother went on: “They will be married in a year or so.”

“May I offer my congratulations?” He looked at me as though the prospect of my marriage was a mild source of amusement.

"You may," I said, "and thank you for them."

"It is unexpected news."

"It was not all that unexpected to us," said my grandmother. "Pedrek and Rebecca have been good friends for years."

He nodded. "The Stennings will be leaving shortly," he said.

"Are you staying there . . . at High Tor?"

He smiled. "Yes. There is plenty of room. It is not a small house, you know. And we have business to discuss. Some furniture belongs to my family . . . but most of it in the house is theirs."

The coffee had come. I noticed his renewed interest in Madge and I thought to myself: It is a habit with him. He assesses all females. How different he was from Pedrek. When Jean Pascal married, his wife would be wondering all the time if he was unfaithful.

Over coffee we discussed the house.

He said: "My family are a little uncertain at the moment. They are leaving Chislehurst."

"Oh," I said blankly. "Did they plan to come back to Cornwall?"

He paused. I had betrayed my eagerness to possess the house. Mr. Pencarron would say that was a foolish thing to do before a prospective seller.

He smiled at me and went on: "No. They will not come back here. The Empress kept a little court at Chislehurst of which my family were a part as they were of the Imperial Court before the *débâcle*. She has suffered much in exile . . . the loss of her husband and now after the death of her son in the Zulu war she finds it difficult to be happy there and wants to move. She is to go to Farnborough and my parents will give up their place in Chislehurst and go with her."

"So . . . not to Cornwall," I murmured.

"No . . . no. That would be too far away. They will go to Farnborough."

"The point is," said my grandmother, "what of High Tor?"

He smiled at us blandly. "Yes . . . I am sure they will sell."

My grandmother and I exchanged glances of triumph.

"When will it be on the market?"

"If you are interested, you shall have the opportunity to buy before we put it there."

"Thank you," said my grandmother. "That's what we hoped."

"Well, are we not friends?"

"I am sure my husband and the Pencarrons will want to look at the place."

"But naturally. Perhaps when the Stennings have left we can start to talk business."

"Excellent," said my grandmother. "More coffee?"

"Please, yes. It is delicious."

I went over and took his cup. He smiled up at me and there was something secretive in his eyes.

"And when is the wedding to be?"

"Oh, not yet . . . not for some time yet. Mr.

Cartwright is at college and will be there for another year or so."

"And when he emerges . . . that will be the happy day?"

"Oh yes . . ."

"It is a pleasure for me to think that my old home will be yours."

When he had taken his leave my grandmother looked at me with shining eyes.

"I don't think there will be any difficulty," she said. "Your grandfather and I want to give you the house as a wedding present, but there will be some argument for I happen to know the Pencarrons want to do the same."

"How lucky we are! We do realize it, Granny. How many people about to get married have such lovely generous grandparents arguing over who is going to give them the most wonderful house in the world?"

"We are all so happy," she said. "Because we are going to have you close to us for the rest of our lives."

There was no talk of anything but the house. On the following Saturday Jean Pascal was invited to lunch. The Stennings were also invited. They talked a great deal about their imminent departure. Pedrek, with his grandparents, was present.

"I hope you will find the perfect place in Dorchester," said my grandmother to the Stennings. "I hear it is a beautiful town."

"We shall not be far from the sea, as we have been here. And we have been so happy in Cornwall, haven't we, Philip?"

Mr. Stenning agreed that they had.

Pedrek and I exchanged glances throughout the meal. Marriage seemed so much closer now that we had a home in view.

After luncheon, when we were taking coffee in the drawing room, Jean Pascal talked to Pedrek and me.

"It's not easy to assess a house when people are living in it. As soon as the Stennings leave you must come over."

"Which pieces of furniture belong to your family?" I asked.

"Some rather heavy stuff. There is a fine old four poster bed which my parents would have liked to move, but it is rather ancient and they were not sure how it would stand up to the journey, so they left it. There are one or two heavy cabinets. Not a great deal. You must come over and see it. When they have gone we'll make an appointment."

"That will be wonderful."

When our guests had gone we were still discussing the house. It had been agreed that the grandparents would buy it between them and it should be a joint present from the four of them.

I said: "We are so lucky."

"Nothing but what you deserve, my dear," said Mr. Pencarron. "Mind you . . . it's got to be right. I'm still suspicious of these old places. There

363

are some who think that a ghost or two make up for a leaking roof and crumbling walls. That's not my idea."

"There may be some repairs needed," said my grandfather.

"We'll get someone down to look at it."

"As soon as the Stennings have left we can give the place a real overhaul," said my grandmother.

In the middle of the following week, I left the house in the afternoon to take a short ride. As I rode out of the stables I met Jean Pascal.

"Hello," he said. "I know you often take a solitary ride at this time and I hoped I'd meet you."

"Why . . . has something happened?" I asked in alarm.

"Only this pleasant encounter."

"I thought perhaps you had come over with some news."

"Actually I came over in the hope of seeing you."

"Because . . ."

"Because it seemed a good idea. Look. You are going for a ride. Why don't I accompany you? We could talk as we go."

"Then there is something. Is it about the house?"

"There is a lot to talk about on the subject, is there not? But there are other things."

"Such as . . . ?"

"General conversation. I always think it is amusing to let that take its own course."

"How do you mean?"

"Let it flow . . . let it come naturally."

"Where shall we go?"

"Not to High Tor. I believe you go there frequently. I mean you ride close by. Mrs. Stenning says she sees you."

I felt a little uncomfortable that my naïve excitement about the house had been noticed.

"I am hoping, of course, that everything will go through satisfactorily," I said.

"I should feel the same myself. It will be your new home."

"Mr. Pencarron wants to have a surveyor to look at it. I hope you won't mind."

"No . . . no. I admire him. It is a wise thing to do. Who knows: the old mansion might be ready to crumble about your ears?"

"Oh, I don't think that."

"Nor do I. But Mr. Pencarron is a business man. He does not go out and say, 'This is a pretty house. I will buy it for my grandson and his wife-to-be.' That I admire. He is a realist."

"And that is a quality you admire very much."

"It is wisdom. Romance, oh, that is beautiful, but the wise man, the realist, he says it is beautiful while it lasts . . . whereas a house must endure . . . it must not be blown away by the first strong wind."

"I'm glad you don't mind Mr. Pencarron taking advice. I thought you might be offended."

"Certainly not. I understand. There is much I understand."

"I am sure you are very wise."

I spurred up my horse and we cantered across a field. We looked down at the sea.

"Do you ever feel nostalgic for France?" I asked.

He lifted his shoulders. "I visit now and then. It is enough. If we could go back to the Old France . . . perhaps I would be there. But not this time . . . the communards . . . Gambetta with his Republicans . . . they have destroyed the old France. But you do not want to hear of our politics . . . our mismanagements. I have made this my home now . . . and so have others. That is France for us. These matters are a bore. I will not speak of them."

"I find them interesting . . . as I do our own politics. When I am in London . . ."

"Oh yes, you are at the heart of politics. In the house of your stepfather and my sister. But you will have to renounce all that. You are going to live the life of a lady of the manor. It is what you have chosen. I want to talk to you. Let us find a cosy inn. We can give the horses a rest and talk over a tankard of cider. How is that?"

"Yes, please let us do that. I am sure you have a lot to tell me about High Tor."

The inn he chose was that one where, not so long ago, Pedrek and I had been. There was the King's head with the dark sensuous face of the Merry Monarch depicted on the sign over the door.

"I believe the cider in here is of a particularly good vintage."

We seated ourselves in the inn parlor with the horse brasses and the leaded windows and cider was brought to us by a buxom girl who claimed Jean Pascal's attention for a few fleeting moments.

"Ha!" he said. "The old English inn . . . a feature of the countryside."

"And a very pleasant one."

"I agree!" He lifted his tankard. "Like so much in this country . . . its women for one thing and chief among them Miss Rebecca Mandeville."

"Thank you," I said coolly. "The Stennings are going at the end of the week, are they not?"

He smiled at me. "High Tor occupies your mind to the exclusion of everything else."

"I admit it."

"You see life at the moment in the glow of romance."

"How do you know?"

"Because I know what it is like to be young . . . and in love. And you are both young and in love with the fortunate Pedrek."

"I think we are both fortunate."

"*I* think he is."

There was a warm glow in his eyes. I thought: He cannot resist flirting with any woman . . . even one who, he knows, is on the point of marriage. It is all part of the way in which he looks at women. I supposed I should be amused and I was, to a certain extent, because we were in an inn parlor with mine host and hostess bustling about in the next room. It would have been different had I been alone with him. I felt safe.

He put his tankard on the table and leaned towards me.

"Tell me," he said. "Have you ever had a lover before the worthy Pedrek?"

I flushed hotly. "What do you mean?"

He spread his hands and lifted his shoulders. Like most of his countrymen and -women—I had noticed it in his sister Celeste—he used his hands a great deal in conversation.

"I mean . . . is this Pedrek the first?" He laughed suddenly. "And now you are going to say I am impertinent."

"You read my thoughts," I said. I had risen from my chair and he put out a hand and detained me.

"Do please sit down. You are very young, Mademoiselle Rebecca, and for that reason you close your eyes to much which goes on in the world. It is not a good thing to close one's eyes. If one is going to live well and wisely . . . to have a good marriage and understand what it is all about . . . one must be wise in the ways of the world."

"I thought we were going to talk about the house. Really, I don't want to . . ."

"I know. You don't want to look at reality. You want to make your pretty pictures and paste them over the truth . . . deluding yourself as you do so. There are people who delude themselves all through their lives. Are you going to be one of them?"

368

"Perhaps they are happy doing it."

"Happiness? Can there be true happiness through shutting one's eyes to reality?"

"I don't know what you are trying to say but I don't think it necessary to continue this conversation."

"You are being a little . . . childish . . . is it?"

"Then you must be bored with my company and I will say goodbye. There is no need for you to leave. I may be childish but I am capable of riding back alone. I ride by myself frequently."

"You are very pretty when you are angry."

I turned away impatiently.

"You are afraid to listen to me," he accused.

"Why should I be afraid?"

"Because you fear to listen to the truth."

"I am not afraid, I assure you, but I find your questions offensive."

"About a lover? I apologize. I know you are a virgin and propose to remain so until your wedding night. That is charming, I know. I was merely hinting that a little premarital experience can sometimes be an advantage."

"I cannot understand why you are talking to me like this."

His attitude changed and he became almost humble. "I am foolish," he said. "That is why. Perhaps I am a little envious of Monsieur Pedrek."

I said with what I hoped was a touch of sarcasm: "Now we have returned to the familiar methods. You complain about my veiling the truth with my romanticism so now I will tell you that I do not believe a word you say. You would use the same words, express the same sentiments, to any woman to whom you happened to be talking at the time. It signifies nothing. It is just idle conversation with you."

"You are right. But in this case it happens to be true."

"So you admit that you, who so admire the truth and think it should be revealed to all, are frequently false?"

Again the lifting of the shoulders, the spreading of the hands. "In France," he said, "a young man's father will arrange for him to take a mistress . . . usually an older charming worldly woman. It is to teach him the ways of the world so that when he marries he will not be *gauche*. You understand?"

"I have heard of this, but we are not French and it would seem we have a different code of morals here."

"I doubt that the English are persistently moral while the French are universally corrupt."

"Is this going to become a nationalistic battle between us?"

"By no means. There is so much here that I love, but there are times when your countrymen can be a little hypocritical, posing as the so-virtuous when they might be slightly less so than they proclaim. I think a little experience before marriage is good for us all, so that when we come to the greatest adventure, which is marriage, we know how to deal with those little crises which arise in the best-regulated unions. In all endeavors, experience is something to be cherished."

"Are you suggesting that I . . . should be trying to gain this . . . experience?"

"I would not dare suggest such a thing. In fact I apologize most sincerely for having raised the subject."

"I accept your apology and now we can drop the matter."

"May I refill your tankard?"

"No thanks. I am ready to leave now. I think I should. There are things I have to do at home."

He bowed his head. "First," he said, "I want you to tell me that I am really forgiven."

"You have apologized and I have accepted it."

"I was very foolish."

"I thought you were so wise on account of all your experience which I am sure has been great."

He looked at me in such a forlorn manner that I could not help laughing.

"That is better," he cried. "I believe I am truly forgiven. You see, I have always admired you so much. Your freshness, your beauty, your approach to life. Do not think I do not admire that innocence of yours, that air of chastity . . ."

"Oh please, you are going too far. I may be innocent and ignorant of those matters in which you are so well versed, but I do know flattery when I hear it. And you have laid it on with a trowel, as I have heard it described."

"So I am foolish, am I not?"

"Listen. You think you understand me. Well, I understand you, too. You are very interested in women. You cannot keep your eyes from them. You are looking for a quick seduction with servant girls and in fact everyone you meet. There are some who say this is natural in young men. It is no concern of mine except that I insist they keep their speculative eyes off me."

He smiled in a rather appealing way.

"I am duly chastened," he said. "I see I have been quite foolish."

"Well, I suppose we all are at times."

"Then we are good friends again?"

"Of course. But please don't talk to me in this fashion ever again."

He shook his head emphatically. "And now another tankard to seal our reconciliation?"

"I have had enough, thank you."

"Just a sip . . . or I shall think I am not well and truly forgiven."

The cider was brought and we lifted our tankards.

"Now we are the best of friends," he said. "And we shall talk about High Tor and as soon as the Stennings have gone you and Monsieur Pedrek will come over and I will show you everything you want to see."

"Thank you. That is what we want."

We talked of High Tor and then he began to tell me about the miniature court at Chislehurst and the members of the French aristocracy who visited the Empress from time to time.

He was very amusing and he had a gift for mimicry which could be very funny, particularly when he was imitating his own formal countrymen and -women.

I laughed a great deal and he was delighted. I could not understand what had made him talk to me as he had in the beginning. However, I believed I had made him realize his mistake.

So after all it was quite a pleasant afternoon.

The Stennings had delayed their departure for a week but at length they left; and it was a Tuesday morning when Jean Pascal sent a message to me at Cador.

He was asking Mr. Pencarron to come over that afternoon at three o'clock so that they could clear up a few points which Mr. Pencarron wished to raise. Would I care to come and join them? I sent the messenger back saying that I should be pleased to.

The girls were there when the messenger came and wanted to know what it was all about.

"It's from Monsieur Bourdon," I said.

"From High Tor?" asked Belinda.

"Yes."

"Are you going over there this afternoon?"

"Yes, this afternoon."

"I'd like to come, too," said Lucie.

"Not today. Perhaps some other time. If we have the house you will be there often. It will be great fun getting the furniture and all that."

"Lovely," said Lucie.

I could scarcely wait and immediately after the midday meal I set out for High Tor.

When I arrived there were no grooms about so I took my horse to the stables and went to the house. I rang the bell and heard the clanging ringing through the emptiness. Jean Pascal opened the door.

"Hello," he said. "I'm glad you have come."

"Is Mr. Pencarron here?"

"Not yet . . . but come in."

We went into the hall.

"It looks bigger without the furniture," I said.

"It is easier for you to see where you want to put your own."

"That table?" I asked. "Will you be taking that away or selling it . . . or does it go with the house?"

"We'll see about that. There are one or two other pieces. You might like to see them and decide whether you want them. Shall we look now?"

"What time did Mr. Pencarron say he would come?"

"He was a little uncertain. He said it would depend on some business at the mine." Noticing my anxious look, he went to the door and opened it. "If I leave it ajar he'll be able to come in. Come up to the first floor and look at this vase."

He paused on the landing while we studied it.

"It's rather fine, is it not?" he said.

374

"Yes, it is lovely and something would be needed at that spot."

We went through to the gallery. "You will have to start a picture gallery," he said.

"I daresay my grandparents will have some of the family portraits to pass on. They have plenty, I think."

"You will start a dynasty."

I laughed as he led the way up some stairs and threw open a door of a room. The curtains were still at the windows and in the center of the room was a large four poster bed.

"Bourdon family heirloom," he said.

"It's very grand."

"The velvet of the curtains is a little worn. The pile has rubbed away over the years."

"You will be taking that away, I suppose."

"I daresay my mother will not want to let it go."

He sat down on it and took my hand so suddenly and firmly that before I realized what was happening I was sitting beside him.

I must have looked alarmed for he said: "Are you just a little uneasy?"

"No," I lied. "Should I be?"

"Well . . . perhaps. Here you are in a house alone with a man whom you know to be a bit of a sinner. After all, he has not really made a secret of the fact, has he?"

I attempted to rise, but he held me back.

"You are a little idiot in some ways, Rebecca," he said. "But I adore you."

"Mr. Pencarron will be here at any moment. Don't you think this is a strange way to behave? You apologized for your impertinence before and I accepted your apology."

"I do not like apologizing very much."

"No one does but there are times when it is necessary. So please do stop behaving in this foolish manner."

His reply was to grip me hard and hold me against him. He bent his head and kissed me on the lips.

I was really frightened then. I tried to free myself but he was stronger than I.

"It's time you stopped being a little innocent, Rebecca," he said.

"You . . . you monster!"

"Yes, I am, am I not? I meant what I said the other day when you were so outraged. It is time someone taught you a lesson."

"I do not want lessons from you."

"That is where you are wrong. You need lessons . . . from someone as charming, practiced and understanding as Jean Pascal Bourdon."

"I think you are behaving in a ridiculous manner."

"You would. You are so conventional. Don't hang on to your conventions, Rebecca. For once do what you want to . . . what your instincts tell you to."

"My instincts tell me to slap your face."

"You might try," he said, imprisoning my hands.

"What do you think you are doing?"

"You know very well what I am doing."

"I'm afraid I don't."

"Then you are not thinking very clearly. I told you what you need. You must know the world. You need to live a little before you tie yourself down to a dull existence."

"I think you are mad."

"I am rather . . . at the moment. You are so deliciously innocent. I am fond of you. I've wanted you for a long time. I was just waiting for the opportunity to show you what fun life can be if you will stop being prim. Let yourself go. Throw away your principles. It will be worth it. It will be an experience you need. Have . . . what do you say? . . . a little adventure, a fling? . . . and then you will settle down with your memories . . . to a dull existence in the country."

"Do you really think I would dally with you? You must be out of your senses. A lecherous man who contemplates seducing every woman he sets eyes on and is so conceited that he imagines he only has to offer himself and she will fall swooning at his feet."

"I think if you and I became friends . . . really friends . . . you would find it a pleasurable experience."

"Take your hands off me."

"I can't. The temptation is too great."

"I never want to see you again."

"Don't be so prim. I assure you it will be most enjoyable . . . irresistible . . ."

"When Mr. Pencarron comes . . ." I began.

He laughed. "So you are naïve enough to think that Mr. Pencarron will come?"

I was struck speechless at the implication of his words.

"That has shaken you," he said with a grin. "Of course, he won't come. He doesn't know about the little rendezvous. No one need know. Come on, my sweet Rebecca, be a sensible girl."

My fear must have given me strength. I got to my feet but he still held me. I brought up my knee sharply; he gave a cry of fury and recoiled. I was at the door. I ran through the gallery . . . but he was close behind me. I was at the top of the stairs. I stood still, gasping, for someone was in the hall. It was Belinda.

I heard myself stammer: "Belinda . . ."

"Oh hello, Rebecca." She stood staring at me. I realized I had lost my riding hat, that my hair was falling about my face and the buttons on my blouse were undone.

She said: "Rebecca . . . you look . . ."

She saw Jean Pascal and there was a silence which seemed to go on for some time. Jean Pascal recovered himself first.

"Hello, Miss Belinda," he said. "Have you come visiting me in an empty house?"

"Yes," she replied. "We went riding. Lucie's here too, out there with Stubbs. I said, 'We'll go to High Tor because I know Rebecca is there. Let's surprise her,' I said."

I walked slowly down the stairs.

"I'm glad you came, Belinda," I said.

"Your hair's untidy."

"Is it?"

"Yes, and where's your hat?"

"Oh . . . I've put it down somewhere."

"We've been looking round the house," Jean Pascal explained, "deciding about the furniture."

"Oh," said Belinda, looking intently from me to Jean Pascal. "It's made Rebecca very untidy."

At that moment Lucie came into the hall.

"Hello, Rebecca," she said. "We've come to see you."

I said to myself: Thank God you did. I never want to see this monster again and I never will.

Jean Pascal was looking at me with a somewhat cynical smile. He said: "I think I ought to tell you where you left your hat. It was in that bedroom leading off the gallery. I'll go and get it."

I went slowly down the stairs. Belinda's eyes never left my face. I wondered what she was thinking.

"You didn't mind our coming, did you?" she said.

"No . . . no, I'm glad you did."

"Can we see round the house?" asked Lucie.

"I think it is time we should be going home."

"Just a quick look," pleaded Belinda.

Jean Pascal was coming down the stairs, carrying my hat. He handed it to me with a little bow. He seemed completely undisturbed.

"We want to see round the house," said Belinda. "It is funny without furniture . . . well, only a bit anyway." She called, "Cooee" suddenly. "Listen," she went on. "It echoes. It reminds you of ghosts and that sort of thing."

"But you know it is only because there is hardly any furniture here," said Lucie.

"Come on," said Jean Pascal, "I'll show you round. Will you come with us, Miss Rebecca?"

I wanted to shout: "No, I long to get away from here. I never want to see you again. You have spoiled this house for me." But what could I do? I had to behave as though nothing unusual had happened.

My thoughts were in a turmoil as I went round the house with them. I was asking myself what I should do. I thought of telling my grandmother. What would be her reaction? I could not say. She would tell my grandfather perhaps. Could I tell Pedrek? What would he do?

I was in a quandary.

I thought: I must do nothing at once. I must think about it. I must never be alone with him again. I would never speak to him unless I was forced to. It could be very embarrassing in the future, his being the brother of my stepfather's wife. Moreover his family owned the house which we were proposing to buy.

I had been a fool to trust him in the first place. I should have remembered that he had tried to coax me into having an affaire with him when we had been at the inn. And because I had shown my contempt for that he had endeavored to force me. I was indeed the innocent he believed me to be. That was what was so humiliating. He had laid a trap and I had blithely walked into it.

I imagined that he would say I had come willingly, I had led him on, and then afterwards I had been scared and accused him of rape. That was what was often said on such occasions. That was how such men as he was behaved; they were without scruples and principles. My grandparents and Pedrek would believe me but when this sort of thing happened there were always those to doubt and condemn.

But I had had a lucky escape . . . thanks to Belinda and Lucie.

I felt sick when we came to the bedroom with the four poster bed. I thought the ordeal would never end.

He stood in the courtyard while we mounted our horses. I would not look at him.

He said: "It has been such an interesting afternoon. A pity it is over so soon."

He gave me his cynical smile as he spoke. I turned my horse away, still thanking God for my miraculous escape as I rode with Stubbs and the girls into the courtyard at Cador.

Evil had intruded into my euphoric dream. The house no longer meant the same to me. I felt unhappy. I did not know what I should do.

If I told what had happened it would be an end of our relationship with the Bourdon family and I thought how awkward that would be for Celeste and for me. I wondered what Benedict would say if he were told.

I could see Jean Pascal's insouciant smile if he were ever taken to task. "It was just a bit of fun . . . a light flirtation. Rebecca agreed to come to the empty house and well, I naturally thought . . ."

Would they believe that it had all been so different?

I was still uncertain what action I should take when the ultimate horror struck and drove all thought of anything else out of my mind.

It was the following Friday and six o'clock in the evening. I was in my bedroom alone, still brooding on that shameful encounter when Leah came to me. She looked very alarmed. Something was very wrong, I knew.

"What is it, Leah?" I asked in trepidation.

"It's Miss Belinda. She's not here . . ."

"Not here? Then where . . . ?"

Leah shook her head. "I don't know. Lucie says she went out to take something to Mary Kellaway. Lucie told her she should wait till morning but she said she was going then. It was a book they had been talking about."

"And she's not come back?"

Leah shook her head.

"Then we had better begin looking for her."

I went to the door and started down the stairs. My grandmother was in the hall.

I said: "Belinda's missing . . ."

"What?" cried my grandmother in alarm.

"Leah says she went out somewhere and hasn't come back."

"Out alone . . . and this hour?"

"I didn't know she'd gone," said Leah. "I would never have let her go alone. Lucie says . . ."

"Where is Lucie?"

"Lucie!" I called. "Lucie!"

I heard Lucie's voice at the top of the stairs.

"Come here quickly, Lucie."

She came. She was breathless and looked startled.

"Where did Belinda go?"

"To take a book to Mary."

"At this hour?"

"I said wait till morning but she said no."

"How long ago?"

"Well, half an hour or more. It was about five o'clock."

"We'd better go down to the village," said my grandmother. "Let Mr. Hanson be told. We'd better get people looking for her."

At that moment Belinda burst in. She ran to me and threw herself into my arms. Her dress was torn and blood mingled with the soil on her face and hands.

"Oh Rebecca," she cried. "It was awful. He frightened me. He was horrible . . . horrible . . . different. I didn't know what to do. I kicked . . . and I screamed . . . but no one came and he held me . . . I couldn't get away . . ."

"Who . . . who?" I cried.

I saw the horror dawning on my grandmother's face.

I said: "Belinda, it's all right now. You're here with me . . . with us all. You're all right now. There's nothing to be afraid of any more. Just tell us what happened."

"I was taking a book to Mary. I said I would . . . in the morning . . . but I took it today. It was near the pool. It was quiet there and then I saw him. He said Hello and I was a nice little girl and he liked nice little girls. It was all right at first. Then he pulled me down and I was lying on the ground . . ."

I felt sick. She hid her face on my shoulder. "He looked different, Rebecca. I didn't know him any more. He tried to pull my frock off. I was right on the ground . . . and he pulled at my skirt. It was all torn . . ."

I stroked her hair. I kept saying: "It's all right. It's all right."

"Then I hit him . . . I hit him as hard as I could. And I jumped up and I ran . . . I ran all the way home."

My grandfather had appeared. His face was white. I had never seen him so angry.

"Did you know this man, Belinda?" he said.

She nodded but could not speak for sobbing.

"Who . . . ?" demanded my grandmother.

"It was . . . Pedrek," she said.

When I look back it is like a series of nightmares

from which I fought desperately to escape. There was no escape. I had to face this terrible thing in the clear light of day, and I knew that I had to accept it.

I could not believe that of Pedrek. How could he, who had always been so kind, so gentle, so courteous, so caring for others, have behaved so? I could not conceive it in any way. And yet there was the evidence of my own eyes. I had heard Belinda's horrific account of what had happened. I had seen the terror in her eyes.

All that night we had sat up . . . my grandparents and I . . . talking . . . endlessly.

I kept saying: "I can't believe it. I can't."

My grandmother said: "Nor I. But the child is so certain. How would she know of such things? How . . . if she had not experienced them? Could it have been a moment of madness?"

"No . . . no," I cried. "Not Pedrek."

I thought of my recent experience with Jean Pascal. In fact when Belinda had been telling her story, my thoughts had immediately gone to him . . . and when she had mentioned Pedrek's name my entire happiness had collapsed about me. I think that was the worst moment I had ever lived through.

How long the night seemed, but we knew it was no use trying to sleep. We had to sit there talking . . . saying the same thing over and over again . . . trying to tell each other that there had been some terrible mistake.

What could we do? How could we question

Belinda further? She was distraught. Leah gave her a small dose of sedative which she kept in her medicine cupboard. At least, she said, it would help the child sleep. She was so disturbed and kept crying out.

So there we sat . . . the three of us . . . trying to tell ourselves it was not true . . . that we should wake up suddenly and find it was only an evil dream.

Leah had taken Belinda into her room. She said the child might wake up in the night and the memory of what she had undergone come back to her. Leah must be there to comfort her . . . to assure her that she was safe now.

At last the morning came—but it brought no comfort.

We were all waiting for the arrival of Pedrek as he usually came about ten o'clock on Saturday morning.

What would he do now? He would know that Belinda had escaped and that she would have given us an account of what had happened. Perhaps he would not come.

He did come . . . riding into the stables as though nothing had happened. He came into the house. My grandparents and I were waiting in the hall.

We all stood up as he entered.

There was no sign from him that this was different from any other week-end when he arrived, full of plans as to what we should do.

"Rebecca!" he cried and his smile embraced us all. He stared at us. "Is anything wrong?"

My grandfather said: "Come into the little room. We have to talk."

Puzzled, he followed us, and my grandfather shut the door.

He said: "Sit down."

Still seeming bemused, Pedrek sat. I felt as though my knees would give away because I was trembling so much.

"What ever is wrong?" asked Pedrek.

"Belinda . . ." began my grandfather.

"Is something wrong with her? Is she ill?"

"Pedrek, do you know what is wrong with her?"

His brow was creased. He shook his head.

"Last night . . . she came running home in a dreadful state. She was molested by the pool."

"Oh, my God . . ."

"She escaped . . . in time. The poor child is distraught. Heaven knows what effect this will have on her."

"What a terrible thing . . ."

"She knows the man."

"Who . . . ?"

There was a brief silence, then my grandfather said in a very stern tone: "You . . . Pedrek."

"*What?*"

"You had better tell us exactly what happened."

"I don't understand."

"She came in and said that you had spoken to her by the pool . . . St Branok's Pool. She said

387

you threw her to the ground, tore her clothes . . . and told her that you liked little girls."

"It's . . . madness."

We were all staring at him. He turned to me. "Rebecca . . . you don't believe . . ."

I was silent. I could not bear to look at him. I just covered my face with my hands.

He took a step towards me but my grandfather barred his way.

"This is a very serious matter," he said. "I don't know what happened . . . what came over you . . . but it is better to come out with it. We might . . ."

"How dare you!" cried Pedrek. "How dare you suggest . . ."

"The child said it was you."

"Bring her here. Let me confront her. She's lying . . ."

My grandmother said: "We cannot have her put to more distress. She is in a terrible state. She was desperately frightened. Anyone who saw her would have realized that . . ."

"I don't know how you can think for one moment . . ."

"Look, Pedrek," said my grandfather. "We don't want to blow this up out of all proportion. God knows, it's bad enough already. Was it . . . was it . . . just a moment of madness?"

"I tell you I was not there."

My grandparents exchanged glances.

"If this comes out," said my grandfather, "it is going to cause a great deal of distress in our two

388

families. I can't understand, Pedrek. You are the last person . . ."

"How can you possibly think . . . Rebecca . . . ?" He was looking at me. I was desperately trying to think of the Pedrek I had known all my life, but I kept seeing his face changing into a monster's. I felt ignorant of men and their ways. I had recently allowed myself to be duped by Jean Pascal. He had said I was innocent . . . knowing nothing of the world. I was simple and trusting and I knew little of the inner lusts of men. I had thought I knew Pedrek as well as I knew anyone, but was I too ready to believe what I saw on the surface? I did not look deep enough. Only a few days ago my innocence and ignorance had lured me into a situation which could have scarred my life. And . . . I could not meet Pedrek's eyes. I was afraid of what I might see there.

My grandfather went on: "Were you in the neighborhood last night?"

"My God," said Pedrek hotly, "is this an interrogation? Of course. I came home from college as I always do."

"Then you would have been with your family . . ." His face lightened. "You are usually at Pencarron about six o'clock."

"Yes, but . . ."

I felt myself go limp with fear.

"But last night you were not?" insisted my grandfather.

"No. I went to see a friend before I left college. It made me late."

"And what time did you get home?"

"It must have been about seven thirty."

There was a terrible silence in the room.

"So . . . you were much later than usual?"

"Yes . . . about an hour and a half."

I knew what my grandparents were thinking. It was just after six when Belinda came running into the house.

"And you came later . . . because you were with a friend. I'm sorry, Pedrek, but would your friend be able to corroborate this?"

Pedrek was growing more and more angry. Could it be the anger of guilt? "This has become an inquisition. Am I in the dock? Do I have to prove alibis?"

"This is a very serious charge. It would be in everyone's interest if we could clear it . . . absolutely."

"I know nothing about it. The child was mistaken. She must have confused me with someone else."

"It's the best way, Pedrek. If this friend of yours will confirm you were with him . . . you see everyone will realize that you could not possibly have been at the pool."

"I was not with him. He was not at home."

"So you did not see him . . . and you came back later . . ."

"Yes, because my visit had delayed me."

We all sat quiet, frightened by the implication of his words.

"So," he cried, "I am judged guilty, am I? Rebecca, how can you believe this of me?"

"I can't believe it, Pedrek, I can't . . ."

He would have approached me but I shrank back and my grandmother said: "We are all very upset. I think we should do nothing at the moment. Belinda . . . fortunately . . . escaped what could have been a terrible experience for her. Understand, Pedrek, we have to think about this. Perhaps when the child has recovered from the shock a little we can discover more . . . but frankly, I should hesitate to question her at the moment."

"I think you had better leave us, Pedrek," added my grandfather. "We must have time to think about this."

He turned abruptly and left us. Through the window I saw him striding to the stables. Something told me that the Pedrek I had known till now had gone out of my life.

The talk continued. Leah was very anxious about Belinda. She said the child was quiet and thoughtful. She kept her in her room for she had nightmares and Leah had to be there to comfort her.

"We should be very grateful for Leah," said my grandmother. "No mother could be more caring for her child."

We had tried very carefully to question her, but when we attempted to she would shrink from us and a look of terror would come into her face.

"It is very important that this should not arouse all sorts of fears in her," said my grandmother. "She is so young and the young are impressionable. It is a dreadful experience for a child to undergo."

"Granny," I said, "I do not believe that Pedrek would do this."

She shook her head. "People do strange things. Nobody really understands another person completely."

We could think of nothing else. The sordid matter took complete possession of our minds. We should take some action, we knew.

I could not eat; I could not sleep; and my grandparents were as worried as I was.

That evening, after I had gone to bed, but not to sleep, my grandmother came to me.

"I guessed you'd be awake," she said. She drew her dressing gown about her and sat down close to the bed.

"We have to do something, Rebecca. We can't go on like this."

"No," I said, "but what?"

"For one thing, Belinda ought to get away. Leah says she keeps talking about the pool and that time they drained it because they thought you were there and they brought up a murderer."

"Where does she hear such tales?"

"People talk. They don't realize that children hear these things. You know there is that superstition about the pool. They get garbled versions. However, what I think is that Belinda should get away from here, and—much as I hate it—you go, too."

"Go away . . ." I repeated.

"Yes. In London or Manorleigh, Belinda will be far away from the scene. Leah thinks she should not go to the pool again. I can't imagine that she will want to . . . but sometimes that sort of thing has a strange effect . . . and the thing is to put it behind her as quickly as possible. In London or Manorleigh life will be entirely different. She will forget. She is only young. But here . . . she never will."

"I can see some reason in that."

"And you, my dear, what of you and Pedrek?"

"I don't believe . . ."

"You don't want to believe . . . but half of you does. Tell the truth, Rebecca. You know you can tell me."

"Yes . . . I think you are right."

She nodded. "If you got away for a while, I think it would be good for you. You were so fond of Pedrek. I know how you feel. And now . . . you are beset by doubts. You are trying to force yourself not to believe . . . and in your heart you do."

"I don't know."

"Time may help. If you stay here you might do something you would regret for the whole of your life."

"What?" I asked.

She lifted her shoulders. "You might decide that you believe him. You might marry him . . .

and then find out hidden things you hadn't dreamed of. On the other hand you might reject him . . . and you might regret that all your life. Go back to London or Manorleigh. Ask yourself how much you care for Pedrek. Look this thing straight in the face . . . don't shirk any possibility. Discover how much you care for Pedrek. Take Belinda with you. Look after her. She is in need of help as much as you are, my darling."

She put her arms round me.

I said pathetically: "Everything was so wonderful. There was the house . . ." I shivered. The house would never be the same to me again. I would always remember that terrifying scene with Jean Pascal. He had besmirched the house—but Pedrek had ruined my future happiness.

I knew my grandmother was right. I could not stay there. I had to get away.

There was another reason why I knew we must go, which was made clear to me by Leah.

My grandmother and I were discussing Belinda with her and my grandmother asked her if she thought the child was growing away from her experience.

Leah stood up very straight, her hands clenched.

"Will she ever be able to grow away from it?" she demanded. "Oh, Madam, Miss Rebecca . . . sometimes I feel I could kill him."

"Leah!" I murmured.

"Oh yes, Miss Rebecca, that is how I feel.

What has he done to our child? I see the terror in her eyes. She whimpers in her sleep. Sometimes she calls out. It will be a long time before it goes away. These men, they . . . they should not be allowed to live. If I see him . . . I could not trust myself."

"You must not talk like this, Leah," said my grandmother. "It may well have been a mistake. Perhaps she was frightened . . . she did not see very well."

Leah looked at my grandmother as though she thought her a little stupid.

"She saw . . ." she said. "Men . . . they are not what they seem. They are wicked. They think only of themselves . . . their need of the moment. Their victims mean nothing to them." I had never seen her so vehement. "They submit them to their will . . . and then cast them aside."

"Dear Leah," said my grandmother, "you have always been wonderful with Belinda. You will know how to help her through this. She will need such careful treatment."

Leah was fierce. "I will not have her questioned and cross-questioned. She must forget quickly . . . it is the only way."

"Leah is right," said my grandmother.

Leah nodded and when I looked at her eyes, wild with hatred, I had a horrible conviction that she meant it when she said she would kill Pedrek.

Afterwards my grandmother said: "She was so fierce. Of course, she has looked after Belinda since she was a baby and regards her as her own child. I can see great trouble growing out of this. I do hope it is not going to be known. It will kill Josiah."

"It isn't true, Granny, I know it in my heart."

"I feel the same. After all these years . . . we know Pedrek and it is not plausible. And yet if it were so . . . there are other children to be thought of . . . protected."

"I know there is some explanation."

"I feel that, too. We must not act rashly. Your grandfather feels we should wait a few days before taking any action."

Wait? What could we do by waiting?

But I could see that it was imperative for us to get away. It was what I needed, too.

I wrote to Pedrek. I made several drafts of the letter before I produced the final one.

Dear Pedrek,

I am going back to London. I cannot stay here. I have been so unhappy since this happened. I know you have been, too. At the moment I am bemused and I don't know what to say. My grandparents think I should get away for a while. I don't want to believe it. I am trying not to. Sometimes I think how absurd it is and then . . . at others . . . I am so unsure.

Do try to understand. Give me time.

Rebecca

He wrote back to me:

Dear Rebecca,

I see that you doubt me. I cannot understand how you could possibly believe this of me. I had thought you loved me. I can see now that I was wrong. After all these years you don't know me if you think I could molest a child. It is a cruel fabrication of lies. But you prefer to believe others rather than me.

Pedrek

I wept over his letter. I wanted to go to him, to comfort him, to tell him that, no matter what he had done, I still loved him.

But I could not do it. I knew that I would always be watching him for signs. I thought of the weakness of men. It was no use setting them up on pedestals and thinking of them as perfect gentle knights. They were not like that. Oddly enough memories of Benedict Lansdon kept coming into my mind. I remembered the love I had witnessed between him and my mother, and yet he had married his first wife for the goldmine she brought him. My mother had known this and forgiven him.

That was different. My image of Pedrek had been changed and when I thought of him I would see the lust I had witnessed in Jean Pascal's eyes, and the two seemed to merge into one.

I was not ready at this time to make a decision.

So I left Cador with Belinda, Lucie, Leah and Miss Stringer, for London.

As the train took us nearer to London I wished that I had not left. I felt a yearning to be back there. I think if I could have seen Pedrek then I should have told him that I believed there had been some hideous mistake. Now that I was away from him I seemed to see more clearly that he could not have been guilty of such an act.

I looked at Belinda. She was pale and sat back in her seat with her eyes closed. Lucie looked a little bewildered. We had told her that Belinda was not well and we must be careful not to upset her.

Miss Stringer was unaware of what had happened. I feared she would have insisted on an open accusation of Pedrek. I could imagine what her verdict would have been.

As for Leah, her attitude had become more protective. She hardly took her eyes from Belinda. I wondered whether she blamed herself for not noticing that the child had left the house to go to Mary Kellaway.

I wanted to tell her that no blame attached to her. We all knew how strong-willed Belinda could be, and if she wanted to go and visit Mary she would have found some way of doing so.

And so we reached London.

Benedict was at home. He had not been told of the reason for our arrival. I said to my grandmother: "There is no need to worry about that. He will not notice whether we are there or not."

The carriage was waiting for us and in a short time we drew up before the house which had never seemed like a home to me. I felt so miserable. There was nothing I wanted to do so much as to take the next train down to Cornwall.

Belinda seemed a little happier as we went into the house. They had been right. It was necessary for her to get away.

There was a great deal to do . . . unpacking, which I wanted to do myself . . . and getting the children fed and settled in.

I noticed that Belinda ate what was put before her. She seemed very tired and I left Leah to put them to bed.

Celeste was pleased to see me; but even she brought up memories of Jean Pascal, although the horror I had felt in that bedroom at High Tor was sunk in insignificance by my greater tragedy.

I wondered—as people do at such times, about matters which seemed of small importance beside the great tragedy—what would happen to the house.

That set me thinking of those happy times when we had talked of living there.

I dined with Benedict and Celeste. The talk was mainly about Cornwall and my grandparents. Benedict was always interested in Cornwall which made him melancholy for he would be reminded of my mother. It was in Cornwall they had first known each other when she was a child. He always looked sad and nostalgic when he spoke of it and I was sure Celeste was aware of this.

As soon as the meal was over I wanted to escape to my room. I think Celeste would have liked to talk to me but I could not endure this on that night. I kept thinking of Jean Pascal—after all, he was her brother—and I wanted to put that out of my mind if possible. I was reminded that there would be occasions when he came to this house and I should have to avoid him.

There were so many unpleasant dilemmas ahead of me and I just wanted to be alone to think.

Celeste said: "Of course you are tired. We will talk in the morning," and I was grateful for that.

As I was making my way upstairs I passed the door of Benedict's study and as I did so the door opened and he came out.

He said: "Rebecca . . . I'd like a word. Do you mind?"

I followed him into the study, and he shut the door.

He looked at me quizzically and said: "Something is wrong, isn't it?"

I hesitated. "Well, Belinda has not been very well."

"No, so I gather. And you? You don't look well yourself."

"Don't I?"

"You seem surprised about something."

"Oh . . . I am surprised that you noticed."

"I do notice." He smiled. "I want everything to be . . . all right for you."

400

"Oh, thank you."

"I know I haven't been very demonstrative, but that doesn't mean I'm indifferent."

"Oh, doesn't it?"

"No. I wish . . ." He shrugged his shoulders. "I want you to know that if there is anything . . ."

"Anything?"

"Any way in which I could help . . ."

"I don't need help, thanks. I'm all right."

"Well, don't forget. Your mother would have wanted us to be friends. She always did."

I was astonished. He was looking at me almost pleadingly.

He went on: "I'm here, you know . . . I just want you to realize that if I can be of any use . . . well, I'm here."

For a moment I forgot my misery. What on Earth had happened to the man? Of course, there had been an election in March and Mr. Gladstone, his hero, was now Prime Minister. Perhaps that would mean a post in the Cabinet for him. It must be that which made him feel on good terms with the whole world. He had even noticed me . . . and Belinda.

A week passed and the tragedy seemed as close as ever. I brooded for hours when I was alone in my bedroom. I should have stayed in Cornwall. But Belinda had had to get away and how could she have gone without Lucie and me, for Lucie was my responsibility. She had no claims on Benedict. I could not have let her go without me. And yet my heart was back in Cornwall with Pedrek. I wanted to write to him to tell him that whatever he had done made no difference. Anything else would not have been the same. If he had been a thief . . . even if he had killed someone . . . but to me *this* was so revolting that I could not bear to think of it.

I had a talk with Celeste who had her own problem to face.

She said: "You are unhappy but you do not want to talk about it."

I shook my head.

"Is it a love affair?"

I nodded.

"Someone in Cornwall. It must be Pedrek Cartwright. I always thought what a delightful young man he is. Has it gone wrong then?"

"Yes," I said. "It has gone wrong."

"My poor Rebecca. And you love him?"

"Yes."

"It is so sad. Life is cruel, is it not? To love and to be rejected . . . that is a terrible thing."

I was silent thinking of Pedrek. It was I who had rejected him. We had said our love would last forever and at the first ill wind it had blown away.

"At least," she went on, "you find out in time . . . not like . . ."

I was drawn away from my own tragedy to hers.

She said: "It hurts too much to talk, I know. But it is too soon. As time passes the hurt does not go away . . . but it is easier to talk. And you suffer, too . . ."

I put out my hand and took hers.

She went on: "Sometimes I wonder how I will endure it. It is better when he is away. Then I can deceive myself . . . a little. But when he is here and shows so clearly . . . Why did he marry me? I ask myself."

"He must have loved you or he would never have done that."

"It was done . . . how you say? . . . without thought."

"On the spur of the moment. Oh, but I do not believe he would act rashly in such matters. He must have thought you would be happy together."

"Perhaps. At first . . . I thought we might . . . but he is obsessed by a dead love. He cannot forget."

"Does he still go to the locked room?"

She nodded. "And I am sad and lonely waiting for a husband who does not want me."

"My poor Celeste."

"I need to be loved. I am not one to live alone."

"Perhaps in time . . ."

"In time? It is years since she died . . . but she is still with him. It is as though she is in this house. I do not know how long I can endure . . ." She stared into space. "I could take a lover . . . or take my life . . . he would not care . . ."

"Oh, Celeste, please don't talk like that."

"You see . . . I love him. I want him as he . . .

wants his dead wife. We are in a maze . . . both of us . . . searching for the impossible."

"Perhaps it will come right in the end."

"Perhaps," she said. "That is a word which does not fill me with hope."

"It may be it is wrong to care for people too much. One gets hurt."

She nodded.

"He must have been fond of you to marry you," I insisted.

"He needed a wife. I could entertain his guests. It is a help in his career. I am like the first wife. He married her for the goldmine."

"I think he cares for you, but you see . . . there was this special feeling for my mother . . . and he just cannot forget her."

"She is there all the time."

"Yes, I know . . . a shadowy third!"

And between Pedrek and me was the memory of a small girl running to me . . . her eyes wild, her clothes torn . . . as certainly as Benedict's obsession with my mother was between him and Celeste.

It might well be that I had been right to get away. We should never have been happy with that shadow between us. It would have flashed into my memory at odd moments throughout my life.

I was glad when we left London for Manorleigh.

Mrs. Emery was shocked at the sight of me. "My goodness me, Miss Rebecca," she said. "You do look pale . . . and I believe you've lost some weight. Yes, I'm sure of it . . . and you were like a beanpole before. That's Cornwall for you. Well, we'll have to see what we can do. We'll get some color back into those cheeks and a little more flesh on the bones."

I would sit at my window and look down at the winged-footed Hermes, at the pond and the haunted seat under the oak tree. If only my mother were here, she would tell me what to do.

Oliver Gerson called. The children and I were pleased to see him. He was one of those people who only have to appear to dispel melancholy. He expressed his great delight in our reunion. He kissed hands all round. Belinda seemed to step right away from her tragedy on his first visit. She jumped about him. Lucie was almost equally delighted.

"This is a joyous reunion, I see," he said. "I am deeply aware of my own delight but it is gratifying to see that it is shared."

"Why didn't you come to Cornwall?" demanded Belinda.

"I had my duties here. I am not a man of leisure."

"I know," said Belinda. "You work for my father."

"Which is very fortunate because it gives me an opportunity to be with his charming family now and then."

His eyes met mine and he smiled warmly. "I wondered when you were going to return from Cornwall," he said.

"It was a long time," said Lucie. "And then Belinda got ill."

"Oh dear me." He was all concern, turning to Belinda.

"I'm all right now," she said. "What are we going to do?"

"Well, first I shall have a conference with your father. After that I shall be free for an hour or so. Could we ride . . . as we did in the days before you deserted me?"

"We didn't desert *you*," said Belinda firmly. "It was just that we had to go to Cornwall."

"And now you are glad to be back."

Belinda did one of her joyous leaps and nodded.

"Well, as they say, all's well that ends well. Now, if Your Majesty will excuse me . . ." He made an elegant bow in Belinda's direction which delighted her. ". . . I will get to my duty and later we will ride together . . . all of us, the Misses Rebecca, Belinda and Lucie . . . and I shall be their guide."

"Hurry," commanded Belinda.

He bowed more deeply. "Your wishes shall be granted, my Queen."

How he charmed her! He came frequently to the house and every day she looked for him. She seemed to have completely forgotten her unhappy experience in Cornwall and reverted to her old self.

He was right when he said he would be a frequent visitor and on those days when he did not come Belinda would be sulky and very difficult to

406

handle. Leah was wonderfully patient. How devoted she was to that child! To Lucie too, I supposed, but Lucie was more docile and she was always making excuses for Belinda.

We often rode at Manorleigh and Oliver Gerson's company was a help even to me. He was constantly devising competitions for the children, tests in riding and observation so that each ride was full of interest for them. They were always on the alert for what he had decreed they must watch for and he instilled in them a competitive spirit which Miss Stringer said was good for them. She too had fallen under the spell of the Gerson charm.

One day we found an inn with a creaking sign over the door: The Hanging Judge. Belinda was immediately intrigued.

"What does it mean? Is it because he's hanging up there?"

"Oh no, no," said Oliver. "He's the hanging judge because he hanged people by the neck."

Belinda's eyes were sparkling.

"Come on," he said. "We'll go in and have a little refreshment."

I was uneasy about taking the children into such a place, but he took my arm reassuringly. "They'll love it," he whispered. "It will be something new for them. I'll make sure it is all right."

He exerted his charm wherever he went. He talked to the landlord's wife; she nodded conspiratorially and we were all seated in the parlor with its oak beams and air of adventure.

Watered-down cider was brought for the children and we all sat there drinking. Neither Belinda nor Lucie had been in an inn before. Their eyes were round with wonder and it was clear that they thought it a great adventure.

Belinda demanded to know about the hanging judge and he told them that the Duke of Monmouth, the son of Charles the Second, thought he had more right to the throne than the King's brother James, and how there was a battle and Monmouth was defeated and his men captured and brought before the cruel hanging judge.

"There are gibbets all over the West Country," he told them; and they listened spellbound.

I thought: How they love horror! I could only think it was because they did not fully understand it.

"You think of the most lovely things," Belinda told Oliver Gerson.

When they reached home they chattered to Miss Stringer about the hanging judge and the Monmouth rebellion. She was delighted.

"So instructive," she said. "So good for them. What a delightful man!"

My dreams were haunted by Pedrek. I kept recalling that look of dawning horror on his face when we had confronted him with our suspicions. My first thoughts were of him each morning when I awoke, and he seemed to be beside me all through the day.

I said to myself: I must see him. I must tell him that I believe in him. That whatever he has done, I love him.

I knew there had been a mistake.

I would write to him. I would ask him to forgive me for distrusting him. But I did not write. Between me and that letter was the face of Belinda . . . distorted with fear . . . her wide innocent eyes showing so clearly that she could not entirely understand what had happened to her.

In the midst of my uncertainty there came a letter from my grandmother.

My dear Rebecca,

I hope you are feeling a little better. I think you did right to get away—and in any case it was necessary for Belinda. It has been sad for us here. Pedrek is leaving Cornwall. I think it is best really. I think we all need to get away from that terrible time . . . to try to see things in proportion.

He is going to Australia. There have been discoveries of tin in New South Wales and they are asking for mining engineers to go out there. Of course, Pedrek has not finished his course at the college but he has attained a degree of knowledge and there are of course his grandfather's connections in the mining field and that will stand for a good deal. He needs to get away. We simply could not go on as we have been after all that has happened. He will be leaving almost immediately and I don't know how long he will be away.

The Pencarrons are very upset. They don't know what it is all about. They think there has been some big quarrel between you and Pedrek and they are very sad.

Your grandfather and I have felt very uncertain. We could not bring ourselves to tell them. I think it would have killed his grandmother . . . and what Josiah would have done, I cannot imagine. They worship Pedrek. Then we wondered whether we should have done something about it . . . whether it was our duty to. It is such a terrible thing . . . What if some other child . . . ? On the other hand we could not really believe it somehow. As I said to your grandfather even suppose he lost control for a moment he would have learned his lesson.

He looks so unhappy . . . so terribly sad and bewildered in a way. It is such a wretched business and I know, my darling, how you must be suffering. It is best for you to be right away from it.

We can only wait and see. Try not to grieve too much. Perhaps there will be some explanation some day. However it was best that you should leave here and I think that he should get away, too.

I only wonder whether we have done the right thing . . .

The letter dropped from my hands. Gone away! To Australia! As my parents had in search of gold. My grandmother had gone there too and met tragedy . . . and now Pedrek had left to look for tin and get away from a situation which had become intolerable.

Who would have believed that in such a short time life could change so drastically?

I should have written to him before. I should have told him that I loved him and would go on doing so no matter what had happened.

But it was too late now.

He continued to haunt my thoughts. Where was he now? Had he left Cornwall? I could imagine the heartrending farewell between him and his grandparents.

Morwenna came to see me. She was distraught.

"What does all this mean between you and Pedrek?" she demanded.

"We decided we couldn't marry . . . for a while."

"But why? You were so happy . . . so looking forward to it . . . why, you had almost got the house."

"I know . . . but it changed. We realized that we had made a mistake and it would be wrong to . . . to er . . . rush into it."

"I can't believe it."

I looked at her sadly. I could not explain to her. I could not show her how bewildered and unhappy I was. She and his father would be completely shocked if they knew.

So I let them think that I was fickle. They could not believe that it was Pedrek who had changed his mind.

And now he was going to Australia . . . the home of his birth. I could see the fear in Morwenna's eyes; her attitude had changed towards me. She was cold and withdrawn.

But I could not tell her. The terrible event at the pool had resulted in misery in all directions.

Mrs. Emery said: "I don't know what's the matter with Mrs. Cartwright. She seems changed. It's because her son's going out to Australia, I suppose."

"Yes, I suppose so," I said.

She looked at me and shrugged her shoulders. They had all guessed that there had been an understanding between Pedrek and me and knew that this was so no longer.

"These matters are for them they belong to," was her judicial summing up. "It's for them to decide and nobody else's business." She looked at me almost tenderly. "And you've got to take a bit of care of yourself. We don't want you ill, Miss Rebecca."

"I'll take care," I promised.

I imagined how they all discussed the matter round the kitchen table and conjured up reasons for my wan looks.

There were times when I almost walked out

of the house and took the train to Cornwall that I might see him before he left and urge him not to go . . . to tell him that no matter what had happened I wanted to be with him.

Would he accept that? He would not want me to say "no matter what." He wanted me to have the utmost belief in his innocence. This I instinctively knew would be his terms.

I loved Pedrek. I knew now how much. But I had grown up. I had discovered lust in the bedroom at High Tor and I knew men could change when that lustful urge was upon them. I had learned that it takes a long time to know people and I was asking myself, Did I know Pedrek? Did I know every aspect of him?

The fact of the matter was that I could not be sure. And what he was asking from me was absolute belief in his innocence.

It was an impasse. I hesitated . . . and so he would go to Australia.

There he would try to forget me . . . and I must try to forget him.

Blackmail

An air of excitement pervaded the house. I often had talks with Mrs. Emery and found it comforting to sit in her room and chat desultorily about little matters of the household and to drink a cup of tea from one of her special cups.

She was aware of a great deal of what was going on.

One day she said: "Mr. Lansdon is especially busy these days. Emery and me . . . well, we're interested in politics . . . and we're keeping our fingers crossed for Mr. Lansdon."

"Oh . . . why?"

"Well, there's this Cabinet reshuffle, isn't there? And since his party's in . . . who knows? I reckon Mr. Lansdon's made for some high post. Emery thinks the Home Office."

"Does Mr. Emery think that Mr. Gladstone will stay in power?"

"Oh yes. The Conservatives are not the same now that that Mr. Disraeli's lost his wife. I reckon a man wants a woman behind him."

"I'm not so sure. He did some important things *after* her death. It may be that he's devoted everything to politics now she has gone. What about his getting control in the Suez Canal and proclaiming the Queen Empress of India and cleverly averting war with the Russians and bringing Cyprus into the Empire? He did all that after his wife died."

"Yes, but he was never a happy man since and a man needs to have a happy home life. There's Mr. Lansdon . . ." She shook her head sadly.

I thought: They know everything about us. They know that Benedict does not love Celeste and that he still mourns for my mother, and that I have come back from Cornwall sad and troubled because my engagement to Pedrek is broken. All these things they know of us and they discuss them at meal times when they are all round the table together. No, Mrs. Emery would not allow that. It would be between herself and Mr. Emery when they were alone in their room. But the servants would be all eagerness to learn; they would listen at every opportunity; they would watch; they would garner their information and compare with each other; then they would doubtless draw their garbled conclusions.

"It's no good looking back," said Mrs. Emery. "Your dear mother is dead and gone and more's the pity. If she were here . . . how different everything would be. The present Mrs. Lansdon . . . she tries. She could be good for him . . . if he'd let her be. But he keeps looking back."

"Perhaps in time."

"Time. That's what saves us all. No use nursing your troubles, Miss Rebecca. That's what I always say . . . and it will be wonderful for Mr. Lansdon if he gets a post in the Cabinet. Emery and me . . . well . . . we'll be that pleased."

"Yes," I said. "I wish . . ."

She looked at me expectantly but I did not finish.

She was silent. She was a very understanding woman and I think she had the good of the family at heart. She really would like to see Benedict in the Cabinet and happy in his domestic as well as public life; she would like to see me recovered from my wounds and happily engaged to a suitable someone.

She and Emery wanted to have a happy as well as a successful household over which to rule in the lower regions.

Benedict was in London and Celeste with him. Oliver Gerson came down once or twice but his stays were brief. He told me that Mr. Lansdon was so busy in the House that business matters were left to him.

I was pleased to hear Belinda's laughter. She really seemed to have forgotten. Leah said she never referred to it now and that she slept peacefully and was her old self.

When I went to the children's room to say goodnight she suddenly put her arms round my neck and hugged me tightly.

"I love you, dear darling sister Rebecca."

Such expressions of affection from Belinda were rare and made me very happy.

I went over to Lucie's bed. She hugged me too. But then she often did. "I love you too, Rebecca," she said.

I was very comforted.

It was a few days later in the early afternoon, a time when the household was usually quiet. Mrs. Emery returned to her room to—as she said—put her feet up for five minutes. I don't know what Mr. Emery did—probably took a nap in the Emery bedroom. The house had a somnolent air.

I was going upstairs and as I passed the locked room, I thought I heard a sound. I went quietly to the door and stood there for a few moments . . . listening.

I felt a tingling sensation in my back. Benedict was in London. Mrs. Emery was in her room, and I knew that someone was behind that locked door.

It was so much my mother's room . . . her brushes, her mirror . . . her clothes . . . just as she had left it. I must be mistaken. I stood very still . . . listening. And then came the faint rustling sound.

I was trembling. Did the dead really return? Once I had had the feeling that my mother came back to me. That was when I had fancied that she had wanted me to take in Lucie. Fancy? Imagination? I had always had a vivid one. I had been intrigued by the story of Lady Flamstead who had returned to comfort the child whom she had never seen. Perhaps if people left especially loved ones behind they had to come back. My mother had left Benedict and she had left me. I knew how deeply she had loved him and I had been the center of her life until she married him.

These thoughts flashed into my mind as I stood there, tingling with excitement and apprehension.

I took the handle of the door and turned it very quietly. The door was locked. Yet . . . someone was in there.

I stood for a few more seconds and then I went very quietly along to Mrs. Emery's room.

I knocked. There was no answer for a few moments and then she said sleepily: "Who's there?"

I went in. She was dozing by the fire and was startled to see me.

"I'm sorry to disturb you, Mrs. Emery, but I think there is someone in the locked room."

She continued to look bemused and was clearly not yet awakened from her doze.

"Locked room . . ." she repeated.

"Yes. I distinctly heard someone there."

She was recovering herself. "Oh no, Miss Rebecca. You must have fancied it. Unless Mr. Lansdon's come home unexpectedly and none of us heard he had."

"I can hardly believe that. Have you got your key?"

She jumped up, looking alarmed, and went to a drawer, opened it and held up the key in triumph.

"Then it must be Mr. Lansdon. But I tried the door and it was locked."

"You didn't speak to him, did you? He wouldn't have liked that. He wouldn't have wanted to be disturbed."

"No, I did not. I was very quiet. I can't believe he was in there."

"I'll go up to his room and see if his things are there. But we should have heard him if he'd come from London. There would have been the carriage from the station and all that bustle. There always is."

"Let's go at once, Mrs. Emery. Bring the key. Let's go into the room. Someone may have broken in."

She nodded grimly. But first we went to Benedict's room. There was no sign of his arrival.

Mrs. Emery was looking uneasy.

"I must assure myself that there is no one there, Mrs. Emery," I said.

"All right then, Miss Rebecca."

We went to the room and she unlocked the door. I caught my breath in amazement. Oliver Gerson was sitting at a little bureau near the window. There was a tin box at his feet and it looked as though he were going through some papers.

He stood up and stared at us.

"So . . ." I stammered. "It was you . . ."

"Miss Rebecca . . ." He looked a little startled for the moment. I fancied he had paled beneath his bronzed skin.

I said: "What are you doing here? No one is supposed to come here. How did you get in?"

He smiled at me and then he was the charming

419

easy-going Oliver Gerson. He put his hand in his pocket and held up a key.

"But there are only two. Mrs. Emery has one."

"This is the other," he said.

"Mr. Lansdon's? So he gave it to you."

"I came to get some papers and take them back to him."

"Papers?" I said. "But this was my mother's room."

"He keeps some papers here . . . rather special papers. He wanted me to find them and take them to him."

"Oh," I said, feeling deflated.

Mrs. Emery looked very relieved.

"You look really scared," he said. "Did you think I was a ghost?"

Mrs. Emery said: "Mr. Lansdon always wanted the room locked. He was the only one who went in . . . bar me to clear. I wonder he didn't say."

"Oh, he didn't think it was important. He knew my coming would not excite much curiosity. As a matter of fact I have nearly finished."

"Did you bring any luggage, Mr. Gerson?" asked Mrs. Emery. "I'll see about a room . . ."

"No . . . please. It is just a day visit . . . to get the papers and get back with them. They are wanted urgently."

"Well, I expect you'll want something to eat before you go back to London."

"I dropped in at an inn for some ale and a sandwich. I was in rather a hurry."

"How did you get into the house?"

"The back door was open and as everyone seemed to be out of the way I got on with the business. I knew where to find everything."

"Well, you'd like something, I daresay. A cup of tea . . . or that sort of thing?"

"How very good of you, Mrs. Emery; always so thoughtful for our creature comforts. I was saying to Mr. Lansdon what a treasure you are. But I can't stop. I'm in rather a hurry. I have to get back to London."

He was putting some papers into a case.

"You found what you wanted?" I asked.

"Oh yes. Everything."

"So you will be leaving immediately?"

"I regret that I must. Mr. Lansdon can be a very impatient man."

"Belinda will be disappointed."

He put his fingers to his lips. "Sh. Not a word to her or I shall be severely castigated when I next see her which I hope will be soon."

He smiled at me warmly. "Well, much as I regret it, I must be off. Sorry I gave you a bit of a scare."

"It wouldn't take me long to brew a cup of tea," said Mrs. Emery. "The kettle's on the hob in my room."

"Mrs. Emery, you are an angel of mercy as well as a treasure, but duty calls."

He closed the case and we went out of the room. He locked the door and put the key back into his pocket.

"*Au revoir,*" he said and was gone.

Mrs. Emery said: "Well, I could certainly do with a nice cup of tea after that. You really had me scared, Miss Rebecca."

"It was a bit hair-raising to hear someone there."

"I'd say. It was a good thing it wasn't one of those girls. They would have had hysterics . . . you can bet your life."

"I'm glad we found the explanation."

We went to her room. "What a nice young man he is," said Mrs. Emery, looking intently at me. "Always a smile and a cheery word. He's as friendly to the tweeny as he is to the rest of us. And the children just love him."

"Yes," I agreed, "particularly Belinda."

"Poor mite. She looked really seedy when she came back." She looked at me intently and added: "I think he's sweet on you."

There was a little smirk about her lips. I guessed she was thinking he might provide the solution to my troubles.

It was about a week after that incident that Benedict came to Manorleigh. Oliver Gerson came with him.

They had not been in the house more than twenty minutes when the trouble started.

Benedict was in his study and the children at their lessons in the schoolroom. Belinda was very excited because Oliver Gerson was in the house and she guessed that we should all go riding together as we did when he was here.

I was mounting the stairs when I heard angry voices coming from the study. I paused. Then I heard Benedict saying: "Go. Go at once. Get out of this house."

I stood still, horror creeping over me. For the moment I thought he must be talking to Celeste.

Then I heard Oliver Gerson: "Don't imagine you can talk like that to me. I know too much."

"I don't care what you know. You are finished here. Do you understand? Get out."

"Look here," said Oliver Gerson. "You can't do this, I tell you. Don't imagine that I shall just go meekly. You can't afford that, Mr. Benedict Lansdon. I repeat . . . I know too much."

"I don't care what you know. I won't have you here. You must be mad if you think you can blackmail me."

"You can't afford to be so high and mighty. All I ask is what would be expected: after the marriage . . . partnership. It would be good for you, too. Enable you to be free of the whole unsavory business. It's not good for your political image, you know. You won't want certain things known. The Devil's Crown, eh? What goes on . . . Mr. Benedict Lansdon, the owner of the most disreputable club in Town. Come, come, be reasonable."

"I would not allow my stepdaughter to marry you, no matter what you threatened to do."

I could not have moved then if I had wanted to. They were talking about me. I tried to calm myself. It was vital that I understand what this was all about.

"And . . ." went on my stepfather, "if Rebecca knew what you are you wouldn't have the ghost of a chance with her."

"She knows me well enough."

"But you admit you have spoken to her."

"I tell you it is only a matter of time. I am almost there, and she'll be ready to defy you. Think again."

"I tell you I will not have it."

"Isn't it her decision?"

"I am her guardian. I will forbid it. I have no doubt you have been a charming suitor and in the event of failing with her you have your eyes on Belinda. You'd have to wait a long time for that one. But get this out of your mind. You are not getting a foothold in this family. I know too much about you and now you are indulging in attempted blackmail, I tell you it is the end."

"You can't do it, Lansdon. Just think what it means. It put an end to your grandfather's political ambitions. Can't you learn from him? This Devil's Crown affair. It's damning."

"How . . . how did you . . . ?"

"How did I discover? Never mind, I did. Think again. You'd better be careful. You'll be better off as my stepfather-in-law, you know, than if certain things came out into the open."

"Get out of this house."

"Do you think you can push me out like this? What of my contracts?"

"It will be arranged through lawyers."

"Don't think I shall go meekly."

"I don't care how you go as long as you go."

"It's not the end of this, Benedict Lansdon."

"It's the end of our association, Oliver Gerson."

I knew the door was about to open and I sped upstairs. I stood on the landing above looking down. I saw Oliver Gerson stride down the stairs.

I still stood there in a dazed fashion. Benedict came up the stairs and saw me.

"Rebecca!" he said, and I realized at once that he knew I had overheard at least something of what had been said.

"You were listening."

I could not deny it.

"Come into my study," he said. "It is time we talked."

I followed him in. He shut the door and stood looking at me for a few seconds.

Then he said: "Sit down. How much did you hear?"

"I heard him threatening you, demanding a partnership . . . and then something about marrying me."

He said: "How could you marry a man like that! Did you imagine yourself in love with him?"

I flushed. "No. I certainly did not."

"Thank God for that. I couldn't make up my mind. You were with him a great deal. All those rides with the children . . . all that gallantry."

"You . . . noticed that?"

"Of course I did."

"I'm surprised. I thought you were quite oblivious of our existence."

"Belinda is my daughter. You are my stepdaughter. You were left in my charge. Of course I am aware of you. I blame myself for allowing him to come here."

"I gather he is a close associate of yours. It was natural that he should come here."

"I guessed what he was after when he paid so much attention to you."

"He wanted a partnership in your business, I gather, and he thought if he married me it would help him to get it."

"That is so."

"He did ask me to marry him some time ago. I declined."

"He is so sure of himself that he thought in time you would change your mind."

"He made an error of judgment."

"I am glad of that. He has a certain superficial charm. I should have seen through him before. When I told him I would never allow him to marry you, I think he lost his head. He saw his careful plans coming to nothing . . . and then he tried to blackmail me. You heard it. You might as well understand the position clearly . . . particularly as you are concerned."

"I am a little shocked. I don't know what to think."

"You couldn't see the motive behind all the gallantry."

"What surprises me most is that you were aware of it."

"Do you think I am blind?"

"To your family . . . yes. I know you are very astute in other matters."

"Your welfare has always been my concern. You were left in my care by . . ." He faltered a little. "By your mother. I looked upon it as a trust. I know that you resented me right from the moment we were married. I tried to understand it. She explained it to me. She said that because you had no father you and she had been particularly close. You didn't want change. We never got together, did we? And then . . . she died."

He turned away and I said: "I know. I lost her too."

"She was . . . everything I wanted . . ."

I nodded.

"There has been animosity between us . . . It was not my wish . . ."

"I see that now."

And I was seeing a completely different person. He was vulnerable as I had never thought of him before. He might be the stern ruthless man but he had his weaknesses . . . and he had loved my mother and needed her . . . he needed her now.

I was sad and lonely. I had lost her, as he had, and then I had thought I could have a happy life with Pedrek, and now I had lost him, too.

He said: "We should try to help each other, you and I . . . instead of which . . ." He was silent for a short while and then went on: "There was only ever one trouble between your mother and me. It was these clubs. She hated it when I inherited them from my grandfather. She wanted me to get rid of them. I should have listened to her. It was the only time there was contention between us. She knew my grandfather. He was an adventurer. Everyone said I was like him. But I think there is a difference. I should have listened to her. I should have got rid of them long ago."

I said: "I heard something about . . . was it The Devil's Crown?"

"Yes . . . I was considering acquiring it. Gerson believes I already have. He does not know as much as he thinks he does. I can't imagine how he has so much information about my affairs."

A sudden memory came back to me.

I said: "Do you keep confidential papers in that locked room?"

"Yes," he said.

"So it is not entirely a shrine. I thought you kept it as it was because . . ."

"I did," he admitted. "Then it occurred to me that it was just the place to keep secret documents."

I was surprised that at such a time I could feel a twinge of amusement. I supposed that was typical of him, that in the midst of his emotions he could think of such a thing. He had made that shrine to her memory and he could at the same time use it as a secret cache for important documents. I seemed to see my mother's face smiling indulgently, whispering: "Yes, but that is Benedict."

I said: "You kept private documents in there yet you let Oliver Gerson have access to them."

He stared at me in amazement. "No. Never," he said.

I went on: "He was here in that locked room." "When?"

"Not very long ago. I heard noises there and I made Mrs. Emery get her key. We went there and he was there with some papers before him . . . at the bureau. He said you had given him your key."

He was incredulous. "He must have got hold of Mrs. Emery's key."

"No. She had hers. We had gone in with that and found him there. He had locked the door on the inside."

"I can't believe this. My key has never left the ring on which I keep it."

"Well, it was not Mrs. Emery's because she had hers."

"I am astounded, Rebecca. I can't imagine how this could happen. There are only two keys."

"If one of them had been in his possession for a while couldn't he have had another made?"

"That's the answer. He must have stolen one of the keys at some time."

"It seems the only reasonable solution."

"And he has been examining papers . . ."

"Does that make any difference to what he can bring against you?"

He shook his head. "You know so much now, so let me tell you this. The clubs which my grandfather started and owned for many years brought him great riches. He was a clever man who loved adventure. Life without risks would not have been exciting enough for him. He enjoyed what he did. Some would say he was a rogue . . . but many loved him. I have realized that we are different. I am not of his caliber. I have inherited some of his qualities . . . but not all. You know my ambitions are great. They mean more to me than that fortune which comes through questionable channels. For some time I have been working on disposing of the clubs and concentrating entirely on politics. As you know I made a fortune from the goldmine. I still have a small interest in that. Money is no problem. It was just the thought of more that tempted me. Now I am following the advice which she gave me . . . all those years ago. I shall dispose of my interests in the clubs. That is what Gerson does not know. He has worked for me for some time. He is ambitious. He plans to have a big share by acquiring a partnership . . . well, you've heard all that."

"And this attempt to blackmail you, what harm could it do you?"

"This Devil's Crown which I was considering adding to the others . . . is more than just a night club. There are activities going on there which are quite unsavory. I think it is possibly the haunt of drug traffickers. It was that which decided me that I wanted to get out."

"So you are not caught up in anything of that sort yet?"

"Nor do I intend to be. I shall not be acquiring The Devil's Crown, I think."

"Then Oliver Gerson's threats are groundless. He could bring nothing against you."

"Well, he could always remind people of my connection with the clubs."

"And that would harm you?"

"If I were in the Cabinet, perhaps."

"So you think it wise to get out?"

"I should have listened to your mother long ago. But I am so pleased you are not involved with him."

"There was never any intention on my part to marry him, but if there had been . . ."

"Oh yes," he said with a faint smile, "you would have rejected my advice. I anticipated conflict so I am only too delighted that there is no need for it."

"But if I did decide to marry . . ."

The smile deepened. "You would not be prepared to listen to me."

"I should expect to make my own decision."

"And if your choice had fallen on an unsuitable person such as Oliver Gerson, I should have done everything in my power to prevent the marriage because . . . well, I should feel it would be what your mother would have wanted. I wish . . ."

I looked at him waiting for him to go on.

"I wish," he continued, "that I knew how Gerson got that key. I can't tell you how pleased

I am that you are not involved with him. That pleases me more than anything."

He meant that. I was amazed.

It was a turning point in our relationship.

Missing Person

Leah was in the garden with the children and I was just about to join them when a telegram arrived.

I glanced at it and saw that it was addressed to Leah. I took it to her at once. She was startled and took it from me with trembling fingers. Like most people who received them she was immediately thinking of bad news.

She read it and stared at me.

"Is something wrong, Leah?" I asked.

Belinda ran to her and took the telegram. " 'Your mother very ill,' " she said. " 'Asking for you. Come if possible.' "

I snatched the telegram from her. Belinda had read it correctly. "Oh Leah," I said. "You must go at once."

Leah looked round in a bewildered way. "How can I? The children . . ."

"Of course we can manage. Don't you think you should go? She is asking for you."

Leah nodded dumbly.

"You could catch the evening train," I went on. "It would get you to Cornwall in the morning. Someone will meet you. Don't worry about what's happening here. We can manage."

She seemed very undecided but at length she agreed that she must go.

I kept thinking of Mrs. Polhenny . . . ill. I wondered what had happened to her. The last time my grandmother had mentioned her, everything seemed as it always had been.

A few days later I had a letter from my grandmother.

"We are all a little shocked by the death of Mrs. Polhenny," she wrote. "She was so much a part of the place and it is hard to imagine that we shall not see her any more. She was riding home from one of her cases when the wheel of her old boneshaker seems to have come into contact with a stone of some sort. It must have been a sizeable one. Unfortunately she was at the top of Goonhilly Hill and she came hurtling down. You know how steep it is. She fell and cracked her skull. They got her to the hospital in Plymouth but by the time she reached there she was in a bad state. A messenger came to tell me that she was asking for me . . . urgently. She wanted to say something very important to me. They had already sent for Leah.

"I scarcely recognized her when I saw her. She did not look in the least like the Mrs. Polhenny we knew. She looked old and frail lying there wrapped up in bandages.

"They left me with her, for somehow she implied that was what she wanted. I was surprised that it was allowed but I think she was too far gone for anything to matter. It was so strange,

434

Rebecca, she seemed really afraid. You know how we used to say her place was secure in Heaven. She was always the virtuous one, you remember, on very special terms with the Almighty. We used to say she had her place booked in the Heavenly Choir. And then . . . there she was. There was no doubt in my mind that she was a very frightened woman.

"She put out a hand to me. I took it. Hers was cold and clammy. She was very feeble but the light pressure on her fingers told me she wanted me to be there. She kept saying, 'I want . . . want . . . want . . .' I replied softly, 'Yes, Mrs. Polhenny, I am here. What is it you want? I am listening.' 'Have to . . . have to . . . ,' I could not make out what she was trying to tell me but I knew it was something on her mind. Then she started to make queer gurgling noises. I thought she needed help so I called for the nurse. I was sent out of the room and the doctor came in. That was the end, and I never knew why that urgent call had been sent to me. I waited at the hospital and a little while later they came out to tell me she was dead.

"I can tell you it was a terrible shock to us all. I think we had believed she was immortal. We expected she would still be riding that old bone-shaker up and down the hill when most of us were no more. Oh, how I hate change!

"How are you getting on? We think of you all the time. Pedrek has now arrived in New South Wales. His grandparents are sad without him. They say he will probably be away for two years.

"How I wish it could all have been different!"

I could scarcely read on. This terrible thing had ruined not only Pedrek's life and mine but all those who loved us.

Leah had returned from Cornwall. It was difficult to tell what her true feelings were. She had always been such a secretive person. She had found her mother dead when she arrived. There had been a certain amount to clear up. She had to arrange the sale of the furniture and other matters. My grandparents had been helpful and had insisted that she stay at Cador while all that was done.

The children were delighted to have her back. Belinda had been a little sad because Oliver had left so abruptly. I wondered what her reaction would be when she realized she was not going to see him again. His visits had always been spasmodic so, for the time being, she had no notion that anything was wrong and I did not give her any intimation. I thought the longer the time lapsed the easier it would be.

Then Tom Marner arrived.

Benedict told me about him. Since that day when I had had a glimpse of a different aspect of him, there had begun a growing friendship between us. It was as though a high barrier had been removed; but there were still others.

We were at dinner. There were only three of us: Benedict, Celeste and myself.

He said: "By the way, Tom Marner will be coming. He's now on his way over."

I imagined Celeste, like myself, had no notion who Tom Marner was.

"He's a good sort," went on Benedict. "A bit of a rough diamond, but he's a fellow one can trust. By the way, he's the man who bought the goldmine from me."

"And he is coming here?" asked Celeste in some alarm.

"If he's a good sort we shall enjoy meeting him," I said.

"I think you will be interested and amused. Honest . . . down-to-earth, no compromise."

"I know," I said. "The heart of gold under the rough exterior."

"I think you have the idea."

He looked faintly embarrassed as he did when he mentioned the mine. He guessed, rightly, that I should be thinking of the way he acquired it.

"I didn't sell outright," he went on. "I retained a small interest in it."

"So it is really a business visit," I said.

"You could say that. There are certain matters we want to discuss."

"Will he be staying in Manorleigh or London?" asked Celeste.

"Manorleigh first, I should think. And we may go up to London. He'll probably be here in a couple of weeks."

"We will get ready for him," said Celeste; and we went on to talk of other things.

I made use of the Australian's coming when Belinda talked about Oliver Gerson.

"It's funny," she said. "He went away without seeing us. He didn't say goodbye and it's ages since he came."

"Well, now we are going to have another visitor."

"Who?"

"Someone from the Outback."

"What's the Outback?"

"The wilds of Australia."

"Will he be painted red and blue with feathers in his hair?"

"That's North American Indians," said Lucie scornfully. "He's Australian."

"What do you know about it?"

"More than you do."

"No quarrelling," I said. "You will both have to be very polite to Mr. Marner."

"What's he like?"

"How should I know? I haven't seen him. He owns a goldmine."

"He must be very rich," said Belinda in awe. "Gold is worth a lot of money."

"Does he go down the mine?" asked Lucie.

"I don't know."

"Of course he does," said Belinda scornfully. "You have to go down to get the gold. So who will be getting it when he's not there?"

"He will have people managing it I daresay."

"Oh," said Belinda, impressed.

"Tell us about Australia," wheedled Lucie.

"I don't remember much. I was only a baby when I left."

They loved to hear the story, although they had heard it many times before of how my parents went out to Australia and lived in a little shack in a mining township, and how I had been born in Belinda's father's house which was the only place suitable for babies to be born in.

The subject of Australia was constantly referred to after that and the coming of Tom Marner brought a certain expectancy into the house.

Benedict's description of the rough diamond conjured up an image of a rather brash character who gave little attention to dress or manners; in fact the antithesis of Oliver Gerson. I wondered what Belinda's reaction would be. I was hoping that she would be diverted by him because she was talking of Oliver Gerson very frequently now and expecting that he would shortly be with us.

She had been so overwhelmed by the Gerson charm that I was sure she would find the Australian's manners a great contrast; and it seemed hardly likely that the rough diamond would go out of his way to win the approval of a child.

And then he arrived. He was very tall with a skin burned to bronze by the sun; and his bright blue eyes seemed to be screwed up as though he was still protecting himself from it even in our climate. His hair was bleached to a light blond —the sun again. I think the children were a little disappointed. They had expected him to look like a miner—at least their idea of one, basing it on the tin miners they had seen in Cornwall. He was quietly dressed in a navy blue suit, the darkness of which made the effects of his outdoor life almost startling.

"This is my wife," said Benedict.

He gripped Celeste's hand. "I've heard about you. Pleased to meet you."

"And my stepdaughter."

My hand was shaken.

"And the rest of the family . . ."

The children came forward and held out their hands to be shaken.

"How's everything going?" asked Benedict.

Tom Marner winked and put his finger against his nose. The children who were watching closely were clearly intrigued.

"You don't look like a miner," Belinda said boldly.

"That's 'cos I'm got up like a sixpenny doll . . . just to meet you folks. You should see me on the job." He gave Belinda a wink which made her giggle.

I could see there was an instant liking and I rejoiced. He'll take her mind off Oliver Gerson, I thought.

And so it proved. Tom Marner was a blessing.

He was the epitome of the rough diamond. Goodness shone out of him and one was immediately aware of his sterling honesty; he was good-tempered, easily amused and had a friendly easy-going attitude towards everyone.

Mrs. Emery secretly told me that she didn't

think he was quite the sort she expected in the house but there was no doubt that he appreciated what was done for him and he had a smile for everyone.

"He don't seem to know the difference between Miss Belinda and the servants. He called that tweeny 'Chickabidee' the other day, and I heard him call Miss Belinda the same."

"The children like him," I said. "And what is nice he has time for them."

"Yes, he seems fond of the little ones."

Miss Stringer had doubts as to the effect he might have on the children's manners and their use of the English language. They were saying "Good-o" now and talking about things being "dinkum."

I said I did not think it would do much harm.

He certainly brought a change to the household. I heard him and Benedict laughing together. Celeste found him an easy guest. He went riding with us and his expert horsemanship won Belinda's admiration—I might say adoration. He and his horse seemed like one. "You live on horseback in the Outback," he told them. He was skillful. He could tie amazing knots; he could make lassos. He taught them how to throw them round trees and had them practicing for hours. "It's not trees you want to catch though," he explalned. "It's cattle . . . or someone who's come to rob the homestead."

We were all fond of him in a very short time.

He did talk business a great deal with Benedict,

just as Oliver Gerson had done, so it did seem to me like a replacement for Belinda and I really believe she accepted him as such, for I noticed she ceased to talk so often of Oliver Gerson.

It soon became obvious that Tom Marner enjoyed the company of the children. As soon as they went into the garden he would be there with them. Leah was pleased about this. She had changed since the death of her mother but I was not sure in what way it had affected her. I imagined there had never been great love between them. It was hard to think of anyone's loving Mrs. Polhenny. In fact I had always been under the impression that Leah wanted to get away from her and I could understand that.

I wished Leah was more communicative. One could never understand what might be going on in her mind. I had tried to talk to her on one or two occasions but had never made any headway. Her devotion to the children was wonderful —particularly to Belinda. She understood Belinda's difficult nature better than any of us. Even she seemed to blossom a little under the influence of Tom Marner and I had heard her laugh quite heartily several times and join in the merriment he seemed to generate.

Celeste seemed relaxed in his company, so it was a very pleasant visit.

Sometimes I heard his cry echoing through the house: "Cooeee" and Belinda or Lucie would answer in the same way, and run to find him, anticipating some excitement, some story of the Out-back, or the fun of riding with him.

He was a lover of nature and his admiration for his own country soon became apparent.

He used to tell them stories of how the first fleet went out to Australia. "Prisoners . . . all of them . . . who had committed some petty crime . . . or no crime at all." He talked of how the convicts had suffered during the long haul across the ocean. How they had been lined up on deck when they reached that sun-drenched land, to be chosen as slaves and to work out their time of exile. He described the golden gorse and the eucalyptus trees, the colorful birds, the rosellas, the grey- and red-crested cockatoos called galahs, the kookaburra with its laughter, the one they called the laughing jackass.

We would often hear cries imitating the kookaburra. "It would be useful if the children were lost," said Miss Stringer, "or when one wanted them to come in from the garden."

She also approved of the history which was wrapped up in Tom Marner's racy conversation; so even she was not averse to his presence in the house.

All this talk of Australia naturally made me think even more of Pedrek. I wondered what he was doing out there and how often he thought of me. He would be reproaching me, I knew, for doubting him. In my heart I did not . . . and yet there was that niggling fear.

For the rest of my life, I thought, I shall go on

longing for him, believing in him . . . or would there always be that faint uncertainty?

But something told me that even if it were true, if I had loved him enough I should never have deserted him. Was not understanding . . . and forgiving . . . the very meaning of love? What did they say? In sickness and health. If this were a sickness, I had not been there to understand him or help him.

But he had been so horrified that I could not believe him. I did, I wanted to cry out. I did. But somewhere in my mind was that damning doubt.

How sad life was! There was Celeste who could look so sorrowful. Why could not life be simple . . . easy . . . as it seemed to be with people like Tom Marner?

I liked to be alone with my thoughts—far from happy ones, it was true. Sometimes I was on the verge of writing to Pedrek begging him to come back and let it be as it was in the past, so that we could get on with the future we had planned.

But in my heart I knew it could never be as we had planned. Always there would be the memory. I think my encounter with Jean Pascal—who mercifully had not visited his sister since—had made me more conscious of the horror of a victim in that situation. I would never forget the terror on Belinda's face, her bewilderment, her horror.

The children's preoccupation with Tom Marner gave me the opportunity I needed for a little solitude and I often rode out alone. I found a certain solace in the quiet of the country lanes, though Pedrek was always in my thoughts and I believed that our parting would cast a gloom over my life for ever more.

One afternoon I was on my way back to the house when I passed The Hanging Judge. I paused to look at it and remembered that occasion when Oliver Gerson had taken the children there, and how thrilled they had been to drink watered-down cider out of tankards.

As I approached two people emerged and made their way to the stables.

I stared after them. I could scarcely believe my eyes for one of them was Oliver Gerson, the other Celeste. I felt apprehensive. Celeste . . . meeting Oliver Gerson . . . secretly! It must be secret for he was not allowed into the house. What could it mean? I knew she was the sad and ne-glected wife . . . but Oliver Gerson!

I guessed it would be embarrassing to us all if they saw me so I turned abruptly and rode off in the opposite direction. For the rest of the day I wondered about what it meant.

I could see terrible trouble ahead if what I feared might be the case. Was she seeking conso-lation? And if she were to whom would she be more likely to turn but to a man who had great charm at his fingertips and a great deal of sympa-thy to offer to his enemy's wife. They would have much in common for they would share resentment towards Benedict. Both would have considered themselves to have been badly treated by him and it was very likely that they would want their revenge.

Was it any concern of mine? I asked. My stepfather's affairs were for him to sort out.

Yet something had happened to our relationship in the past weeks. I had a strong feeling that my mother was close to me . . . that she was urging me not to quarrel with him . . . to do all I could to help him.

Why did I get these fanciful ideas? It was due to living in a house in which it was said there was a ghost whose story had some resemblance to my mother's.

Benedict and I were the two whom she had loved dearly and I could not get out of my mind that there must be ties which even death could not break.

It had been one of her dearest wishes that Benedict and I should be friends.

I thought a good deal about Celeste and Oliver Gerson. I had heard him attempt blackmail and I was aware that he was an unscrupulous adventurer. Would Celeste know this or would she be only aware of that overwhelming charm, which I imagined would bring some balm to a woman who thought herself to be unwanted?

I decided to talk to her.

I asked her if she would come to my room because I wanted to show her something, but when she arrived, unsuspectingly, I thought it best to come straight to the point.

"Celeste," I said. "I know it is none of my business, but I was passing The Hanging Judge the other day . . ."

She was startled. She turned pale and then the color rushed into her face.

"You saw . . ."

"Yes. I saw you come out with Oliver Gerson." She did not answer.

"You know of course that Benedict has forbidden him to come to the house?"

She nodded.

I said: "Celeste, please forgive me . . . but . . ."

"I know what you are thinking. You are quite wrong. I went to see him because . . . well, you know he left the house in a hurry."

I nodded.

"He had found some lace mats in his luggage . . . only small things. He said he had swept them up at some time when he was getting his things together. He thought they might be valuable . . . special lace and so on . . . and he wanted to return them."

"And he did? And are they valuable?"

"I don't know. I'd never seen them before. I did not know they were missing. I just put them back in the room which had been his. Surely you didn't think . . ."

"Not really. But, you see, Benedict having quarrelled with him . . ."

"Benedict never talks to me of that sort of thing. Mr. Gerson said there had been some misunderstanding. He didn't want Benedict to know

447

that he had seen me . . . and he thought our meeting like that was the best way of returning the mats."

"He could be rather dangerous, you know," I said.

"Dangerous?"

"Well, there was this quarrel. I thought he would not be coming to the house again."

"He did tell me that he had been badly treated."

"And you believed his side of the story."

She shrugged her shoulders.

I did not know how far I could go and it occurred to me that I was getting into dangerous waters. Benedict had spoken to me on the spur of the moment, in the heat of his anger against Oliver Gerson and because he knew that I had overheard enough to piece some story together. He would trust my discretion. Perhaps I was going too far now.

"I don't think it is wise to see him," I finished lamely.

"It is good of you to worry about me, Rebecca. I'm all right. I would never take a lover . . . if that is what you are thinking. I love Benedict. I always have. I wish I didn't. I'm a fool, I know, but I do. He is the only one I want. It's not easy . . . being here with him when he shows so clearly that he does not love me.

"Dear Celeste, forgive me."

"There isn't anything to forgive. I'm so glad you are here. You've helped me a lot. Sometimes I am so wretched, Rebecca."

"You can always talk to me."

"Talking helps," she admitted. "You understand how it is."

"Yes, I understand. I meant forgive me for thinking . . ."

"You mean about Oliver Gerson?"

"I think he could be a dangerous man," I said.

It was always interesting to drink a cup of tea in Mrs. Emery's room. Her all-seeing eyes missed little. I knew at once that something excited her.

She poured out the tea in her special cups.

"My goodness, Miss Rebecca, that Mr. Marner is a one, isn't he? You can't help noticing that he's around . . . singing that one about kangaroos and things. You'd think you was in the wilds of Australia. But you can't help liking him. He's got a smile for everyone . . . no matter who. Mind you, he's not exactly what I'd call a true gentleman."

"It depends on your definition of a gentleman, Mrs. Emery."

"Oh, I know one when I see one. I've always worked for them. But he's a bit of a caution. That Miss Belinda thinks the sun shines out of his eyes."

"She is apt to get these feelings for people . . . and mostly men."

"She'll be a little Madam when she grows up, I shouldn't wonder."

"Some children are like that. They are attracted by people and put them on a pedestal."

I was rejoicing that her adoration for Oliver Gerson had waned and that Tom Marner had clearly stepped into his shoes.

"It does you good to hear them all laughing away," she said. "Another cup?"

"Thank you, Mrs. Emery. It's delicious."

She nodded, gratified.

"Have you noticed the change in that Leah?"

"Leah?" I queried.

"A bit of a misery, I used to think. Might have had all the troubles of the world on her shoulders. Well, she's changed. Now there she is laughing away with the children and that Mr. Marner. Do you know, I heard her singing the other day."

"What . . . Leah?"

"I couldn't believe my ears. She used to go round with that mournful face as though she was going to a funeral. Now chatting away she is . . . and she was always such a close customer."

"I'm glad. Mr. Marner seems to have made himself very popular."

"I suppose he'll soon be moving on."

"I'm afraid so. There will be lamentations in the nursery."

"Miss Belinda will be very sorry . . . that Leah, too. By the way, it's good news about the shuffle. That's what Emery calls it. Something to do with the government. It seems it's really coming now . . . after all the talk about it."

"You mean the Cabinet reshuffle."

"Emery knows all about these things. I reckon he ought to have gone in for it himself. He thinks there's a good chance of something coming out of it for our gentleman."

"Mr. Lansdon?"

"Who else? It's not only Emery. There's a bit in the paper. Emery cuts bits out and saves them, you know. Emery would like the Foreign Office for him but he doesn't think there is going to be a change there. The Home Office would be good. Or the War Office . . . Emery says."

"You're very ambitious for him."

"Emery's a very ambitious man."

I could not help smiling at this perfect example of the joys of reflected glory.

"We're keeping our fingers crossed . . . Emery and me . . ."

I was still smiling. A session with Mrs. Emery was as refreshing as her tea.

When I was passing Benedict's study, he opened the door suddenly and stood smiling at me.

"Rebecca, could you spare a moment?"

"But of course."

"Then come in."

I went in, he indicated a chair and I sat down. He took his place at his desk and we sat facing each other.

"I thought I'd let you know," he said. "I am definitely out of the club business. The deal has gone through."

"That must be a great relief to you."

"Yes, it is. The Devil's Crown decided me. I only wish I could have done it years ago."

"I hear there is a possibility of a Cabinet post."

"A possibility," he admitted. "There's only a hint at the moment, but I think there is almost certain to be one."

"Well, good luck."

"Thank you."

"The Emerys are very eager for your success."

He smiled. "I gathered that from Emery."

"They are very loyal."

He nodded. "And one needs loyalty in this business."

"It's very acceptable in any."

"I thought I'd tell you about the clubs because of our little talk the other day. It was what your mother would have wanted."

We were silent for a moment.

Then he said: "By the way, Gerson hasn't been prowling round, has he?"

I had a quick vision of him, coming out of The Hanging Judge with Celeste.

"Around the house . . . no, I shouldn't think so."

"That's good. I never discovered how he got that key. I should like to know. I don't suppose I ever shall. But that sort of thing shakes one. I've always been so careful."

"Yes," I said. "It's a mystery."

I rose. Our conversation seemed to have come

452

to an end and our relationship was still such that there was embarrassment between us.

I said: "I'm glad about the clubs. I am sure it is for the best."

He nodded. "I thought you'd like to know."

I went to the door and as I did so, he said: "You shouldn't be so much in the country. You should be in London . . . getting out and about. That was what your season was for."

"I prefer to be in the country."

"Might you not regret it later?"

I shrugged my shoulders.

"Has something happened?" he asked.

"Something happened . . ." I repeated stupidly.

"You seem withdrawn lately. Brooding on something, are you?"

"I'm all right."

"Well, if I can help . . ."

I shook my head.

"I really think you are making a mistake in shutting yourself away like this. What's happened to Morwenna Cartwright? Wasn't she supposed to launch you into society?"

"That was at the time."

"Well, it goes on, doesn't it?"

"I think I am supposed to be launched now."

"It's no good shutting yourself away in the country."

"I assure you I'm all right."

"If it is what you want . . ."

"It is."

"Are you sure there is nothing wrong? Nothing I can do to help?"

"Thank you. There is nothing."

He looked at me quizzically. He was trying hard to put things right between us. He would be telling himself that he ought to do it for my mother's sake. He had now sold out of the clubs because that was what she wanted him to do. No. It was not because of that. Had he not clung to them for all these years? No, he wanted to become a Cabinet minister and as such he could not be involved in them. I must not forget that he had kept his secret papers in what was supposed to be a shrine to my mother.

In the midst of his sentimentality, Benedict would always be practical.

I went out and closed the door.

Benedict had gone to London and Celeste had not gone with him.

She had been very quiet and I was wondering whether she was seeing Oliver Gerson. I had a twinge of conscience because when Benedict had asked me if I had seen him round the place I had said no. What else could I have said? It would have been tantamount to a suggestion that there was some sort of relationship between Oliver Gerson and Celeste.

It was midmorning when Mrs. Emery came to my room. I knew something dramatic had happened by her expression.

"What is it?" I cried.

"It's Mrs. Lansdon . . ."

"What of her?" I asked in alarm.

"She's not in her room. Her bed hasn't been slept in."

"Could she have gone to London?"

Mrs. Emery shook her head. "It seems as if her things are all there."

"You mean she has just walked out . . . taking nothing."

"As far as I can see, Miss Rebecca."

"I'll come up there."

I went to their bedroom. The room was in order. The maid had turned down the bed as she did every evening and it was as smooth as it would have been when she made it on the previous morning.

I turned to Mrs. Emery in dismay.

"She must have gone last night," she said.

"Gone? Gone where?"

"Search me," said Mrs. Emery. "She could have gone anywhere."

"What has she taken with her?"

"Nothing as far as I can see. Better get that Yvette. She's always been her personal maid. She'd know what's going on."

"Let's get her right away."

Yvette came.

"When did you last see Mrs. Lansdon?" I asked.

"Why, Mademoiselle, it was last night."

"Do you know where she is now?"

Yvette looked blank. "She send for me when

she is ready . . . to dress her hair . . . I wait till I am called. This morning . . . she has not call. I think she does not wish for me . . ."

"Did she seem all right last night?"

"A little quiet . . . perhaps. But then . . . she is so . . . now and then."

"She didn't say she was going to meet somebody?"

"No, Mademoiselle. She say nothing to me."

"Do you not bring her something in the morning . . . tea . . . chocolate . . . coffee?"

"If she ask, yes. If not, I leave her. She likes to sleep late some mornings."

"Will you look at her clothes, Yvette, and tell me if anything is missing?"

She went to the cupboard and the wardrobe; she opened the drawers.

"No . . . nothing . . . there is only the grey velvet she was wearing last night."

"So that is the only thing that has gone?"

"Yes, Mademoiselle, and the grey shoes she wear with it."

"Her coat?"

"There is a coat which go with the grey velvet. That here. Some of her clothes go . . . last week. She gave them away to people in the cottages . . . as she does . . . always. There is nothing else missing."

"What about her handbag?"

"She have a beautiful crocodile one now. Yes, that is here."

"It would seem that she went out without anything but what she was wearing."

"Perhaps she take a walk."

"Last night? And was she in the habit of taking walks?"

Yvette shook her head vigorously. "Non, non, non," she said emphatically.

I told Yvette that she could go and when she had left I turned to Mrs. Emery. "This is very mysterious," I said. "Where can she be?"

Mrs. Emery shook her head.

"What are we going to do?" I asked.

"Perhaps she went for a walk and has fallen and hurt herself . . . not able to get back to the house. Yes, that's the most likely."

"We'll get Mr. Emery to organize a search. She has to be here near the house. Yvette says she did not go for a walk. But you never know. The impulse may have taken her. We've got to start looking without delay."

We found Mr. Emery who immediately took charge. Tom Marner joined in. He was very efficient. When the grounds had been explored and yielded nothing the search went on farther afield.

The morning was passing and there was no trace of Celeste. We could not delay telling Benedict any longer.

A message was sent off to London explaining that his wife was missing.

I sat in Mrs. Emery's room. I could see how worried she was.

"The servants will be talking," she said. "This will get round. Oh, where is she? If only she'd come walking in! Emery's worried. The papers will have a field day with this, he said. It could do Mr. Lansdon's chances a lot of harm. The way things look, Miss Rebecca, I don't like it at all."

"I'm not surprised. Nor do I."

"She's just gone. She doesn't seem to have taken anything. It would have been better if she had."

"Why?"

"Well, then we should have known she had gone of her own free will. As it is . . ."

"Mrs. Emery, what are you thinking?"

"I'm thinking that this isn't going to do him any good. If she'd left him for someone else . . . well, that's not very nice . . . but he can't be blamed for it . . . though the papers would try to make something out of it. You can see this is just about the worst time it could happen."

"Last time . . ."

"Yes, I know all about that. When he was standing for Manorleigh for the first time. His wife died and there was a bit of a mystery about him. They blamed him and it cost him the seat."

"I remember hearing about it."

"If there's a scandal about this it will all be brought up again. There will be a lot of raking over the past."

"Mrs. Emery, she must be somewhere near. She wouldn't have run away from him without

458

anything . . . only the clothes she was standing up in."

"I can't think what it means."

"Nor can I."

Mrs. Emery went on: "It looks to me as if she didn't leave the house of her own free will."

"How could it be otherwise?"

"If she'd gone at night and taken a case full of some of her things with her . . . it would make sense. But she's gone with nothing and we've searched the gardens and round about and still . . . no sign of her."

"I don't know what explanation there can be," I said.

"It frightens me," added Mrs. Emery.

It frightened me, too.

Benedict returned, and we began to realize how serious the matter was. He questioned every one of us and there was no doubt that Celeste had left the house on the previous night taking nothing with her. The search had been extended and she could not be found.

We knew that it could not be long before the news was out. It came sooner than we expected.

"Wife of prominent M.P. disappears. Tragedy-haunted Benedict Lansdon is the centre of a new mystery. His wife, Mrs Celeste Lansdon, is missing from her home in her husband's constituency of Manorleigh. As she appears to have taken nothing but the clothes she was wearing there is alarming speculation as to what has happened to her. It will be remembered that Benedict Lansdon's first wife died during his original and unsuccessful campaign in Manorleigh and there were suggestions of foul play. It was, however, afterwards proved that she was suffering from an incurable illness and took her own life. Unlucky Mr Lansdon is now at his home in Manorleigh where extensive enquiries are being made, and there is no doubt that the mystery will soon be solved."

There was a hush over the house. The servants were talking in whispers. I could imagine the theories which were being circulated. I saw the expressions of excitement . . . suppressed into concern, of course, but they were there. They were hoping for startling developments. I wondered how many of them knew of the strained relations between the master and mistress of the house.

I also wondered what would be revealed when the press intruded on us and its members talked to the servants . . . always the most informed of detectives, keeping a close watch on our lives. What would the police get from them? I could imagine the questions . . . and the answers.

Tom Marner was a boon to us during that time. He took the children off our hands. They went riding with him and he was often in the nursery. I would hear their laughter which sounded odd in a house of fear.

We felt so helpless. What could we do? What had happened to Celeste? If only she would walk into the house and tell us she was well. If only we knew. It was so frustrating. She had just disappeared without a trace.

The first few days had passed and speculation was rife. The police had called. They spent a long time with Benedict. They asked some of us questions, including myself. Had I seen her the night she disappeared? Had I noticed anything unusual?

No, I told them. There had been nothing unusual.

"Had Mrs. Lansdon seemed distressed . . . afraid? Had she mentioned that someone had been threatening her?"

"Certainly not."

The questions frightened me. They held a suggestion of foul play.

Did I know any reason why she should suddenly walk out of the house?

I did not. She was not a great walker. We had both said goodnight and gone to our respective rooms.

"What was the time then?"

"About nine o'clock."

"Did anyone see her after nine?"

I thought no one had.

Yvette was closely interrogated. Everything had seemed as normal, she said.

"Was there any reason why Mrs. Lansdon should leave home?"

There was none that she knew of.

I guessed that they had not ruled out the possibility of murder.

Jean Pascal arrived at Manorleigh. It would have been impossibly embarrassing meeting him had it not been for the terrible tragedy which dwarfed everything else into insignificance.

He looked distracted and grief-stricken. He talked to Benedict in his study and when he emerged he was pale and clearly disturbed. He told us that his parents were very worried. They were neither of them well enough to travel and he would have to go straight back to them but would keep in close touch.

He did have a word with me before he left.

"Don't think too badly of me," he said. "I've repented. I am truly sorry, Rebecca. I misjudged you. I have meant to come here on one or two occasions, but could not imagine how you would receive me."

"I am afraid it would not have been very graciously."

"So I guessed. This is a terrible business. We did not see very much of each other recently but she was . . . is . . . my sister."

"If anything comes to light we shall let you know immediately."

He frowned. "Was everything all right between . . . them?"

"What do you mean?"

"Well, she seems to have disappeared."

I said, "Mr. Lansdon was not here when it

happened. He was in London. We had to send for him."

"I see."

"You can be sure," I reiterated, "that we shall keep you informed of whatever happens."

"Thank you."

I could not help being relieved when he left.

A week had passed. There were paragraphs in the paper.

"Where is Mrs Lansdon?" The headlines stared out at me. I could imagine how the matter was being discussed all over the country.

My grandmother wrote. "This must be distressing for you right in the midst of it. Would it be possible for you to come to Cornwall for a while?"

I shivered at the thought. There were too many memories in Cornwall. I should be constantly reminded of Pedrek . . . and there his grandparents would have to be faced. I was glad to be out of London to avoid meeting Morwenna and Justin Cartwright. I believed they blamed me for breaking off the engagement which had sent Pedrek to the other side of the world. I could not bear to think of facing any of them. I could never explain what had happened and to be in Cador would make the bitterness all the more vivid.

Besides, I had to be here. For some strange reason I thought Benedict might need my help.

I could not imagine why I should feel this.

He had always been my enemy. I understood the veiled suggestions which were circulating. He was a ruthless and ambitious man, and his wife had disappeared. Why? Had she been an encumbrance? Had he plans which did not include her?

A member of the press had cornered Yvette. They discovered through subtle questioning that the relationship between the husband and wife had not been a happy one.

We read in the papers: "He never had any time for her, said her personal maid. She was very upset about it. She was seen crying. She seemed desperate sometimes . . ."

Yvette was horrified when she read the papers. I guessed that her sometimes imperfect English had led her into saying more than she meant to reveal.

"I did not say it . . . I did not," she cried. "He kept on . . . he make me say that which I do not mean . . ."

Poor Yvette. She had not meant to cast suspicion on her mistress's husband. But of course this was seized on. There were sly hints. One of the less reputable papers printed a piece about him.

"The member for Manorleigh is unlucky in love . . . or should one say marriage. His first wife, Lizzie, from whom he inherited a goldmine which has made him many times a millionaire, killed herself; his second wife died in childbirth, and now his third, Celeste, has disappeared. But perhaps there will be a happy ending to this one.

464

The police are pursuing their inquiries and are hopeful to solve the mystery soon."

A week passed and there was still no news of Celeste. The police were searching for her. Emery came in with the news that they had been digging up Three Acre Field by the paddock because it looked as though the earth had been freshly turned over.

That was a terrible time. I was afraid that they would find Celeste buried there.

Nothing was found and there was silence for a few more days.

The news of Celeste's disappearance was replaced by that of the Cabinet reshuffle as worthy of the headlines. I don't think anyone was surprised that there was no place in it for Benedict.

The news was in the papers that morning.

"No place in Cabinet for M.P. whose wife has mysteriously disappeared. Mr Benedict Lansdon, the M.P. for whom all seemed set fair for a high post in the Cabinet, has been passed over. Police intimate they may have an answer to the riddle shortly."

How subtly cruel they were in linking up his being passed over with his wife's disappearance. We all knew it was the reason why his hopes had been blighted, but to stress it seemed unnecessary. It was almost like pronouncing Benedict guilty of killing his wife, which was of course what they were suggesting.

Benedict had taken the papers to his study. I was very sad at the thought of his reading those cruel words and a sudden impulse came to me. I knocked at his door.

"Come in," he said.

I went in. He was sitting at his desk with the newspapers spread out before him.

"I'm sorry," I said.

He knew what I meant for he replied: "It was inevitable."

I advanced into the room and slipped into the chair facing him.

"It can't go on," I said. "There has to be news soon."

He shrugged his shoulders.

"Benedict . . . do you mind if I call you Benedict? I can't call you Mr. Lansdon and . . ."

He smiled wryly. "It seems a strange matter to worry about at such a time. You can't bring yourself to call me father or stepfather . . . I always understood that. Call me Benedict. Why not? It makes us more friendly. Perhaps that was one of the reasons why you wouldn't accept me. You couldn't find a name for me."

He laughed but it was mirthless laughter. I knew he was desperately upset and worried.

"What is going to happen?" I asked.

"That is something I cannot tell. Where can she be, Rebecca? Have you any idea?"

"Where should she go . . . just as she was? She has taken nothing . . . her handbag . . . she is without money."

"It looks as though something happened to her. The police think she is dead, Rebecca."

"How can you be sure?"

"You must have heard. They have dug up Three Acre Field. Why should they do that? Because they expected they would find her there."

"Oh no!"

"I am sure they suspect murder."

Of course, he had been through something like this before when his first wife had died of an overdose of laudanum. It had made him acutely aware of the hints and innuendoes, just as it had made him doubly open to suspicion.

"But who . . . ?" I began.

"In these cases the husband is the first suspect."

"Oh no. How could it be? You were not here."

"What was to stop my coming to the house, letting myself in . . . going to the room we shared . . . taking a pillow . . . pressing it over her face and then . . . getting rid of the body?"

I stared at him in horror.

"I didn't do it, Rebecca. I knew nothing of her disappearance until I received your message. Do you believe me?"

"Of course I believe you."

"I really think you mean that."

"I can't understand how you could think for a moment that I could believe anything else."

"Thank you. It's a very sorry business. Where will it end?"

"Perhaps she will come back."

"Do you think she will?"

"Yes . . . I do. I think she will."

"But where from . . . and why? There's no sense in it . . . no reason."

"Mysteries are always like that until they are solved."

"I've gone over and over it in my mind. Possible solutions . . . but I can find none good enough to believe. Oh, it's a wearying subject, and I am to blame, Rebecca, I am responsible for this as surely as if I had smothered her with a pillow."

"You must stop talking like this. It's not true."

"You know it is true. You know I have made her unhappy, don't you?"

"Yes."

"Did she confide in you?"

"A little."

"You see . . . whatever she has done . . . I am responsible. I should have tried harder."

"It's hard to try at love."

"I should never have married her, but I thought it might work. It was foolish of me to try to replace Angelet."

"No one could. But you could have found some happiness with her. She loved you absolutely."

"She was too demanding. Perhaps if she had been less so I could have managed better. But there is no excuse. I have suffered something like this before, Rebecca. If I thought I had killed her with my indifference . . . with my love for Angelet . . . I could not live very easily with the knowledge. How could life have been so cruel? I thought I had everything I wanted in life . . . we both wanted that child . . . she did very, very

468

much . . . and then it was all snatched from me. Why? And all for . . . Belinda. Why am I telling you all this?"

"Because we are now friends . . . because I can now call you Benedict."

A faint smile played about his lips. Then he said: "But what of you, Rebecca? You are not happy. Before all this . . . I noticed it."

"*You* noticed?"

"I wanted to ask what had happened. But we were so withdrawn, weren't we? There was no friendship between us. We were like potential enemies ready to go to war with each other at the slightest provocation."

"Yes," I agreed, "we were like that."

"I have let you see right into the heart of me," he said. "What about you, Rebecca?"

"I have been very unhappy."

"A love affair, was it?"

"Yes."

"My poor child, how can I help?"

"Nobody can help."

"Couldn't you tell me?"

I hesitated.

"If you do not," he went on, "I feel that we have not really found this new friendship which means so much to me."

"I don't think you would have approved perhaps. You wanted a grand marriage for me . . . because I was your stepdaughter."

"I . . ."

"There was that costly London season."

"It was then, was it? Some perfidious man?"

"Oh no. I always thought you would try to prevent our marriage, for after the cost of that season you would have wanted me to marry a duke or something like that."

"All I wanted was your happiness because that was what your mother would have wished."

"We were going to be married."

"You and . . . ?"

"Pedrek . . . Pedrek Cartwright."

"Oh. A nice young man. I was always interested in him because he was born in my house. I remember it well. What happened?"

I was silent for a few moments, not wishing to speak of it.

"Tell me," he insisted. "I find it hard to believe that he would behave badly. What was it, Rebecca?"

"It's . . . it's hard to talk of."

"Tell me."

I found myself telling. I described that terrible scene when Belinda had come running in to us with that horrific story. Benedict listened in blank amazement.

He said: "I don't believe it."

"We none of us could."

"And that child . . . Belinda . . . she told you this?"

"She was so distressed. If you had been there, you would have seen . . ."

"And you confronted Pedrek with this?"

"He came the next morning . . . just as though nothing had happened . . ."

"And what did he say?"

"He denied it."

"And you believed the child and not him?"

"If you had seen her crying and distressed . . . her clothes torn."

"And she said it happened at St Branok's Pool. That's significant."

"It happens to be a lonely spot."

He seemed to be looking far away. "I remember it well," he said.

He seemed very thoughtful. Then he said: "Did it occur to you to doubt the child?"

"I told you how she looked. She was distraught. She had obviously been molested."

"There is something odd about this because something happened years before you were born when your mother was a child. I was not much more. It was at the pool of St Branok. This is what I find so odd about it. A murderer had escaped from jail. He was under sentence of death for having raped and murdered a little girl. This is something I never told anyone but I am telling you, Rebecca, because I think it could have a bearing on this matter. When your mother was a little girl she came face to face with this murderer at St Branok's Pool."

I caught my breath in horror.

He went on: "I came in time. I went for him and he fell and struck his head on a boulder. It killed him. We were young and frightened and

471

we did not know what to do. You are shocked. You are stunned. These things come suddenly upon you. We dragged his body to the pool and pushed him into the water. I know it is dramatic . . . sensational, the sort of thing one sometimes reads of in the papers, things that may happen to other people but should not to us. We kept our secret . . . your mother and I. It is a long story. Perhaps it was all part of the bond which held us together. It certainly influenced our lives. It was the reason for our parting. You see while it drove us apart it forged the unbreakable bond. You would have to live through it to understand it. But let us think of your problem. Does it not seem odd to you that a similar thing should have happened to Belinda?"

"Yes," I said. "But it is a lonely spot. There is only one small cottage nearby. It is a place where that sort of thing could happen."

"Might it not be that an imaginative child who had heard the story might have conjured it up?"

"But the look in her face . . . her clothes . . . Besides, nobody would have told her the story and if she had heard it she would not have understood what it really meant."

He was silent for a while. He seemed to be considering. Then he said: "Would you take a piece of advice from me?"

"I would certainly listen to it."

"Pedrek is in Australia now, is he? He was so hurt and disgusted by your suspicions that your

472

engagement was broken off and he went away. Is that the story?"

"Yes," I answered.

"Go to your room now and write to him. Tell him that he must come back. That you are wretched without him. That's true, isn't it?"

"Yes, but . . ."

"Do you want to live your life regretting . . . ? You love him, do you not? I know you have been together a good deal. It was not a sudden attraction. It has grown gradually. It has deep roots and you really love him. I know that. Yours could be a wonderful marriage. When you have the chance of happiness, you must not turn from it. You must hold on to it. Never let it be your fault that it ended."

"I know I shall always be miserable . . . but always, too, I shall think of Belinda coming in from the pool . . . that terror in her . . . the horror of it."

"Write to him. Tell him you made a mistake. Don't be afraid to admit it, for I know you have made a mistake. Tell him that you want him back, that you believe in him. Tell him that it could not be otherwise. Write to him . . . write today."

"Perhaps I should think about it."

He had risen from his chair. He came towards me and I stood up to face him. There was an earnest look in his eyes.

"Believe me. I am right," he said. "I know how much you care for him. There will never be anyone else for you. Don't lose this, Rebecca.

Some of us make big mistakes which ruin our lives. Tell him how much you love him. Do not say whatever he has done you will love him. Tell him you do not have any shadow of a doubt now about that crime of which he was accused. Tell him you believe *him* . . . completely. Put your trust in him. Tell him you know he is innocent and beg him to come home."

"But . . . I am not sure . . ."

"You will be. I know you will be. I think I am going to prove to you that I am right, but first of all you must send that letter . . . send it to him . . . without delay. I can see now how I can help you. That is why you should not wait. This is what your mother would want. Think of her. If she is looking down on you she will have mourned for the loss of your happiness. She wanted you to be happy so much. She cared so much for you. Rebecca, we have to live without her. Let's see if we can help each other to do that. You look a little happier already.

"It is the thought of writing to Pedrek."

"Go then . . . go now and do it."

Benedict is one of the most forceful men I ever knew. I could understand how it was that, among all those men who went to Australia to look for gold, he found it. He was a man who would always succeed at whatever he set himself to do. He may have been ruthless, but that was necessary if he were to reach his goal; he had a way of enforcing his beliefs until one accepted them as one's own.

In spite of the turmoil in the house and the terrible shadow which hung over it—and in particular over Benedict—he could give his mind to my problem and I felt happier than I had ever since the day when Belinda had run in from St Branok's Pool.

Benedict had convinced me. I could not believe that Pedrek was guilty and there must be some other explanation.

I sat down and wrote:

Dearest Pedrek,

I love you. I am so miserable without you. It was all so quick. I could not face it then, but now I believe in you. I have always believed in you. I *know* that it was all a mistake and will be proved to be so in time. I want you back. Please believe me. We will face whatever has to be faced together. I know we can just as I know you are innocent of what you were accused. We will prove it in time, but now . . . I believe in you and we have each other.

So please, *please*, come back to me.

Your ever faithful Rebecca.

Perhaps it was a little hysterical. Perhaps it did not convey all I felt. But it was sincere. Benedict had had that effect on me. He had made me see my true feelings. He had made me believe in Pedrek.

The letter was posted.

Would he come? Would he forgive me for doubting him?

Just as I knew he could never be guilty, I knew he would come.

Benedict said to me: "Have you written to Pedrek?"

"Yes."

"Telling him you believe in him."

"I have."

He smiled. "I want you to come to my study."

I went with him. He sent for one of the servants and when she came, he said: "Will you go to the nursery and bring Miss Belinda to me here, please?"

"Yes, sir. I'll tell Leah to bring her."

"There is no need for Leah to bring her. She knows the way."

In due course Belinda came. She looked a little uneasy and suspicious and not without that certain bellicosity which I had noticed she assumed in Benedict's presence.

"Shut the door and come in," said Benedict.

She obeyed somewhat unwillingly.

"Now," he said, "I want to talk to you. Cast your mind back to that time when you were at St Branok's Pool."

She flushed scarlet. "I . . . I don't have to talk about it. It's, it's bad for me. I have to forget it."

"Perhaps you can forget it later. Just at the

moment I want you to remember it. I want you to tell me exactly what happened . . . I mean the truth."

"It's bad for me, I don't have to remember."

"But I want to know."

She was afraid of him, I could see, and I felt sorry for her. He was remembering that she was the child whose coming had brought about her mother's death, and for that he could not forgive her.

"Come along," he said. "Let's talk, shall we? Let's get it over."

"It was Pedrek," she said.

"We'll start at the beginning. Why did you go to the pool? You weren't supposed to go out at that time alone, were you?"

"I went to take a book to Mary Kellaway at the cottage."

"Did you see Mary Kellaway?"

"No . . . he was there first."

"What happened to the book?"

"I . . . I don't know. He just . . . jumped at me."

"Did Mary Kellaway tell you about the murderer who was found in the pool when they dragged it?"

"No, that was . . ."

"Not Mary Kellaway. Then someone else?"

"Mary Kellaway used to tell us old stories about the bells down the pool and knackers and ghosts and things."

"I see. Then who told you about the murderer?"

"That was Madge."

"Madge?"

"One of the maids at Cador," I said. "She was
often with the children."

"So Madge told you about the murderer, did
she?"

"Yes." She smiled, remembering and momentarily forgetting her fear. "He'd been in the pool
for a long time."

"Did she tell you whom he murdered?"

"Yes, it was a little girl . . . well, not really very
little. She was about eight or nine."

"About your age. Did she tell you what he had
done to the little girl?"

She was silent.

"She did, didn't she?"

"Well, she said not to tell. She said we were too
young to understand."

"But you are clever and you did."

She was rather pleased at the suggestion.

"Oh yes," she said. "I did."

"You didn't like Pedrek Cartwright, did you?"

"I didn't mind him."

"I want a truthful answer. Why did you go out
that evening, Belinda? Where is the book you took
to your friend? What happened to it?"

"I . . . I don't know."

"You don't know because there wasn't a book.
You didn't see Pedrek at the pool, did you?"

478

"I did. I did. He attacked me . . . just like the murderer did . . . but I ran away."

"Why, Belinda?"

"Well, I didn't want to be . . . done that to, did I?"

"I mean why did you do it?"

"I didn't do anything. I only ran away."

"It's no use lying any more. You went to the pool. You tore your clothes. You put soil on your face. You even scratched yourself. It was acting, wasn't it, and you liked acting. It was a good game, and when they were all worried about you, you came back and told those dreadful lies."

"I didn't. I didn't. I hate you. You've always hated me. You think I killed my mother. I didn't. I didn't want to be born."

I was filled with pity and took a step towards her, but Benedict signed to me to stand back.

He said gently: "I don't blame you, Belinda. I never have. I want to be good friends with you. Let's try, shall we?"

She stopped crying and looked at him.

"We'll help each other. I'll help you and you'll help me. Your mother would be very unhappy if she knew we were bad friends."

She was silent. He went to her and knelt down beside her.

He said: "Tell me the truth. Tell me everything. You won't be blamed for I am sure you had a reason for what you did. You love Rebecca, don't you?"

She nodded vigorously.

"You don't want her to be unhappy, do you?"

She shook her head. Then she said: "It was because . . . because . . ."

"Yes, yes?"

"It was for her."

"For Rebecca?"

She nodded again. "She was going to marry him. I didn't want her to. I wanted her to marry Oliver. We could all have lived together. It would have been nicer for her . . ."

"I see. So you did it because you thought you knew what was best for Rebecca? You are not very old, you know, to judge for other people."

"I knew it would be lovely if we could all live together. What . . . what are you going to do to me?"

I went to her then and took her hands in mine.

"Do you hate me?" she asked.

I shook my head.

"He's gone away, hasn't he? He's gone to Australia."

"Yes."

"And you didn't want him to. You do hate me."

"No. I understand now. But it was a wicked thing to do. You must never do anything like that again."

"It was only a game."

"A game which has hurt a lot of people."

"But I did it for you."

"You knew you were wrong though, didn't you?"

She started to cry again.

"But," I went on, "you'll feel better now you have told us. It's always good to confess. Now you can start again."

"I'm sorry, Rebecca. Oliver would have been fun to have with us and he would have married you. We don't see him now."

"But there is Mr. Marner. You like him, don't you?"

"But he'll go back to Australia."

"Perhaps not for a little while." I turned to Benedict. "I think I should take her back to Leah. I'll tell Leah what's happened."

She suddenly flung her arms round my neck. "I did it for you as well," she said.

"As well as for yourself. I know."

"And Lucie, too. She liked him."

"I understand. Now we are going to forget all about it. But promise me you won't ever do anything like that again."

She shook her head and clung to me.

"Come on," I said. "Let's go now."

She did not look at Benedict as I led her out. I left her with Leah.

"There has been a bit of an upset," I said. "I think she needs to be alone with you. She will tell you about it. I will later. But just now . . . soothe her, Leah."

Leah always seemed to understand. She took Belinda in her arms.

I went back to Benedict's study. He was waiting for me.

481

"How did you know?" I asked.

"She's a strange child. I know she is my daughter but she bears no resemblance to her mother or to me. She is like a changeling. I have watched them from my study window sometimes. I find Lucie more appealing. Belinda bears me a grudge."

"You have ignored her."

"I know. I couldn't forget. If she had been a different child . . ."

"It was a terrible thing to do . . . to let a child feel she has caused her mother's death. I know it is not the first time this sort of thing has happened, but it should never be."

"I know. I am to blame. But there is something about her which . . . in a way repels. Celeste told me that she took your mother's clothes and played the ghost. It shows a strange quirk in her nature."

"It is because you have aroused this feeling of guilt in her."

"I have done so much that is wrong. But it was so premeditated. She stole the key from Mrs. Emery's drawer to get the clothes . . . it was not a matter of dressing up on the spur of the moment. It was *planned*. She knew it would cause distress and I guessed—though it was only a surmise—that this was another of her well-thought-out schemes. She is devious."

"She is clever to deceive us all."

"You were too ready to be deceived."

"It is because of her youth. I would never have thought she knew about that long-ago murder."

"Foolish people talk to her. There was that

maid. You can imagine her version. Then the little girl whose father had been in the mine accident. She would be interested in stories of disaster . . . legends . . . bells at the pool. The salacious Madge would corrupt the mind of the young. They would not fully understand, but they would know enough to give a girl like Belinda the material she needed for her game."

"I feel a little lightheaded."

"You see why I wanted you to get this letter off to Pedrek? I did not want you to write to him later and say you had discovered the truth. I wanted that letter to go first. I wanted you to show your faith in him . . . the depth of your feelings . . ."

"I don't know what to say to you. I can't help feeling happy although . . ."

"Well, at least there is a little brightness now. I feel happier too. Believe me, it grieved me to see you so sad."

He took my hands and gripped them hard.

"I don't know what to say to you," I began.

"Then say nothing. We'll talk . . . we'll talk a lot . . . later."

The Devil's Crown

Feelings of elation mingled oddly with a terrible apprehension. This was a house of shadows with a menacing cloud hanging over it. And so it would remain until Celeste was found. But there was something miraculous in my new relationship with my stepfather, and the manner in which he had dealt with my unhappiness filled me with tender admiration for him.

It seemed that he, who had always before been on the fringe of my life, had now walked into it and swept aside all obstacles to my happiness. He had always given an impression of power, and how astute he was for as soon as he was aware of what had happened, he had guessed at the truth and exposed it in a masterly fashion.

I wished that I could do something for him.

I wrote to Pedrek telling him what had happened, making sure, as Benedict would have advised me, that he knew I had written my previous letter before the revelations.

Then I wrote to my grandparents, the Pencarrons and Morwenna and Justin. I told them all that I had already written to Pedrek some days before the truth was known, that I believed in him and hoped he would forgive me for doubting him even for a short time; and I was waiting to hear from him that his feelings towards me had not changed.

I knew what joy that would bring them all. We could now be together in harmony just as we had been in the past.

I asked them all not to think too hardly of Belinda. She was only a child and it had been a great tragedy for her that she had lost her mother before she could know her. We must all try to understand that.

"I have talked to Benedict," I wrote. "And he wants to do everything he can to make a harmonious family life for us all. At the moment, of course, he is terribly worried and unhappy with this fearful mystery hanging over us. But I am convinced that the truth will come out soon."

I wondered how long it would take for my letter to reach Pedrek and for him to reply. It was a long way for a letter to go—to the other side of the world.

Meanwhile it was the waiting period. I could not believe that Pedrek would not come back to me. But then he would not have believed I could think him guilty of such a monstrous crime. He must have been bitterly and deeply wounded. Did that sort of thing leave a scar forever?

My grandparents wrote of their delight. How understanding they were! They spared a little sympathy for Belinda in spite of the havoc she had wrought in our lives.

"We must remember that she is only a child,"

wrote my grandmother, "and I suppose she did it for your happiness as well as her own. She, in her simple innocence, thought she could play God and direct your lives. At what a cost to poor Pedrek! Let us hope that he will soon come home and that you will be happy together."

And it was Benedict who had done this. But for him I should not have written that letter. Only he could have made Belinda confess the truth.

How I wished that I could help him!

For some time I had felt a twinge of guilt because I had never said anything about that occasion when I had seen Celeste and Oliver Gerson together at The Hanging Judge. Was it of any significance?

How could I know? But in a case like this any small detail could be of importance. Who knew which were the key pieces to fit into the puzzle to complete the picture?

I could not bring myself to speak to him of Oliver Gerson. He hated the man and would not have him in the house. Understandably since he had tried to blackmail him. As for Oliver Gerson, the thought had occurred to me that he might be responsible for some of the pieces which had appeared in the press. I could well imagine his revelling in supplying damning information. I was sure he was delighted to see Benedict in trouble.

I could not believe that Celeste was dead. I awoke one morning. I had been dreaming, but it was as though a revelation had come to me. In my dream I had seen Oliver Gerson, with a malicious expression on his face. I heard his voice: "Don't think I shall let this pass."

I had the firm conviction that Oliver Gerson could tell us something.

He would never help Benedict, but what of me? He had been courteous and charming to me always. Of course, he had thought I was a good proposition. He had planned to marry the step-daughter and so acquire a share in the business. That had been his motive. Most girls would have been impressed by him and very likely delighted that he had planned to marry them.

Was he so bad? Benedict had married his first wife for the goldmine she brought him. When one grew up one realized that people's characters were made up of many facets.

Oliver Gerson had been so good to the children, amusing them, playing their games. They had both adored him—Lucie as well as Belinda—but Belinda was more fierce in her emotions. She loved with passion and hated with venom. Therefore while to Lucie he had been Nice Mr. Gerson, to Belinda he had been godlike.

If I could see him now . . . How? I did not know where he lived. He would, of course, still be connected with the clubs. His had been an important post there. He had been Benedict's right-hand man; and now that Benedict was no longer working for them, he would still be there with the new owners.

I had heard the names of some of them: The Green Light, The Yellow Canary, Charade and

The Devil's Crown, but that last was the one Benedict had not acquired.

I could find out where the clubs were situated. I knew they were all in the west end of London. It would not be very difficult; and as soon as the idea occurred to me I decided to put it into practice.

I felt so much happier than I had for a long time. I was sure I should be hearing from Pedrek soon . . . and I owed this to Benedict. He was the one who had made me do the right thing and then set about to prove that it was not only the best for me but the truth. He had given me a chance to be happy again, and I longed to do the same for him.

Just suppose Oliver Gerson knew where Celeste was. It even occurred to me that she might have run off with him. Perhaps they had eloped together to some other country. I could try to find out. Some of his associates at the clubs might know.

I would go to London. I would make the excuse that I wanted to be with Morwenna who was so pleased that we had discovered the truth and that her son was exonerated.

Normally I should have been beset by pleas from the children to come with me. Lucie wanted to, but I told her I had a great deal to do and I should not be away for long. Belinda showed no desire to accompany me. She had been very subdued since her confession.

Leah told me that I need have no qualms about leaving the children at this difficult time. Belinda was clearly relieved that the truth had been revealed. "She had it on her mind, Miss Rebecca," said Leah, and added, determined to protect her darling: "She meant well."

"Yes," I replied, "the road to Hell is paved with good intentions."

"Poor mite. It's her father. That hurt her a lot, you know. And he was the one who got it out of her. She's terrified of him."

"On this occasion it was a good thing that she was."

"Don't you worry, Miss Rebecca. I'll look after her when you've gone."

"I know you will, Leah."

She smiled and I remembered Mrs. Emery's words when she had described the change in her. She no longer looked as though she were going to a funeral. Poor Leah! But she certainly did seem happier. What an effect parental attitudes had on children. There was Belinda—as she was because she resented her father's attitude towards her. And Leah? What had life been like in that shiningly clean cottage presided over by the self-righteous Mrs. Polhenny? No wonder she was secretive . . . shut in on herself.

But she seemed to be growing away from that a little now. There was truly a new softness in her face for the whole world and not just for Belinda.

Morwenna was delighted when she heard I was to stay with them for a week or so. So in due course I left Manorleigh for London.

I was warmly welcomed by both Pedrek's

parents, and all the coldness which had existed between us for the last months was swept away.

Morwenna kissed me and said: "Thank you for your letter . . . particularly the one you sent to Pedrek . . . before . . ."

I smiled. What a lot I owed to Benedict.

"I feel sure he will be home soon," said Morwenna.

Justin came out to greet me. It was like a happy reunion. We talked about Pedrek for practically the whole of the first evening. He was finding Australia interesting but Morwenna fancied he was homesick for Cornwall.

"My father is so delighted that he will be coming home soon," she added.

"Has he said he is coming home?"

"There has not been time to hear yet, but he will . . . of course he will."

I prayed he would and that he would forgive me for my doubts. I did have some dark moments when I wondered whether I had wounded him too deeply that even if the wounds healed the scars would show.

We put off talking in any depth about the disappearance of Celeste and the terrible position Benedict was in; but it was there all the time, hanging over us, reminding us that we were inclined to let our happiness over Pedrek's release from suspicion make us forget.

Morwenna said: "I suppose you will want to do some shopping while you are here?"

"I daresay . . ."

"I shan't be able to come with you as I should have liked. I have one or two engagements, made before I knew you were coming."

"I understand that . . . and I'll get round quicker on my own."

I wondered what they would say if they knew I proposed to visit The Yellow Canary the next day.

I spent the next morning with Morwenna. Justin had gone off to his office where he worked on the consignments of tin which were sent to various parts of the country and the Continent.

In the afternoon Morwenna went out, full of apologies, to fulfill an engagement. I told her I should be perfectly all right.

It was a bright and sunny afternoon and as soon as Morwenna left, I went out, hailed a cab and asked to be taken to The Yellow Canary. The cab driver looked rather surprised at such a request coming from a respectable looking female in the middle of the afternoon.

We drew up before a building in a rather narrow side street. On the wall by the door was the model of a yellow canary, so I knew I had come to the right place.

I alighted and went to the door. I rang a bell. After a few moments a hatch was drawn back and a pair of eyes were looking at me.

"Yes?" asked a male voice.

"Could I speak to the manager?" I asked.

"We're not open."

"I know. But I want to make some enquiries."

"You the press?"

"No. I'm a friend of Mr. Oliver Gerson."

I fancied that made some impression. He paused. "I could tell him you called."

"When will he be here?"

"I don't know. Comes and goes. Wait a minute." He opened the door and I stepped into a dark little lobby. I was confronted by a flight of stairs.

"Does Mr. Gerson know you're coming?"

"No. But I have to get in touch with him. It's urgent."

He looked at me for a few seconds as though summing me up. "I'll tell you," he said at length. "He might be at The Green Light. Yes . . . he's likely to be there."

"The Green Light? Where is that?"

"Just a few streets from here. All the clubs are close. It's club area, you see. I'll tell you how to get there. It's simple. Turn to your right and go along to the end of this street, cross the road and you'll see Lowry Street. The Green Light's on the right. You can't miss it. It's got a green light outside."

"Like your yellow canary."

"That's right. You might well find him there at this time."

I thanked him and came out into the street. He had given me clear instructions and it was not difficult to find The Green Light.

The door was open and I went in. There was a similar small dark lobby and a flight of stairs. A woman came out of a side door.

"Good afternoon," I said.

"Good afternoon. Can I help you?"

"I'm looking for Mr. Oliver Gerson. Is he here?"

"What name is it?"

"Miss Mandeville."

"Could I ask what it's about?"

"It's a personal matter."

She looked at me suspiciously. "He's not here, I'm afraid."

My heart sank. "Could you give me an address where I could get into touch with him?"

"Well, I couldn't do that, but if you leave your name and address, I'll get a message to him."

"I'm staying with friends and I may not be in London for long. Would you tell him it is urgent."

Then I heard a voice say: "Why, it is! What a surprise, Rebecca!"

Oliver Gerson was coming down the stairs.

"It's all right, Emily," he said to the girl. "This young lady is a friend of mine."

"Oh," I cried. "I am so pleased to have found you."

"As pleased as I was when I gathered you were looking for me."

"I thought you would still be in the club business."

"Yes, when the new people took over they wanted me to stay on and look after the management. I did so . . . on my own terms. But this is no place to entertain a lady like yourself. There's a tea place round the corner. We'll be comfortable there and you can tell me to what I owe the pleasure of this visit."

He led me out of The Green Light and we walked to the end of the street while he told me how well I looked and as beautiful as ever— no, more so.

It was the typical Gerson charm and I did not believe a word of it; but I had to admit it was pleasant and I felt—as I always had—that he would be easy to talk to.

We crossed a road and in the next street was the little shop. Tables were not too close together and they were already serving tea though the place was not very full.

"Good afternoon, Mr. Gerson. A table for two?"

"Not too public a one, please, Marianna."

"I know, sir."

She smiled roguishly and gave me a speculative but friendly smile.

The table was in an alcove rather apart from the others.

"Ideal," said Oliver. "Now bring us some tea and some of those superb scones of yours, please."

She gave him an almost tender look and I thought, He may be a blackmailer and all sorts of a villain but he knows how to make people happy. Belinda . . . Lucie . . . and even the woman in the shop.

When tea was brought the waitress received a charming smile from him and I noticed that she served him as though it were a special pleasure to do so.

"Now tell me what this is about?" he said.

"Do you know anything about Celeste Lansdon?"

A smile curved his lips. "I know that she has made quite a stir. It's hardly a secret. Poor Mr. Lansdon! I can't help feeling sorry for him. He's in a rather nasty position. There's no doubt about that."

"You hate him, don't you?"

He shrugged his shoulders. "I've been annoyed with him."

"He has suffered a great deal through this."

"It won't do him much harm. You'll see. He'll pop up again."

"He has lost his chances in the Cabinet."

"Well, he lost his seat once, didn't he . . . over that first wife of his. And yet . . . there he was . . . all set for getting to the top. It's all part of life . . . anyway the life of a man such as he is. He's down . . . then he's up. And the ability to fall and rise again . . . that's the mark of a strong man."

"You sound rather pleased about his troubles."

"You could hardly expect me to go into sackcloth and ashes, could you?"

"No . . . but perhaps a little sympathy."

"I am afraid we are not all as good as you obviously are."

"Do you know anything about Celeste Lansdon's disappearance?"

"Why should you think I would know about it?"

"I saw you with her once. You were coming out of The Hanging Judge."

"I did not see you. I wish I had."

"So . . . I know you were in touch with her."

"Poor girl! He treated her badly, didn't he? He neglected her. She was very unhappy. You can try people too far. What a juicy scandal it is! In view of his past history particularly. He was lucky to get out of the club business when he did."

"You have stayed in it."

"My dear Rebecca, I am not a budding cabinet minister. I can live my own quiet life and as long as I am on the right side of the law, I am in the clear."

"Providing you don't indulge in a little . . . blackmail?"

He was taken aback for a moment or two and I went on: "I overheard a conversation of yours. You were offering to marry me in exchange for some partnership. Do you remember?"

"Listeners do not often get the entire story. Marrying you would have been no hardship, but I did think that having family ties with Benedict Lansdon would have been advantageous, especially when the lady in question was the most charming I was ever likely to meet."

"I'd rather you dispensed with the gallantry."

"It's genuine. I am very fond of you. I like your spirit. You are bold to come rashly to night clubs . . . even by day. They are no place for a respectable young lady."

"I gathered that. But you must know that

Benedict has . . . and still is . . . suffering a great deal."

"It can't have been easy for him. Do you care so much about that? I gathered that he was not one of your favorite people."

"That has changed. He has done a great deal for me. I want to help him if I can."

"A great deal . . . for *you?*"

"Yes, he has helped to put things right between me and the man I hope to marry."

"This lucky man is . . . ?"

I made an impatient movement, and he went on: "I mean he is the lucky one . . . the luckiest man on Earth. Is it Pedrek Cartwright?"

"Yes."

"And he has done this marvelous thing? What is in it for him?"

"Nothing. You don't understand. He could not bring himself to forget the past . . . the death of my mother . . . now he is breaking through. He and I . . ."

"It's very touching," he said with a hint of cynicism.

I half rose. "I can see it is no use . . ."

"Of course that's not so. Listen to me. I want to help you."

"Do you really mean that?"

"From the bottom of my heart."

"You are so superficially charming, I admit, but I do not know how much I can believe."

"You can believe that I would do a great deal to

help you.' He looked so sincere that I really did begin to believe him.

"Tell me about Pedrek," he said, and rather to my surprise I found myself relating what had happened in Cornwall, of the part Belinda had played in ruining our lives which might have been forever had it not been for Benedict.

"That child! What a wild creature she is! I was fond of her, you know."

"And she of you. In fact it was because of you that she did this terrible thing."

"She's got imagination, that one, but I am amazed that she went so far as that . . . even for my sake."

An idea suddenly came to me.

I said: "Did she by any chance help you to get the key to the locked room?"

He smiled at me provocatively.

"She did, of course," I said. "Why didn't I think of it? She stole Mrs. Emery's key, didn't she?"

He continued to smile.

"And she brought it to you. You had a copy made. Then she returned it to Mrs. Emery's room."

"Sounds plausible, doesn't it?"

"Oh, how could you! To use a child in such deception!"

"What a devoted little creature she is. I had to see those papers, you know. I had to be sure of my facts."

"And you found out that there had been negotiations for The Devil's Crown."

"How clever you are. There is no need for me to tell you because you know already. Oh yes, Miss Belinda would do a great deal for me."

"Her feelings are rather superficial," I said with a touch of malice. "She has now transferred her devotion to another male visitor to the house. An Australian, who owns a goldmine out there. He tells racy stories about the Outback and has quite pushed you out of her mind."

"Well, perhaps it is for the best. And Benedict got to the bottom of it, did he? Why?"

"For the satisfaction of seeing me happy."

"He has turned over a new leaf then?"

"We are all turning over new leaves. It is a good thing to do. There might be more to gain from helping people than from taking revenge for petty slights. Will you help me?"

"You believe that I am involved in this, don't you?"

"I heard you say you would take your revenge on him, that's why."

"My dependence on him is over, you know."

"And you have had the satisfaction of seeing that there was no place in the Cabinet for him."

"Was he very upset?"

"It was you who said he takes blows calmly and he did in this case. But he has changed. If only there could be some answer to this riddle . . . he might find some happiness."

"Providing it was the right answer. I heard that they were digging near the house."

I nodded. "The ground appeared to have been recently disturbed and it gave them ideas."

"And nothing was revealed."

"No. I do not believe she is dead. Oh, if only she would come back."

"Do you think they would live happy ever after, if she did?"

"I think if he would try . . . and she would try . . . they might. I told you he had changed."

He took my hand which was lying on the table, and pressed it.

"You are a very nice girl, Rebecca," he said. "I should have been lucky if it had all turned out to plan."

"I should never have married you. There was always . . ."

"The lucky Pedrek."

"I think he has not been very lucky so far. When—and if—he comes back I intend that he shall be."

"I am envying him more and more. Do you know, I should like to help you."

"You see now why I wanted to find you. It just occurred to me that as you had been meeting Celeste you might have known something."

"Where are you staying?"

"At the Cartwrights' . . ."

"The lucky Pedrek's parents' house. I know it. How long shall you be there?"

"No more than a week."

"You have come to London on a quest. You want to solve the mystery of Celeste's disappearance. You want to do it for him because he has been so good to you. He has turned over a new leaf and will be the loving husband and stepfather. He will take the wayward Belinda to his heart and you will all be as one happy family."

"Please don't laugh at me."

"I am not laughing. I am overcome with admiration. It means a lot to you, does it not?"

"A great deal."

"I think it was so noble of you to come on your pilgrimage of detection. I will do all I can to help."

"How? Do you think you can?"

"Who knows?"

I said: "I think I should go now."

"You are disappointed."

"It was a faint hope. It just occurred to me that she might have said something to you."

He looked up from his teacup and smiled at me.

"Thank you for the tea," I said, "and for listening to me."

"I will settle with Marianna and then we will find a cab and I'll take you home." He paused and smiled at me. "Don't be alarmed. I shall not attempt to oppose the ban and shall make no attempt to darken doors."

We came into the street and were soon driving along.

"I am afraid you are a little disappointed in me," he said. "How I should love to be of use."

"I believe you would if you could," I told him.

"Then you don't think I am such a villain after all?"

"No."

"Blackmail? Seeking betterment in shady ways . . ."

"I have discovered that many people who may be a little unscrupulous in some ways can be very good in others."

"What a lovely view of human nature! I should hate to change it."

We drove in silence for some little way then he went on: "Ah, here is your destination. I will remain in the cab. I think there is just a possibility that you may not wish me to be seen."

"It is just that . . ."

He raised a hand. "I understand . . . perfectly. I'll make sure that you are safely in the house, then we shall trot discreetly away."

"You are so kind and thoughtful."

He took my hand and kissed it. *"Au revoir,* sweet Rebecca."

I went into the house.

Two days later I received a note from him. It came by hand and was dropped through the letter box. I was glad that I was alone and no explanation was needed as to who my correspondent was.

He was asking me to meet him at three o'clock that afternoon at The Devil's Crown.

I was taken aback by the proposed venue, but I subdued my uneasiness, at the prospect of hearing something about Celeste.

I arrived there on time.

I was apprehensive as I stood before the building. It was not very far from The Yellow Canary and The Green Light and bore a resemblance to them . . . a tall, shabby building on the wall of which was the sign, the Devil with cloven feet and horns, and a crown on his head.

I noticed the big brass knocker with a decoration at the top of it. When I looked closer I saw that it was a crowned devil's head.

I knocked and in a few moments the door was opened by Oliver Gerson.

"I knew you'd be here promptly," he said. "Come in."

I stepped into a small room which was empty of furniture. He opened the door and led the way into another room. Like the first it was empty. I was beginning to feel apprehensive. He realized this and said: "I have a reason for bringing you here. I'm sorry. It is not very attractive, is it? It's empty actually. We have only recently acquired the premises. Plans are in progress for redesigning the whole place."

"Why did you ask me to come here?"

"I can explain to you here. I can see you are uneasy. Don't be. You are perfectly safe with me

503

and I think you are going to be glad I brought you here."

"It's . . . a very strange place."

"Are you thinking of the devil at the door? That is meant to give people a little shiver as they enter."

He laid a hand on my arm. Instinctively I drew back. I could not help being reminded of Jean Pascal and wondering if I had been foolish enough to wander into another such trap.

"Could we go somewhere to talk?" I suggested. "That teashop?"

He shook his head. "It was necessary that you should come here. You must not be afraid of me. I know I am all sorts of a rogue and an adventurer in a way. I climbed to the position I hold now . . . and not always by the straight and narrow path. Benedict's grandfather was interested in me. He recognized my talents and said he would exploit them. I had a position of some responsibility in his day and of course continued in it when Benedict took over."

"I know all this . . . and that you jeopardized that position. That was unwise surely."

"Ah, but he couldn't turn me out. I was too well entrenched. However, that's neither here nor there. He's finished with us now and I am still here. But I am wasting time, aren't I? You want to know why I brought you here."

"You are going to tell me something about Celeste, I hope."

"I want to prepare you . . . gently. I don't want

to give you too much of a shock. You saw us at The Hanging Judge. Yes, I was meeting her. No . . . not what you are thinking. It was not a love affair. I was sorry for her. I'm not so bad really. There is a little good in the worst of us, you know. I am capable of feeling sorry for someone in distress, and she was certainly that. She confided in me. She wanted to talk to someone who was sympathetic . . . and worldly enough to understand the situation. So we talked . . . and then we used to meet occasionally. Then . . . Benedict threatened to ruin everything for me. I was furious with him. He would not find it easy to be rid of me. There were others concerned and they knew my value. I recalled that other affair of his . . . his first election when he lost through the scandal about his wife. I was furious. I wanted above all to make him pay. It became an obsession."

"Go on."

"I thought I would spoil his chances. I knew how much he wanted that Cabinet post, and I thought, as it happened before through wife number one, why not do it again through wife number three?"

"So you arranged that . . ."

"She was to disappear. Not run away openly. That might not have had the desired effect. But suppose she disappeared . . . taking nothing with her? Suppose it could look like murder?"

I stared at him incredulously.

"You . . . you've hidden her. You know where she is. She's alive."

He nodded.

"Where is she?"

"You'll know soon."

"What a wicked thing to do!"

"Has he not been wicked? Did he not make his first wife unhappy? He has not cared for his daughter. He has made a little monster of that child. And was he a kind stepfather to you . . . for all those years?"

"It was largely my fault. He might have been different if I had let him."

"I can see you are determined to make excuses for him. He should be made to see that there are others in the world beside himself. Oh, I know he has turned over a new leaf. Well, he has been punished. You think he has been punished enough. Perhaps you are right."

"I wish you would tell me everything . . . now."

"You have come at the right moment, Rebecca. You know how fond I am of you. The partnership was not the only reason. I wanted you . . . and I want to do something for you now. I want to make you happy. I hope your lover comes back to you. I hope you set up that harmonious family atmosphere in Manorleigh and in London. I hope you are able to console your stepfather for the loss of his post. I've had my revenge on him, so that score is settled. It was a good one. It harmed him as he tried to harm me. Now I am ready to finish with the business, and you are going to help

506

us out of a rather difficult situation. Celeste is here."

"Here? In this place?"

He nodded. "She has been here all the time. It was most convenient. You see, the place is empty. At the top is a flat . . . with kitchen and facilities. It was here when the club was running and was for the manager's use at those times when he wanted to remain on the premises. It was just what we needed. Celeste had the notion that if she went away . . . disappeared for a while . . . Benedict might want her back. She thought it might revive some affection for her. The idea became an obsession. I helped her . . ."

"Persuaded her to put it into action, I suspect. It suited your plans for revenge."

"How well you understand! Yes, naturally I was intrigued by the idea."

"So you helped her make up her mind. You showed her how it could be done."

He lifted his shoulders. "She fervently believed . . . at the start . . . that it would change his feelings towards her. It was what she wanted more than anything. She was ready to go to any lengths to reach that end. I suggested this as a place of refuge . . . She was enthusiastic about the idea. She smuggled a few essential clothes out of the house. I brought them here. She told her maid she was giving them away to some cottagers. I made this place habitable for her."

"What a terrible thing to do!"

"Yes. Quite ingeniously worked out, though.

507

But it's over, and we have to get her out of here. We have to have a plausible story. Not easy . . . but if you will help, we could achieve that. I know I can trust your discretion. I have thought of a plan and when you see the wisdom of it, you will agree to it, I am sure. We have to think of the press who will be avid for the story. She can't stay here as the work is to start on the building very soon."

"When can I see her?"

"When I have told you the plan. You are staying with the Cartwrights. Go back to Benedict's house and stay a night there. Say you had something to do in your room there . . . some things you want to sort out . . . something like that. In the morning, Celeste will return there. She will be dazed and uncertain. She will not know what has happened to her because she has lost her memory. She walked out of the house on that night but she did not know where to. She must have had money in her pocket . . . enough to enable her to buy a rail ticket to London. She got into conversation with someone on the train . . . a woman who by chance had a boarding house. She told her she could not remember where she was going. The woman befriended her and she stayed with her some time . . . she cannot remember how long. She was obviously of good family and the woman believed that in time she would be rewarded—in fact, Celeste had told her this would be so. She merely wanted a temporary refuge while she was trying to remember who she was. She used to walk round the streets looking for her home. She knew she had one . . . somewhere. Then suddenly, passing Benedict's town house she recognized it and some memory came back to her. So she presented herself and you happened to be there. You are overcome with joy. You get her to bed. You send for the doctor. As you talk to her some memory comes back and she knows you, of course. You send for Benedict. He comes. Happy reunion. Celeste is back in the family circle and this damning mystery is over."

I listened with incredulity to all and said: "It is very wild. No one will believe it."

"You can make it plausible enough."

"Surely . . ."

"It is the only way, Rebecca. Imagine the press getting their hands on this. Do not bring more scandal on Benedict. Lost memory is the only answer. Play it carefully as you go along. She has been ill. They'll probably say it was through his neglect of her, but that will pass, when he shows himself to be the devoted husband. It's easily done. Loving looks in public . . . a little pressure of the hands . . ."

"Take me to her."

"Follow me."

He led the way to the stairs and we started to climb. It was a long way up. Right at the top of the tall building we came to a landing. He went to a door and knocked. It was opened immediately and there stood Celeste. She looked pale, thin and very distressed.

She flew at me and we were in each other's arms.

"Oh, Celeste," I cried. "I'm so happy to see you."

"Rebecca . . . it's been so terrible. I should never have done it."

"Never mind," I said. "It's over. Oliver has been explaining to me."

He stood by watching us.

"Now we must be practical," he said. He turned to Celeste. "Rebecca has agreed to help us."

Celeste smiled at me pathetically and I felt great sympathy for her. I wanted so much to make her life a happy one. I wondered if she and Benedict would be able to forget all that had gone before. I did not know whether that was possible, but at least we could hope.

"Oliver has been telling me how and why you left. We've got to forget that, Celeste. You've got to come back. Dreadful things have been said in the papers."

Oliver broke in: "Now we are going to work this out so that our plan is perfect. It must sound right."

He produced a bottle from his pocket. "There are glasses here," he said. He went to a cupboard and brought out three. "A little sip of brandy is what we need. Yes, even you, Rebecca. You have had a shock."

We sat at a table and he poured a little of the spirit into each glass.

He gave me his tender smile. "Celeste," he said.

"Rebecca is going to help us sort this out. I aim for you to get back to your husband's roof, and there will be a happy reunion. Rebecca wants you all to be as one happy family and as we are fond of Rebecca we must give her what she wants if that is possible. Now listen closely. Rebecca is going back to your husband's house. Tomorrow I shall take you out in a cab and drop you two streets away. You will then walk to the house and ring the doorbell. Rebecca will let the maid answer it but she will be close at hand. She will show great amazement at the sight of you. She will be a little tearful and very emotional . . . and certainly bewildered. The house was familiar to you . . . you were trying to remember . . . you began to recognize it as your home . . ."

"I hope this will work," I said. "It does not sound natural to me."

"We will make it work. They are not difficult roles to play. It is very important that this should work out. If the press got hold of the truth there would be the most horrific scandal . . . and great trouble."

"Trouble for you?" I suggested. "Goodness knows what the penalty would be for hiding someone whom the police are trying to find."

"I think I could extricate myself with some plausibility. A lapse of memory leaves everyone innocent. It is the way to get the smallest amount of press coverage."

"Celeste," I burst out. "I am so happy to have found you!"

"I wasn't sure whether I wanted to do it or not," she said. "Sometimes I hated him. I wanted to have my revenge on him . . . and then I wished I hadn't. What did the papers say?"

"The police are looking for you, Celeste."

She shivered.

"Yes," said Oliver. "And on second thoughts I think we had better leave here at dusk. We will not trust to a cab. There would be the driver to consider. He might remember something. I hadn't thought that we might be seen. I will bring my own carriage and drive it myself. Celeste will arrive at the house just as it is getting dark . . . this evening. You must go back at once, Rebecca. Tell them you have to stay at Benedict's house for a night or so and leave as soon as possible. You must be there when Celeste arrives. You have to help her through this. Just get her to bed . . . send for Benedict . . . and make sure you stay with her. She'll show that she wants you there. It is imperative that you play your parts right."

"Then I must go at once," I said. "I have to make arrangements to go to the other house and there is not much time if Celeste is coming back this evening."

He nodded.

I turned to Celeste. "It is going to be all right. It must be there. I'll be there when you come. Don't worry."

"Benedict . . ."

"He will be so glad to see you."

"He doesn't want me."

512

"He's changed," I said. "He has changed with me and he'll change with you too. All this has changed him."

She clung to me and it was some seconds before I could extricate myself.

"I'll take you out now," said Oliver to me. Then to Celeste: "Be ready. Only a few hours now."

We descended the stairs

I turned to Oliver and said: "I shall have to tell Benedict the truth."

"Why?"

"It won't work otherwise."

"But . . ."

"I must," I insisted. "He will see that that is the only way to avoid more scandal. There might be holes in the story . . . there probably are. It sounds wild to me. If he knew . . . he'd realize the need to play it the way we are doing. He'll help us."

"And what will he think of me?"

"At least you helped us in the end."

"So you would put in a good word for me, would you?"

"I would indeed . . . and I thank you. In fact, I am most grateful to you."

"I'd do a lot for you, Rebecca. I know how you wanted this. But at the same time we had to get her back, somehow."

"So . . . I shall tell him."

"If you think you must. I can see how he would probably probe, and he might find something we'd overlooked which would give the whole show away."

We left The Devil's Crown and in a short while I was driven back to the Cartwrights' house.

There was no time to lose. I went to my room and put a few things into a bag. I came downstairs and was relieved to see that Morwenna had returned.

I said: "Morwenna, I want to go to the house . . . and to my room there. There are a few things I want to get together to take back with me to Manorleigh. It will be easier for me to stay a night or two there."

"Are you going now?"

"Yes," I said, "at once. I want to get on with it. I ought to be returning to Manorleigh soon."

"Will you be all right . . . none of the family being there?"

"Yes, perfectly all right."

So it was easier than I thought.

I arrived at the house and told the servants that I would be there for a night or two.

The afternoon seemed long. I thought it would never pass. And then . . . the knocking was reverberating through the house. I went downstairs. I was standing at the foot of them when the maid opened the door. I heard her give an exclamation of amazement and I hurried forward.

"Celeste!" I cried. "Oh . . . Celeste!" I rushed at her and embraced her.

She looked pale and quite bewildered. "Rebecca," she murmured.

514

I turned to the maid. "Mrs. Lansdon's come home!" I cried. "She's here . . . she's safe." I was trying to imagine how I would be feeling if this were a surprise to me.

There were several people in the hall now. They were all staring at Celeste as though she were a ghost. The butler and the housekeeper arrived. I turned to them.

"She's ill," I said. "I'm going to get her to bed. Let hot-water bottles be put in the bed. She's shivering. Get the doctor. Send for Mr. Lansdon. I'll tell you what to say. Send at once . . . and for the moment say nothing to anyone . . ."

I wrote a message. "Come at once. We have astounding news. Very necessary you are here."

"There must be no mention of Mrs. Lansdon's return to the outside world as yet," I said. "We must wait to see how Mr. Lansdon intends to handle this."

They all listened in awe.

The dignified butler bowed his head. He was the sort of man who would show little emotion in any contingency. I think he saw the wisdom of my reasoning. Nobody wanted the press here until Mr. Lansdon arrived. It was so easy to say something which would be regretted afterwards.

I got her to her room. They were fussing about with hot-water bottles. When they had gone I helped her undress and to get into bed.

I said: "Say little, Celeste. You are doing well. You looked quite bewildered and dazed."

515

She replied: "I feel it. Oh Rebecca, I'm so frightened."

"It's going to work out. Just say nothing. Don't answer questions . . . if they are awkward. We'll work it out."

"Benedict . . ."

"He'll understand. I shall make him understand."

"Oh, Rebecca!" She was sobbing in my arms.

"Listen, Celeste," I said. "This has been a terrible time but it is over now. Everything will be different from now on. I know it."

She looked at me with a certain confidence and I felt quite humble. I was talking to give myself courage for I was as apprehensive as she was.

The housekeeper tapped on the door. I went outside so that Celeste should not hear what was said.

"The message has been sent off to Manorleigh," I was told, "and the doctor will be here very soon."

"Thank you, Mrs. Greaves," I said. "This has been a terrible business. Mrs. Lansdon has clearly lost her memory."

"I've heard of such cases, Miss Rebecca."

"She'll be all right. It is coming back a little now. I gathered that she recognized the house as her home which is a good sign."

"Poor lady. She must have gone through a good deal."

"Yes, but we'll get her better. When Mr. Lansdon comes . . ."

"Of course, Miss Rebecca. Ah. There's someone at the door. It must be the doctor."

I went down to him. I knew him because he had been to the house once or twice before.

I said to him: "A most extraordinary thing has happened. I am sure Mr. Lansdon would not want it known until he himself has had time to deal with the matter. He will be here very shortly for he has been informed. Mrs. Lansdon is here."

He was taken aback.

"Yes," I went on. "It appears she lost her memory."

"So . . . that is the explanation."

"Dr. Jennings, I know I can rely on your discretion. It is rather important that no one knows she has come back until Mr. Lansdon is here. In view of his position and all the fuss there has been we should not be able to deal with the press."

"I see," said the doctor. "Yes, of course."

"He will want to see you, I expect, when he arrives. But in the meantime I thought you should visit Mrs. Lansdon. She is in a weak state and questions seem to upset her."

"I understand. Let me see her. I'll give her something to soothe her. I expect she wants rest . . . and when she has had it . . . we'll go on from there."

"Let me take you to her."

I went into the bedroom. Celeste looked scared. I said: "It's only the doctor, Celeste. He's going

517

to give you something soothing to make you sleep. There is nothing to worry about now. You're home and safe."

I remained in the room with the doctor. I was terrified that he might ask her some question and at the moment she seemed in no state to deal with a complicated situation.

However he was both soothing and tactful. He gave her a dose which he said would make her sleep. We left together. He shut the door and said to me: "She's very muddled, isn't she? What a mercy she saw the house and recognized it. It's clearly a case of loss of memory."

"It will come back, I hope."

"Gradually. But it may take some time."

"I am so absolutely delighted that she has returned."

"It has been a trying time for the whole family. But this is the best thing that could have happened in the circumstances. She doesn't seem to be ill physically. It is just this mental block. It happens now and then."

"You've had experience of it, I daresay?"

"I did have another case . . . once."

"And the person in question recovered . . . completely?"

"Yes . . . in time."

"I am so relieved. Mr. Lansdon will be here soon, I hope."

"That would be a considerable help, I should imagine. The more people she knows about her, the better. Familiar surroundings will be a great help."

When he left I was deeply relieved. We had passed the first hurdle.

I went back into the bedroom. Celeste looked at me sleepily.

I sat down by the bed. She reached for my hand and clung to it. In a few moments she was in a deep sleep.

I sat there for what seemed like an eternity . . . waiting for Benedict.

At last he came. I heard the cab draw up at the door and saw him alight. I sped down to the hall and when he came in I ran to him.

"Rebecca!" he said.

"Benedict, something has happened. Come to my room."

He followed me there. I shut the door and faced him.

"Celeste is here," I said.

"Here!" He stared at me unbelievingly.

"I found her . . ."

"What? Where? How is she?"

"She's in her bed . . . fast asleep. I sent for the doctor. He's been and has given her a sedative. He said she needs a great deal of rest. She's been through an ordeal."

"What . . . ?" he repeated. "How . . . ?"

"I'll tell you from the beginning," I said, and I

told him. He listened incredulously but I could see the tremendous relief he felt.

"I must see her," he said at length.

"She's sleeping now. But come. I can see you find it hard to believe she is here."

I took him into the bedroom. She lay on her bed looking very pale, her lovely dark hair spread out on the pillow.

"How young she looks," he said.

"I must talk to you, Benedict. When she wakes I want you to be thoroughly prepared. Please come back to my room."

I had never seen him as he was then. He was like a man in a dream. He must be finding it hard to believe that this was actually happening to him.

"I've thought so much about this," I said. "And so has Oliver Gerson. I know you hate him, but he is clever. He has done what he intended to do—stopped your getting into the Cabinet. He is satisfied."

"He could be prosecuted for his part in this . . . helping to hide her, aiding and abetting her . . . keeping information from the police."

"That all has to be forgotten. It will be worse for you if you allow bitterness to prevail. No one is guiltless . . . you would be blamed as much as any. You neglected her . . . made her so unhappy that she could contemplate such a thing. You've kept that locked room. How could you . . . in a house where she is living? She loved you far too much . . . more than you deserved. So please forget bitterness and thoughts of revenge. You are as much to blame as Oliver Gerson who has repented apparently. Through him I found her. And he has helped us. It was his idea that she should feign loss of memory. It's the best way, Benedict. So . . . forget resentments. Oliver Gerson has gone out of your life. You apparently said things to him which he could not forgive and he has had his revenge. We have to think about the press. They will be on your heels. I suggest that you tell them she has returned and that she was suffering from a loss of memory. At the moment she is not certain what exactly happened and the doctor has given orders that she must not be disturbed and bothered with questions. She needs medical attention and care."

He nodded and smiled at me in a quizzical way. "I see," he said, "that you have worked it out in a logical way."

"We must, Benedict. We have to think of her. Life has to be made worth living for her. This should never have happened. You would have had the Cabinet post for which you craved if it had not. There would never have been this scandal and all the terrible suspense and horror we have endured during these weeks."

"I know. You are right. It is my fault. I have behaved badly . . ."

"That will change, won't it?"

He said in a low and husky voice: "I can try, Rebecca."

"And you will. Promise me."

He took my hands in his and drew me to him. I put my arms about him.

"It has changed for us. It must change for her," I said.

He did not speak. I think his emotion prevented him.

"I think, Benedict," I went on, "that you may have brought happiness back to me. If I can do anything to repay you . . ."

"Why, Rebecca," he said, "you have become my guardian angel." Then he laughed— uncertain laughter it was true. He held me at arms' length. "Thank God for you . . . stepdaughter."

"Let us thank God we have each other," I added.

I took him to the bedroom they shared together. She was lying in her bed, drowsy but awake.

"Celeste," I said softly. "Benedict is here."

She was fully awake at once. She sat up in bed looking fearful. He went to her and took her in his arms.

"I am so glad that you have come home," he said.

She clung to him.

I said: "Don't be afraid, Celeste. Benedict is so happy because you have come back. He knows everything now. He understands . . . and there is nothing to fear."

I closed the door on them.

I wanted to sing for joy. I knew in time all would be well.

Confession

So much happened during the next few days. It was wonderful to see Celeste looking happy. She now knew that Benedict was fully aware of all that had happened and there were no reproaches. He accepted his own guilt and gave the impression that he wanted to take care of her. As for her, she seemed to be living in a blissful dream.

The doctor was delighted with her progress and said it would be better not to mention the incident unless she did herself. Benedict dealt with the press and of course there were the expected headlines in the papers.

He was now represented as the joyous husband emerging from his terrible ordeal with courage and dignity. I was reminded of Uncle Peter who would have said this would be good for his image after all. There was nothing people liked better than a happy ending to a love story.

Of course, it was a pity it had come too late for the Cabinet reshuffle, but as Uncle Peter would have philosophically pointed out, there would be another time and with the enhanced presentation of a grieving husband now rejoicing in the return of his wife who had been suffering all the time from amnesia, he would give him a better chance than ever.

I talked to him when we were alone and said I should go back to Manorleigh before them. I wanted to have that room unlocked. I wanted to take out my mother's things and to change it some way. Mrs. Emery would help me.

I was surprised and delighted when he agreed. He and Celeste would stay in London for a few more days. He was devoting himself to her as he never had before, talking of politics, drawing her into his life; and she responded like a flower opening to the sun and her happiness brought back her beauty and a certain gaiety of which until now I had been unaware.

Then I returned to Manorleigh.

There was great rejoicing there because of Celeste's return. The children asked excited questions about her. I told them she had been lost because she could not remember where she was, and they listened round-eyed.

"Then she was in the street and saw the house and she remembered," I told them.

"How could you forget who you were?" demanded Belinda.

"People do . . . sometimes."

"Does she remember it all now?" asked Lucie.

"She is beginning to . . . and soon she will be here."

Belinda was thoughtful; I wondered what was in her mind.

I was soon in Mrs. Emery's room drinking a cup of tea.

"I think there will be a change, Mrs. Emery," I said. "Mr. Lansdon was very upset, you know."

"You can say that again," said Mrs. Emery.

"It has made him realize that he didn't know how much he cared for her."

Mrs. Emery nodded.

"It took a lot to do it," she said severely.

"Mrs. Emery, there is the locked room. It's not going to be locked any more. I want you to help me deal with it. We'll get to work on it right away. I am going to take out all my mother's clothes . . . everything that's personal . . . everything that was there when she was alive."

Mrs. Emery sighed with relief. "Does he know?" she asked.

"Yes. I suggested it to him. He sees the point. I said by the time they arrived there would be no locked room."

"That's good, that is. I never liked the idea myself."

"I thought if we could turn the furniture round a little. Perhaps take some things away. The bureau there which contains his papers must stay for him to deal with. But let us take all the clothes away. Perhaps there is something in the attics with which we could replace one or two pieces of furniture. Not much . . . just enough to make a difference . . . to make it an impersonal sort of room."

"I know just what you mean, Miss Rebecca. You just say when you're ready to start."

By the next day we had changed the room considerably. I had packed up my mother's clothes and they had been taken up to the attics. I took her initialled brush to my room; and by the time we had finished there was nothing there to remind people that it had once been her room.

Everything was now ready for the return.

There had been no reply from Pedrek. I told myself there had not been time but there was a niggling fear in my mind as to whether he would come back. Perhaps I had wounded him too deeply when I had doubted him.

I refused to allow myself to harbor such thoughts. It is too soon, I told myself. He will come back. He must. Benedict and Celeste had another chance and there must be one for Pedrek and me.

I noticed that Tom Marner was a little subdued. I wondered why and made a point of being alone with him while the children were with Miss Stringer at their lessons.

I asked him if anything was wrong.

He paused for a moment. Then he said: "I've had such a wonderful time here and received such warm hospitality. I didn't want to go when all that upset was on but now it's over and everything's all right . . . I'll have to be thinking of making my way back."

"I suppose you have managers to look after the mine."

"Oh yes . . . surely . . . but I can't stay forever. And now the lady's back where she belongs
. . . well, it seems to me that I ought to begin to
make tracks for home . . . and I don't like it . . .
much."

"We shall be very sorry to see you go. I can't
imagine what Belinda is going to say."

He smiled. "Ha. I'll be sad to go. Reckon
I've stayed too long already. But I just had to wait
and see what happened. Now it's all in the clear
. . . well, I should be off."

"You sound very reluctant to go."

"It's been good here. Don't know when I enjoyed myself so much."

"It's always sad when visits like this come to
an end, and we have to say goodbye. But I daresay
you'll be coming over again."

"I reckon," he said.

So that was it. He was going and although
he wanted to get home he did not want to leave
England. It was gratifying and we should all be
sorry, for we had grown fond of him.

I did wonder about Belinda. Oliver Gerson
first, then Tom Marner. She was going to be very
upset.

Celeste and Benedict returned. All the servants
were in the hall when they came in. It was quite
an emotional scene.

Celeste looked radiant. I had never seen her
look so beautiful. I knew the reason, of course. It

was Benedict. I hoped he was not merely playing a part, expiating his sins: I hoped he really was beginning to care for her deeply.

There was great rejoicing. I had arranged for Emery to bring champagne from the cellar and everyone in the house drank to the joyous return of Mrs. Lansdon. Celeste replied charmingly, thanking them all for their kind welcome. "I think I am almost well now," she told them.

They clapped with pleasure.

There would be a dinner party to which the agent and many of the important people in the neighborhood who worked for the party, would be invited.

Normally Celeste would have been apprehensive at the prospect, but she was changing. She had more confidence now. Benedict said he loved her and she was proud to work with him in his career.

I would never have believed they could have changed so quickly. It was like a miracle.

And the evening was a success.

It was not only Celeste who was so happy; Benedict was too. At least I believed so, though I did now and then wonder if he were playing a part.

Sometimes his eyes would meet mine and some understanding flashed between us. He really was finding consolation; he was shutting out the past. I knew my mother would be there always in his heart; she was the one he would always yearn for, but Celeste was there, warm, loving and living . . .

and she would comfort him; she was helping him and he would love her more as time passed.

It was now known throughout the household that Tom Marner would soon be leaving us. Everyone was sorry. He was such a jolly person, treating all as though they were important to him. "Such a pleasant gentleman," commented Mrs. Emery, "even if he is not quite out of the top drawer."

I laughed and said I never thought of people being in drawers.

". . . as the saying goes," added Mrs. Emery, somewhat reprovingly.

Miss Stringer said: "The children are very upset . . . both of them . . . but particularly Belinda. She keeps asking about ships and how far Australia is. I heard her telling Lucie that they have stowaways on ships and I have the idea that she fancies herself as one of them. That child's imagination is phenomenal."

Belinda was certainly intense in her feelings. Hadn't she tried to ruin my life and Pedrek's because of her infatuation for Oliver Gerson?

I tried to find out how deeply her emotions were engaged with Tom Marner. She was always asking questions about the goldfields.

"Fancy you being born there, Rebecca," she said. "Lucky you!"

"I don't think it was considered to be very lucky. It was not the best of places to be born, I assure you."

"I wish I'd been born in a goldfield. Is it a long way to Australia?"

"It's right on the other side of the world," volunteered Lucie.

"You go in a big ship. There are lots of people on it and they have stowaways."

"What do you know about stowaways?"

"That they stow away. They get on the ship when it's in port and they hide themselves and when the ship gets out to sea they come out and they can't be put off."

"They could and they are . . . at the next port."

"Well, the clever ones wouldn't come out until they got to Australia."

"They would never be able to hide for so long."

"Clever ones could." Her eyes were speculative.

"You're not thinking of trying it, are you?" I asked.

"It would be a great adventure," she said, her eyes shining.

"You wouldn't like it. If they found you they would make you work until they could put you off."

"I wouldn't mind working, would you, Lucie?"

"No, I wouldn't mind."

"Peeling vegetables, washing up in the galley, swabbing the decks?" I asked.

"I'd swab the decks," said Belinda. "Lucie could wash up and do the vegetables."

"You're talking a lot of nonsense," I said.

But I was worried about Belinda. She had a way of bringing her fantasies into reality.

531

Something was happening to Leah. She was very preoccupied with her own thoughts. I spoke to her once or twice and she did not answer. She would start suddenly and realize that I had asked a question and would not have the faintest idea what I had said.

I went up to the nursery while the children were once more in Miss Stringer's care, for I thought there would be a chance of having a quiet word with her. I found her there, sorting out the clothes. She was holding one of Belinda's nightdresses in her hands and I saw that she was close to tears.

"Leah," I said, "something's wrong. Why don't you tell me? I might just be able to help."

She paused, biting her lips . . . holding back her tears.

I said on impulse: "Is it because Mr. Marner is going?"

She stared at me and I saw that I had stumbled on the truth.

"My poor Leah," I said. "You have let yourself fall in love with him, haven't you?"

She nodded.

"Oh, Leah, I'm so sorry. I am sure he would not have led you to believe . . . you see, he is so friendly with everybody."

"I know. But he was specially friendly with me."

"I am so sorry. I am sure he would be most upset if he thought you had taken it this way."

"He's not upset, Miss Rebecca. He's asked me to marry him and go back with him to Australia."

I opened my eyes wide. I ran to her and kissed her.

"Well then," I said. "What is there to be sad about? You love him, don't you?"

"Oh yes, I do. I love him dearly. He's the most wonderful person I ever knew. I couldn't believe he'd notice me . . . like that."

"Leah, you are a very beautiful woman. You are good and kind too. Of course he fell in love with you. But why the sadness?"

"It's Belinda. I can't bear to leave her."

"My dear Leah, I know how fond you have grown of her. It's natural. You've looked after her since she was a baby. But you have your own life to live. It happens sometimes. People who look after children get so attached to them that it's a wrench to leave them. But you have your own life to lead. You'd have to break away some time."

"I couldn't leave her. I just couldn't . . ."

I thought how strange it was that Belinda, that rebellious child, should have inspired such devotion.

"It's like making a choice," she said. "I don't know which way to turn."

"Have you told Mr. Marner this?" I asked.

She shook her head. "I told him . . . I don't know what to do. He thinks it's because I'm not sure of my feelings for him. He says he'll give me time . . . but it's running out. He's got to get back and he wants me to go with him."

"But you must go, Leah. You love him, don't you? It's your future."

"I can't seem to choose between them. It seems either way I'll be miserable."

"Oh Leah, it's the whole of your life with Tom Marner. I'm sure he'll be the best of husbands. You'll have a wonderful life with him . . . Belinda . . . she's so unpredictable . . . she could change in a week. Besides, in time, she'll have her own life."

Her face crinkled with pain.

"Be sensible," I said. "Think what it means. Your future . . . your marriage . . . your own children. You can't give all that up for someone else's child."

I thought she was going to burst into tears. "I don't know what to do," she said. "I just don't know."

"Go and think about it. I am sure you will come to the right decision."

I left her then. I was certain that she could not give up all that marriage with Tom Marner would mean for the sake of someone else's child.

It was two days later when Benedict came to me and told me that Tom Marner wanted to talk to us.

"*Us?*" I said in surprise.

"You, me and Celeste," he said.

"Is it about Leah?" I asked.

"Yes, she is with him. It looks as if this is

534

something serious. Come along to my study. They will be there shortly."

We went and Celeste came in—the new Celeste, the radiant wife, no longer the outsider. I felt a glow of pleasure every time I saw her.

"I wonder what this is all about?" she said.

"I think Tom Marner wants to marry Leah and Leah wants to marry him."

"Oh, that will be very . . . very . . . how you say?"

"Suitable?" I suggested.

"That is just what I mean."

They came. Leah looked very emotional and Tom Marner was more serious than usual.

"Sit down," said Benedict, "and tell us all about it."

There was a brief silence. Tom Marner looked at Leah and smiled. "Go on," he said.

Leah seemed to brace herself. "It was when I went to High Tor to do the tapestry. It was the first time I had been away from home."

"I remember your coming to us," murmured Celeste.

"Yes . . . you were there," went on Leah. "To me it was all so different . . . I had never been away from home before. They were all friendly to me . . . especially Monsieur Jean Pascal . . ."

I drew a deep breath. I could never hear that name without experiencing a tremor of fear. I was guessing what was coming.

"I . . . I thought I was in love with him. I believed that we would marry. Please understand.

535

I knew nothing of the way things really are. I had lived all the time with my mother who was always talking about sin and burning in hell and such things. I knew I had sinned . . . but somehow it happened. There was never any talk of marriage . . . but I thought that when people did as we had, they would be . . . in time . . ."

"We understand, Leah," I said.

"In time I finished the tapestry. I went home . . . back to my mother. And then I found I was going to have a baby. You knew my mother . . ."

"I knew her well," I said. I could imagine the scenes in that cottage, the fear of Leah, the rage of her mother. She who found sin wherever she looked in those around her now discovered that her daughter was to be the mother of an illegitimate child.

"She told me I was wicked," went on Leah. "I would go to hell. Our reputations would be in ruins. She started making plans. She would send me away. I could fend for myself."

"So much for her Christian charity," murmured Benedict.

"You must not judge her harshly," said Leah. "She thought she was right. It came out when she talked to me . . . she was so upset . . . the secret somehow escaped. She had had a very hard time. She called herself Mrs. Polhenny, but she had never been married. Something similar had happened to her. When she was sixteen she was seduced by the squire of the village in which she lived. There was a child . . . me. Her parents were

536

shocked and sent her away to an aunt where she pretended she was a widow. The aunt was a midwife and she learned her profession . . . and in time she came to the Poldoreys and practiced it. I was about five years old then. What had happened was on her mind to such an extent that she became fanatically religious. She thought she was saved and she saw sin in everything and everyone. I could understand her horror . . . and I was very sad that I had brought more sorrow to her.

"She kept me locked up in the cottage. She said I had gone to stay with an aunt in St Ives. There was no aunt in St Ives."

"I thought I saw you once at the window," I said. "Just a shadow . . . you were there . . . and gone."

"Yes," she said. "I saw you. I was terrified. I did not know what I should have done if I had been seen and my condition discovered. Then she had this plan. She said she could never hold up her head in the towns again if it were known that her own daughter was a slut. She would do anything . . . anything . . . to stop its being known. So she had this idea. Jenny Stubbs had gone about believing she was pregnant for a long time. She longed for a child. Being a midwife, my mother would be able to put her plan into action. Jenny had had a child once before. My mother would examine her and tell everyone that Jenny was indeed pregnant. She would attend her and let it be known that Jenny had her child. That child would be mine. The more she thought of it the better it seemed. She could get rid of my child, and my virtue, at least outwardly, would be retained."

"So . . ." I cried, "Lucie is your child."

"It didn't turn out like that. Your mother had her child at this time. She died and not much attention was given to the child at first. She was a sickly little girl. My mother believed she could not live more than a few days . . . weeks at most. She was always fond of children and it was only when they began to grow up that she saw them as imps of mischief. Then she did this thing. She took Mrs. Lansdon's sickly baby and gave her to Jenny and my child she put in the nurseries here. Mine was a strong and healthy child and it seemed the best thing to do. My child would have the advantages Jenny Stubbs could not give her . . . and my mother was, after all, her grandmother. She thought she had settled everything in the best way. We did not know that Lucie would grow stronger and live."

I looked at Benedict. He was as shocked as I was.

Tom Marner said: "So you see . . . Belinda is Leah's own child."

"And that means," said Benedict, "that Lucie is mine."

There was a long silence. I believe everyone was too bewildered by what we had heard to say anything just yet.

It was Tom Marner who spoke first. "Leah told me all this and I persuaded her that she must tell you. We are all concerned and we have to work out what is to be done. You can understand how Leah feels."

"You are right," said Benedict. "But this is a great shock to us all."

"I'll tell you what we want," went on Tom. "Leah and I want to take Belinda with us to Australia."

That evening we sat together in the drawing room—Benedict, Tom Marner, Celeste and I. After her confession, Leah was too upset to join us.

"I still find it hard to credit this story," said Benedict. "Who would have believed that the midwife had such a devious mind?"

"I would," I said. "But she did have it on her conscience at the end. I know now why she was so anxious to see my grandmother when she was dying. She was going to confess to her. If she had we should have known of this long ago."

"Leah can't be parted from her child," said Celeste.

"That's for sure," added Tom.

"I always felt drawn towards Lucie," put in Benedict, as though talking to himself. "Perhaps there is something in this relationship between a parent and child even when they are unaware of that relationship."

"I am very fond of Lucie too," said Celeste.

We talked for a long time . . . well into the night. Tom Marner was passionately persuasive.

He wanted to take Leah back with him and he wanted Belinda too. "She's a strange one," he said. "She needs special handling." He was smiling to himself. He would know how to do the handling and, having seen the comradeship between him and Belinda, I believed him. Moreover Belinda would never be happy if they left without her. I had thought she showed signs of fondness for me. I believed she did care for me . . . a little. But Leah was first with her and I guessed that place could be shared with Tom before long.

I think we were all beginning to realize that when Leah and Tom went to Australia, Belinda, that strange changeling child, would go with her mother and the stepfather she would have chosen for herself.

The wedding followed very soon. There was no point—nor time—for delay, Tom said. Belinda and Lucie were bridesmaids.

Belinda was brimming over with excitement. She talked continually of Australia and the perfections of her new father.

It was a little churlish perhaps to those of us who had cared for her all these years, but she was genuinely happy and so excited that she could not hide her feelings. We all understood.

After the church ceremony we went to Manor Grange for the reception.

As I came into the hall one of the maids called to me. Her eyes were shining and she said in a high-pitched voice, "There's someone called to see you, Miss Rebecca. He's in the little room."

I went into that room where Benedict listened to the complaints and suggestions of his constituents. A man was standing there, his back to the window. He looked different. The sun had tanned his skin to a light bronze and he seemed older.

"Pedrek!" I cried.

And then we ran to each other.

The embrace was breathtaking. I managed to say, "You have come home then. I have been so longing for news."

"I thought it better to come myself."

"At last! It's been so long."

"Never mind. It's now that counts. I've loved you through it all, Rebecca."

"And I you."

"Never doubt again."

"Never . . . never . . . never," I said.

There was so much to be told . . . so much to plan for.

Leah, Tom and Belinda were to leave soon after the wedding and there came that moment when we had to say goodbye.

Belinda was like a wild-eyed sprite. She could not stand still.

"We'll come back to see you," she said. "And you can come out to see us. My father says so . . ."

She jumped up and put her arms round my neck.

"I do love you, Rebecca," she said a little rue-fully, as though apologizing for her enthusiasm. "I will come back and see you." She hugged me more tightly. "And now you can marry that boring old Pedrek."

"Thank you. I shall," I told her.

The publishers hope that this
Large Print Book has brought
you pleasurable reading.
Each title is designed to make
the text as easy to see as possible.
G.K. Hall Large Print Books
are available from your library and
your local bookstore. Or, you can
receive information by mail on
upcoming and current Large Print Books
and order directly from the publishers.
Just send your name and address to:

G.K. Hall & Co.
70 Lincoln Street
Boston, Mass. 02111

or call, toll-free:

1-800-343-2806

A note on the text
Large print edition designed by
Kipling West.
Composed in 16 pt Plantin
on a Xyvision 300/Linotron 202N
by Marilyn Ann Richards
of G.K. Hall & Co.